DEATH FOLLOWS

THE FALLEN GODS SERIES
BOOK ONE

DEATH FOLLOWS

HANNAH RACHEL

Death Follows
Book 1 of The Fallen Gods Series

Content Warnings

Death & Violence
Torture
Substance Abuse
Mental Health Themes (Anxiety, PTSD)
Graphic Language
Explicit Sexual Scenes
Blood & Gore
Parental Abuse
Death of Parent

Pronunciation Guide

Characters

Ameria – Ah-MEER-ee-uh

Gregor – GREG-or

Keenan – KEE-nin

Inara – IN-ah-rah

Delyth – DEL-ith

Toross –TOR-ahs

Narses – NAHR-sis

Corro – COR-oh

Beor Svariti –BAY-or Svar-EE-tee

Haemir – HAY-meer

Mereena – Mer-EE-nah

Torvin – PET-rah

Callum – Cal-uhm

Serafelle – SER-uh-fel

Malvolia —Mal-VOH-lee-yah

Vishah – VEE-shah

Locations

Litherion — Lih-THER-ee-on

Serenya – Ser-EN-ee-yah

Araelia –Ah -RAY-lee-yah

Eadrias – EE-dree-ahs

Nyasa – Nee-AH-suh

Lunestra – Loo-NESS-truh

Aeros – ER-ohss

Balrath – BAL-rath

Other

Dranoq – DRA-nock

Svarog – SVAR-ahg

Glossary

Locations

Elemental Lands: They consist of the Fire Kingdom, Earth Kingdom, Water Kingdom, and Air Kingdom.

The Fire Kingdom: The capital city is Litherion and it is the largest of the kingdoms. The north is lush with greenery and many plants, whereas the south is mostly desert and dry land. Rain does not often fall in the south. The Fire Kingdom does not get very cold, except near the border with the Air Kingdom. Fire Fae are the more elite of elementals: Power is status. The poor are likely to have less magic than the nobles. The Fire King, Toross, leans more toward dictatorship and being a conqueror. The Fire Kingdom has always had tense relations with the Water Kingdom.

The Earth Kingdom: The capital city is Eadrias. The kingdom consists of rolling fields, forests, flowers, and every type of plant. Earth Fae are more likely to be healers and are welcomed in all kingdoms because of that skill. The Earth Kingdom has a positive relationship with the Fire Kingdom.

The Air Kingdom: The capital city is Araelia. This kingdom is the coldest of all and is the only one where it snows. The Air Kingdom has always remained generally neutral, only aligning with others or engaging in conflicts, etc. if it benefits them.

The Water Kingdom: The capital city is Serenya. which sits on an island off the coast. The Water Kingdom has tense relations with the Fire Kingdom. Water Fae have always been more welcoming and lead with fairness. They are innovators and embrace new ways of living.

The Western Isles: These are four islands off the southern coast of the Water Kingdom. They consist of the Sun Court, Astral Court, Moon Court, and the King's Island. The Isles and the Elemental Lands tend to stay out of each other's business except for trading goods. Not much else is known about the Isles.

History

Many millennia ago, the Elemental Lands worshipped and celebrated the Gods. There were no closed-off kingdoms, and the Elemental Fae lived amongst each other across the continent. One day, the gods disappeared, and the fae grew tense. The four Elemental kings and queens broke the continent up and thus began the separation of fae. The Elemental Fae eventually gave up on the Gods and began celebrating the land and magic itself.

The Realm of The Living
Earth Kingdom
Eadrias
Fire Kingdom
Litherion
The Restless S
Water Kingdom
Serenya
Air Kingdom
Araelia
Dread The Forest
The Zlavrov Wastes
The Abdorian Dunes
Qesa
The Western Isles
The Elemental Lands

The Realm of The Living
The Elemental Lands
Balrath
Kings Island
Warrior Camp
Sun Court
Nyasa
Astral Court
Moon Court
The Western Isles

Dedication

For those who have hit rock bottom and
clawed their way out.
You're a badass.

Prologue

For seven millennia, I have not set foot in this realm. But, my dearest love is almost gone, and I must carry out her final wishes.

My feet traverse wondrous streets and I take in all that the God I am here to see has created. This new world he has molded for himself, for her, is astonishing. I imagine she is gazing down upon him with pride.

I reach the steep steps that lead up to his black moonstone palace. As I climb, I can feel how slow, how weak, my body has become. My soul does not have much time left. Once things are set in motion, I can rest and soon reconnect with my wife.

Reaching the top, I even out my breaths before shoving open the heavy ebony wood doors. The clanking of the heavy iron chains that hang from them echoes through the empty halls. The lack of guards is not surprising, for he is immortal.

I wander the halls, my shoes scuffing the dark marble flooring as I take in the dusty paintings and cob-webbed artifacts. The chandeliers emit a dim light, and fixtures on the wall cast a deep red glow.

At last, a pale man crosses my path. "Where is your King?" I ask, my deep voice commanding his attention. The man staggers a bit, some of the liquid in his goblet splashes to the floor, the red of it blending into the black flooring.

His clawed finger points over his shoulder while his deep crimson eyes survey me, "Back that way, to the left."

I side-step him and make my way around the corner. Voices reverberate through the darkening hall. I follow them to a set of double doors, and striding right in, I'm met with naked lifeless bodies scattered throughout the room, blood pooling from open wounds on their necks, wrists, and thighs. Creatures tangle with one another on alcoved beds lining the walls, doing what they do best behind slightly sheer silver draperies.

I walk straight ahead, to the God I have come to see. He lays upon a silk-covered platformed bed, a man sucking his cock while he feeds from a woman's neck. "I see you have been enjoying yourself all these years."

His teeth rip from the woman's neck and he tosses her limp body from the bed. He releases a groan when he sets his eyes upon me and shoos away the man pleasuring him. The God wipes his mouth with his fingers and licks the smudged blood off with his tongue. "What are you doing here?"

"We need to talk." I stare into his eyes, their entirety consumed by a dark maroon red.

He lets out a deep sigh, "Well, if you're here then I assume it must be important." The God stands, slips on a black robe, and then pads his way past me. "Follow me."

We saunter down the hall I'd just been in, to another set of double doors. He pushes them open and waltzes inside with me on his heels. With a wave of his clawed fingers, the doors shut behind me, and then he motions to the chair in front of his polished onyx desk.

I take a seat and the God plops down into the tufted chair behind the desk, "Why are you bothering me, Svarog?"

Wasting no time, I explain the actions I took to suspend the war and the ramifications it caused. And then I tell him why I'm really here — what Lada did that set her death into motion.

His eyes narrow, "Why are you telling me this?"

"Because, you are the only one who avoided the spell. You are the only one who remembers."

"You come here and drop this into my lap, expecting me to up and leave to fulfill this prophecy. I do not care what happens to everyone else. They can all continue suffering in their deserved punishment."

I do not want to hurt him, but I must. The fate of this entire universe depends on it. "She would care."

Shock forms across his face, morphing to hurt, and then anger. "Yeah, well she's dead!" He slams his fist, a crack spreading across the desk from the impact.

"You know she was dedicated to putting Perun on the throne."

"And look where that got her," he spits.

I release a heavy breath and fish the stone from my pocket, placing the marquise-shaped chrome diopside gem on the desk between us. Its vivid green color shines brightly against the onyx.

"You are the only one who can do this, and it must be now. The others will begin waking because of what my wife did. Because these," I nod to the gemstone, "are now here in this realm."

The god plucks up the stone with his fingers, "Is this really…"

"Yes."

The God's shoulders slump as he continues to fidget with the gem, "Why me, Svarog? Why can't it be someone else?"

I observe the God before I answer, hearing the exhaustion in his voice. The tragedies he's faced throughout his already long life weigh on him. Losing an eternal mate is — I think of Lada, my eternal mate, likely taking her last breaths as I sit here. It is the most soul-shattering experience a deity can go through. It's no wonder he's locked himself away for well over a millennium.

"I had asked my wife that same question. She'd just smiled at me and said that you deserve a new purpose, a new life. Happiness. I think she's right."

He looks up from the gem, the whites of his eyes having returned, the maroon now contained to his irises. "I am sorry for your loss, Svarog." His voice is uncharacteristically soft.

"Do not feel sorry for me. I will reunite with her soon. With me no longer on the throne, my time has come as well." I get to my feet and he rises with me, stone still in hand.

"That stone acts as a portal. Get your affairs in order, I will wait in the city and we will head out. I've located the world where important players reside. We have much to discuss when we get there."

Chapter One
Ameria

The sound of choked sobs and dripping blood pooling at my feet fills my ears. I wipe the stained scalpel with a small black cloth and toss both onto my table of instruments. Tucking the ginger strand of hair that fell out of my braid behind my ear, I peer over my shoulder at the man laying naked and restrained on the metal table.

Six perfect squares have been carved from his chest and three of his fingers have been broken, all of them now missing their nails. My eyes dart back to the small clock that sits on my little steel table. It's only been a half hour since I walked into the torture room and saw the nobleman I retrieved from his home three days ago strapped down.

"I'm telling you, please! I don't know who else is involved. Just myself and Lord Reeve. I swear it!" Lord Meldrick stutters from the immense pain I've been inflicting upon him.

"Really now?" The King's face lights up with a cruel smile. "Would you swear it on your wife's life?" Toross taunts while leaning over the stone edge of the interrogation room viewing balcony.

"I swear," Meldrick breathes heavily, "I swear on my wife."

"You do know what will happen to her if you're lying?" The King smirks. Lord Meldrick starts to sob again but doesn't speak further. I pluck up a larger knife, already knowing what comes next. My eyes find those of my father, his golden crown glinting in the torchlight beside him, and he gives me a slight nod before he stands.

With a deep breath, I steel myself. My dark magic stirs in excitement. It likes this part, the death. I turn fully toward the Lord and with a quick swipe of my knife, blood gushes from his throat. His dying gurgles mix with the fading footsteps of my father and his two council members as I watch another rebel take his last breath. I release my magic, which flutters in delight, as if it just devoured this man's soul, and then creeps back down to the depths of my well.

I gently place the knife back on the table and take off my blood-splattered apron. My father and his council members have already gone down the stairs and exited the square room made of ebony brick that's seen death for more than a millennium. I hurriedly wipe most of the blood off my hands on a clean cloth before rushing after them.

Their voices echo off the stone dungeon walls but the words they speak are muffled background noise to me, lost in my thoughts. Over a hundred years of torturing people, most of them citizens of my own Kingdom, and the aftermath never gets easier. Letting the darkness take over most of my consciousness while I kill helps, but the more I do, the more it feeds the magic. These days, it has been harder to ignore its clawing and nagging to be fully released.

My silent brooding falters when I slam into someone. Haemir. "You should really watch where you're going," he says, his green eyes softening. I shake my head, snapping myself out of my internal struggle. I hadn't even noticed that I exited the dungeons and was in the guards' hallway, my feet guiding me out of habit. Closing my eyes, I snake my arms around my best friend and bury my face in his chest. His clove and cinnamon scent grounds me like always. Arms gently encase me. "Come on, let's go spar for a while."

I say nothing as I let Haemir lead me down the hall to the training room.

Haemir hits the mat with a grunt. The steel of my blade presses up against his tan-skinned throat as I pin him to the ground. My lips curve up into a smirk, "For a member of the guard, that was pretty sloppy." Lifting myself off him, I reach out and help him up.

"First of all," he grunts as he rises to his full height, "I had heavy training all day and now we've been at this for hours. I'm fucking tired, hungry and grumpy." He pauses and grumbles under his breath, "and horny." Haemir heaves a long sigh while running a hand through his shoulder-length, wavy auburn hair and strides toward the rack of blunt training weapons.

"Excuses, excuses my friend," I huff while following him, wiping sweat from my brow. We have been sparring for hours and it's barely helped push away any of my emotional turmoil. I hand him my practice daggers, "You're right. You should go rest, see Mereena." She is Haemir's mate and my only other friend. We've all been friends since childhood and then one day the bond between them sparked. It wasn't a surprise to any of us though, as they have been inseparable since they met.

I, however, am glad I haven't met my mate. It would just give my father another chance to control me. Maybe I'll reconsider if I ever get out of here and go live a peaceful, free life somewhere in the mountains. Perhaps by the ocean. A secluded cottage in the forest? It doesn't matter, it's all just a dream, one that will likely only come true in the afterlife. After I've left this realm forever, either by my father's hands or by my magic consuming me whole.

Haemir wraps an arm around my shoulders and places a friendly kiss on my head. "Do you need anything before I go?" he asks, concern showing in his downturned brows.

I give him a small smile. "No, I'll be fine. Tell Mereena I'll see her at the library in the morning."

With a squeeze on my shoulder, he starts to back out of the room in a hurry, surely about to sprint back to the housing he has been provided on the palace grounds. "If you need anything, you know where we'll be."

Crossing my arms, I stare blankly at the wall of weapons. My dark magic is tucked away and quiet, but my deeds still haunt me. A few more hours of training and a drink or two might solve the problem.

Usually, training helps push away thoughts about how much blood is on my hands, but if I'm honest, Haemir is a big reason for that. He and Mereena have become the only good left in my life. If I didn't have them to ground me, I would have fully turned into the sadistic dictator my father has become by now. I feel that I'm not too far off at this point.

A small noise behind me puts my senses on alert. The distinct smell of mint and sage hits my nose just as I feel movement in the air to my right. Years of meticulous training kick in and I duck, avoiding an arm that flies above my head. Twisting my body, my fist connects with the hard planes of Torvin's stomach, earning a heavy grunt. He grabs my wrist before I can pull it out of reach and tugs, kicking my legs out from under me. We topple to the ground, his body pinning mine.

"Get off me Torvin," I grit through my teeth.

"A little slow this evening, Ameria," he says, his mouth quirking up to the side.

My lips curve into a wicked smile and I uncurl my fists. Letting flames coat my palms. I hold them close to his hands which are restraining my wrists against the mat. My smile grows wider as I watch him start to squirm under the heat while attempting to use his air magic to put out my flames. He can't though, because my magic is more powerful than his.

Snarling, Torvin jumps off me while shaking out his hands. "Always so hostile!"

My flames extinguish and I hop up off the floor. "What do you want Torvin?"

The six-foot-three brute of a man stalks forward to crowd my space. "Your father has summoned us to his office."

With an inward groan, I push past Torvin who easily catches up to walk alongside me, and we stroll silently through the halls to my father's office. Being so late into the evening, and if only Torvin and I are being called in, it can only mean we'll either be sent to take someone out or kidnap them. The King has a few offices scattered throughout the palace, each one used for different purposes. Based on the direction we're heading, to his private wing, it further confirms what I suspected my activities for the rest of the evening would be.

The hallways of the palace are quiet save for our boots hitting the polished beige stone. This place has always been a bore to me. Everything is either beige, white, or gold. The only color in here is from the occasional bouquets of flowers placed by my father's current lover.

The doors to the King's office are, of course, stark white with flame engravings. I grip the gaudy gold handle and swing the door open. My father lounges in a chair by the crackling fire, my sister sitting opposite him in a matching plush chair. Small bouquets of flame azaleas and tansies sit atop the mantel with his collection of worldly trinkets. Bookshelves line the walls, and his wide cherry oak desk sits in front of the floor-to-ceiling windows that overlook the back gardens.

Torvin bursts through the door behind me, hitting my shoulder with his arm on the way in. I flick my eyes in annoyance and shut the door as he takes his place in the middle of the room. A stack of parchments sits on the table between my father and sister. "What are you doing here Petra?" I ask, trying to keep my tone indifferent as I come to stand in front of Torvin.

She flips her soft caramel hair over a perfectly tan shoulder and opens her mouth, no doubt to say something snarky, but

Toross answers before she has the chance. "Petra is beginning to learn the ways of the Fire Kingdom, just like any future Queen should." She shoots a pompous smile my way as he says this.

Petra is my half-sister and also a cousin. My father, the prick he is, had an affair with my mother's sister Queen Thea of the Earth Kingdom not long after I was born. This resulted in a pest of a younger sister who came to live here after my mother died. She inherited fire magic, so my aunt sent her to the Fire Kingdom. Our father decided she'd make a better Queen and I a pet that could be ordered around. What irks me the most is that she resembles my mother, and I received all of our father's genes except for my eyes.

I was fifteen when my mother died, and the pain caused me to release a magic this land had not seen for thousands of years. The few who witnessed my outburst were executed so that none would know the power I could wield. From then on, my father encouraged the use of my dark magic. He made me practice wielding shadows so I could spy and taught me efficient and brutal ways to get people to talk. He viewed me as a tool and molded me as such. One hundred and sixty years later, I have become the perfect weapon.

"You two are to go retrieve Lord Reeve this evening. That folder has all the information you need" the King announces while swirling his goblet of wine. "I expect to be informed when you return and a report on what you've found."

I snatch the folder before Torvin can. He throws me a glare and I smirk while flipping it open. "What would you like us to do with him when we bring him back, Your Majesty?" Torvin asks in his perfect kiss-ass tone.

My father waves a jeweled hand in the air as he takes another sip of wine. "Throw him in the dungeons' lower levels for now."

Torvin nods, "Will do, my King." He bows and heads to the door.

Toross finally glances up from the fire to me, clearly looking for verbal confirmation. "Yes, Your Majesty," I respond with a small dip of my head. I turn and march through the door Torvin is holding open. Once we're out and halfway down the hall, I close the folder and abruptly stop. "Here," I shove it into his hands. "I'll meet you by the eastern servants' doors in fifteen." I hear him mumble something under his breath, but I've already walked away in a rush toward the wing I share with Petra.

I bust through the doors to my suite in a fit of rage, startling a poor maid who was exiting my room with laundry. Muttering an apology, I storm into my closet, reaching for the button that's hidden behind a display stand holding my old tiara from when I was a child.

As wood paneling slides back on the back wall, I push past all the frilly dresses I rarely wear and step into my secret room.

The sets of black leather armor I wear for these late-night excursions line the wall to the left, my regular training outfits to the right, and some of the finest enchanted weapons claim the back wall. My mother's black steel sword displayed right in the middle.

A room full of "gifts" from my father. I learned quickly that these were not presents from the heart, but rather bribes. If they did not work, he beat me until I folded like a towel. It's been a while since he's had to punish me like that. Last time, he locked me in a confining pitch-black cell afterward. My wounds would have become infected if Haemir hadn't risked his life to bring me a couple of Mereena's healing elixirs. Since then, I decided that it's easier to just toe the line and do what he says, like a good little pet.

I hastily change into leathers and slip on my boots, their ebony black making my pale skin look as white as the moon. Preferring daggers over swords, especially in my line of work, I reach for my favorite slightly curved blades and strap them to my hips. These are enchanted to never chip or dull. A gift I received last month after the longest torturing session I've ever completed.

The panel wall shifts back into place as I enter my main closet again and push the same hidden button. Removing the band at the bottom of my braid, I shake out my hair with my fingers and redo it, the tail hitting between my shoulder blades. Staring in the mirror, I let out a disgruntled snort, slip on my hood, and tie my mask around the bottom portion of my face, hiding everything but my mother's green eyes and the dark circles accompanying them.

I stand in front of my suite's double doors for a moment and reach down into the depths of my well. I poke at my magic and it stirs awake, slithering up to crawl just beneath my skin. A chill creeps up my spine and I take a deep breath to steady myself. Shadows swirl around me and I portal to the hallway where I told Torvin to be. Keeping my shadows cloaked around me, I survey him already standing by the door. His broad frame takes up most of the narrow hallway as he leans against the wall, his black hair hanging partially across his face.

Torvin's matching leathers mold perfectly to his thighs, accentuating his butt. He may be an asshole but damn, if he isn't nice to look at. Shoving those thoughts away – because that would be an awful idea – I ease my way in front of him. I stand there with my arms crossed and let the shadows fall away.

My lips twitch, satisfied with the small jolt he makes as I appear. "Shit. I hate when you do that."

I snort and uncross my arms to open the door. "Let's just get this over with."

Chapter Two
Ameria

Sweat drips down the back of my neck as we jump from roof to roof, heading to the outskirts of Litherion, the capital city of the Fire Kingdom. Lord Reeve's estate is east, just outside the main city limits. I shimmy down a drainpipe and jump into a back alley with Torvin landing right behind me. We're nearing the edge of the city where the buildings are set farther apart, which means we'll have to go the rest of the way on the ground.

"Alright shadow lady, time to use your magic," Torvin whispers behind me. I roll my eyes but do it anyway, cloaking us both in darkness. We sneak effortlessly out of the city, unseen.

We make it to the estate and hide in the forest surrounding the house, waiting for Lord Reeve to arrive home. "We need to search his office when we're in there," Torvin says while resting against the tree next to me.

"I read what we need to do, this isn't my first time," I spit.

"I was just reminding you," he grumbles.

I'm about to curse him out when I hear horses and a carriage come down the road. I cloak us again and we make our way out of the trees. Luckily, the moon is hidden behind clouds, making this part easier.

Not one but four people exit the coach and I stop dead in my tracks. "He's not supposed to have anyone with him," I whip my head toward Torvin, "let alone his whole family," I hiss.

Torvin stiffens, fists clenched, as his wide eyes dart between the house and the family heading toward it. "Okay, new plan. We'll have to grab him when he's alone. Our sources say he stays up later than his family anyway, so we'll just have to improvise and jump at the first chance we get. We'll need your shadows to muffle the sound too."

"If I use my shadows to do that, I can't use them to get us all back to the palace."

"What good is your magic if you can barely use it?"

My jaw drops. The fucking asshole. "What exactly have you contributed?"

He cocks a smile, "My devastatingly good looks and muscle, obviously."

I throw him a scowl and ignore his cocky remark, "I have used my magic almost all day, I don't have much left in me." This is a monumental lie. I can feel an endless stream of magic coming from my well, but the longer I use it the harder it is to ignore its need to be used. Plus, it's better for others to not know how much I am truly able to wield.

He groans and pinches the bridge of his nose. "Fine. We'll steal the carriage and just burn it when we get back to the palace to get rid of the evidence."

"What if someone sees the carriage go into the palace?"

Torvin's face is in mine in seconds. "You've got a better idea, Princess?"

I grit my teeth, knowing I don't. "Don't call me that. And fine, let's go."

We're still cloaked as we find an unlatched window on the ground floor, thanks to a maid who was likely paid heavily, and climb in. The voices of his family tell me that they are all still on the ground floor. I don't do well sitting around so I take the opportunity to search for his office. The report said it was on the main floor in the back of the house, so I tug Torvin by his arm, signaling him to follow and stay within my shadows.

I stay close to the floor when we enter the hallway so the fae lights don't catch my movement. All the rich have automatic fae lights, and even though we are cloaked in shadow, they can still pick us up. The office is easy to find as it's the only door in the hallway that's closed. I freeze as voices emerge at the other end.

Lady Reeve and her two children come into view, Lord Reeve on their tail. I can't make out the hushed sentence he speaks to her, but her response is loud and clear, "Oh no, you sir are coming up and helping tuck them into bed!" His wife sneers with a glare while shooing the children up the stairs. I bite the inside of my lip to fight a snicker as the bastard slumps and trudges up after them.

"Do you think opening the door will set off the two lights above us?" Torvin whispers.

My lips draw into a tight line as I peer at the lights, my nose scrunching in annoyance. "Maybe. I can at least try." I scooch over so that my back is fully against the door. Staying as still as possible, I bend my elbow and bring my left arm in as close to my body as I can. Slowly, I rotate my shoulder so my forearm is out to my side and the back of my hand rests against the door.

As I ease my arm up toward the knob, I silently thank Haemir for forcing me to work on shoulder mobility. My fingertips graze the knob, and I turn it. The door clicks and cracks open. Torvin eases his way closer to the door and we lock eyes as he uses his fingertips to push it the rest of the way. The lights stay off and we both release a relieved breath. Hastily, we move the rest of the way into the office and shut the door behind us.

"Might as well search while we wait," Torvin says as he stalks over to the desk, tapping the small light that sits on the desk to turn it on.

We start carefully rummaging through his stacks of parchment and drawers, looking for anything that could prove his involvement with the rebellion. The report I read before coming here said that it's suspected he is slowly funneling money into their pockets, so any documents showing his finances would be perfect.

"I'm not finding a single thing." Torvin says while searching the cabinets at the bottom of the bookshelves that line both side walls.

"Neither am I," I grumble. "He's careful, I'll give him that."

Footsteps sound from the hall, heading straight toward the office. Torvin carefully closes the cabinet he was looking in and swiftly tucks himself into the corner of the room. I tap the light off and take the other corner, readying my shadows to swallow the room in darkness and muffle the sound the minute Lord

Reeve enters.

The door cracks…

It's not Lord Reeve.

His wife walks into the dark office and heads for the desk, completely unaware of our presence. I shoot a wide-eyed glance toward Torvin, able to make out his equally panicked expression through the hallway light filtering in. Just as she taps the light on the desk, I make the split-second decision to release my shadows around the room.

She screams but outside my magic, no one can hear her. Torvin, now understanding my plan, rushes over and knocks her on the back of the head with the pommel of his dagger. Her body thumps to the floor. "Merriam?" I whip my head up as the door opens and light pours in. While the light cannot pierce my shadows, it's still evident the room is enveloped in unnatural darkness. Lord Reeve's eyes bulge, and then he runs.

"Shit. New plan!" I yelp as I unsheathe a dagger and book it after him. I catch up and we tumble to the floor as I tackle him. He manages to get a kick in but unfortunately for him, I'm not a man and am unaffected. A crunching noise comes from his face as I shove it into the marble flooring. I slam the back of his head with my dagger hilt and he at last falls still. I let out a hefty sigh.

"Mommy? Daddy?"

My heart drops and I peer up to where the voices came from. "Shit," I hear Torvin mutter from behind me. The two children are staring through the banister at the top of the stairs. I wince. Don't scream, don't scream, don't scream.

Blood-curdling screams echo through the foyer and the two

of them rush out of sight. My head sags between my shoulders as I groan. "You find the girl, I'll take care of the boy first," Torvin says as he walks past me.

I leap up the stairs after him. "Don't hurt the boy." I hiss.

Torvin pauses and glares back at me, "I'm not heartless you know." I return the glare and climb past him, taking two steps at a time.

I find the girl's bedroom and smother it with shadows so that she cannot see but I can. It's not hard to find her with the sniffles coming from under the bed. I now wait for Torvin to come, suffering through the sound of a family I'm tearing apart.

My mind floods with the memory of a time I hid under my bed, the first time my father hit me because I accidentally broke one of his antiques. My mother almost brought the whole room to the ground with her vines. Footsteps pierce my thoughts, and I'm brought back to the present, finding Torvin already standing at the door. I allow him to see into my shadows and point to the bed, grateful that he didn't see me lost in one of my flashbacks.

I feel the air shift and a moment later the sniffling stops. With parents from the Air Kingdom, Torvin is able to render someone unconscious without hurting them by quickly cutting off their oxygen supply.

Releasing my shadows, I gently pull the little girl out from under the bed and place her under the covers. I stop by the door and look back at the child. "They're going to remember."

"There's not much we can do about that," says Torvin, standing next to me.

I shoot him a glance, "You know what he'd have us do."

"They're children," he spits at me.

"I know," I hiss back, "I'm not saying we do it either. But.." My words trail off as I remember the few times my father has ordered the execution of a youngling and made me do it. Those deeds will forever stain my soul.

"We'll have to report it," he finishes the sentence for me.

I turn and leave the room, heading for the stairs. "Let's worry about the mother first. She didn't see us, but she saw my magic, which is a problem."

"We'll have to bring her with us," Torvin responds as we rush down the stairs. I release a sigh while looking down the hall toward the office, Lady Reeve's feet sticking out from behind the desk. "I'll bring her out after I search the office. You take him and load him into the carriage."

My jaw clenches at his commands but I comply, just to avoid arguing, and start dragging the lord's unconscious body to the front door.

"We really messed up tonight," Torvin heaves as Lord Reeve's body hits the dungeon floor with a heavy thump making dust fly. I put his wife in the cell a few doors down so that they can't see each other, making it more torturous for him when he wakes.

"Yeah." My tone is bitter as I lock the cell door after he exits. "We did what we could though."

We ditched the carriage in the forest right outside the palace's back entrance before hauling the unconscious couple to the dungeons, telling a guard on the way to get rid of the carriage.

I start walking down the hall toward the stairs to exit when Torvin cuts me off by slamming my back into the stone wall. My dagger is at his throat in seconds. The small flicker of torchlight on the wall by my head highlights the side of his angered face and the natural silver-blonde that's growing in at the roots of his dyed black hair. "Your father won't see it that way," he growls. Baring my teeth at him, I push the dagger into the skin of his throat, enough to make a small trickle of blood appear.

"Back off Torvin."

"You know what," he pushes off me, taking a step back, "you can give your father the report for once." With that said, he turns and hastily stomps away.

Bile stings the back of my throat as I watch him disappear, the handle of my dagger digging into my palm under my stiff grip. Since Torvin arrived a few months ago, I have managed to avoid giving my father the reports just in case there was something he wasn't happy about. Whatever luck I had has just ended because he's going to be pissed. And nothing is more terrifying than the wrath of the King when he's angry.

I make a small detour to the large kitchen on my way to my father's wing. I haven't had dinner yet and at least one bottle of wine will be necessary after speaking with him. Maybe two. I have the staff send food and wine to my suite and then make the long trek to the Western wing.

The guard knocks on the King's suite doors as I try to calm the ache in my chest and wipe my sweaty palms on my cloak. My magic perks up at my distress but I manage to keep it at bay, for now. "Come in," my father's voice floats from somewhere behind the closed doors.

It's eased open for me, and I step through, squaring my shoulders before I walk down the small hall before me. The King lounges in front of the fire reading through stacks of parchment. "Father, I've come to relay the report," I state, begging my voice to stay steady and calm. He looks up, waiting for me to continue. I clear my throat, "There wasn't any evidence that he's directly working with the rebellion. It seems he's being very careful. We retrieved Lord Reeve and locked him in the middle of the southern cells." I take a deep breath. "Unfortunately, we ran into some complications."

Toross tosses the parchment he was holding onto the table. "What kind of complications?" he barks.

I swallow hard. "The report said he would arrive home alone, but his family was with him. We changed our plans, but they were disrupted by Lady Reeve walking in instead of her husband. We managed to knock her out, but she saw the magic used and the children witnessed the capture of their father."

My heart feels like it's going to come flying out of my chest as my father slowly rises from his seat. "What did you do with Lady Reeve and the children?"

"We brought Lady Reeve with us and put her in a different cell. The children though, we rendered them unconscious and put them in their rooms."

Flames burst from the King's hands. The tips of his red hair spark and his amber eyes glow like molten lava. "You useless pig of a child." He stalks toward me, his steps scorching sizzling tracks on the rug in his wake. "Do you know how much of a problem this is going to cause me? The children will spread word that their parents are missing. The rebellion will go into hiding. This could ruin everything!"

His fist comes lightning fast. My nose cracks and I am face down on the floor. Blood from my nose dribbles down into my mouth and onto the pristine white carpet. Flashbacks to the last beating flood my vision. "I'm sorry father! We did what we could in the moment."

A foot collides with my side, and I instinctively curl in on myself. "That's King to you, pet." Another kick, and another. My breaths become rough and ragged as my ribs start to snap. A slight reprieve comes when his foot halts and a rattled whine leaves me. A lock clicks open and my body stills, stiffening with what's to come. My tear-stained gaze finds my father at the box I know all too well.

"Please, it won't happen again. I'll fix it," I beg as my father gently closes the lid and turns, enchanted blade in hand. Calmly, he walks toward where I still lay curled on the ground.

"You will fix it. And may this remind you so that it doesn't happen again." He gives a short, sharp whistle and the two guards from outside come rushing in. They grab my arms and restrain me on my knees with my back facing my father.

My dark magic comes slithering out of its hole. It crawls under my skin, begging to take over. I try to keep it from doing so, but as the blade makes its first swipe upon my back…I let my magic consume me.

Chapter Three
Ameria

Stumbling into my suite, I kick the doors closed behind me and collapse to the floor. Blood drips slowly from my nose as I stare out at the beige and gold-accented room. He'd broken it on the first hit but on the way back to my room I reset it – a skill I learned long ago. Besides the broken nose that will leave me with a pair of swollen purple and blue eyes tomorrow, he kept much of the damage to areas that would be concealed by clothing. I'll have Mereena heal most of it in the morning with her array of magical ointments. The new wound on my back though…

I cringe, still feeling the slow slice of his enchanted blade over and over again. A third cut right along my spine this time, to match the other two he gave me when I was younger. The pain has stopped for now, my body already healing the broken skin into an ugly scar that will forever taunt me like the others. That's the enchantment of his special blade – it leaves a permanent scar on a fae's body and every so often it will feel like acid fire is burning underneath it. A torture to last a lifetime.

My magic is nowhere to be found. All I remember is bits and pieces of searing pain, but not as much as I should have felt. At this point, I couldn't care less that I let my magic have full control of my consciousness. That's a problem for another day, when I haven't just been beaten to a pulp.

Easing my way onto my hands and knees, I slowly crawl over to where my food and wine are waiting on the table in front of the cream-colored couch. Each movement has me wincing in pain from my ribs. They'll take the longest to heal. After I manage to haul myself onto the couch, I stuff some bread into my mouth. Swiping the bottle of wine off the table, I pull the cork out with my teeth and let it fall into my lap. I practically chug the stuff, letting the sweet wine flow down my throat and coat some of the pain radiating throughout my body.

The stew is cold by the time I finish the wine, but I eat it anyway and pop open the second bottle. A groan crawls up my throat as I stare at the doors to my bedroom in front of me. To get up and crawl to my bed or not?

My body clearly made the decision for me, since I wake up still on the couch, my head bent back at an unnatural angle. My head lolls to the side and I hiss as splitting pain radiates through my brain. By the light coming through the curtains, I can tell it's mid-morning. Which means I'm going to be late to meet Mereena in the library.

With a deep exhale, I haul myself up, kicking the empty wine bottle by my feet in the process, and carefully make my way to the bathroom knowing it's going to be an exceptionally long day.

The large leather-bound book hits the library table with a thunk, and I sink myself into a chair with a huff. Mereena sits across from me, her nose in some new herb book she found on a recent trip home to the Earth Kingdom. She's an earth fae but was born here on the palace grounds because her mother relocated here when mine married my father. After my mother died, hers went back to their home kingdom, but Mereena chose not to leave.

Mereena takes after her mother who had a knack for healing magic. Over the years, she's become skilled at crossbreeding different plants and inventing new mixture combinations. Her thirst and excitement for plants and knowledge is one of the things I love most about her.

It has been a few days since Torvin and I screwed up our mission. Mereena immediately set to healing me when I entered the library that day. I'd tortured answers out of Lord Reeve this morning after letting him stew in the dungeons. He cracked like an egg with only a few swipes of my blade and words of harm toward his wife.

I'd questioned her separately and it turned out she was a part of the rebellion as well, which meant immediate death. My father had me execute her in front of her husband before I killed him too. I'm not sure what became of their children but I'd rather not know and sit in ignorance.

The questioning revealed that apparently, a special shipment was said to arrive in a small docking town off the coast of the Water Kingdom this week. A weapon that allows its wielder to magnify his or her magic was reportedly aboard. We also added a few more names to the roster of known rebels, whom I'm sure Torvin and I will be sent out to collect soon.

The King was furious and ordered some of his spies to try and intercept the shipment. It was likely for naught, however, since the Fire Kingdom and Water Kingdom don't have good relations.

The Elemental Lands have four kingdoms - Fire, Earth, Water, and Air. We've always had a tense relationship with the water fae so it's no surprise to me that it looks like they're aiding the rebellion.

Even before the continent was broken into the four kingdoms, when all the elemental fae lived among each other, the water and fire rulers never got along. Again, this is not really a surprise since I'm sure my ancestors were all pricks just like my father.

I came right here after the session in the dungeons. Since mates can speak to each other in their minds, Haemir had told Mereena to bring one of her calming medicines to the library for me. It has done enough to settle my magic a bit, but hopefully escaping into one of my favorite books will help ease it further and I can detach from my emotions.

Worrying on my bottom lip, I flip open the book. When I was younger, my mother would read me various stories about the Gods that our land used to worship. Since then, it has been my favorite topic partly because when I read it, I feel like my mother is reading alongside me.

No one worships the Gods anymore. Instead, we celebrate the land and the magic it continues to provide for us. All traces of the Gods in the Elemental Lands disappeared many millennia ago, according to history books and rumors. Now, all we have are their myths.

I will my muscles to relax and let my eyes drift over the pages I've read many times before. This particular story is about a war between the Gods that went on for years. They battled and slaughtered each other in hopes of taking the throne and becoming the King of Gods. Svarog, the King at the time, was passing the realm on to one of his sons, but another disagreed with his father's choice and so the war began.

The story doesn't have an ending, which continues to plague me. They probably all killed each other and that's why they disappeared and we stopped worshiping them. Who knows.

"I don't know why you read that nonsense," Mereena mutters and my gaze snaps to her. Her nose is still stuffed in her new book, but she pauses to annotate something in the margin.

With a small grumble, I flip the book closed. "Because it's interesting, Mereena." My eyes wander up to the golden-domed ceiling and take in the faint flames etched into it. "It makes me wonder what life was like when we did worship the Gods. If they really roamed the lands granting miracles and gifting unique magic to people."

Mereena snorts, "I'm sure it involved a lot of unnecessary, time-consuming ceremonies." I bring my gaze back down and smile at her scribbling away on a notepad.

I decide to change the subject. "Getting a lot of new information about your plants?" I ask, resting my chin on the heel of my palm.

My friend finally looks up and squeals, a wide grin spreading across her face. "I can't believe I found this book. I mean, there are some flowers in here that I never thought to use for certain remedies." A small gasp emanates from her and my brows raise in amusement. Her eyes widen, "How would you like to try a tea that knocks you right out? There might be a few side effects but nothing too damaging I don't think."

I squint my eyes at her. "First of all, absolutely not. Second of all, isn't that what Haemir is for?"

"What am I for?" Haemir says as he walks through the rows of bookshelves behind Mereena. "You know, besides the obvious bedside manner."

I make a disgusted noise in the back of my throat at his comment. "Mereena wants to try one of her new experimental concoctions on me again."

Haemir bends down to kiss his mate and takes the seat next to her. He cringes, "Honestly, I wouldn't mind taking a break from her experiments." Mereena's mouth falls open and she smacks his arm. "I'm sorry my love," he chuckles while holding his hands up in defense, "but sometimes the side effects are a little too much."

Mereena clicks her tongue and scowls, "I always fix you afterward. Don't be such a baby." I snort to myself, watching them bicker. "Well, how about it Ameria? It's just one little sleeping tonic!"

I aggressively shake my head, "Oh no, I've had enough of your little sleeping tonics Mereena. The last one had me out for three days!"

"I was eventually able to wake you up," she defends.

My eyes narrow, "Key word being, 'eventually'."

"Anyway," Haemir drawls, dragging Mereena off her chair and into his lap, "have you seen the post today?"

I lean back in my seat and cross my arms. "No, why?"

"Apparently, the Western Isles are holding their warrior competition this year and it starts in about a week."

The Western Isles are a cluster of Islands west of the Elemental Lands, not too far from the Water Kingdom. They're pretty elusive, the fae from the Isles. The only contact our lands have with them is for trade and the annual meeting between all the Kings and Queens. They also regulate who can cross their borders, and everyone must travel there by ship since non-residents can't portal their way in or out. Mostly, the Elemental Lands and Western Isles have stayed out of each other's way.

"And your point is?"

Mereena and Haemir share a look with each other. "We think you should enter," Mereena whispers.

My jaw slackens in a moment of shock and then I snort. "Yeah, okay. Let me just pack up and head on over there."

"We mean it Ameria," Haemir's tone is stern. "This could be your one chance at freeing yourself from this life, from your father. We know you've been thinking about it more lately."

I instantly swallow us in my shadows to mute our conversation. "Are you crazy? Anybody could hear you! And what, you think I can just leave without his knowledge? He'd catch me before I even made it onto the ship," I hiss back at him.

"We see the toll these past months have put on you. For fuck's sake he's started to beat you again! Who knows when he'll tire of you and you'll suddenly be the one on that metal table getting your skin peeled off," Mereena says, angrily pointing her finger at me.

Haemir sighs, "Once you enter the competition your father can't touch you anymore. It's literally written in the rules. You should know that by now considering that you've played with this idea since the last time it was held," he raises an eyebrow, daring me to disagree.

He is right, I have thought about it. In my one hundred and seventy-five years of life, they have only held the competition twice. Who knows if I'll be alive for the next one? The rules of the competition are that once you join, you are considered to be in the process of becoming a Western Isles resident. This means that whatever crimes you committed here in the Elemental Lands become void.

The rulers here don't seem to bat an eye when the competition comes around, likely because those who enter either die or are no longer an Elemental citizen and no longer their problem. The event draws a lot of criminals and mercenaries for that specific reason.

My mouth forms a tight line as I briefly consider it. "I can't just leave you two here. If I somehow make it, Toross will take it out on you two and I can't allow that." I look away from the two of them cuddled into each other, unable to stomach possibly losing them. "Enough people have been hurt because of me."

"We would go with you," Mereena says softly.

I stand while dropping my shadows. "I'll think about it. I should go get cleaned up before my duties at the Summer

Solstice Luncheon in an hour." I leave my friends who are still canoodling and head to my suite, but first I stop by the kitchens and grab some wine. The need to wash off the grime from this morning is as strong as the need to drown it from my mind as well.

Following Petra around the luncheon was not what I had in mind. It's more like babysitting since she has never bothered to learn how to defend herself. I'd arrived assuming I was going to do my usual sleuthing in dark corners and watching people from the wrap-around balcony above the ballroom. Turns out my father wanted me to personally follow her around in this horrendous guard uniform. The metal clanks as I walk and it has started to give me a headache. While I'm thankful this thing covers my face, it's as hot as the underworld.

Petra has greeted every lord, lady, dignitary, and so on with a gentle dip of her head and a perfectly curated smile. Sometimes I'm grateful that it's not me having to put on a fake smile in front of all the wealthy assholes of this Kingdom. She hasn't said a word to me. Why would she? I'm just her dog for the night. We rarely talk to one another anyway.

Lucky for me, she retires early and I can get out of this uniform. It's a hassle but I make it out of the thing and kick the stupid helmet halfway across the room where the uniforms are kept.

I'm in my usual leathers and up on the balcony seconds later thanks to being able to portal. The stronger your magic, the higher the likelihood you'll be able to portal. Some can only do small distances, and some can't do it at all. I never portal with my fire magic because it's unnecessary when my shadows can take me further. Plus, portaling with fire isn't exactly discreet.

I take a couple of laps around the balcony and find the few lords my father wanted me to keep an eye on. I take up a spot in the darkest area I can find and watch the three of them. It's boring work since they're quite unlikely to do something right under my father's nose, but I make mental notes of who they talk to and for how long. Interestingly, they don't speak to one another. However, I notice that two of them make small glances toward each other, and note that in my head as well.

As I continue to watch my marks enjoy the party below, my brain wanders to my earlier conversation with Haemir and Mereena. I can't believe that they're suggesting I enter the competition. The last time it was held I was old enough and I had thought about it. Haemir nudged me a little then, but it was not like how they're trying to convince me now.

Back then, I was too scared to leave, especially without them. But this time they say they'll go with me. Can they really do that? What happens if we're caught? There's no doubt their lives would be in danger by default. My father would torture me by going after them since he knows how important they are to me.

"Knew I'd find you here." My body jolts at the sound of Torvin's voice. Muttering a curse, I glance his way as he comes to stand next to me. I'm a little peeved that I was so in my head that he was able to sneak up on me. That doesn't happen often because my magic usually warns me by abruptly rising from my well. This afternoon, it has been a little too quiet.

"Where else would I be?" I snark and continue resting against the pillar as if he hadn't spooked me.

"Heard your father was pissed about the report."

"Yeah. Thanks for that by the way," I huff, sending him a quick glare.

"I'd had enough of his disapproval, and it was time for you to take some of it for a change," Torvin grunts as he takes up a position against the other pillar.

This time, I study him a bit longer. Understanding floods me. "I didn't know he showed his displeasure to others the same way he does with me," I say.

He makes a noise in the back of his throat but doesn't say anything. We watch the party for a while, not uttering a single word to one another. Believe it or not, this is one of the more pleasurable moments I have with Torvin, working in comfortable silence next to him. When he first started working with me, he would try to get me to talk. I quickly shut that down, though he still sometimes tries to converse with me.

After a while, Torvin speaks, his voice quiet, soft. "What happened to the children?" My heart clenches and I have to fight the tears that well up. "I don't know, but I'm sure nothing good," I whisper.

We fall back into our usual silence until the party begins to wind down. I gather my courage and push off the pillar to go report to my father. The last thing I want to do is go see him. There's nothing he could possibly be upset about this time because tonight was uneventful, but the past couple of days since being beaten are still very fresh in my mind.

I'm half covered in shadow when Torvin grabs my wrist. My shadows halt and I look into his ice-blue eyes. "Tell me what you've observed, and I'll go give him the report this time." My brows jump upward, but instead of arguing that I don't need his pity, I let him.

Chapter Four
Ameria

After snarfing down some meat stew, I rush to change clothes as Mereena and Haemir wait in the living area of my suite. My thin-strapped, bright yellow silk dress flows just past my knees. I shake out my typical simple braid and let my ginger hair fall free in waves.

I fix my belt pouch around my hips, grab the half-drunk bottle of wine off my vanity, and waltz out to where my friends sit drinking one of their own. Mereena, in her matching but vibrant orange dress, pops up out of her seat and links arms with me. Haemir stands with his arms spread wide, a bottle in hand. "Ah, my two rays of sunshine!" His smile is radiant as he strides over to drape both arms around our shoulders and shove us toward the doors.

"In a hurry, are we?" I snort.

"I don't want to miss all the free alcohol!"

"Haemir, you're already drinking free alcohol."

"Yes, yes, but it tastes different when you're dancing around a fire."

Mereena scoffs and pushes her mate off of us. Reaching for the door, she drags me by the arm out into the hallway with Haemir fumbling behind us.

The three of us hurry through the servants' halls to avoid others and make our way to the stables. My beautiful black stallion Rasha, a single white splotch on his hind quarters, is already saddled and ready to go. Shoving my bottle of wine into the waiting stableman's hand, I fling myself up onto my horse. I snatch the bottle back and take a generous swig.

"Which town are we off to Ameria?" Mereena asks while bringing her horse up next to mine.

Haemir pulls up in front of us to lead the way as I grin, "Bellmoore is the best of the best celebrations this year my friends." With that, I give my horse a kick and take off.

We arrive at the edge of Bellmoore where the festivities are already well underway. My friends and I finished our bottles on the ride and are ready to have more. Two large bonfires blaze in the darkness, illuminating the hundreds of fae dancing around them.

Haemir takes our horses and ties them to the designated poles in front of portable troughs. As he does that, I close my eyes and take a deep breath, inhaling the smell of smoke and various foods, while letting the music float through my ears.

I grin wildly, grab Mereena's hand, and take off running toward one of the fires. "Get us some drinks, will ya Haemir?" I yell back at him over my shoulder. We giggle as the two of us join the circle of dancing fae around the fires, twirling and swinging our hips to the beat. I let the magic of the land wash over me and let myself feel free, even if it's only for the night. Reality can wait.

Haemir has finally caught up with us and he shoves a drink into my hand before stealing Mereena away to dance. It's a sweet-smelling wine and I take three long gulps. The drums pound through the air as I drink and continue to dance, changing partners every so often.

At some point later, I stumble out of the spirited crowd for a breather, having lost sight of my two friends long ago. The cool summer air feels blissful against my sweaty body. A group starts to line up before a stall and I poke my head around them trying to figure out what's being sold. My eyes flare wide when a woman walks away with a bag full of peach candy strings. It's the most delicious candy and my summer favorite, made only in the Earth Kingdom. Giddy with joy, I hop right in line to get my sugary bag of sweets.

"I figured this is where we'd find you!" Mereena startles me while flinging her arms around my waist and giving me a squeeze. I squeeze her back. "I saw a man walk by with three bags of those things and I knew I'd be able to spot you."

"The man's teeth looked like he didn't need three bags of them though," Haemir chimes in, dragging Mereena against his chest and clasping his arms around her front. The two of them share a drunken, passionate kiss.

I scrunch my nose and step up to the older woman running the cart. I purchase four bags, two for me and two for my friends who still have their tongues down each other's throats. I cough to get their attention and push them out of the way.

After handing the giggling lovebirds their bags, I rip into mine, my mouth already salivating just from thinking about the sweets. The minute the sugary candy touches my tongue, a moan slips from my throat. Bouncing on my toes, I flail my arms in the sky with a peach string half hanging out of my mouth, "Gods these are so fucking good!" My words come out mumbled, with my teeth still holding onto the candy.

In the turning of my happy little dance, I find my friends feeding each other their candy. A disgusted noise rumbles in the back of my throat and I rip the candy string in half with my teeth. "Must you two be so nauseatingly cute?"

Mereena pouts, "Oh, Ameria. Don't worry, you'll find your mate one day."

I recoil, my face twisting, "Who said I wanted one?"

"Please, like you expect us to believe that with the number of romance novels you have stashed underneath your bed where you think nooooo one can see them," Haemir snorts.

My mouth falls open and I slap his arm, "What are you doing under my bed you nosy ass?"

His head flies backward in laughter. "The maids love to talk. All the guards know about your little stash too."

I can feel heat flood my cheeks but with a scoff, I push through my two friends and stomp my way to one of the beverage stalls. Do I enjoy reading about two people finding each other against all odds and falling in love? Of course I do. It's cheesy and cute and I'm not a total monster. Realistically though, I know it will never happen for me. Given my current situation, it would just be another way for my father to have a tighter grasp on me. It's best if I just stick to keeping casual sex partners and disregard romance entirely.

The second I get my hands on a cup of sweet wine, I chug it, washing down the five peach strings I shoved into my mouth while in line. I fling another two coins at the man and he hands me another. Wandering around the field, I watch people eat, dance, and drink. How I wish things could have been different for me...

I could run. Right here, right now. I could just up and leave the Fire Kingdom. These thoughts have crossed my mind many times. But then I think about Haemir and Mereena. Hell, I've even thought about what would happen to my sister if I left. Dozens of maps are seared into my brain, just in case one day I do flee and never look back. In the end, I doubt I'd make it very far without my father or one of his spies finding me. My friends would be executed, and I'd be tortured in ways I don't even want to think about.

A little girl runs by me, skids to a halt, and whips her head back in my direction. She grins, showing off a gap where her first canine will soon grow in. I smile back as she trots toward me. Hanging around her elbow are crowns made of vibrant red flowers. "This would look so pretty in your orange hair!" She holds out one of the crowns, "May I miss?"

I smile and nod, "Of course." Kneeling, I let the young girl place it atop my head. As she does, I notice the flowers are poppies, which do not grow here in the Fire Kingdom. She must be of Earthen descent, where all sorts of flowers and plants grow. I touch the crown on my head and stand, "Thank you very much, young lady. Here," I fish a silver from my pouch. "Your hard efforts should be rewarded."

The smile slips from my face as a memory of my own mother flits through my drunken haze. I heave a large breath and tip back the cup of wine, enjoying the slight burn in my throat. Shaking my head, I clear my mind of all the constricting thoughts and eye the crowd. Tonight is a perfect night to find someone to tangle with in a dark part of the field. My bare toes wiggle in the soft grass in anticipation. I shamelessly lost my slippers a few hours ago.

"Looking for someone?" a deep voice rumbles from behind me, hot breath caressing the tip of my ear. Startled, I jump with a yelp and spin around, tripping over my own feet. Strong hands grip my arms, keeping me from tumbling to the ground.

Steadying myself, I peer up at the fae man looming over me, which honestly isn't uncommon because I'm relatively short for a fae. His long, silver hair is a stark contrast against his deep umber skin, and it is tucked behind an ear adorned with gold jewels. Words suddenly become lost to me as I stare into those golden brown eyes. A brow rises, "Are you alright?"

I blink. "Oh, uh, yeah." I clear my throat with a shake of my head, "Yes. Sorry." Gods was I making a fool of myself.

"My name is Callum," he says with a smile and a slightly dramatic bow. "Would you care for a dance?"

Finally coming back to myself, I smirk, "I think I would." Throwing back the rest of my wine, I take his hand and drag him closer to the bonfire, throwing my cup in a waste bin on the way.

Callum pulls me into his arms and we spin in circles to the

beat of the drums. "So, my beauty, do I get the honor of knowing your name?"

A snort escapes me. "Do you talk like this normally, or are you just trying to woo me?" He lowers me into a dip. "Also, the name is Ameria."

His chest reverberates with a pleased hum. As we continue dancing, he leans down to whisper into my ear, "A beautiful name, to match a beautiful woman."

I snort, "Trying to flatter me, are you?"

"Is it working?"

"Possibly." I survey him, curious to know which Kingdom he comes from. My mind is already running through the possibility of seeing him again after this. "So, what Kingdom do you live in, Callum?"

He furrows his brows, "Do I really look like I would be from this ridiculous land?"

My head jerks back, but then realization dawns on me. My feet stumble and I stare at him, my mouth popping open a little. "You're from the Western Isles."

"I'm surprised it wasn't obvious. Just look at me." Callum smirks.

I ignore his baiting comment, "I didn't think anyone from the Isles would bother coming to the Elemental Lands."

We spin again, twirling away from the heat of the fire. "Not many do, but I had some business here to attend to."

He spins me. "And what business would that be?" I ask, extra curious as to what business would bring a Western Isles fae all the way here.

Callum smiles slightly, "Ah, that would be classified, my beauty." He spins me again but this time drops my hand. "It was an absolute pleasure meeting you, Ameria, but I must take my leave now."

"Oh…you're not going to stay for a while?" I question while watching him slowly back away.

"Unfortunately not. I was just heading home and when I laid my eyes on you. I had to stop and meet you first." He grins, though something about it seems off. "I'm quite glad I did. Perhaps you and I will meet again." With a wink, he finally turns and strides away. I stand there with mixed emotions, watching him until he disappears fully into the throng of people.

I sigh, feeling quite disappointed that I won't be having my way with him in the field after all. I grumble, maneuvering my way through the dancing couples to find my friends cozied up on a log drinking more wine. Mereena's face lights up when she sees me and Haemir looks like he's trying to smirk but is too drunk to do so. I snatch the wine cup right out of his hand and down it. "Hey!" He whines. I hand it back to him empty and plop down on the log next to Mereena.

Her smile fades, "What's wrong? This is supposed to be a happy night, not a grumpy one!"

"Plus, I saw you go off with that big handsome-lookin' fella for a while," Haemir teases, wiggling his brows. "You know, he looked soooo familiar too," he says, slurring his words and draping his arm over his mate's shoulders.

Annoyance flashes on Mereena's face, "Don't listen to him. He's gone up to at least twenty people tonight telling them they looked familiar." She places a hand on my arm, "But seriously, what's wrong? Did it not go well with that hunk of man?"

I ponder for a split second on whether or not to tell her about my interaction with Callum. Shaking my head, I decide now is not the time to bring it up, especially if they start trying to convince me to enter the competition again. "I just ended up not being that interested is all."

The halls are quiet as the three of us wander back to my suite. I'd convinced them both to stay in the guest bedroom across the living area so that we could all have breakfast together. We make it to the east wing when Torvin appears out of one of the rooms attached to the main hall – a room that happens to be Petra's. I stumble a few steps as I come to a halt. His shirt is loose and rumpled in places, undone a little, showing off his pale chest. Haemir and Mereena stop a couple of feet in front of me. Mereena's wide eyes bouncing between him and me.

I swallow a hard lump in my throat as Torvin takes a few steps toward me. "It uh… it's not what it looks like," he mutters.

A bark of laughter escapes me at the typical male line and I cross my arms. "Really Torvin? Getting with my sister? I didn't know you'd stoop so low."

Torvin clears his throat, "I, uh." He hesitates, his eyes darting between me and the shocked faces of my friends.

I raise my palms, "You know what, I don't want to know." That's something I'd rather not picture. Grabbing Mereena by the arm, I drag her with me to my suite, ignoring the hushed whispers between him and Haemir behind me. I have no idea when the two of them became so close but I'm too drunkenly annoyed to care.

What little respect I had for Torvin just went out the window. I didn't think he'd be the type to climb his way to the top by sleeping with the future queen but here we are. Though, if my father ever found out, Torvin would likely be burnt to a crisp.

Chapter Five
Ameria

My head is throbbing. Sinking further into the warm water of my tub, I massage my temples as last night plays on a loop in my head. First, meeting someone who was actually from the Western Isles, and then Torvin looking guilty as sin coming out of my sister's room. It should concern me that seeing him leaving her room so disheveled has put me in my feelings more than I'd care to admit.

Why not me? The thought crosses my mind. He's with me all the time, why wouldn't he go for me instead? Am I too much? Grumbling, I sink further and dunk my head under the water to wash away these pointless thoughts.

When I finally emerge into the suite's dining area, my friends are already eating a late breakfast. Mereena, of course, already has her new book splayed out in front of her.

Her head pops up. "There she is! We were wondering if you were going to show before the food went cold." From beside her, Haemir grunts around the food he's shoveled into his mouth. I plop into the seat across from them with a huff. "I made you my special hangover cure, as always," she says, nodding to the little vial next to my water glass.

"Thank the fucking Gods." I pop off the top and knock it back. A shiver crawls up my spine and I grimace from the sour taste, but my head immediately begins to clear, and my stomach begins to ease.

The room is quiet while we eat, the clanking of our utensils the only sound filling the air. I feel their watchful stares because they likely want to ask me about the Torvin and Petra situation. After getting ten minutes of side-eye, my fork clunks onto my plate. "What?" I snap at them.

Mereena eyes Haemir who raises his hands, one still wrapped around his spoon. He swallows his mouthful of food, "Nothing, nothing. It's just…" he glances toward his mate, "the competition is nearing." I blink with a start, not expecting that to be the subject they were going to bring up. I honestly had forgotten about it already.

"We really think you should enter," Mereena adds.

I squint at them. "Why are you two pushing this so hard? You know people die in that thing, right?"

"Yes, but you could also die here, so what's the difference?" Haemir replies dryly. Mereena elbows him with a scowl.

"That's nice Haemir, thank you," I scoff.

"Look, Ameria," another glance at her mate, "we have decided to leave. Not just the palace but the Fire Kingdom."

My jaw slackens and my eyes dart between them. "You're leaving me?" My voice rasps. Mereena winces, hurt crossing her face. I should feel bad making them feel guilty for leaving, but selfishly I don't. They're all I have.

"That is why we are pushing you to finally leave too, Ameria. We know that when we go, things will become much more difficult for you since we won't be here to give you the support you've needed all these years." I take a deep breath, Mereena's words sending a punch to my gut. My gaze drifts toward the open window, snagging on the sheer gold curtains blowing in the wind while feelings of helplessness and fear flood my mind.

Rarely do I acknowledge how much I depend on my two friends to keep me grounded and how much of a burden it probably puts on them. It has always been easier to ignore the fact that I place my happiness and livelihood in others because I have nothing other than my two best friends. I literally have nothing else in my life that brings me joy.

Now here I am, finally having to face those facts.

"Where will you go?" My voice comes out as a whisper. My eyes don't leave the fluttering curtains. Curtains I want to rip from the rod along with half of the other gold shit in this room. A room that's now starting to feel extra confining, the walls slowly closing in on me. It feels like a horse is sitting on my chest. I can't pull in a deep enough breath and tears begin to well up in my eyes, my throat constricting with holding them at bay. I hear words being spoken but they don't register.

I shoot up from my chair so fast it falls to the ground behind me. My friends are staring at me wide-eyed, Haemir already halfway out of his chair as I blurt, "I have to go." I'm out the door of my suite in a matter of seconds. My feet don't stop as they carry me through the halls, down three flights of stairs, and out a servants' side door. Not until I reach the stables past the garden to the west. My entire body bubbles with a brewing storm of the emotions I've worked hard to keep locked away for so long. The darkness in me swirls with anticipation, a dam waiting to burst free.

I haul myself onto Rasha and kick him into a gallop through the forest lining the back walls of the palace grounds. We don't stop until the cliffs overlooking the ocean come into view and my shadows are now pulsing under my skin. I leave my horse and fall to my knees in front of the lone yew tree I planted for my mother. This is one place of mine that my father never bothers to touch. Perhaps he did love her, in his own twisted way.

The hold on my magic breaks and it leaks from my body. Darkness trails the ground around me, like a deep mist on a humid morning. As much as I try to keep my tears at bay, my resolve splits in half and they stream down my face. My fists clench the grass, tearing out pieces as my nails dig into the earth.

All these years I've yearned to escape, to leave this cursed palace and my cruel father. My mother wouldn't want this life for me, and neither should I. She was strong enough to stand up against him. It seems that courage didn't carry over to me.

As I stare out over the vast ocean, the two choices lay clear before me. I can stay in this rotten place, working for a rotten King and an even worse father. Without my two friends, I'd eventually give in and surrender the rest of my morality. My other option is to finally make the leap and leave. Entering the Western Isles competition is the only way of escaping the clutches of Toross once and for all, making me untouchable to him.

Haemir had been blunt, but he was right. The difference between dying here versus in the competition would be that I at least tried to leave. At the end of it all, that is enough for me.

Slinging myself up onto Rasha, I tear back through the forest with only one thought in my mind: I would rather die on my own terms than stay here and die at my father's hands.

"I'll do it," I heave out between breaths, leaning against the open door frame I'd just burst through. I ran as fast as I could from the stables to the small apartment cottage that is provided to all the captains of the guard.

Mereena hops up from the chair, her book falling to the floor, and throws herself into my arms forcefully enough to knock me back a couple of steps. Pulling away, she flings me further into the main living area and slams the door behind me.

Haemir is on his feet, the sword he was sharpening forgotten on the table. "You truly mean it?" He asks, hopefulness seeping into his voice.

I nod and he pulls me into a hug, my head falling to rest on his chest. "I'm happy you're finally doing something for yourself," he whispers into my hair. My arms, around my best friend's waist, squeeze in response.

"In that case, there's actually something more we need to tell you," Mereena's voice comes softly from beside me. I feel Haemir's body tense. Removing myself from his arms I look between the two of them. Haemir seems to be more on edge, making my heart rate pick up.

Mereena takes my hands, "Haemir and I -"

"Are expecting!" He cuts her off. A whoosh of air leaves her and she shoots him a withering look.

My chest tightens with so many emotions that are hard for me to express. "That's why you're leaving, isn't it?" I whisper. Shaking my head, I pull Mereena into a big hug, dragging Haemir with me. "I'm truly so happy for the two of you. I didn't even know you were trying."

"We weren't," he says with a huff of laughter. I squeeze them both harder. "Alright, now that that's out in the open, we should discuss specifics." Releasing them, I nod agreeably. "I had hoped you would agree to leave, so I took the liberty of including you in our plans."

"How hopeful of you," I chuckle.

Haemir shrugs, "We'll all travel to Qesa and board a ship together. However, since we can't go with you to the Isles, we'll part ways in the Water Kingdom."

"Where will you go once you're there? What happens if my father comes after you both?" I shift nervously on my feet.

"Don't worry about us, we have some…" he pauses for a split second, "friends there that are hosting us until we find a permanent residence." I narrow my eyes. I didn't know they knew people in the Water Kingdom. Before I can inquire about it, he continues, "Once you're in the Western Isles, all you have to do is register and you'll officially be free."

I cross my arms while snorting, "You make it sound so easy."

"Well, why can't it be? Easy is what we need right now. Nothing elaborate."

My fists clench and unclench. "Nothing with my father is easy. If he finds out before I can get my name in, if he even catches a whiff of a hint that I'm planning something, we're all fucked. Maybe we need something a bit more elaborate."

"That is why we leave immediately before he can suspect anything. Tonight." Mereena pipes up from the arm of the chair she's resting against.

I straighten, my brows rising, "Tonight?"

"The competition starts soon, we need time to travel and the faster we all get to where we need to go the better," she responds, tucking a lock of brown hair behind her ear.

"We hate having to ask you, but the only way to get to Qesa fast enough is for you to portal us. I know you hate using that magic too much but it's the fastest way to get us there by morning," Haemir says cautiously.

I wave my hand, "It's fine. If it gets us there fast enough then it's worth using." The shadows within me flutter in excitement and I take a deep breath, feeling them settle down.

Haemir nods. "Pack light and meet us back here after sundown."

I stand in my closet with an empty bag at my feet, staring at most of the fancy clothes that go unused these days. I rarely ever wear the jewels either, so there's not much I need to pack. Everything is tainted by my father's false words and promises. Pushing past the pretty and expensive dresses, I press the button to my hidden room and step inside.

After shoving different black outfits as well as my favorite daggers into my bag, I heave it over my shoulder and turn to leave. Yet, my gaze snags on a particular black steel blade still displayed in its place on the wall. My mother's sword. I've never used it or even wielded it. It just sits there collecting dust. The only time I've ever touched it was when I shoved it into Haemir's hands and told him to hang it.

My mother had said a man who visited the palace in Eadrias when she was pregnant with me, gifted it to her. She was a force when she wielded it while training with her main guard, Neera. The day it had been passed down to me by Neera before she left to go back to the Earth Kingdom, I vowed to never use it.

The blade doesn't deserve to be used for my father's gain. Though, now that I'm leaving, maybe one day I'll feel worthy enough to use it. Taking a deep inhale and squaring my shoulders, I snatch it off the wall. While I'm at it, I also pluck up a smaller, more concealable dagger, and stride out of my secret room for the last time.

I still pack quite a few jewels into my bag before I leave the closet as I likely will need some funds on my journey and once I complete the competition. If I make it out alive.

I've eaten dinner and am all ready to go. Now here I stand uncomfortably in front of a set of white double doors. I close my eyes, take in a deep breath, and knock. I know she's here because she always takes dinner in her room.

There's muffled shuffling before the door opens. Her maid turns to let my sister know it's me. "Let her in," Petra's voice lethargically calls from within. "And please leave us Erra," she tells her maid. The door shuts behind me and I'm left standing awkwardly in the middle of the room while my sister lounges on the couch before a dying fire.

"Are you going to just stand there in silence or are you going to ask me why Torvin was here last night?"

I clear my throat. "That's not why I'm here, but now that you mention it," I shift on my feet, "why was he? I didn't think you'd slum it with some no name."

Petra stands and waltzes over to her drink cart. "No need to be jealous sister, we didn't even touch each other." Sipping the wine she'd just poured, she finally turns to face me. Her sun-kissed face is void of any emotion but annoyance. I fear that's her permanent state. "Why are you here then, Ameria? You have never bothered to come speak with me before."

I'd come to try and make amends before I leave tonight, but her attitude is making me second-guess my choice. I swallow and take a few steps toward her. "I um, brought you something." The metal on the small dagger is cool against my fingers as I take it out of my boot. I hand it to her hilt first, but she just stares at it. With a scoff, I close the distance and shove it into her hand.

"What is this for?" she questions, cautiously glancing from the dagger to me.

"I figured you might need it one day, I don't know," I shrug. "It's perfectly concealable, so you can hide it easily and it's enchanted to always hit your intended target."

"I have guards to take care of that for me."

I fight an eye roll. "Yeah well, maybe one day they won't be there, and you might have to protect yourself," I answer, exasperated.

Her eyes thin to slits as she stares at me and then slowly places the dagger on the drink cart. "Okay."

"Look," my eyes fall to anywhere but her as I gather the courage to do something I don't ever like doing – talking about my feelings. "I know we haven't always gotten along. But just take care of yourself and don't let Father corrupt you too much."

There's a long enough pause that it makes me glance up at her. Petra's face is hard, her lips drawn in a tight line. "So, you're finally leaving then." I just stare at her, shocked that she knows my plan and also concerned that she'll ruin everything. "It's about time." I let out a heavy relieved breath.

Petra downs the rest of her wine and places the glass softly on the cart. "Well then," she takes a step forward, her red robe making a swishing sound as she does. "You are right. We haven't gotten along, and it's your fault." My head jerks back like I've been slapped in the face. I open my mouth to argue but she raises a hand stopping me. "I was forced to come here, yes forced. You think I wanted to leave my home and all my friends? I was comfortable in the Earth Kingdom. But when I found out that I was to have a sister, a half-one at that, I was thrilled. Silly, naive me thought I'd at least get to have a friend in this," she gestures around the room, "place. But then I met you, and you immediately turned me away. Then, I find out I am to take your place as heir and because of that, I thought you hated me. Now that I'm older, I know that's not really why. Is it?"

My shoulders sag, "No."

"I deserve to know why you hate me so much."

"I don't hate you." I shake my head, "I - I resent you. For

everything. When you came here, I only saw you as the result of my father's betrayal and what has made it worse is that you look exactly like my mother."

"None of that is my fault. It's unfair to judge me as such," she spits.

"I know."

A muscle in her cheek twitches with the clenching of her jaw, "You're more like him than you think." My stomach sinks and my cheeks heat with anger and shame. "Perhaps, wherever you are going, you will be able to unlearn all that he has ingrained in you." With that, she turns her back to me and wanders back to the couch.

I stand stunned for a moment, taking in the blow she just dealt me before I remember where I am to be. As I reach for the door, Petra speaks again but this time in a soft tone. One that I've never heard her use before. "Don't worry about me sister, I can take care of myself. I am made of iron, fire, and claws. He cannot corrupt me. No one can."

Chapter Six
Ameria

My pack hits the floor with a thunk as I enter my friends' small cottage. I'd immediately scooped up my things when I got back to my suite from my sister's and receded into my shadows to get here. Mereena is at the table stuffing some last things into her two bags, one overflowing with different herbs, elixirs, and pouches. Haemir emerges from the bedroom door, "Alright, we almost ready?"

"Just a few more things my love," Mereena answers, hastily shoving things into her second pack. I help her finish and we gather at the door.

Calling my shadows, I notice it takes less effort than usual to conceal the three of us but I don't take the time to dwell on that now. Under the cover of darkness, we make haste around the dimly lit areas of the palace grounds to get beyond the warded barrier that prevents portaling in and out. I feel us pass the border and instantly transport us to the city of Andosas, which is a little more than halfway between Litherion and Qesa.

The city streets are quiet except for the few children who

are playing in the torrential downpour, a rarity for the more southern portion of the Fire Kingdom. My hair is braided tightly and tucked underneath my hood, just in case there are any Kingdom guards around that could recognize me. My mother's sword, which is strapped to my back, feels heavy, my body exhausted from the exertion it took to portal the three of us. I've never moved this many people such a distance.

I hand Haemir some coin to go find us a room while Mereena and I take up a spot at an empty table in the corner of the first inn we spotted. A busty woman comes sauntering over, plunking down two mugs of ale. "Friend says you'd be liking some food as well. Stew is all we got."

Mereena nods, "Stew sounds wonderful, thank you." The woman whisks away right before Haemir, ale in hand, slides into the booth and snakes an arm around Mereena.

"We got the last room. I'll take the floor and you two can take the bed. We won't be here long anyway." He takes a sip of his ale, eyes scanning the room over the rim.

My eyes wander as well, taking in the different patrons: Plenty of travelers and what look to be some drunken regulars, with the waitresses giggling at their jokes and swatting away roaming hands. "When do we need to be in Qesa?" I ask without taking my eyes off the room.

"Ship sails after sunrise. We'll need to leave before first light."

The waitress comes back with our food, and I eat while continuing to watch my surroundings. My friends are discussing something in hushed murmurs but I pay no attention to their private conversation. After shoveling the rest of my food into my mouth and draining my mug, I heave myself up from the bench. "Got the room key?"

Haemir hands me a skeleton key. "Third floor, third room on the right." Slipping my bag over my shoulder, I make my way up.

The room is rather small, the slope of the roof making the place feel even tighter. Haemir will have to duck to avoid hitting his head. I toss my things to the ground at the foot of the bed, my mother's sword falling atop it all, and I sink down onto the mattress.

As I stare at my feet, my elbows resting on my knees, the room around me falls away and suddenly I'm back home. I'm fifteen again and my parents are arguing in the dining room. The doors are too thick to hear what the fighting is about but the next thing I know, there's blood pooled around my knees. Her severed head, mere feet from me. Moments later, I'm in the dungeons, an angry man strapped to the metal slab I know so well. A knife forced into my hand. What follows is pain, so much pain.

I feel hands gripping my arms. I'm being shaken. My vision comes back to the present and Haemir is on his knees before me. Thick shadows cover the room. He takes my face between his hands and draws my attention to his unwavering gaze. "You're okay." My lashes flutter and I can feel my magic dissipate.

My hands meet his, "I'm okay." He nods sharply and stands. Mereena is already sitting next to me on the bed, her arm snaking around my waist. I fold into her and sigh.

"That hasn't happened in a while," Haemir's voice wavers.

"I -" I heave out a breath. My friends both look concerned, and it makes me uncomfortably vulnerable. I shoot to my feet, "It's fine. Everything is fine. I'm uh, going to go prepare for bed." I grab a small bag out of my pack and rush to the attached bathing chamber that's no bigger than a broom closet. My back hits the wall and I wait for my shaky breath to even out. I have not been sucked into my past like that in a long while. The last time was about ten years ago after my father ordered me to perform multiple executions one after the other, including one of my maids.

I take the outside of the bed, leaving the side against the wall for Mereena, and Haemir sleeps on the floor. We all settle in, but I cannot sleep. My magic hasn't calmed since being pulled back into that memory. It doesn't help that my body is buzzing from anxiety. I finally left home. I made the leap and now I just have to get to the boat and make it to registration.

In the morning, I'm up and moving before my friends. My mixed emotions are at an all-time high. The sky is still dark, and I give a snoring Haemir a kick in the arm. "Wakey, wakey, you brute." He grumbles and so does Mereena who turns her back toward me. I hop on the bed and give her a big smooch on the cheek. "Wake up my friends, it's time to get the hell out of here!"

Haemir groans while sitting up, scratching at the auburn stubble growing on his chin. "You're never this energized in the morning, Ameria."

I splay my arms out to the sides, "Well, first, I didn't even sleep. Second," I snatch the blanket off Mereena who curses me under her breath, "I can taste my freedom from here so let's hop to it. We leave in five minutes."

The rain has stopped and our footsteps squelch in the mud as we leave the inn. We duck down an alleyway and I portal us the rest of the way to Qesa, arriving right outside the main market street that leads directly to the docks. We head straight for it,toward the market which is already bustling with early morning customers. "We should probably stock up on some food for the sail," I say over my shoulder.

A low whistle escapes from Haemir. "It has been a long time since I've been here."

I snort, "Oh, I remember. I convinced your captain at the time that I needed you on an assignment and we both woke up hungover on top of some roof. Not far from here actually."

Mereena clicks her tongue though she's smiling a little. "You heathens."

My arm loops around her neck, "If you weren't back in the Earth Kingdom that month visiting your mother, I would have dragged you along as well. But poor Haemir here needed an outlet since his little mate was gone for so long." I pout toward him. Mereena and I giggle at the scowl he sends us both.

"Okay, you two can get some food, I need to find some specific ingredients while we're here." Mereena starts speed walking toward a section of the stall-lined street. "I'll meet you at the docks!" she calls back.

I purse my lips and squint my eyes after her. "Should one of us go with her?"

Haemir huffs a laugh and adjusts the pack on his shoulder.

"She'll be fine. Best to let her zip about. Come on." We start picking through the stalls that have food you can eat without being cooked. "So…"

I side-eye him, "So?"

"Should we talk about what happened last night?"

"I don't think that's necessary, no," I grumble while taking a bag of apples from a man.

The two of us continue down the street peering at the different goods. I dodge a child running from an angry man shaking his fist. "Ameria, that has never happened while you were awake…unless you're keeping it from me."

"No, Haemir. I haven't kept anything from you." I shrug, "I think I may have just been in shock from actually leaving." He makes a noise like he wants to disagree and say more but I shoot him my death glare and he decides against it. I don't need to tell him that my magic hasn't settled since then. There's no need to worry him.

The line for fresh bread is surprisingly only a few people deep so I wait by myself while Haemir is off at some trinket stall he saw a few minutes ago. I figure two hefty loaves will be enough for the three of us over the few days of travel. I hand my coin over to the baker who happily provides me with a sample of poppyseed bread. Quickly, I stuff it into my mouth before Haemir comes back and notices I received free food.

I'm browsing a few trinkets when he sidles up next to me and dangles a golden chain in front of my face. "You think Mereena will like it?"

My eyes narrow at it. "Doesn't she already have something

like that?"

He shakes his head, "Definitely not like this." Clicking the locket open, a small image projects from it. A memory, I realize. Haemir, Mereena, and I were in the Earth Kingdom during our thirties at Mereena's mother's home. The three of us were crammed onto a small couch in front of a fire, giggling and drinking spiced wine, our noses still pink from the snowball fight we'd just had.

It was one of the last times my father lengthened my leash a bit. I've not been back to the Earth Kingdom since. I've not been anywhere else either, and excitement thrums through me at the possibility of seeing more of the world soon.

He snaps the locket closed and I peer up at my best friend who is smiling softly down at me. Tears prickle at my eyes, my throat starting to hurt from holding them back. I clear it, "This is..." I shake my head, "This is really, really thoughtful Haemir."

He laughs and loops his arm around my neck, leading me down the street. "You're our best friend, Ameria, and you're about to go participate in an epic competition. She'll need something to look at when she misses you. I thought about getting you one, but I know you don't like wearing jewelry."

My face scrunches up, "You're right, I don't. It gets in the way of fighting." We laugh and Haemir squeezes his arm around my neck, locking me into his side like he used to do when we were younger and drags me down to the docks.

"There you guys are! What - oh, for God's sake, you two are such children." Mereena greets us as I'm emerging from Haemir's hold and I turn, tripping him so he stumbles into a stack of wooden crates.

We're howling with laughter as we finally come to stand in front of her. "You know, we're supposed to be keeping a low profile," she says, arms crossed and foot tapping like an annoyed mother. Haemir and I cease our laughter, and I fix my hood, which partially fell off my head.

"Alright, which one is the ship?" I ask, scanning the lineup of vessels in front of us.

"That one," Haemir points to the closest.

I nod. "Perfect, let's go." I lead us up the gangway onto the ship. Mereena procures some parchment and hands it to a burly man who looks like he's in charge.

"You three'll be in the fourth cabin, down one level, portside. Got two washrooms, one on each end." I nod my head in understanding, but it must not have looked confident enough because he points to the left side of the ship, "Portside." And then stalks away to yell at some poor crew member.

"Okay then, shall we go check out where we'll be staying?" I say somewhat excitedly yet already a little nauseous from the slight rocking.

"We'll meet you down there, I want to take one last look at the Kingdom," Mereena says.

"Sounds good." I smile at them and make my way down to the first lower level of the ship.

The room is easy enough to find, now that I know what Portside means. I kick open the door and step inside. Throwing my pack to the ground, I head straight for the porthole and look out. All my eyes can see is endless ocean. My mind wanders to the sights I'll see – once I win this competition of course. There's no other option — I have to. I'll win, and I'll be free. The thought of seeing the Western Isles thrills me. I wonder what they're like, what the people are like. Do they have different customs, food, clothing? A small smile spreads across my face, a peaceful one. I finally did it, I finally left. I can taste the freedom already.

The scent of mint tickles my nose and my magic perks up. My dagger is immediately in my hand and I whip around, finding Torvin standing in the doorway.

"Torvin." I look at him cautiously.

"I'm sorry, Ameria."

My eyes widen, "Wha-" My words are cut off as all the air inside my lungs is stolen. I drop to my knees, the dagger clattering to the floor as I claw at my chest and neck, begging for the air to return to me. Torvin kneels in front of me and clamps heavy steel cuffs on my wrists. My magic winks out and I finally gasp a full breath of air. He moves behind me and hauls me to my feet, just in time for a figure to come through the doorway.

Chapter Seven
Ameria

"After everything I have given you, this is how you repay me?" My father spreads his arms out wide. He clicks his tongue in disapproval. "No matter, I'd already traded you away the other night for something much dearer to me anyway. Now, you've just made transporting you to your new owner a lot easier for me."

My immediate thoughts slip to Haemir and Mereena. Panic courses through my body. Did they escape? Are they being imprisoned as I stand here helplessly?

"You know, when a very old acquaintance offered something I've long been searching for, I had to decide which weapon was worth more to me. This," Toross unsheathes a gleaming gold sword from his back, "won without question."

"Screw you." I spit out and lunge forward, but Torvin yanks me back.

My father laughs. "Oh child. How I'd hoped you would turn into the true weapon I needed, but unfortunately, you have failed me, just like your mother." A pure, primal snarl rips from me.

He waves me off. "Perhaps your new owner will turn you into what I could not."

"I'm not some pet to be traded and owned. I'm a fucking person… your daughter," I sneer.

"Wrong. Petra is my only daughter. You have been my pet since I started training you to be one. I owned you and now someone else does. There is even a contract officially signing you over." He slides his sword back into its sheath. My insides are roiling with anger and hurt. I'd thought that maybe there was some humanity left in him, but clearly I was wrong.

"Enjoy your trip, Ameria. I'm sure I'll see you around once in a while." He turns and begins to walk out the door.

I yell after him, "One day Father, I will come for you. Your death will be at my hands and I will claim your soul!"

All I hear is his fading laughter as he moves further away. My head whips to Torvin, "You -" I'm cut off by a blow to the head that knocks me out.

Breakthrough

I wake up in short bouts throughout the sailing to throw up from the rocking of the ship and be fed. I found out from loud crewmen that we're headed directly for the Western Isles. The blow of being so close to freedom hits hard.

The guards barely utter more than two words to me but I don't have the energy to talk to them anyway. In the rare moments of lucidity, all I do is think about Haemir and Mereena and whether they were able to escape. For all I know, they could be locked in a cell somewhere, or dead, and I'm able to do nothing about it.

The days blur together, but I know when we've arrived by the sound of seagulls and the extra shouting. Two guards drag me up to the deck and I blink against the full sun beating down on me. I'm pushed to the front of the ship where they remove the chain between my wrists but keep the magic-nulling cuffs on.

I take this moment to try and come up with a plan. I'm weak, underfed, dehydrated, and my magic is locked away tight. While this makes me feel like an empty shell, I still have my resolve and I'm not entirely useless without my magic.

Any plans of escape rush out of me like a tidal wave when ten men dressed in gold uniforms march up onto the deck. I roll my eyes at the sight of more fucking gold. They surround me, caging me in like I'm some sort of wild animal. I manage to smirk at them. It seems they have been thoroughly warned of how dangerous I can be.

My hood is thrown over my head and I'm ushered down the gangway to the end of the dock where a white and gold carriage awaits. I'm almost thrown into it with the door snapping shut at my heels.

Two guards are inside along with… "You!" I spit in Torvin's direction. They securely attach my cuffs to the floor with chains. "What are you doing here?"

He peers out the window as he says, "Seeing your father's deal to completion."

I sneer at him as the carriage jerks to a start, "I knew you were a fucking kiss ass."

The ride starts bumpy but smooths out over time. Torvin doesn't acknowledge my existence the entire trip, which at this point I welcome. He's lucky my hands are bound, or I would have choked the life out of him by now. The two guards, however, don't take their eyes off me. I smile wildly beneath my hood, appearing as menacing and insane as possible. One of them clenches the hilt of his sword a bit tighter and I chuckle.

The carriage curtains are drawn shut except for the small sliver Torvin is looking out. I try to see as much through the bit of exposed window as I can. It looks like they're hauling me through a city, but I only manage to catch small glimpses of brown and red brick roofs and blobs of pedestrians.

We come to a stop and my chains are detached from the floor. They shove me out of the carriage and into another large group of guards. I blink against the sun as my eyes wander up the massive run of steps to the pristine white and gold-domed palace at the top.

My legs ache from being dehydrated and malnourished as we climb toward the looming palace and walk across the courtyard to the main entrance. As we enter the building, I swallow a dry lump in my throat. I allow myself a small moment of fear before I pull myself together. I can't let any weakness show, especially here.

I get a glimpse of the front hall before I'm ushered through small hidden passageways and deserted hallways. A large gold-lined staircase leads up to a landing where it splits into two smaller ones going off in opposite directions. A marble statue stands against the back of the platform in front of a window.

Chandeliers of crystal and white embellishments hang from the ceiling in front of the glass window. It all reminds me so much of home that the urge to hurl all over the perfectly polished floor is strong.

We stop in front of wide-set double doors made from genuine gold with a sun carved into the middle. My nose scrunches at the opulence as a guard knocks, the sound echoing throughout the hall. Both doors automatically open and I'm pushed into an office. It's a lot larger than I expected. Low shelves stuffed neatly with books line both walls to the sides, paintings, maps, and weapons displayed above them.

At the back of the room, a solid gold desk sits atop a raised platform and standing behind it by the three looming windows, is Callum. He watches me while sipping a dark liquid from a crystal glass.

The doors behind me shut and I lose all sense of sanity. Laughter bubbles up hysterically out of me. It all makes sense now. That's why a Western Isles fae was in the Elemental lands. Also, Haemir mentioned that he looked familiar. He was the dignitary my father was entertaining that very day. I can't believe I didn't put it all together.

"Something funny, Princess?" he says, stepping away from the windows. His silver hair is tied back, showing off his one golden-bejeweled ear.

My laughter dies off and I sigh, "So, what? Your business in the Elemental Lands was to acquire me?"

Callum smirks while swirling the liquid around in his glass, ignoring my question, "Your reputation precedes you. Even here in the Isles, word about the Shadow of Death – that's what they call you if you didn't know – has spread like wildfire."

I snort, "That's a ridiculous name."

His eyes wander to the space behind me. "I assume you're here for the rest of the payment?"

My head whips around and I see Torvin, who had been standing by the doors the entire time, come forward. "Yes, my Lord."

Callum picks up a sealed letter, flicks his wrist and it disappears, appearing in Torvin's hand. "My men have gathered what the King asked for. It's in a warehouse in the arts district. They will take you there and help load it onto the ship for you."

Torvin nods and turns to leave. He sends a sympathetic look my way before he exits, the heavy doors thudding shut. If looks could kill, he'd be a dead man.

I turn my attention back to Callum, who is staring at me with a tilt of his head. His eyes are squinting a little, like I'm some riddle he's trying to solve. "Come, sit," he motions toward the chair on the other side of the desk. I don't move. "Would you like me to force you to sit, like a petulant child? That would be quite embarrassing, no?" I grit my teeth, damning me and my ego. Straightening my back, I glide as confidently as I can with chains around my wrists to the chair and reluctantly sit, crossing one leg over the other.

With a wave of his hand, a glass appears before me filled with the same dark liquid he is drinking. I glance between him and the glass. "Don't worry, it's safe. It would be counterproductive for me to drug my investment."

I hesitate briefly before picking it up, my chains rattling and clanking against the gold desk as I do. I take a sip and choke on the burning liquid as it hits the back of my throat. Grimacing, I place it back on the desk. Callum chuckles, "It's called whiskey. It's some special drink the High Lord in the Moon Court created. Not for everyone though."

He knocks back his drink and slides the glass onto the desk, "I'll cut to the chase, Princess. I purchased you because I need someone with a particular set of skills and that happens to be you. Who better to have in my pocket than the Shadow of Death herself."

My hands ball up into fists., "I am not some object to be bought and sold," I spit.

"Aren't you though?" The corner of his mouth twitches upward.

My anger gets the best of me and I'm on my feet leaning over the desk. "I refuse to be used like an object by another egotistical pig of a man!" I snarl.

A gasp rips from my throat as my body is yanked back into my chair and restrained by bright yellow bands of light around my chest and middle. Callum slides into his tufted chair on the other side of the desk. "Get over it. I paid for you which means I own you. Do not test me because from where I'm sitting, I hold all the power here. You are mine to use as I please."

My mouth opens to refuse again, but another yellow band of light slaps over my mouth. Growling from my chest, I attempt to wiggle free of the restraints, but it's no use. My hands are also still bound, so I'm currently at his mercy.

"Now that I have your cooperation," he smiles, showing off his perfectly white teeth, "let me tell you what's going to happen." Callum leans back, placing his crossed legs on top of the desk and clasping his hands in his lap. "As you know, there have been stirrings of rebellion in your home kingdom. It seems that some of that nonsense has spread to the Isles. I have a few main suspects, larger players, but it's your job to confirm my suspicions and gather any information you can.

I've entered you into the Western Isles competition. First, because if you're going to work for me, you will need more training and that's the best place to learn. Second, you'll be spying on the contestants and trainers."

My blood is boiling, and I'm aching to tell him how I truly feel but can't because of the band of light around my mouth, so I convey all my "fuck you" emotions into my eyes. "Nothing to say? Good." He grins and stands. Making his way around the desk he grabs my wrist, "And to make sure I have a little insurance for when you're off at the competition that you won't say anything to anyone, run away, or lie to me..." My eyes squeeze shut and I groan as a burning sensation spreads across my wrist.

The restraints fall away, and I pull my arm out of his grasp. On the inside of my wrist is a deep red brand depicting some sort of flower. Callum twists my arm to see the brand. "Hmmm. A marigold. Interesting." He drops my hand.

"I thought the other person had to agree to the deal to solidify a brand?" I scold. Most fae avoid doing these kinds of deals anymore, and things are sorted using contracts now. It seems here in the Isles, they still participate in the old ways of doing deals.

Callum shrugs. "Our brands are different. Plus, this isn't a deal since you already have to do as I say. This is just making sure you don't screw me over." My lips thin in anger. "Anyway, here's what's going to happen. In the morning you'll be escorted to the competition check-in and then enter through the gate to the High King's island where training will be held. When I need you, I'll find you. For now, just focus on befriending contestants, gathering information, and learning the important skills you'll eventually need to be a better asset to me."

"It seems I have no choice in the matter." I deflate and slump further into the chair. Callum's answering grin makes my insides squirm.

I thought I'd be brought to the dungeons or stuffed into a room the size of a broom closet. Surprisingly, I was wrong. My room is half the size of my suite back in the Fire Kingdom, but still lavish. A four-poster bed covered in silk sheets and fluffy blankets sits against the back left wall. Food has been laid out by the unlit fireplace and a bath is already drawn for me in the attached bathing chamber.

The chains hanging from my wrists have been removed but the magical cuffs continue to be an accessory. However, it could be much worse than having to wear these cursed things.

As I peel off the crusty clothes I've been stewing in for days, a piece of parchment falls from my pants pocket. Kneeling, I pick it up.

"M & H are safe."

That's all it says. Unfortunately for whoever sent me this note, I don't believe them. In my dirty, naked state, I frantically search the room for any ink to write with, but of course, I come up empty. Maybe the lodgings where the competition training is held will have supplies. Then, I can send a letter to my friends and see if they are, in fact, safe.

I slip into the bath and scrub away the days at sea. The water dirties enough to where I'd just be sitting in my own filth so, as nice as the warm water feels, I hop out and throw on the white nightgown that was laid out on the bed.

After stuffing food down my throat and cleaning my teeth – which feels absolutely divine – I chuck the anonymous note into the fire I started. I'd never created a fire with a flint before, so it embarrassingly took a few minutes.

I plop into the chair and hug my knees to my chest, finally having the time to think about the events that have transpired.

Technically, I am free from my father. I'm stuck still being used as a weapon, sure, but so far Callum has been less cruel than I expected. He has given me a room, food, and a chance to learn new skills. All I have to do is what I'm best at and pass along information. It's not the ideal situation, but maybe Callum will prove to offer me more freedom than I had back home.

I grumble and shake my head. No, fuck that. I don't want to belong to anyone but myself. I'll just have to wing it, take this situation day by day and see how lenient this brand is. I glance down at the red flower on my wrist. Brands disappear once the deal is completed, so perhaps this one will fade away at some point and that will be my opportunity.

With a groan, I sink lower into the chair and wish I had some wine to drown my sorrows in. Hell, I'd even take that whiskey shit.

Chapter Eight
Ameria

I'm escorted out of the palace the same way I came in – via back hallways and through the front pearly gates. Equally as many guards are around me as last time but now they're more spread out, likely so people can gawk at me. I don't know where any of my belongings are, which irks the hell out of me since it's everything I own now.

I'd been forcefully awakened by a maid who rudely ripped off my blankets, and threw black pants, a top, and a hooded cloak at me. I was shoved into my boots and ushered out the door. A measly block of cheese and a hunk of bread were all I was given to eat on my way out. I had to argue with her to allow me a minute to clean my teeth.

Glancing over my shoulder to peer at the colossal, gaudy palace, I see Callum standing on a balcony, glass in hand. He raises it slightly, and I can feel his pompous smirk from here. I whip my head back around and continue walking.

I'm stuffed into a carriage similar to yesterday's, but I'm gratefully not chained to the floor this time. Three guards are perched on the seats around me and I look out the window as we make our way through the streets. Peach-, sand-, and white-colored buildings become more tightly spaced the further into the city we travel. The green lawns and courtyards become smaller and then nonexistent, the lush grass turning to cobblestone.

The carriage lurches to a halt and I'm once again pushed out. This time I turn and snarl at the guard who pushed me, and he has the intellect to take a step back. We're at the edge of the city where the forest meets ramshackle wooden buildings. Dozens of men and women wearing black leather armor with an eight-pointed star surrounded by a braided circle on the chest are lining the forest's edge. I'm shuffled to one of them.

"Name?"

I open my mouth to answer but the guard on my right does it for me. "Ameria. No last name."

The man with papers looks me up and down, "Fair enough." He nods to the gate, "Hand her over to the two warriors there and they'll take care of the cuffs once she's on the other side." It's then that I realize those checking in around me are also wearing cuffs. It must be a safety precaution since it's common knowledge that most of the contestants are known to be criminals or other unsavory types.

The gray stone archway looms high above me. Symbols in a language I don't recognize are carved into the moss- and vine-covered stones. Two male warriors stand on either side. One is tan-skinned with short blonde hair and the other has long black locs pulled into a messy bun high on top of his head, with two left to hang in front of his deep umber face.

"She's all yours," says the same guard who decided he needed to speak for me earlier.

The two warriors nod and grab hold of my arms while the guards who escorted me practically flee, likely glad to be done with their babysitting duties. The dark-haired one runs his hand over some of the stones and the space inside the gate is filled with dark space. Then, white twinkling lights burst to life sparkling throughout, as if the night sky just opened up in front of me.

I'm jerked forward and a blinding light surrounds me as I step through. For a moment, nothing exists. No sounds or smells. The only thing assuring me that I didn't just die are the two strong grips on my arms. The light disappears as fast as it came and I'm facing a different-looking forest.

The trees are taller than any I've ever seen. The canopy blocks out the sky, making the area dim and eerie. As I'm led through, the trees become sparser and eventually disappear altogether. My eyes widen and my mouth falls open at the sight before me. Rows and rows of large beige tents stretch out into the distance and various elemental fae are sitting on wood stumps around unlit campfires. The grass has been removed leaving only dirt. Throughout the camp are large wood and metal structures similar to the ones guards back home use to exercise on.

The two warriors who escorted me begin to remove my cuffs when another stops them, an eight-pointed star on his chest. "Don't remove those yet. She has to see the King before she gets settled." My heart drops for a moment, thinking that they are going to take me to my father but then the rational part of my brain reminds me that I'm currently on the High King's island and it's him I am going to see. That thought doesn't settle me much though.

Again, I'm hauled by the arms to a black tent that sits at the bottom of a large three-tiered hill. A castle made of smooth, dark gray slate looms menacingly at the top. I'm brought through the tent flaps, and the two men escorting me promptly let go and leave.

The inside is covered in lavish furs and silk curtains drape from the ceiling to the floor. Across from me stands an extremely tall, slender older fae man with deep bronze skin. His hands are in the pockets of his strange, pleated pants as he surveys me. His facial features are cold and sharp. Based on all the brands covering his bald head and those peeking out from the collar of his shirt, I assume he must be much older than he looks.

"Welcome to the Western Isles, Princess." His voice is rough but oddly welcoming, though I flinch at the direct title – at the fact he knows who I truly am. "My name is Beor Svariti, High King of these lands." He pauses and I blink at him, my face a mask of indifference. If he expects me to bow to him, he will be gravely disappointed.

"I am aware of the arrangement between you and the

Sun Lord. However, I couldn't care less about whatever it is you're doing for him, as long as it doesn't interfere with my competition. You are here to learn new skills, compete, and hopefully live to become a warrior of these lands. I will have no distractions and I expect you to take this seriously. Is that understood?"

I lift my chin and nod, "I planned on entering this competition before the arrangement with Callum."

Beor smiles genuinely, which greatly contrasts his stoic appearance. "Good." He approaches me and with his heavily branded hands, he removes the cuffs. I gasp and fall to my hands and knees as my magic floods me. "The skills you learn here Ameria will no doubt help you in the future." I glance up at him with heavy breaths. "I expect monumental things from you."

Rough hands haul me to my feet and a random warrior escorts me from the King's tent, pointing to me in the direction of where to go.

Walking through the rows, my eyes scan the crowd and immediately notice all the different kinds of fae gathered here. I realize that few fire fae are here, which is a surprise. After wandering down the fourth row of occupied beige tents, I start to get frustrated at the lack of vacancy. "There's an open one right there," a soft voice floats to me from behind. I turn around and find a woman sitting in front of the unlit fire looking at me and pointing to a tent across the way.

Her skin is a warm reddish-brown and the jet-black

twisted braids falling to her waist are streaked with an emerald green. Little silver clasps adorn some of the front pieces. I give her a polite smile with a muttered thanks and head to the tent she indicated.

It's larger and nicer inside than I expected. There's a bed that could comfortably fit two people on the tapestry floor, and satin fabric of taupe and silver hangs over the bed. It flows down to drape behind it, separating this area and whatever is on the other side. There are two neatly folded piles of clothes on the bed. One consists of black cotton pants and matching thick strapped tops. The other has long black silk nightgowns. My brows raise at those – definitely unexpected. At the end of the bed on the floor are simple but sturdy lace-up boots.

I wander around the draped curtains and find a silver tub sitting right up against the curtains and a sink across from it. I search around the tub, perplexed as to why there isn't a faucet for running water like the sink has. Maybe I'll have to ask for steamed buckets to fill it.

Trudging back to the bed, I plop down with a defeated sigh. It's then I notice all my belongings are sitting on the floor in the corner next to a plain silver body-length mirror. I shoot up so fast that I trip over my own feet and land on my knees before my things. My hands rummage through to make sure everything is accounted for. My weapons are the only things missing. Frantically, I look around the room for them and spot my mother's sword and enchanted daggers sitting on the small writing desk. Beneath them is a stack of plain parchment.

My heart leaps and I pull out the chair, pushing the weapons out of the way. I take one of the pieces of parchment but don't find any ink and quill, just an unusual metal stick-like thing. Holding it up in front of my face to examine it, I touch my finger to the tip and it comes away with a dot of ink on it. My brows spike up. Dragging it across the paper, it leaves a long streak of ink. I let out a huff of laughter, "Huh. Isn't that fucking handy."

I begin writing my letter to Haemir and Mereena, asking if they are safe and unharmed. I throw in some brief information about what happened on my part, just in case they don't already know, and tell them I still made it into the competition. The brand on my wrist prevents me from telling them more but at least I can inform them of my whereabouts. I sign it like all my letters to them before, "A", and fold it up nicely. With a flick of my wrist, it disappears.

Fidgeting with the ends of my hair, I bounce my knee and watch the tiny clock on the desk as I impatiently wait to see if I get a response. The letter I wrote isn't returned to me which puts me at ease knowing they aren't dead or somewhere unreachable.

A head pops into my tent startling me. "Hi! I didn't mean to spook you, my name is Inara," says the woman who had pointed me toward this tent, smiling warmly. My first thought is to snap at her about barging into someone else's space without asking first, but I'm then reminded that Haemir and Mereena were just as bold. Plus, I'm supposed to be friendly.

The snarky reply dies on my lips and I stand to meet her. "I'm Ameria."

Inara sticks her hand out so I politely shake it. "Food is being served so I thought perhaps we would head there together."

I shift on my feet but manage an awkward tight-lipped smile, "Sure." If I am to spy on the other contestants, I'll have to suck it up and be social, be friendly – which is entirely out of my comfort zone. Besides having my two best friends, I'm quickly reminded how friendless I truly was back home.

Inara loops her arm through mine and pulls me from the tent. We approach two large pavilions with a buffet of tables piled with food. There's a spread of everything: meat, vegetables, rice, and potatoes. My mouth instantly waters.

I scoop up nearly everything and pile it onto my plate. Trailing behind Inara, I'm brought to a crowded picnic table. My stomach bottoms out in anticipation of meeting so many people at once. I'm so used to being alone, I forget what it's like to socialize. As I take the seat next to Inara, she introduces me to the rest of the group. Each of them offers a warm hello and then returns to eating and resuming their interrupted conversations.

"These are some of our tent neighbors. Most of us got here yesterday," she says while popping a potato wedge into her mouth.

A large burly man with short brown hair and a scruffy beard that has a piece of rice stuck in it turns his attention to me. "The name's Gregor. Happy to be the hell out of the Earth Kingdom. I believe I'm in the tent next to yours," he grins, his upper lip disappearing into his thick mustache. Gregor motions with his thumb to the small pale silver-haired woman next to him. "This here is Delyth. She's in the tent on the other side of mine."

Delyth smiles, "Nice to meet you, Ameria!" Her piercing blue eyes dart to Gregor. "You know, you have a piece of rice in your beard, you pig," she says, wiggling a finger at his face.

He scowls at her but wipes his beard with a hand, knocking out the grain "Leave me be, woman." As I push around the rice and vegetables on my plate, a warm body slides onto the bench next to me.

"Took ya long enough to get here Keenan. You're lucky I was able to save ya a tent," Gregor grumbles.

"Now, now. You know I had that errand to run in the city before coming," Keenan retorts. His dirty blonde hair is tied back, showing off his golden skin. He turns to me and gives me a dazzling smile. "And who is this lovely redhead?"

"None of that you fool, you're a taken man." Gregor flings a potato at him.

Keenan catches it and pops it in his mouth. "Starla knows I'm just a flirt, nothing more!"

My nose crinkles but I answer him anyway. "I'm

Ameria." I glance between the two men, "So, you know each other then?"

"Oh, we go way back, don't we Gregor?" Keenan smirks.

Gregor's mouth quirks up, "Yeah, we've worked the same jobs back in the Earth Kingdom."

Everyone returns to eating and conversing but I mostly stay quiet, chiming in here and there. My interest in Gregor and Keenan has been piqued, and I'm intrigued to see if I can find out what their professions were before coming here. Plus, what kind of errand would an Earth fae have in the Sun Court?

After eating, everyone decided to gather by the fire pit in the middle of our group of tents, but I declined, preferring to hole up alone in mine. I know I should probably be out there getting any bit of information I can for Callum, but I've had enough socializing for the day. I'll try to make more of an effort tomorrow.

Kicking my boots off, I walk over to the bath, and to my surprise, it's full of water. I hum to myself as I dip my hand in and find it deliciously warm. Perhaps someone filled them all during dinner.

I strip and hop right in, letting out a deep exhale. The events since leaving home start to play through my mind and my heart aches at the fact that I still haven't heard from my friends. My thoughts continue to wander as I soak. Bringing my wrist in front of my face, I stare at the brand. My thumb traces over it. All he wants is information. I can do that. I'll have to settle for doing what I'm told for now and keep my focus on winning the competition. Once this is all over, I can figure out the rest.

Chapter Nine
Ameria

I tumble out of bed in a tangle of sheets as a loud bellowing rings throughout the air. Groaning, I crawl to the entrance of my tent and poke my head out. The sun hasn't risen yet and warriors in less official clothing than yesterday walk through the camp blaring horns. I sit back on my heels and rub the sleepiness from my eyes. Heading to the bathing area, I get ready for the day, dressing in the black clothing and boots they provided.

By the time I'm done braiding my hair, Inara has already entered my tent. Bold that one is.

"Morning Ameria. Ready for some breakfast and our first official day?" Inara holds open the tent flap, smiling brightly.

I cover my mouth, hiding a yawn. "How are you so peppy at this hour?"

She shrugs and we walk out together, "I'm used to waking before the sun every day."

For breakfast, we head to the same pavilions as last night, which is quite a hike from our far row of tents. This morning, women are handing out bowls of porridge and a slice of bread.

Delyth waves us over while scooching to make room on the bench next to her.

"Good morning you two!"

"Morning" Inara and I say in unison while taking our seats, though my tone is less enthusiastic than hers.

Delyth shovels a spoonful of porridge into her mouth. "Are you ready for training to begin today?"

"That depends on what exactly this training entails," I mumble before forcing some of the bland breakfast down my throat.

"I assume at some point they'll probably teach us about the different courts and their magic. That I'm definitely looking forward to," Inara says.

I nod my head in agreement. I'm also looking forward to learning more about the Isles. We only get so much information in the Elemental Lands. Most of this place is still a mystery to us.

We finish eating while trying to guess what the next forty days will look like and then the three of us follow the gathering crowd out to a vast field just beyond the pavilions where ten warriors are waiting. I take them in, seeing it's a good mix of men and women. I'm not used to seeing women in the military, considering my father never allowed them to join the guards or his army.

One of the male warriors steps forward. "Today marks day one of the competition. You'll be here for exactly forty days and if you win both trials at the end, you will undergo a special ceremony where our land will officially mark you as a resident of the Western Isles. Throughout your time here, you'll improve your fighting skills and learn to wield different types of weapons. On top of that, you will experiment with how to use all four of the elements." Murmurs echo throughout the crowd. We're going to use the other elements? How is that possible?

"I know you all have questions about that, which we will get to, don't worry. For today, you'll be broken up into ten groups with two trainers who will assess your skill level. We'll be coming through the crowd to point you in the direction of your group. Tomorrow, you'll be assigned to a warrior and work one-on-one with them until the day of the trials.

"Now, let's go over the rules. No brawling. If you have an issue with someone, take it to the ring and spar it out. You are allowed to practice your magic any time with the exception of meal times and we encourage you to learn from each other. If you have personal relations, do so discreetly. You're here to train, not fuck," he smirks. "Lastly, part of the Northern forest is off limits. You'll know which part if you get close to it because there is a magical barrier."

Hushed whispers spread through the crowd with questions of how we're going to wield other magic and why part of the island is off limits. I'm separated from the people I've met so far and of course, my group has one of the few fire fae here. I stay far enough away from him for fear he'll somehow recognize my likeness to the Fire King, however, I still keep him in my sight at all times.

One of my group's assigned trainers is tall and slender with golden blonde hair.

"My name is Jalek, I'll be assessing you today along with my friend Narses here." He nods in the direction of the approaching trainer and I recognize him as one of the warriors who escorted me here. "Now, everyone follow me," Jalek hollers while turning to lead us to the edge of the field where it meets the trees.

When I pass by Narses, who is surveying the group, his eyes land on me. I keep walking with my attention focused forward in hopes he doesn't want to chat. My hope is quickly shattered as he falls into step with me while coiling his black locs on top of his head. "Well, hello again."

"Hi," I monotone, wondering why he's decided to single me out.

"I've been wondering why the King wanted to see you," he says while peering down at me.

Ah, that's why. "Have you now?" Narses continues to look at me expectantly with his stormy gray eyes. "Well, you'll have to keep wondering because that's between him and me."

He clicks his tongue, "I'll figure it out eventually." I set my pace faster before he can ask any more questions I can't even answer and quickly catch up to the rest of the competitors.

We're gathered in front of a setup consisting of tall block-stone walls and metal objects among a bunch of intimidating-looking things. I'd seen a lot of the guards back home use equipment set up like this, creating a course they would all run through over and over again. Mereena and I would sometimes sit on the balcony that overlooked the training field and watch all the attractive, sweaty men. I smile slightly with a shake of my head at the memories. A pang hits my chest at the thought of her.

"We'll stretch first to warm up and then you'll each run through the course so we can get an idea of how physically capable you are." Jalek motions to the setup behind him. He and Narses lead us through various stretches that have most of us grunting in pain, making it blatantly obvious that none of us stretch enough.

Watching the first few people go through the course gives me a good idea of what to expect and I make some mental notes for when it's my turn. They all slip and slide in the mud, get torn to bits by the thorny vines that wrap around some of the tight spaces meant to squeeze through, and are rammed by spinning metal contraptions that stick out of the ground. Luckily, those who have gone through it already are much bigger than me. My small stature will definitely work in my favor, but I don't have my shadow magic to rely on to get past some of these obstacles.

It's my turn to go and I'm joined by a large man who immediately sets to climbing. I puff up my chest and start on the first stone wall, using the cracks and divots to climb up and over. Easy. I approach the thorny vines that are arranged in a zig-zag pattern, and I make it through with only a few scratches. The next task doesn't look as easy.

The spinning metal contraptions hit me, blow after blow. One hits my stomach so hard I fly onto my back, knocking the wind out of me. I regain my breath and sit up to find Narses chuckling to himself. I don't know why he's chosen to latch onto me but it's annoying as hell. Throwing him my best "piss off" look, I continue through the rest of the course, determined to finish as fast as possible and be done.

After getting hit more times by the damn moving metal tubes, I collapse onto the ground at the finish line, embarrassed, exhausted, and panting like a dog. "Get up and get back in line!" Jalek roars at me. With the little pride I have left, I haul myself up and limp back to the lineup.

The rest of the morning we continue to run the course while learning different ways to get through. When the sun was highest in the sky, we broke for lunch but instead of heading to the pavilions, food came to us along with a healer to fix any wounds.

I was beyond grateful to have a chance to rest and eat. My training back at the palace was very different from this. It was less rigorous, which tells me that this competition is going to be much harder than I thought.

The afternoon portion begins, and we are instructed to display our magical abilities. I decide it's best to dampen my fire magic for multiple reasons. One, because little old me shouldn't be going around showing off royal-level magic. And two, every single time I try to wield more fire than I'm used to, it rages out of control and someone has to help me put it out. I watch the other fire fae throw a decent-sized fireball and figure a smidge larger than that will suffice. I can still show off a little bit.

When it's my turn I straighten my shoulders, anxiously aware of all the eyes currently on me, and fling a large fireball at the sandbag target. I let it fully engulf and then smother the flames easily with a wave of my hand. Originally, I hadn't planned on putting it out too, but my ego wanted to one-up some of these men.

Jalek comes around with a maroon elixir, one I've never seen before. "Every day, you will receive a vial like this. It helps you access the elements you do not possess. It wears off overnight, but you'll receive it at breakfast every morning." He hands me mine and I down it with everyone else. It has no taste, but I can feel a peculiar magic pulse throughout my body. I wonder how these are made; this magic feels unlike anything I've ever felt before.

"Go find yourself an area in this vicinity and work on your known ability only. Narses and I will come around to observe and give pointers." Jalek motions to the portion of the field we're in.

I choose a spot near the forest edge and I wonder what kind of boost this elixir will give my already strong fire power. Starting small, I make fireball after fireball. The first thing I notice is that it comes to me easier. The second thing I notice is that my other magic feels stronger. I stomp that down quickly, but it seems harder than usual. That's the last thing that needs to be released right now.

Ignoring it the best I can, I focus only on my fire and go through my daily magic training exercises. My fire cyclones are larger and less wild, the fire spears are faster, and my shield walls spring up quicker and presumably are more solid. Movement catches my eye, and I dissipate the cyclone I was working on as Narses comes to stand before me.

He cocks his head to the side, "You dampened your abilities in the lineup."

I glance toward the others practicing their magic and shrug,

"I don't know what you're talking about."

The corner of his mouth ticks upwards, "Why?"

Smirking, I produce a flame that slowly crawls up my arm, eventually covering it entirely. I look at him, "Better to have people underestimate you, no?" His stormy eyes trace my flame-covered arm.

"I supposed that's a strategy." He hums. I pull back on my magic and it dies out, leaving my skin perfectly unharmed.

My feet drag to the pavilions for dinner as I think about how tedious the rest of the afternoon was. I practiced the same things over and over again, hiding how much more powerful my abilities are so no one questions my background.

I pile food onto my plate and make my way over to the table where my tent mates are sitting. My gut churns as I'm not used to socializing this much with new people. They're all deep in discussion about their first day of training when I sit. Delyth is beaming ear to ear in her muddied clothes. "I was able to create a wind wall that surrounded my entire body. Impenetrable and everything!"

"That's incredible Delyth!" Inara grins. "Some of the other water fae in my group and I decided to work together to see how big of a water ball we could make." She snorts, "It ended up falling and soaking us all and our trainers." I manage a small laugh along with her and Delyth, wishing I had seen that spectacle.

"How did your day go Ameria?" Delyth asks while popping a potato into her mouth.

My nose scrunches up when I think about what to say.

"Those stupid metal tubes were a pain in my ass. Literally."

She dramatically groans, "I have a feeling we're going to see a lot of those wretched things."

The three of us continue to talk about the possibilities of tomorrow as well as the interesting elixir that we were given. They too have never felt such magic before. Tonight, no one was up for a late-night fire, exhausted from the demands of the day, so we retired to our tents.

After bidding my two new companions farewell, I stripped myself of my dirt-covered clothes and boots and climbed into the tub, again already filled with hot water. I could have stayed in there forever but once I was done scrubbing the caked-on mud and grime off my body, the water was a murky brown.

Lying in bed, I think about how another day has passed without hearing from my friends. My body aches and my mind races, still mostly about Haemir and Mereena but also about how I was able to taste freedom for a few moments in Qesa, but then end up in the same position as I was before. A pet with a new owner. Gods, I could use a drink right now.

Chapter Ten
Ameria

I'm actually looking forward to individual training this morning as the group dynamic poses a couple of hurdles when it comes to my magic ability. I don't want anyone to know how much fire I can wield; they'll get suspicious of my lineage. I can't risk someone seeing my other magic either.

After breakfast, everyone begins lining up in front of a handful of trainers holding parchment and pointing people in different directions. I start to make my way to one of the lines when I'm cut off by a large broad-shouldered man. "Ameria, right?" he asks, arms crossed and forehead creased as he looks his nose down at me.

"Yes?" My eyes narrow a little.

He nods in confirmation, "You'll be training with me. Come on." I stutter with the beginnings of confused words, but he's already started walking away so I rush to catch up to him. His muddy brown hair is cut shorter on the sides, letting the top front half hang partially into his eyes.

I'm led north, past a bunch of other training pairs and into part of the forest that surrounds the camp. We trudge through the brush together in silence. I've opened and closed my mouth a few times, trying to find something to say or ask why we're heading so far away from camp but in the end, I decide to be quiet. The trees finally open to a rather large clearing. Stopping at the edge, my trainer finally faces me. "My name is Corro. Every morning after breakfast you will meet me here."

I cross my arms and glance back the way we came, "Why are we so far away from everyone else?"

"Narses suggested it," he replies monotone. Corro motions for me to follow him further into the clearing and I do while questioning why Narses would suggest a private training area. Not that I should be complaining — I'm rather grateful to be away from prying eyes.

I'm instructed to start stretching and Corro chimes in sporadically, reminding me to fix my form or pushing me deeper into a stretch. He also shows me a few advanced ones that have my muscles screaming in protest.

"Alright, show me what you can do with your fire magic," he demands, crossing his arms in front of his chest. I pause to decide if I should show him everything I've got. I figure it would aid me best to show him exactly what I can do, but I stay within my known limits and don't go past the point where I can't control it.

I run through my typical routine — hurling fire spears, throwing up walls of fire, whirling cyclones, basically everything I'm able to do. He whistles, "Not bad." Corro looks me up and down and then clears his throat, "There's another reason why we're out so far, and it's not because of your suspiciously strong fire magic." He side-eyes me. "It's because of the other magic you possess."

The blood drains from my face, my stomach dropping like a rock. No one is supposed to know about this magic. If Narses is the one who told him to train me away from others, that means he also knows about it. But how?

"Don't worry, I'm one of a few who know your secret. We're secluded because it's been suggested that you continue to practice that ability as well."

"Who told you?" I question, wondering if Beor told them or if they work for Callum.

"The High King thought it was important for us to know about your special magic. All he told us is that you can wield shadows." I don't like that they know about my magic, but I can live with it as long as they don't know about who I truly am.

I wring my hands as I think about entertaining the idea of using it. The magic perks up in response and begins to crawl under my skin, sending a chill throughout my body. Corro nods at me, "Show me what you can do with it."

"But, it's light out." I motion to the sky.

"That's fine. I still want to see, show me." My lips thin into a tight line but I call my shadows up, covering myself in them. I portal myself behind him and tap his shoulder. He whips his head around, "Is that all?"

I shift on my feet, "Well I can block noise from within my shadows and allow other people in them with me but yes, that's it. I don't particularly like using this ability."

"Who trained you?"

"No one. I learned everything on my own."

Corro laughs unenthusiastically, "It shows."

I scowl at him, "Well excuse me, I didn't exactly have anyone to teach me." It's not like my father would let anyone see my magic other than a select few. How would one specifically train this magic anyway, it's not like the elements.

"Would you allow me to feel your magic?" he asks, closing the distance between us.

My eyes narrow up at him towering over me. "What do you mean?"

"I have a special magic as well. It was gifted to me by my High Lord. It allows me to do many things but one aspect of it lets me examine other magic by…" he pauses, "borrowing it, in a way. You'll be able to send some of your magic to me through touch."

I consider his words carefully, "You mean steal it?"

Corros smirks and shakes his head, "No, I'm borrowing it. I'll give back whatever I take from you, don't worry." I'm quiet while I weigh the risk of handing my powers over, even briefly. "It's the only way I'll be able to see if I can help you or not."

"Who says I want the help?"

"You would be a fool to not grow such an ability," Corro hisses, his mossy green eyes piercing into me.

I grit my teeth. "Fine." Flinging out my hand, he takes it. Whatever he starts doing, it feels like a magnet. The smoke-like black threads of my dark magic resist him tugging at them, but I urge them forward and they flow to where our hands touch.

Both our eyes are wide as Corro pulls his hand away to examine it. It's black, as if he dipped it in a bucket of paint and it streamed down his forearm creating swirling drips that fade to nothing. Shadow leaks from his hand, cascading to the ground like a waterfall.

Something inside me cracks at seeing him use my magic. "Okay. Give it back."

He huffs a laugh, "So you want it after all?"

I swallow a lump in my throat, "I feel, empty, without all of it." My voice comes out barely a whisper.

His face falls and he clasps my hand. I feel my magic rush back in, threading itself with my essence. It flows through my veins, wraps around my bones, and clings onto my soul as if it never wants to leave me ever again. My body sighs in relief.

Corro's hand returns to its tawny-beige color. "Magic outside of the regular elements is different. It's more volatile and the way you train it is not the same. If it was anything else, I'd be able to help. But this…I don't know how to help train this kind."

My body deflates, as some tiny part of me was hopeful that I'd be able to learn more about this magic. "Have you ever released this magic without meaning to?" he asks.

"Yes," I admit.

He nods like he expected me to say that. "That happened to me when I first got my magic as well. I can't teach you how to grow or wield it, but I can at least give you a tool to help you try to control and calm your magic in those kinds of situations."

I begrudgingly accept his help, not that I think I really have a choice in the matter. Corro points to the grassy floor of the clearing, "Sit." With a small sound of annoyance at being commanded like a dog, I plop my butt to the ground. I haven't had a tutor in magic since I was young so this is going to take some getting used to.

Corro sits directly in front of me with his legs crossed and I mimic him. "I'm going to teach you a breathing technique that's helped me not just with calming my magic but also in stressful situations. Close your eyes and focus on just your breath."

After Corro taught me his simple breathing exercise, which was just inhaling for four seconds, holding it, and then exhaling for four, we began with the earth element. He said it might be the easiest to start with since I told him my mother wielded that magic. He was very wrong as I spent the entire morning sitting on the ground trying to make a flower bloom over and over again.

Lunch came to us and afterward, Corro had me meditate for hours to "connect with the ground." For the first hour, I thought it was bullshit but then I finally started to feel the ground beneath me: The worms and bugs digging throughout, the living movement from each blade of grass. Eventually I was able to somewhat connect with the surrounding trees. I had no idea that Earth wielders could feel so much.

As the day progressed, Corro wasn't as grumpy as he initially seemed. He cracked a few jokes even though they weren't particularly funny. At dinner, I found out that Delyth also began with the earth element. I was glad to hear that she struggled with it as well and that some of the others had a hard time with the magic they started with too.

My heavy body collapses onto my bed, my belly full and energy entirely depleted. I haven't been this tired since I started training my fire magic at ten years old. I forgot how much it takes out of you.

I jolt upwards in a daze. The fae lights around the tent are harsh on my eyes and I wave my hand to dim them with my basic magic. I'm unsure of how long I dozed but the camp outside is deathly quiet so it must be late. I unlace my boots and throw them to the side of the tent near my desk.

A folded piece of parchment sitting on the surface has me doing a double take. I stumble to my feet and rush over with my heart in my throat. Instantly, I recognize the handwriting as Haemir's and I audibly sigh while falling into the chair. The note is brief, but it tells me they're safe and unharmed.

Flipping the parchment over, I write a reply, asking them where they are. With a flick of my hand, I send it off and sit here for a few minutes to see if they respond right away but nothing arrives.

The next afternoon, food is delivered to the clearing by the same woman as yesterday. My morning consisted of working on upper body strength and Corro taught me a new fight sequence. We now sit eating our turkey legs and vegetables in silence. I figure it might be worth asking him some questions and get to know him. I am to be gathering information after all. The way to do that is to befriend people. However, I don't have the best experience with doing so.

I slip into my spy mode instead and examine him like I

would any target my father might assign me. I start with what I know: he's one of the few here who know about my magic, which means he's somehow important enough to have the same information as the High King. He also mentioned yesterday that his High Lord gifted him power, so he must be of high rank. It's possible he's from the Sun Court, but there are also other courts I don't know about yet.

"Why do you keep looking at me like that?" Corro mumbles, startling me.

"Nothing, I just…" I quickly pick something that's been on my mind, "I was just trying to figure out if you're from the Elemental Lands or here."

Corro hums and chucks the bare bone of his turkey leg into the trees and brush behind us. "I'm originally from the Water Kingdom but I came to compete many years ago."

My interest piques at where he's originally from. The Water Kingdom has always had tense relations with the Fire Kingdom, and it's almost clear they are working to aid the rebels. Perhaps he is a good person to gather information from. "How many years ago?"

"Six hundred."

My brows rise, "You're over six hundred?" I squeak. Gods, he's a lot older than I thought.

Corro nods and takes a large sip from his water skin, "Six hundred and fifteen."

The green bean I was gnawing on falls from my mouth as it drops open, "You were only *fifteen* when you competed?" He was almost a baby when it comes to fae years. Most of us don't even come into our magic until a few years before then.

"Yes, I was," he says matter of fact.

"You were just a child."

"A child that had to grow up fast," he says with a shrug. I open my mouth to ask more questions, but he stands abruptly. "Finish your greens and meet me on the other side of the clearing." And then he takes off without waiting for confirmation from me.

I wash down the last of my green beans with a few gulps of water. Well, there goes my idea of getting information from him since he was just a child when he left the Water Kingdom. Clearly, it's a sore spot by the way he immediately shut the conversation down.

Heaving myself up off the ground, I meet him at the various exercises he's set up to practice more earth magic.

"This afternoon we'll continue to work on manipulating earth materials that already exist before you learn how to create something from scratch. Remember that the point of learning the other elements is to understand how they work and use that knowledge to defend yourself and others against it." Corro side-eyes me with a raised brow, "Meaning, it's okay to not excel at it." A pointed reference to yesterday when I ripped the poor flower out of the ground in frustration multiple times. Taking a deep breath, I face the wall of vines he's created. Pulling on the magic from the daily elixir, I begin to manipulate the vines to untangle them. One immediately whips out and smacks me in the face.

"Agh, fucking hell." I rub my cheek and hiss, sure that there's a mark blooming already.

"Release the magic more slowly," Corro's voice floats to me from somewhere behind.

I let out a frustrated exhale and shake out my hands. *Okay, let's try this again.* Releasing the magic more slowly, I focus on the wall of vines and begin untangling them one by one. It takes deliriously long but I finally do it. My arms fall to my sides, already exhausted.

"Well, took longer than I expected but you got it." Corro comes to stand next to me. "Get some water and then come back and put the vines back the way they were." Grumbling, I trudge over to my water skin and drink deeply. The rest of the day I deconstruct and reconstruct the same damn wall of vines too many times to count. I did eventually get faster at it, slowly requiring less effort than I'd used in the beginning.

On the way back to camp Corro strides up next to me, "You did well today."

I snort and cast him a side glance." All I did was move vines and I'm exhausted. I haven't practiced magic like that since I was a child."

"It's only your second day wielding magic that isn't yours. As you practice more, it'll get easier."

My brows scrunch in thought. "Why do we have to learn how to use them? Why not just learn defense techniques against them?"

"For multiple reasons. The hands-on experience of wielding different magic helps you understand how to properly defend against it. Also, after winning the competition, our land might gift you with more magic during the special ceremony."

My mouth pops open and I quicken my pace to keep up with him. "We might get more magic?"

He nods once and I notice him glance toward my feet and our strides slow down. "Sometimes it's another element or the land chooses which court you should be in and gifts you that magic. Occasionally it's more rare magic."

My boot catches on a root and a I stumble a bit. "You mean like yours?"

"Sure, but I didn't get my power from the land remember."

"Right," I pause, "is that something the land gifted your high lord?"

He flashes a wide grin at me, "Nope." His pace then quickens and I try to catch up to him again, but another root gets my boot and this time I fall onto my hands and knees. Damn these stupid roots. Cursing under my breath I stumble to my feet and wipe the dirt from my hands onto my pants. "Wait!" I call after him. "I have more questions!"

"You have over a whole month to ask them. Save them for later!" He calls over his shoulder.

I start walking again but make no effort to catch up to Corro. My mind floats in thought. When he said he left the Water Kingdom at fifteen, I figured that he wouldn't be a good target for information. Then he mentioned his High Lord again, and now I'm curious. Who is this High Lord who has the natural power to *gift* magic like that?

Chapter Eleven
Ameria

It's not my fault they told me to practice near the trees," Gregor grumbles as he stuffs the last of the food into his mouth, his eyes rolling.

A snort escapes me because I remember setting many things on fire when I was first learning magic. "Fire can be a little unpredictable when you're first learning. I can't tell you how many things and people I accidentally set on fire when I was younger."

He grunts, "It's a lot different than earth magic, that's for sure."

"As someone who is learning that now, I can agree."

Keenan appears behind Gregor and places a boot on the bench next to him, resting an elbow on his knee. "You'll never guess what I found out from a group of trainers." We all turn to him as he pauses to wait for us to guess.

"Just tell us and be done with it Keenan," Gregor says, pushing his empty plate away.

Keenan deflates a little but continues, "Well, apparently

there's a tavern not far from here that they built years ago. A full working bar!"

My body perks up, "A bar? Where?"

He smiles and points behind me, "A mile east."

Gregor hops up like he has fire under his ass, "Well, what are we waiting for? Let's check it out."

"What are we checking out?" Inara chimes while walking up to the table, Delyth in tow behind her. I'm unsure of where the two of them have been during dinner.

"I guess there's a tavern not far from here. You two want to join us?" I ask while swinging my legs over the bench and getting to my feet. My belly is full and I'm ready to drown myself in alcohol that I've been dearly missing.

"Count me in!" Delyth smiles.

"Me too," Inara adds and I notice the small longing look she makes toward Delyth.

We follow Keenan's lead along with some other groups of people who also heard about the tavern. I'm practically jumping out of my skin the whole way there, itching to finally get some alcohol in my system. It has been too long, and my night sweats are starting to keep me up at night. The only relief I've had was the journey here when I spent most of my time unconscious.

My eyes wander to the few tent mates who decided to come along, distracting the growing need to become inebriated. Everyone has been nice so far, which is helping me get out of my comfort zone. However, I'm supposed to be spying on them. I should try not to get too attached, since I'll be stabbing them in the back and all.

I wonder how much information I can withold from Callum as a recurring thought crosses my mind: how I'd rather the rebellion win over my father. Over Callum. It's not like I haven't thought about aiding them in the past, but I was too afraid of getting caught. And if the rebels I caught and tortured recognized me and blew my cover…

My hand finds the brand on my wrist as the cabin-like building comes into view. I push away the wandering thoughts and decide to deal with my problems another day. It's time to get drunk.

The minute the door opens, the muffled sounds of people grow into a roar. Holy Gods, half the camp must be packed in here. My group and I maneuver our way through the basic tables made of wood and the sea of people to the bar that's built right in the center.

"Should we have brought money?" Delyth shouts over the noise.

"It's free!" shout some people who overheard her. Indeed, they are right. The booze is free, and I think I might be in heaven.

Gregor has snagged a round table that was just vacated, and we pile into the chairs quickly before others try to take it. I notice Delyth claims a seat right in Inara's lap, which is a quick development and explains that interesting look Inara sent her way earlier. She catches my eye and I arch a brow. Her arms squeeze Delyth a little as she winks at me. Smirking, I raise my glass in her direction and finally take a large gulp of much-needed wine.

"You're cheating, I fucking know it, Keenan!" Gregor bellows while slamming the cards he acquired from somewhere in the tavern onto the table. We've all made it to our second round of wine and it's clear that this stuff is a hell of a lot stronger than what we have in the Elemental Lands. We're all drunk off our asses.

Keenan holds up his hands, "No, you're just shit at the game Gregor."

"It's true Gregor," I lean my body in his direction, my arm resting on the table, keeping me from falling over. "You haven't won a hand all night." I eye him over the rim of my mug and drain the rest of my drink.

He scowls in my direction and swipes up my cards from the table, "Says the lady who also lost!" I click my tongue while waving him off with my hand and glance toward the people who are dancing. Keenan and Gregor continue to argue while I search for Inara and Delyth, but I don't see where they have gone.

The remainder of our tent mates arrived not long ago and I spy one by the bar flirting with some woman. The rest of us sit around the table enjoying seeing Gregor get angry at every hand he loses.

It's the early hours of the morning by the time a handful of us make it back to camp. I collapse onto my bed, my head swimming with four mugs of that deliciously strong wine. A giggle bubbles up my throat. The trainers are probably going to put us through hell tomorrow. I smile to myself, knowing that it was worth it because I'm drunk, happy, and can't focus on any of my problems. Just how I like it.

I heave into the bushes, but nothing comes out, likely because I already spilled my entire breakfast an hour ago after sparring with Corro. He's a hundred and ten percent pissed at how hungover I am and he's definitely making me pay for it.

This morning has been extra hell for me without Mereena's hangover elixir. Boy, am I really missing that. "Just one teensy tiny break?" I plead as I collapse against a tree. I haven't had to deal with a hangover like this in Gods know how long. This morning while I was peeling off the dirty clothes I slept in, all the thoughts I had before getting drunk came rushing back.

I've been chastising myself ever since for forgetting to get any useful information in case Callum comes calling. Everyone is always loose lipped with alcohol in their systems, and I missed a perfect opportunity. Hopefully, there will be another soon. On top of that, I still haven't heard back from my friends, which is only adding to my ever-growing stress.

A shadow blocks the sun that's been scorching me all morning. "I don't particularly think you deserve a break." I look up to see Corro towering over me with his arms crossed and a look that makes me feel like I just kicked a baby animal.

"Not even a tiny one?" I hold up my fingers with a small space between them.

"You're having one right now. Give me five more laps and I'll think about giving you another." I groan and before I can peel myself off the ground, vines shoot down from the tree and yank me to my feet.

Damn, he's a real asshole today. "Alright, alright." I start jogging, my head throbbing to the beat of my feet.

Five laps later — and a break for heaving up the water I drank too quickly after the fourth lap — Corro takes mercy on me and lets me lay on the ground for five minutes. A boot kicks mine far too soon, "Get up and let's spar again."

I moan into the grass that my face is plastered in, "Has it been five minutes already?"

"It has been six. You're welcome for the extra minute. Now, up."

Flopping onto my back, I haul myself off the ground. Begrudgingly, I trudge over to where he's waiting and get into a fighting stance. Just like earlier, he doesn't hold back. The minute I get my fists up he comes at me. Corro throws a right hook and I manage to duck, trying to avoid it. Except it never passes over me. I notice my mistake too late when his knee connects with my face, his hand pushing my head right into it.

Pain explodes through my face at the same time I hear a loud crack. The next thing I see is the blotchy blue sky above me, my back resting against the ground. The blood dripping down the back of my throat makes me want to vomit again. I'm flipped over onto my stomach and I hack out the blood, letting it gush into the grass. "You definitely broke my nose," I say, my words strangled as I grapple with the fresh yet familiar pain.

"You're taking it a lot better than I thought you would, to be honest," Corro says, crouched beside me. I grunt in response. Unfortunately, I'm quite familiar with a broken nose.

"Is there a reason you decided to fuck up my face?" I spit out more thick blood.

"You could have stopped me. It's not my fault that you're too hungover to think clearly or move fast enough." I sit back onto my heels while wiping the tears from my eyes and cheeks.

Sighing, I get into the usual position that helps me set my nose. Corro stands, "I'll send for the…" My hands move quickly, cracking the bones back into place. Instantly, I'm heaving up whatever water and bile is left in my stomach and waiting for the disorientation from the pain to go away.

"Did you just fucking set your own nose?" he says in disbelief.

I manage to sit upright and take deep breaths through my mouth. "Yup."

"You should have let a healer do that so you don't mess it up, making it harder to heal."

Waving him off, I slowly get to my feet. "Don't worry, I've done it plenty of times. My face is still as beautiful as ever." I flash him a smile that I'm sure is full of blood.

Corro comes to loom over me and examines my nose, "How many times have you done that?"

"Too many to count my friend," I pat him on the shoulder and wipe the blood that still trickles from my nose with the back of my hand. "Is it lunch yet?" I ask, wiping the blood off on my sweat-soaked shirt.

He shakes his head and I grumble. My stomach hurts more than it did before now that it's fully empty. Corro surveys me, a crease on his forehead, "Before lunch gets here, let's practice some of your shadow magic."

My back stiffens, "What? Why are we going to practice that? I thought you couldn't help me?" My insides swirl with dread at my magic's excitement.

"Because," he says while crossing his arms, "based on your previous statements about it, I assume you haven't expelled any of it since you've gotten here." I gnaw at my lip and glance toward the trees. Truthfully, it has been longer. I haven't used it since I left the Fire Kingdom. My power rumbles within me and I wince.

Corro's voice pulls my attention back to him, "Thought so. The less you use it the more it'll build and become unpredictable. Plus, who knows what else you can do with it. You'll never know if you don't use it more." I grunt with defeat. Part of the reason I drank so much last night was to try and tame my magic from bubbling over.

I spend the rest of the morning bouncing about the clearing in my shadows, sometimes bringing Corro along with me. For the remainder of the day, I practice more earth magic and finally get the hang of creating vines that don't already exist.

The walk to my tent after dinner feels longer than usual, and I can't wait to have a nice hot bath and crawl into bed. I'm looking forward to getting the rest my body is currently crying out for. My dark magic instantly perks up as I enter my tent, and standing before me is the reason why.

Chapter Twelve
Ameria

Callum looks my way, a piece of parchment hanging between his fingers. "I didn't expect the Shadow of Death to have friends." He waves it before flinging it back onto the desk. My stomach sinks, the letter is new and it could very well contain my friends' whereabouts. Him knowing I have friends means he has something to use against me.

My hands ball into fists and I scowl, "Don't call me that ridiculous name. And what are you doing here?" I change the subject, hoping it takes his mind away from the letter I'm itching to read.

He stalks toward me and I straighten, lifting my chin. I refuse to cower and show weakness. Callum's fingers find a stray piece of my hair that has fallen out of my braid and twirls it while towering over me. My teeth clench at the closeness and I boldly smack his hand away and tuck the strand behind my ear.

He clicks his tongue, "So hostile." My breath slowly leaks from me, relieved that I didn't just earn a reprimand for doing that. My father would have beaten me. Callum takes a step back and looks me up and down. "I'm here to check in on my investment. What have you collected so far?"

My mouth forms a tight line, "It's only been a few days, I haven't collected anything yet."

His disappointment is written all over his face, "I expected better." He takes a deep breath, "Never mind that now, we'll discuss it later. I've also come to retrieve you and your particular set of skills."

Callum grabs my arm and a yellow light swallows us. I find myself suddenly in his office back in the Sun Court. My eyes widen and I stumble a little when he lets go. My mind starts whirring. I thought that portaling in and out of the warrior camp wasn't allowed but I guess I'd never given the idea a thought before this. Maybe - "*You*, cannot portal in or out of the camp if that is what's currently rattling around in that brain of yours."

Well, there goes that. Not sure it would have done me much good anyway since I have this brand marking me. I groan inwardly and turn to him, "What am I doing here?"

His long thick legs stride behind his desk and he begins messing around with some parchment. Lightning illuminates the night sky in the floor-to-ceiling windows. "I have a council meeting and I need you to follow one of the members home afterward and report on what he does."

My brows narrow, "You want me to spy on one of your own council members? If you don't trust him, why not just get rid of him?"

"Yes, I do. And because if he has been corrupted with this rebel nonsense, I can play this smartly and use him to my advantage." Callum shuffles a stack of parchment into a neat pile and shoves it into a folder.

The rain starts hitting the windowpanes and his gaze meets mine. "Your room here has clothes for you to change into as well as all the information you need." He waltzes down the few steps from this desk, folder in hand, "I trust you remember how to get there."

Callum walks past me and to the door, holding it open expectantly.

"*My* room?"

He sighs, "Yes, your room. This is your place of residence now after all. Did you expect I'd put my most valuable tool in a broom closet?"

My feet start moving and I head for the open door, "Yes, actually," I mumble under my breath.

He follows me out the door and the sound of the lock clicking echoes through the silent hall. Sidling into step next to me, he opens his pompous mouth again, "You get all the perks of a high-ranking member of my court, Ameria. You should be grateful that I treat my belongings well."

My entire body thrums with repressed anger and, if I clench my teeth any harder, they'll surely break. There's that word, *belongings*, marking me as an object. Referring to me as something that can be traded back and forth like a bargaining chip. Reducing me to a weapon that needs an owner. To be wielded at my master's command. I'm afraid this is all I'll ever be.

The door that leads to the servants' hallway finally comes up on my right and I reach for the handle, needing to be out of the presence of my new "owner" before I say something I shouldn't. Though, perhaps being dead might not be a bad thing. I chastise myself at that thought. I need to keep going.

"However," Callum's voice stops me in my tracks and my hand grips the handle tightly. I glance over my shoulder and find him right up against my back. Leaning low to my ear he whispers, "I don't like to lose, so try not to fail me." His breath is hot on the tip of my ear and he grips my face with one of his large hands, turning me to look at him. Something flashes in his eyes, "Or you'll find out exactly what it means to be an object owned by me."

I swallow the lump that's formed in my throat, an action he notices and answers with a cruel smirk. His hand drops gingerly from my face and he turns on his heel to continue walking. "See you after your mission!" He calls over his shoulder, the sound of his odd polished pointed shoes clicking in his wake.

The fleeting thought I had that he might be a bit more merciful than my father has gone. Stomping through the servants' halls, I find my way by memory to the room I stayed in the other night. I may have been underfed, dehydrated, and seasick on my last visit, but I was still able to keep track of my surroundings.

Bursting through the doors, I see the room is just as gaudy as I remember. With a huff, I slam the door shut. If I am truly to be stuck in the Sun Court for longer than I plan, perhaps I can bargain to redo this room to an aesthetic that doesn't make me want to vomit. I'm getting tired of seeing gold everywhere I go.

Just like Callum said, the closet is full of black leathers and of course, they fit me perfectly. Unlike the ones I've seen the warriors wear, there aren't any markings carved into the chest of these. This is likely to deter anyone from figuring out who I'm working for.

I plop down into the chair by the unlit fireplace and swipe up the folder sitting on the table. Glancing toward the windows, I see that the rain has picked up now. It's a slight complication but nothing I can't deal with. It'll be easier to sneak around but I'll need to get closer if I want to overhear any conversations.

The folder's contents include a map of the hidden hallways and parchments explaining my assignment. The council member's name is Lord Perrian Sprek and attached is an oddly small yet very detailed and colorful glossy portrait of him. I've never seen anything like this back in the Elemental Lands. I flip the portrait over but it's just plain white on the back.

This isn't the first odd thing I've seen here in the Isles and it makes me wonder how else they're more advanced. They certainly have more access to enchantments here, unlike back home where only those with obscene amounts of money can get them. Even then, they aren't this sophisticated.

Saving my excitement about exploring the Isles more for later, I continue sifting through the information. Callum suspects Perrian is selling information to members of the rebellion. A glance at the clock on the fireplace mantel tells me I have ten minutes to get to the front entrance and find the Lord's carriage.

A small piece of parchment appears on the table in front of me and I drop what I'm holding to read it.

There are daggers for your use in a hidden compartment behind the third panel from the right in the closet.

Watch Perrian for around an hour after he enters his residence and then meet me in my office.

If you don't bring back something of note, I'll be very displeased. And we don't want that.

I roll my eyes as another piece flashes onto the table.

Oh, and I would hurry. The meeting has ended early.

"Shit!" I leap out of the chair and rush to the closet. Finding the panel he specified, I slip the daggers into the different sheaths built into my leathers. I book it out of the door muttering profanities at the High Lord under my breath.

Wrapping the provided black scarf around my head and the lower portion of my mouth, I rush through the hidden passageways. How big is this rebellion? I'd always thought it was just my father being a tyrant and his people trying to overthrow him, with the possibility of the Water Kingdom secretly supplying aid. Now that I know it's reached overseas to the Isles, which are as disconnected as possible from our lands, I wonder what this is all really about. What is the bigger goal?

I have to gather information for Callum sure, but I plan to gather my own too. It's time I keep my options open. Irritatingly, there's nothing I can do until this brand on my wrist is gone. So, I'll do what I must for now.

Cracking the door that leads to the outside, I find that the rain is now coming down sideways and thunder rumbles in the distance. Taking in my immediate surroundings to make sure no one is around, I call upon my shadows. With a deep calming breath, I slide out the door, blend in with the darkness, and head toward the line of carriages.

I release my shadows as I duck behind a bush. Easily, I spot Lord Sprek making his way down the rest of the steps with a guard who is shielding him from the rain. He must have air magic. Sprek and his guard shuffle into the carriage together and take off.

With my head down, I try to blend into the crowded sidewalks and follow them. They turn and I rush across the street to find the path they took, which is less busy but has more illumination from tall fae light poles. Luckily, the buildings are starting to get closer together, so I slip into an alley and climb up a drainpipe that leads to the roof.

Rooftop to rooftop, I follow the carriage, portaling myself when buildings are too far apart to jump. They finally stop in front of a large townhome where two hooded figures stand on the steps, waiting.

Lord Sprek nods to them both as he leads them inside and guards post themselves under the front awning. I slide into the shadows on the roof across the way and observe. A window illuminates in a room on the third story and one of the hooded figures closes the curtains. It's clear he's dealing in some shady business, but whether it's related to the rebellion is still unknown.

I notice that the room they're meeting in is the only one without a balcony. There's not even a ledge one could grip onto. Clever. Still, there's a balcony to each side so I pick one and portal to it. Staying in my shadows I try to listen, but their muffled conversation combined with the rain, makes it futile.

My face scrunches in annoyance and I portal back to the

rooftop across the way to sit and wait. Rain beats down on me as I continuously flip a throwing knife and watch the front door that no one else enters or leaves. I stand to stretch my legs and look for one of the large clock towers I noticed on my way here. It has been forty-five minutes. Just a little bit longer and I can get out of the rain, go back to my warm tent, and collapse into bed. Unfortunately, I have a feeling Callum will be pissed if I don't stay to see the hooded figures come out.

It's been a little over an hour by the time the figures finally emerge. My eyes track them as they walk together down the street. Just as I'm about to get up and go follow them, curious to see where they go or if I can catch a small glimpse at what they look like, one of them abruptly stops and whips their head in my direction.

Panic rises in me, and I double-check to make sure I'm in my shadows and fully blended in. I confirm that they're shielding me and bring my gaze back to where they were, but they're gone. My eyes dart around, panicking, but there aren't any alleyways they could have run to that fast. Unless they can portal.

"Didn't anyone tell you that it's not polite to spy on people?" I gasp and spin around. Both hooded figures stand halfway across the roof, the dark concealing their faces underneath their hoods. How did they manage to sneak up on me? I stay as still as possible, knowing that they can't see me within my magic, though my small gasp might have given me away. "We know you're there."

The one on the left speaks again. Well, shit. I drop my magic and the figure on the right cocks their head. Standing to my full height, I flick two daggers out of their sheaths on my thighs. The man who spoke snorts and takes a single step forward. I hurl a dagger at him but the other figure catches it in the air. The hooded man who took a step clicks his tongue with a shake of his head and plucks the dagger from his companion's hand.

He studies it and then slips it into his own sheath. "How did you know I was up here?" I ask, wanting to know what gave me away so that I may fix it.

He speaks again, ignoring my question completely. "Tell your High Lord that if he wants information, then all he needs to do is look right underneath his own nose." A cloud of mist starts to surround them both.

"He's not my High Lord." I spit. I may unfortunately work for him, but he's not my ruler.

I notice the figure that has never spoken tilt his head again, the mist pausing around them as a flash of lightning streaks the sky in the distance. I can't see past the darkness from the hood covering his face, but I can still feel his piercing stare. The mist resumes encompassing them and I'm left alone on the rooftop.

Chapter Thirteen
Ameria

The storm has dwindled to a light spray by the time I sneak back into the palace. I could have easily portaled but I wanted to enjoy my few moments of freedom, walking the streets and taking in what the Sun Court has to offer at night. Even in the rain, people bustle down the streets. Some converse under awnings, away from the small drops that still fall from the sky. Eateries and taverns are full to the brim with patrons, the commotion inside them filling the air every time a door opens.

It also gave me a chance to think about my interaction with the two hooded figures. How they knew I was there concerns me. I've never been spotted before when hiding within my magic. Whoever they were, I have a feeling it might bite me in the ass in the future. They're clearly a part of the rebellion and now they know Callum has someone with a rare type of magic watching them. They somewhat know what I look like as well, and that makes my stomach swirl with nausea. This could be very bad.

I'm not sure I want to tell Callum about it and I figure that this would be a good chance to find out what my limits are with this brand on my wrist. If I can exclude different bits of information, I will. It's quite literally the least I can do for the rebels.

My leathers are sopping wet but thanks to my fire magic, I've already started to warm myself underneath them. My boots squelch as I trudge through the hidden passageways and side hallways. Guards are stationed outside Callum's office but they automatically open the doors for me.

Callum sits in a chair by a dying fire reading some parchment. "You're late," he monotones without looking up.

My feet stop a few feet away and I fold my arms over my chest, "For good reason."

He at last looks up, his gaze slowly raking over my body. I will my expression to stay neutral even though I can't stand him looking at me like that. "So, you found something of note then?"

"Two hooded figures met Lord Sprek at his home. They met in a room on the third floor but the closest I could get to try and overhear wasn't good enough thanks to how quiet they were and the heavy rain. I waited until they left and I watched them walk away, however, they disappeared before I could follow them." I wait for the brand on my wrist to start burning but it never comes and my body fills with relief.

Callum abandons his reading material with a flick of his hand, the parchment vanishing into thin air, and stands. "Anything distinguishably noticeable about these two figures?"

I shake my head, "No they kept themselves covered completely and dressed in all black. They did seem to be built like men although I've seen some women with a similar physique so, who's to be a hundred percent sure."

He stalks toward me with a sly smile. If I didn't loathe him so much, I'd probably be as enamored as I was when we first met. Despite being a wretched asshole, he's incredibly handsome. His hand is warm as it latches onto my elbow. Light surrounds us and we're back into my plain beige tent.

"Good job." He speaks softly, a smile still on his face. Based on the quick squeeze at my elbow before he drops it and the slight muscle twitch in his jaw, he looks anything but happy.

"I expect you to gather something useful between now and the next time I come to visit." Callum adjusts his posture, standing straighter, and slips his hands into his pockets.

I take a slight step back from him and raise a brow, "Which will be?" My eyes dart to the tent entrance, hoping no one is awake and can hear our voices.

"Undecided. Which should give you motivation to work more quickly, unless you want to disappoint me." His soft smile turns cruel. Light swirls at his feet, "Oh, and before I go. A little side assignment. Get closer to that trainer of yours by any means necessary. I feel he has some useful information floating around in that pretty head of his."

My head jerks back and my mouth pops open, ready to ask what makes him think that but the yellow light swallows him up and he's gone. I'd almost written Corro off because he was so young when he left the Water Kingdom, but now that I know the rebellion has made it over here to the Isles it makes sense. Especially if he's not from the Sun Court, it's possible one of the other courts is aiding the rebels.

Corro is close to a High Lord, so I'll have to figure out which one that is. Maybe Callum suspects that court is aiding the rebels, or at least has crucial information that would be beneficial against them. The question of what this rebellion is truly fighting against floats through my head again because after tonight, I don't think it only has to do with the Fire Kingdom. It must be bigger than that.

With my mind on home, I remember that Haemir and Mereena wrote back. Rushing over to my desk, I find the piece of parchment Callum had likely read. My heart hammers as I hope nothing he could use against me is in it.

A,

We cannot inform you of our current whereabouts but we assure you, we're safe.

M.

That's it? I deflate heavily into the chair and stare at the blank canvas wall. Could they be upset with me? I wouldn't blame them if they were, but this is all I get? Maybe they've decided they like their space away from me and my problems. They've been my friends for over a hundred years and all I get is a measly sentence. And, why can't they inform me of their whereabouts?

I worry my bottom lip with my teeth as I go over the possibilities, trying not to feel so hurt. Maybe they think my correspondences are being read before I get them. Which, now that I think about it, is quite possible. Or maybe, they aren't as safe as they make it seem? A defeated sigh leaves me and I flip the parchment over to write my reply.

I trust you two to let me know where you are when you're able to.

Can you tell me anything else though? How is the pregnancy? Have you seen Torvin since the boat? If you have, I hope you stabbed him for me.

Folding the letter in half, I send it off. As I'm undressing, I realize I left a set of my uniforms back at the palace. The thought of sending Callum a letter and asking him for a favor aggravates me as I'm sure it will come with strings attached. With muttered curses and grumbles, I sink into the hot bath I've been aching for all day.

Entering the clearing the next day, I stumble over my feet at the sight of a very large obstacle course that's set up. My brows rise, "What's this?" I motion in the direction of the course.

"Nothing you need to worry about until after lunch," Corro says as he walks up to me. "Come on, you know the drill. Start your stretches and warm-ups."

I go through my new routine while thinking about how I'm going to get closer to Corro and get the information Callum wants. The best way is obviously to be as friendly as possible, but that doesn't mean he's going to open up about sensitive information, especially in the short amount of time I have with him.

I'm in the middle of a stretch when he comes and pushes my leg farther back than I'm physically capable of at the moment. I hiss a curse and he chuckles, pushing my legs deeper. "You need to work on your hamstrings." I inhale a strangled breath. Mercifully, he eases up on my leg. "Other one." He says with a flick of his fingers, and I begrudgingly lift my other.

After his little torture session, I go through my morning series of full-body exercises. I need to be friendly; it all starts with a conversation, right? "So, besides the daunting course set up, what are we doing this morning?" My words come out through heavy breaths.

Corro drops to the ground from doing his own morning pull-ups and runs a hand through his brown hair. "We're going to work on defending against earth attacks with just your fire magic."

I nod as I hop up from the ground and wipe my hands on my pants, "Okay, that sounds good." I'm pretty excited about this. I've never gotten to fight anyone that has another type of magic. I barely trained with Torvin back home, and when I did, we never used magic.

His eyes narrow, "You're being surprisingly agreeable this morning."

My eyes roll, "Maybe I'm just excited about it." He shakes his head and resumes going through exercises alongside me.

We're standing in the middle of the clearing an hour later where Corro just showed me various earth attacks that I'd most likely encounter among mid-level users. I would have been thrilled if he hadn't demonstrated the attacks by using them on me and I haul myself off the ground after his last one restrained me there.

"Now, most earth attacks should be easy for a fire user to defend against if you've got the right timing and magic as strong as yours." He pauses and gives me a pointed look. I ignore whatever suspicions rattle in his brain and motion for him to continue. "It's the surprise attacks that can be deadly."

For the next two hours, he cycles through all the attacks again and again. My timing gets quicker, and I use my fire magic to either burn vines or fling fireballs through thick walls of dirt. The spears of earth he sends my way have me perfecting my ducking and dodging. Sometimes I'm even able to stop them with a crack of my fire whip or cut them in half with my sword made of flames.

By the end, I'm exhausted. "Those were some pretty cool fire attacks," he says while standing over my crouched position.

I shrug, "I've always seen -" I catch myself before I say my father and correct it, "other people wield the whips and sword before. I thought I'd give them a shot. It was actually pretty easy once I got my magic flowing consistently and with the added boost of the elixir."

Corro nods in approval. "We have about an hour before lunch, so why don't we start the course now." A groan slips past my lips and I get up to follow him over. "There's that enthusiasm you usually give me."

As we stop in front of the course, I get a chance to take it all in. Not only are there moving components, tall walls, and large boulders, but there are bits covered in slick mud. "Is this your way of killing me?"

Corro laughs, "Don't worry. Most of the pointy parts are illusion magic." He grins down at me, "Only the ones that can potentially kill you at least."

The look I give him conveys my thoughts about that but he just shrugs. Cracking my knuckles, I make my way to the start while giving myself a little pep-talk. I manage to make it halfway through and begin walking slowly across a small muddy patch of dirt when thick vines start shooting out of the ground.

They wrap around my ankles, yanking me violently down. My ankles heat to a scalding temperature, and I'm thankful I'm resistant to my own fire magic as the vines turn to ash.

My head whips to Corro who is currently laughing, "There's magic?" I yell.

"Did I forget to mention that? Oh, and you're not allowed to use your fire," he shouts back.

Annoyed that I'm now covered head to toe in mud, I begin to push myself off the ground when more vines strike out and coil around my knees to secure me. Angry growls climb up my throat and I use the small amount of earth magic I've learned so far to wilt the vines, making them rot and fall away.

Except, by the time those are gone, more are snaking around my ankles. I move to rot those as well, but another appears and pulls my wrist down. I grunt as my arm hits the mud, my body wobbling with it. Another growl reverberates through my chest in frustration.

Finally, I make all the vines retreat and get to a standing position. I take one step and to my dismay, more come shooting out of the ground all at once until I'm lying on my back restrained in the mud. The sound of the moving parts in the course comes to a halt and Corro steps into my field of view. I give him my best death glare.

He winces, "That was painful to watch."

My jaw clenches, "Maybe if I had known about this part and

the magic restrictions from the beginning, I wouldn't be in this position." I snap.

Corro smiles, and damn him, it's a nice smile. "The point was to catch you off guard. In a real fight, you have to be ready for anything at a second's notice."

"In a real fight, I would be able to use my fire magic," I retort.

He shrugs, his hands still clasped behind his back, his form still towering over me blocking the sun. "Yes, but again, the point is to learn how by using the different elements."

My eyes roll, "Yeah, yeah. Get me out of these vines Corro."

"I'm sorry," he raises a hand to his ear, "I didn't hear you say please." I continue to glare at him and he laughs. "Fine, maybe if you lay there long enough, you'll learn how to get yourself out." Corro starts to walk away and adds over his shoulder, "Remember, only earth magic."

My head thumps to the ground. I'm too stubborn to give him the satisfaction of begging. The no-fire-magic rule is stupid, but I am certainly capable of getting rid of these vines. Especially now that they're not moving. One by one, I make them slither and rot away.

After what feels like an eternity, I break free and stand up with a long sigh. I stomp my way over to Corro who is sitting atop a rock and enjoying an apple. "That took dreadfully long," he muses through a mouthful.

I slap it from his hand and it rolls across the grass. "At least I got myself out."

Corro's eyes follow the apple and then turn to glare at me. "Yes, but you took too long. Even if you had used your fire magic, you'd still be dead. The moment you let yourself get restrained like that, it's over." My hands ball into fists at my side and he stands to get in my face. "You didn't react fast enough. That wasn't even how quickly a powerful magic user could wield the earth. I went easy on you, but your opponent won't."

Even with my stubbornness and ego, I can't argue with him. My reaction time isn't what it could be. All this time I thought I was good at magic, at fighting, but it turns out I'm just average.

"Now," he points back to the course, "go finish the rest of it."

My mouth falls open, "But, what about lunch?"

"Lunch can wait. Go."

Snarling, I trudge back to the beginning of the course. Gratefully this time through, there aren't any magical parts — just the swinging pipes of metal that knock the wind out of me countless times. In the last portion, I must maneuver around flying daggers. Many of them hit me and if they weren't illusion magic, I would have died many times over.

Just as I cross the finish line, a clicking sound comes from under my boot and a large palette of wood springs up from under the mud, smacking me right in the face. The last thing I remember is the crunch of bone and the iron taste in my mouth as my back hits the ground.

My blurry vision starts to clear away as I blink up at the gray cloud-covered sky. With a moan, I roll my head to the side to see I've been moved and Corro leans against a tree while sharpening a knife. I let out another moan as I fully turn onto my side. "What the hell Corro."

He lets out a laugh and continues to sharpen his weapon.

"Did you put that there just so you could have a good laugh?"

Corro pauses his sharpening to look my way, "No, that palette was there to see how well you can take an unexpected hard hit to the face." The corner of his mouth tugs upward, "Since you've been out for a few hours, we now know you can't."

My eyes widen, "I've been out for hours?" That explains why my stomach is grumbling.

"Yup," he exhales, "looks like we'll have to work on that."

Fully sitting up, my brows crinkle, "And how exactly are we going to do that? Keep hitting me with large pieces of wood?"

A wicked grin sweeps across his face, "Eat your lunch and then I'll show you."

After shoveling food down my throat, I find Corro standing in the middle of a sparring ring he drew with black sand. "You know how to fight decently. However, based on what I've seen in our previous sparring sessions, you weren't taught how to take proper hits in hand-to-hand combat. And, I'm going to guess that whatever your previous employment was, you were used more for your other skills."

I square my shoulders, "I know how to take a proper hit. You saw me do it yesterday when I set my own nose."

Corro shakes his head, "You took the hit but you couldn't get back up. You may know what it feels like to get hit but you don't know how to react to it in a fight-style setting."

I push my sleeves up and mimic his stance. "Fine." We begin to circle each other and then I charge. He side-steps my punch with ease and swings his arm out hitting me. I fall to the ground with an oomph.

As I gasp for air, Corro peers over me. "Come now, I know you can do better than that."

I blink up at him, "You've been going easy on me the past times we've sparred." I stand up and get into stance just in time for him to start throwing punches. I manage to block them all and feel a wave of satisfaction.

It's short-lived, however, as his fist slams into my side and a string of breathy noises tumble from me as I topple over, trying to inhale. "Yes, I have. If you get knocked down, you get right back up, Ameria."

My stomach does a slight flutter at the sound of my name, which he's only used once before. This is a good sign, he's beginning to be friendly with me, for the most part at least. Baby steps.

Wincing at the pain as I stand, I'm right back into a fighting stance. "Why go easy in the first place?"

"I was examining your fight style and ability. Have you ever been in an actual fight before?" I pause to consider, have I really never been in a real fight before? "That reaction tells me all I need to know."

I deflate on the inside, feeling somewhat small. My list of average skills is getting longer and longer. Here I was thinking I knew a lot, but I guess he was right in the assumption that I was used mostly for my other skills.

For an hour, I take punch after punch from Corro but I also manage to land a few good blows on him. I am currently sitting against a tree letting the healer patch me up. If my skills really are lacking, I'm going to need to up my game during training.

No more whining or arguing about making things easier. It's clear I'm going to need all the help I can get to make it through the trials at the end of the competition and even after that, I'll need to be at my best.

Once the healer is done and I've downed the entirety of my water skin, Corro asks her to stay. "You plan on punching me some more?" I ask as he surprisingly helps me up off the ground.

He chuckles, "No, but you're going to run the course until you can get through it in one go." I nod, accepting the challenge, because I want to be a better warrior at the end of all this.

It took me the rest of the day to finally make it through the course and thankfully Corro took out the wooden palette at the end. The healer left to go tend to someone else not long before we started to walk back to camp. For me, it's more like a limp, courtesy of a swinging pipe hitting my knee at just the right angle.

"Listen, you're not that bad of a fighter," Corro starts. "It's just one," he holds up a finger, "I'm older and I've been training since before I was fifteen. And two," another finger goes up, "Western Isles fae are all gifted in the art of speed and strength."

My mouth falls open and I shoot him a scowl, "You didn't think that was important information to share?" He just shrugs. "So, when you won the competition, you got the gift of speed and strength just like someone who was born here?"

Corro nods, "Along with other lesser magics."

I perk up, "Speaking of lesser magics, what are they? Are they different from those of the Elemental Lands?"

"Most of them are the same." He scoops up a stick from the

ground and starts flipping it as we walk. "How we send letters, objects, and such are the same. But there are a few others. We can call things that aren't too ridiculously heavy, like a book or something, to our hands from far away. It's mostly nice when you're feeling lazy or multitasking."

We exit the forest and the camp comes into view, "What else?" I ask, my interest piqued by the differences between our lands.

Corro quickens his pace, "Ask me tomorrow, I'm officially off duty!" I glare at his back and head toward the pavilion for dinner.

Chapter Fourteen
Corro

There he is!" Narses bellows from the corner booth in one of the shoddy taverns we frequent. He's ushering a pouting woman off his lap as I maneuver through the crowd. My body practically falls onto the ripped tan leather seat.

"It has only been five days and I'm already tired of training," I grumble and slug some of Narses' water, which looks untouched.

He hums, "I know it's not like one of your usual missions but Rafael sent you here for a reason."

"Yeah, to babysit." I heave out a long sigh and run my hands through my dirt-filled hair. I desperately need to bathe. My body sags a little more as I think about having to take a bath instead of using one of the showers back home. I don't know how Rafael dreamed up the idea of those things, but they are a godsend – along with many of his other useful inventions.

An empty mug slams on the table, knocking me out of my daydreaming. "What's with you, Corro? You're usually the positive one." Narses motions to one of the waitresses for another.

Her. That's what's wrong with me. It's ridiculous how in just a few days, this woman has gotten under my skin. Leaning my elbows on the table, my head falls into my hands, "I don't want to talk about it."

"Oh, you've got to be fucking with me. You're attracted to her, aren't you?"

I can almost feel him roll his eyes. A disgruntled noise crawls up from my chest but I say nothing because he's right. He's always right. It's almost his secret talent. "I gave you Ameria as an extra assignment to find out more about her and the magic she possesses, not to get your dick wet."

I wish it were only that. The attraction. No, it's something more, and it reaches all the way into the depths of my soul. I'm afraid to name it, to voice it, to acknowledge any of it. I know that when I do, it's game over for me and right now, none of us can afford my feelings getting in the way. Let's just hope I have enough willpower.

"It's fine. Just a minor inconvenience." I lie through my teeth and peer over the rim of my water mug at Narses, who's squinting at me, likely not believing an ounce of it. So, I move the conversation away from my feelings toward Ameria and more to why we are here.

"Speaking of her magic, she briefly allowed me to borrow some of it."

My oldest friend leans forward. "And?"

I grimace, "It was something I've never experienced before. It felt cold, the kind after a freezing winter rain. The kind of cold that seeps into your bones and stays there. It was like all the light in me left." Recalling the moment sends a shiver down my spine. "The magic felt alive, and it didn't want me. It only wanted her. It fought me to return to her." My hand rubs the back of my neck, "Honestly, I was quite relieved to give it back."

Narses has gone still, his eyes are pointing in my direction but it seems like he's looking through me instead, lost in thought or memory. I wait for him to come back to the present, knowing this happens occasionally. At last, he shakes his head and speaks. "That's...very interesting."

He pauses and looks down at his mug, brows drawn together. "This is something Rafael and Damien need to know. In the meantime, continue to get to know her. See if you can learn anything about who she is. If Beor was interested enough in her then so am I. It's just unfortunate that he won't tell me anything."

I nod, as if I have a choice. "Maybe your attraction to her will work in our favor. She hasn't opened up much to the others. Perhaps she needs a little...romance." He winks, suddenly okay with my feelings toward her.

My brow rises, "Are you telling me to use my body to get information? Are you trying to whore me out?"

Narses snorts, "Like you'd have a problem with it. You're always wooing women with your body and charm." He's not wrong. I do like to participate in intimate activities with many women. There's actually a regular here I might have to visit before the meeting later tonight. My insides revolt at the idea but I ignore it.

"Yeah, yeah," I say with a roll of my eyes.

"Just, be cautious with her brother. I don't trust her," Narses says before downing the rest of his ale.

"And why is that?" I question, a tad defensive but hopefully he ignores the tone.

His eyes drift to mine, "Because someone with a power like that is usually always being controlled."

My neck twists with a crack and I roll my shoulders back. The quick fuck I had with Gretta did little to ease my pent-up anxiety. I slip into the back entrance of the tavern and right down the stairs to the lowest level — one of the many secret spots the rebellion uses to meet within Nyasa, the Sun Court's capital.

Each meeting place is located close to a gate so those who cannot portal themselves out have a way to escape, just in case. This spot is new, as we can't sneak so many competitors off the King's Island for long.

"Finally, we can start. Do you know how long we've been waiting for your ass?" Serpent's tone is full of annoyance. I know I'm late, but my cock needed attention before I did something stupid like burying it in Ameria.

I shoot a glare toward Serpent. Her green eyes send a shiver down my spine but I hide it, at least I think I do. She's one hell of a warrior, so it's no wonder the Astral Court wants her. Her looks could kill even the strongest of men. "I was busy."

A snort comes from across the room. Rune is leaning up against the wall, shaking his head at me. His hood is up but unlike the rest of us, who have scarves covering everything but our eyes, his entire identity is shrouded in impenetrable shadow.

He and Vel, the imposingly large figure standing on his other side, are in charge and must keep their identities hidden. They even use magic to change their voices so no one knows who they are. Well, except for me of course.

"Let's get started then, we don't have all night," a member snaps from behind me.

I take a spot against the back wall and it creaks when I place my weight against it. "We'll start with updates from headquarters." Vel begins, "Our shipment of weapons successfully made it to the Water Kingdom. However, some were stolen and put on a vessel headed to the Fire Kingdom. One of our contacts has redirected them and they'll arrive where we sent the others next week."

"This means we have a spy," someone spits.

"Correct."

"Do we have any suspicions of who?" I ask.

"Not entirely, but we suspect it was not someone directly involved in the rebellion, just aiding it. It's possible they were bribed for information. Or tortured, who knows? We have some people in mind and they are already being trailed. I'm confident we'll catch them soon." Vel answers with a nod.

Rune steps to the front, "We have leads on a few possible warehouses that are storing goods for shipment to the Fire Kingdom. We are still locating them all but we have a spy who will be hitting one tonight. Once we get more information, we'll send word."

"Are we supposed to continue babysitting then?" sneers

Gild, another member in the small, crowded room.

"You chose to enter the competition for one reason or another and we made it happen, which means you also chose this mission," Rune answers with authority.

"Yeah, but we didn't know it would mean playing nice with potential enemies. Who is she anyway? Why won't you tell us more about her?" Gild retorts.

"I'm tired of being so nice to someone I'll likely end up killing. It makes me sick having to pretend," Serpent chimes in, her feet outstretched and crossed.

My body tenses at her words. "We need more information about her," I answer a bit tersely.

Her head whips around, pinning me with those eyes, "You're her trainer, why must we also have to babysit?"

I push off from against the wall and open my mouth to answer but Rune inserts himself. "Because it's likely she'll open up more if she feels included and welcome. From what you've all told us so far, Ameria is a bit closed off. Keep making her feel comfortable around you and maybe she'll open up. Corro will do the same."

Serpent scowls but knows not to argue with Rune. "You only have a short time with this mission. Use it well. And, don't forget that your survival at the end of the competition is not certain so...don't die I guess," Vel adds.

"Gee thanks," Gild mumbles.

The meeting ends quickly and I gather the group of competitors, ushering them through the gate back to camp. I wait behind in the forest, allowing enough time to pass so we arrive separately. My mind is swimming. I've always been professional and level-headed when it comes to my missions, but this one is difficult considering my emotions seem to be at an all-time high whenever I'm near Ameria.

With an annoyed grumble reverberating in my throat, I slice my hand through the air creating a blade-like line of water. It cuts through several trees, and I jump out of the way as one of them falls toward me. I cringe at the sight of my tantrum. Releasing a heavy sigh, I begin the walk back to camp.

This is a mission and I need to treat it as such. Ameria is definitely attractive and stirs up intimate emotions, but she's an assignment and nothing more.

Chapter Fifteen
Ameria

It has been two days since I wrote back to my friends and there hasn't word from them since. I also have yet to gather any important information from Corro. Who knows when Callum will show up demanding something useful, which I clearly don't have yet. Just the thought of dealing with him irritates me and I hurl my apple core through the trees.

My anxiety got the best of me this morning after I woke up with my shadows covering the interior of my tent and I decided to send Haemir and Mereena another letter, hoping it'll make them reply.

"Alright, choose a weapon Ameria," Corro says, yanking me out of my spiraling thoughts. The sun is hidden behind clouds today and I'm grateful because the air is so muggy I feel like I'm living in a bowl of soup. Corro has been a bit friendlier the past couple of days, which gives me more of an opportunity to get him to open up.

I survey the weapons littering the ground in front of me: axes, spears, even maces. "Preferably one you've never used before," he adds, halting my hand, which is reaching for the daggers. Fair enough. My eyes wander and I snatch up the spear. "Let's go with this. I don't think I've ever even held one of these before."

Corro nods, "Good choice." He plucks up another spear and motions me to follow him to the middle of our practice space. "So," he clears his throat, "like I said during lunch, learning new weapons gives you a little advantage if you ever have to grab whatever you can find in the midst of fighting. You may not excel at any of them but at least you'll have more of a chance of defending yourself."

I nod, "Okay, yeah. That's actually pretty smart." His brows rise. "What? It is."

The corner of his mouth quirks up, "Wow, look at you agreeing with me. I like it." My eyes roll and I purse my lips, attempting to hide a smile.

Corro starts with the basics, showing me how to correctly hold the spear and how to block different hits. When the light from the sun, still muted by the clouds, is almost behind the trees, he begins showing me how to throw it. "Hold the spear like this," Corro makes an example with his stance. I copy it easily. "Then, hold the spear parallel to the ground. To aim," he points at a tree, "bring your opposite foot forward and the hand holding the spear behind you and…" It wails through the air, landing in the trunk of a tree with a thunk.

My mouth slightly falls open as I watch it wobble. That was… impressive. "Some spears are meant for throwing and some aren't. We're using the ones that aren't for a bit more challenge."

He yanks his weapon out of the tree and heads back to

where I'm gearing up my stance. "I'll have you take a little bit of a running start when you throw yours since you're at a disadvantage with your size." Corro makes a few adjustments to my form and nods. "Alright, give it a shot."

I do a quick little run and launch the spear. It lands nowhere near the tree I was supposed to hit. My cheeks heat and I clear my throat, "That's definitely hard."

He props his fists on his hips, "Yeah, luckily not many people use them anymore but," he shrugs, "you never know. I can't imagine you'll excel very much in using them."

I frown at him, "Thanks for that confidence boost."

Corro snorts, "I'm just pointing out the obvious. They're not meant for people your size, in throwing or in combat."

Feeling a flurry of emotions, mainly embarrassment and frustration because I've never been so monumentally bad at something since I was a child, I retrieve my spear. For the rest of the early evening, I continue to practice throwing and not once do I hit the tree. I do, however, end training with incredibly sore shoulders.

"We're heading to the tavern in a few minutes, you in?" Gregor asks as we walk back to our tents from dinner. I could barely hold my plate with how weak and tired my arms are from this afternoon. I nearly melt with joy and relief at the thought of getting a few drinks in me.

"Absolutely. Let me go freshen up. I spent the morning rolling around in the mud like a pig."

Delyth makes a disgusted noise from behind me, and I turn

to see her sticking out her tongue, "You and me both," she says, plucking chunks of mud off her clothes.

I find my bath all ready for me and I hastily dunk myself and wash off the caked-on dirt and sweat. I have one clean uniform left, which means I'll have to wash the others tonight before I go to bed. I'd have another set if I didn't leave it at the Sun Court palace. Nibbling on my bottom lip, I say screw it and write a note in my nicest possible tone to Callum and send it off, pleading with him to send me the set I left there. I'd sent the leathers back as well, because I don't want those lying around my tent any longer.

On my way out, I see a nice, folded set of clothes with a note on top.

I hope you're collecting valuable information for me. Also, you're welcome.

Clicking my tongue, I burn the note on the spot and leave my tent, annoyingly grateful that he sent them, and so quickly.

Delyth loops her arm through mine and drags me to meet up with Gregor, Keenan, and a few others who have already started walking. I'm still not used to being this social, but they've all been so nice and welcoming that it's starting to become enjoyable, it helps that they're easy to get along with.

The tavern isn't as crowded as the last time but it's still pretty packed. The men grab our drinks as Delyth, Inara, and I secure two tables and push them together.

Keenan sets a mug down in front of me and I instantly take a large gulp. That's when Callum's note flashes in my mind and I look down at my wine. I should probably not drink as much tonight and see if I can get anyone to open up. Maybe get someone to discuss the rebellion. I need something, literally anything, to give Callum next time.

We start playing a card game I'm quite familiar with and after a few rounds, we're all a bit tipsy. "How the hell are you so good at this game, Ameria?" Gregor howls and with a huff, he chucks his cards onto the table. I just won my fifth hand.

I snicker, "I used to play this game with my friends all the time back in the Fire Kingdom." As I slide my cards toward the person shuffling, I notice a shared look between Gregor and Keenan. And finally, I have my opening.

My mouth is barely open when Keenan speaks up first, "What did you used to do for work there?"

I notice everyone around the table is slightly quieter, awaiting my reply. My eyes dart between them, "The group I worked with used to get hired out for different things." The lie slips easily from my lips. The three of us glance at each other while we're dealt another hand. I take a sip of my wine. "You know, we're all automatically cleared of the illegal things we've done once we enter the competition. I think it's safe to openly discuss our past work," I blurt out, already tired of skirting the subject.

Gregor smirks, "Hell, I guess you're right." He places a card down in the middle and picks one up from another pile.

Keenan does the same and lets out a hefty breath, "That's why most of us are here anyway I suspect."

I nod in agreement and throw two cards down before replacing them with another two. "Pretty sure if I didn't get here when I did, my last job would have gotten me killed." Another perfectly crafted lie flows past my lips. I raise my glass and take a big gulp.

A snort comes from Keenan, "Yeah, you're telling me — ow!" He glares across the table at Gregor who's scowling at him.

"Oh for fuck's sake you two," Inara throws her cards down and turns toward me, "What these two idiots are trying to indirectly figure out is what side your group was on. The King's side, or the people's?"

My eyes widen at how direct she is. I knew Inara was bold but this is a different kind of bold. It makes me like her a bit more. I survey everyone around the table and all eyes are on me. "Well, I wasn't and am not on the King's side. That's for sure." Not a complete lie. Was I forced to work for him, yes. Did I ever agree with what he did and who he is? No. I didn't exactly do anything about it though. I was just, complacent. Shame rolls through me at what I've done in my past, and I hide my reaction by taking another sip of wine.

The whole table seems to loose a collective breath. "See, now, was that so hard?" Inara shoots eyes like daggers at Keenan and Gregor with her arms crossed.

Keenan rubs the back of his neck, "Sorry, Ameria. We just weren't sure how to go about asking. Especially if you had said you were on the King's side."

Gregor chuckles, "Yeah, then we'd unfortunately have to kill ya."

I choke on my wine and Keenan pats my back. "Glad we don't have to do that. We actually like you," Keenan chimes.

Inara scoffs and picks up her cards, resuming her turn.

"Glad you don't have to kill me either," I say softly.

Everyone seems to relax after the conversation. Except for me. If they find out why I'm really here, then I'm dead. The only good thing about this situation is now people may in fact start opening their mouths around me. The problem is, I think I'm starting to grow attached to these people. They remind me of Haemir and Mereena. They feel like…home.

Everyone at breakfast this morning is quiet, all incredibly hungover, except for Gregor who is stuffing food into his mouth. Loudly. I'd laughed at him once and immediately regretted it as it made my head hurt so much I wanted to puke. Kind of sucked the hilarity out of it all.

After last night's conversation about what side of the rebellion I was on, everyone seemed to start opening up and sharing the different kinds of jobs they worked. Most of them directly related to aiding the rebellion. I, of course, lied through my teeth every time I had to chime in with a story. Guess my days spent in the library with Mereena paid off.

As the night went on, I lost myself in too many glasses of wine again. It's always so easy, too tempting, to get drunk and get a break from everything that's weighing down on me. Even if it's only for a short time. To forget all the pain I've endured. That I will continue to endure. My fingers rub at my temples as I question my will to live while this hangover absolutely murders my brain. I am again reminded of how much I miss Mereena's hangover concoctions. Maybe if either of them cares to respond, then I can get her to send me a few vials for future mornings like this.

"Your inhaling of food is giving me a headache," Keenan grunts.

"Your presence is giving me a headache," Gregor snaps back, food splattering in Keenan's direction.

"Your bickering is giving me a headache," Inara scolds. Both men look at each other and then mumble apologies.

I run a hand down my face, "Well, today is going to be horrendous again." Delyth, who is face down on the table, grunts in reply.

Gregor finishes his food and lets loose a burp, "I blame Ameria."

"Me?" I yelp, my hand flies from my throbbing temple to chest and I wince from the sudden movement.

"Yes, you. You kept drinking so I kept drinking. By the way, you sure can drink."

I scowl, "I kept drinking because you kept drinking." Technically, I kept drinking because reality started to set in and it's hard dealing with the guilt of betraying them all. All these people around me, seemingly decent people who also hate my father, are all technically part of the rebellion. The very thing I've been ordered to report about. Which means I have to betray all of them and tell Callum.

"You both enabled each other, now shut it," Keenan groans and the whole table grunts in either agreement or mutual pain. Or both.

By the time I make it to training, I'm already sweating buckets and out of breath. On the walk here, I had to stop and throw up my breakfast. Corro is standing in the center of the training area with his arms crossed. "You're late," he spits. I grumble incoherent sounds that try to convey my apologies and drag myself to him.

I collapse to the ground at the finish line of the same course I did the other day. Except today, Corro finally allowed me to use my fire magic. His statements the other day were right, annoyingly. I was too slow and it took me many tries to get through that part of the course.

The sun beats down on me, making me feel like I'm trapped in an oven. I've already puked three times today. Four, if painful dry heaving counts. I pretty much fling myself to the ground where lunch is and start stuffing it down my throat, grateful to be sitting in the shade.

"Maybe if you didn't stay out so late and overdo the drinking, you wouldn't be so miserable today and be of actual use," Corro snaps. I grunt and reply with a wave of my hand continuing to eat.

It's silent for a while, save for the sounds of us both ripping into our turkey legs. The light breeze rustles the green summer leaves. Corro lets out a breath. "You really need to stop drinking so much while you're here, Ameria."

"Everyone else does it too. Plus, it helps me feel better so, no thanks," I reply through a mouthful of meat. Drinking has always been my favorite activity – besides sex– and there's no way I'm giving it up. Especially since right now, it's the only thing that helps repress the dreaded emotions threatening to bubble up every damn moment of my life.

"Really? So, you're telling me you felt good this morning?" And right now? Probably still have a giant headache. You feel "better?"" He air-quotes the last word.

My shoulders sag as I stare down at my mostly eaten turkey leg. He doesn't get it. No one ever does. I can't count how many times Haemir has tried to get me to quit drinking so much. With the amount of shit I've gone through and am still going through, alcohol has been the one saving grace that's helped me handle it all. Deep down, I know it's not healthy and likely a problem, but it's all I have.

"You don't get it." I snap with more venom than I intended. I attempt to soften my tone; it's not his fault he doesn't understand. "It's the only thing that helps me get through everything going on up here," I wave my finger around my head.

"Look," Corro says gently, placing a hand on my forearm, making me still my fingers which were fidgeting with the turkey leg. I meet his gaze. "I know what it's like to feel as if you're drowning and desperate for something to take away all the pain. I did the very same thing. If it weren't for Narses, I would be dead." He removes his hand and looks off in the distance. "It sucks having to feel the heavy things, I know. But the only way to get through it all is to actually feel, Ameria. Pushing it away with alcohol doesn't help. It just mutes it for a while until it comes bubbling up later and then you explode."

I stare at him as if I'm seeing a brand new person in front of me. Someone who is able to describe exactly what the war inside my head feels like. It's odd, seeing him this vulnerable. Not even Haemir shared this kind of openness with me, probably because I never allowed myself to be that way with him. I hate showing emotions and any weaknesses, so have I ever truly opened up to my best friend?

From an early age, all of my softness was conditioned out of me. It's what ended up being best anyway. I couldn't afford to crack. But yet, here I am beginning to crack as I stare at Corro. "You don't drink anymore?" My voice comes out as a whisper.

He turns his head to look at me, his moss green eyes glossy. "I stopped completely a little over ninety-nine years ago. For the past thirty-three, I learned how to moderate my drinking. Once in a while, if I'm celebrating something with my friends, I'll engage in a little more than I should but it's rare. Most of the time if I do drink, it's just one."

"Hm," I hum and glance down at my gristly turkey bone.

Corro grunts as he stands, "Moderation isn't for everyone. Took me sixty-six years to heal what I needed to, and learn how to manage my emotions and whatnot in a healthy way."

I fling my bone into the forest behind me and wipe my hands on my pants. As I watch it fly into the trees out of sight, I think about what Corro had said in his moment of openness. What he's saying, about moderation and actually feeling more emotions other than anger, sounds absolutely miserable. Yet the little butterfly of an idea flits across my mind of trying it out. I've been through worse – and have scars on my back and the three on my belly to prove it.

Plus, Haemir and Mereena wanted this to be a chance at a

fresh start for me. While I can't get out of what I've been forced into, I can at least begin to take control of myself. I bring my gaze back to Corro, who is already staring down at me with a softness that makes me squirm. He stretches out a hand, waiting for me to take it. "I'd be more than happy to help you out Ameria. We can start slow, like I did. Water down your wine a bit and then just go from there."

I take his hand and allow him to help me up, my head throbbing with the movement. Shifting my weight on my feet, I swallow the lump in my throat. "I'll think about it." I don't like asking for help, as it's admitting weakness. Plus, he just told me how to go about it myself. Maybe next time I go out I'll try it and won't need his help.

Corro clears his throat and lets go of my hand, which I've apparently been holding on to for an unreasonable amount of time. "Alright then, let's practice some magic."

I barely had been able to get through dinner without puking again. Even though Corro and I had the mushy heartfelt conversation at lunch, he still pushed me extra hard in training as punishment.

I barely had been able to get through dinner without puking again. Even though Corro and I had the mushy heartfelt conversation at lunch, he still pushed me extra hard in training as punishment.

Chapter Sixteen
Ameria

The next day is more of the same. I run through an obstacle course in the morning and then practice magic in the afternoon. In the few hours before dinner, we spar more with the spear. I've managed to hit the tree only once. I've slowly started to accept defeat at never mastering the weapon, which is hard for me to come to terms with.

My friends have still not answered me even after I wrote them a third letter, mainly just telling them about training. Callum hasn't come to visit yet but I'm sure he'll make an appearance soon. The tenth day arrives and we're informed that every ten days, we'll take what we've learned and spend the morning sparring against each other with magic. Surprisingly, we get the rest of the day off after lunch.

The entire camp is divided into groups of two or three based on the main type of magic and the one they've been trained in thus far. Joyously, I manage to be paired up with Gregor since I trained in earth and he trained in fire this first week.

"The rules are simple," the trainer assigned to oversee our

sparring session begins, "Only use magic. You'll each take turns attacking and defending in your main ability. This is what the past ten days have been leading up to, so give it all you've got." She backs out of the circle we've been ushered into. "Gregor, you will begin."

He wastes no time and vines sprout out of the ground to grip my wrists and tie my legs together. I fall to my knees but calm my initial panic and yank on my fire magic. I heat my ankles at the same time I grab onto the vines holding my wrists. They burst into flames and turn to ash. The ones around my ankles simply wilt against my hot skin and fall limply to the ground. I hop back up to my feet.

Gregor raises his brows, "Not bad."

I smirk and produce a decent sized fireball, flinging it in his direction. It's at this moment I realize we didn't ask what happens if one of us accidentally hurts or kills the other person. To my relief, Gregor throws up a thick wall of dirt, stopping my attack completely.

His next attack is stronger, with four spears of solid earth flying toward me. My flaming sword cuts through them all. He lets out a low whistle of praise. I throw a small cyclone of fire his way. I'm going easy on him but I can't take the risk of going all out. I honestly don't want to kill him. With a sweep of his hand, his own cyclone of dirt and rock smothers it.

Maybe I can go a little harder on him after all. Vines with thorns emerge from the ground, surrounding me in a tight circle. They start to twist around each other above me, getting tighter as the twist gets closer to my head. My flames burst from the ground instantly burning the suffocating cage of thorny vines. Looks like he's decided to go harder on me too.

As I ready my next attack, a blood-curdling scream echoes across the field, and I snap my head in its direction. There, in the distance, an opponent stands with his arms crossed staring at the person in front of him currently burning up in flames. The whole camp has paused to watch the dead body of a contestant turn to ash. Well, I guess that answers my earlier question.

Gregor and I trade a look. He nods and I return it, a silent agreement that neither of us will aim to kill. We spend the rest of the morning attacking and defending against one another until we've exhausted our magic. I only held back a little, and it was a surprise to learn how powerful Gregor is.

By lunch time, we lost five more contestants. Whether it was deliberate or not is debatable. While we ate, I learned that the fire fae who burned his opponent to death is named Lorik and while I doubt he'd be able to hurt me with his magic, I will be staying clear of his path. That's the last thing I need.

Some other contestants at the surrounding tables were talking about taking a gate to a small city here on the island for market day. I rush to my tent to grab some coin as well as my daggers. I'd rather not go anywhere without those.

My magic perks up the minute I step inside. I walk straight past Callum to my desk where my weapons still sit in their sheaths. "To what do I owe the pleasure of your visit, Callum?" A pointless question since I know the reason he's here.

"Now is that any way to speak to your employer?"

I begin strapping my daggers to my hips and thighs and

half turn toward him. "Excuse me, how may I be of service?" I mockingly bow and resume securing my sheathed weapons.

"Such a mood you're in today. I'll let it slide if you have any valuable information for me."

Fully facing him now, I find Callum standing with his hands clasped behind his back waiting expectantly. His silver hair is tied back in one long perfect braid and he's in fighting leathers today. This is a different look for him and it somehow makes him look even more imposing.

My stomach dips at the realization that now is the time I have to betray the people I've begun to befriend. Under normal circumstances, I wouldn't have gotten so close to them, but since it was a necessity for my task, I've started to enjoy their company.

I hiss as the brand on my wrist starts to sting. Callum closes the distance between us, making a noise of disapproval. He grips my chin making me look him in the eyes, "Come now, you know the rules. I ask, you tell."

Clenching my teeth, I pull my chin out of his hand, "Fine." I take a deep breath and the pain recedes like nothing ever happened. "Turns out everyone in this area of tents that I'm in has aided the rebellion in one way or another."

Callum's mouth twitches. "Who, in particular, has aided most."

My mouth forms a tight line, hands balling into fists. "Gregor and Keenan. They're mercenaries from the Earth Kingdom."

He smiles, "Interesting. And what about your trainer?"

I cross my arms, "I think I'm starting to get him to open up but I haven't learned anything yet."

Callum's smile disappears entirely and he crowds further into my space. I attempt to take a step back and bump into the desk. My heart thunders as he towers over me. For a moment I'm back in the Fire Kingdom, and it's my father who looms over me instead. My grip on the desk tightens as I remind myself that it's not him. I'm not at home anymore.

"I told you to get close to him by any means necessary. If you had done what I told you, we'd have information by now."

"I - I'm working on it. I'm being as friendly as possible."

His eyes flash a bright molten gold but it's gone as quickly as it came. "Not nearly friendly enough."

My head rears back as I catch his meaning, "You want me to flirt? To use my body?"

"By any means necessary," Callum grits out before taking a step back.

My grip on the desk doesn't ease but I'm able to breathe a bit easier with him out of my space. "I am not someone you can whore out," I spit with as much venom I can muster. What he's asking me to do is absurd. Not even my father would have asked this of me and that says a lot.

"I own you, remember? That means if I tell you to whore yourself out, then you do so." I can feel an aura of heavy magic radiating off him now and it makes me want to cower, but my dark magic wants a fight.

"And if I refuse?" A cruel smile creeps up on his face. The brand starts burning and I collapse to my knees, gripping my wrist in pain.

"Then that will happen until you submit."

I hold out. I've been through worse torture than this. But the pain starts to spread and becomes so blinding that my body locks up. My brain wants to black out but something about this magic refuses to let me do so. Refuses to let me escape the torture spearing throughout my body. It seeps into my bones.

Tears stream from my eyes as I continue to try and fight through it. Maybe he'll get tired of watching me lay here in pain and stop this agony. But he doesn't. He just stands there, looking down on me, smirking.

It's not long before I choke out the word I know I'm going to come to regret. "Okay."

The pain ceases and I'm left curled up on the ground, still clutching my wrist. "That's a good girl," Callum says, still hovering over me, "I expect something of use next time I see you." Light surrounds him and he's gone.

I'm still on the floor trembling, but no longer in pain and already regretting what I just committed myself to.

I find my new companions at the edge of the camp all waiting for me. "Ameria! There you are, we were wondering what was taking you so long." Delyth skips over, linking her arm with mine.

My stomach sinks with guilt, "Sorry, I had to write my friends back." The lie tastes sour on my tongue.

"Well, let's go already. I'm trying to find a nice woman if you know what I mean." Gregor starts hauling ass into the forest.

"He's quite adamant about that," Delyth mumbles as she pulls me along.

There are a few gates scattered throughout the forest surrounding the camp. Now, I know where two of them are. This one seems to be closer than the one I came through at the beginning of the competition. The gate comes into view and it looks exactly like the other: Made of gray stones with symbols carved into them.

A woman in a healer's robe stands next to the grand archway. "Where would you like to go?" She asks, her voice soft and pleasant as she surveys our group.

"Wherever that market day is happening," Gregor answers.

The healer laughs while covering her mouth, "Today is market day everywhere on the island." She places her hand on the stone and white light consumes the entire inside. "But, I'll send you to the more lively one." She sends a wink in Gregor's direction and he flirtatiously sends one back before walking through the gate.

"I think he may have already found his woman," Keenan whispers as we follow him through.

The bright light fades from my vision and we're smack dab in the middle of a bustling city. Children run by with colorful spinning wheels in their hands. Chatter between citizens lined up to enter through the gate next to the one we came through floods my senses. I can smell dishes with spices being cooked and sweet treats being baked, the aromas wafting out from the many eateries and shops lining the street.

The remainder of our group pushes through behind me and

we're almost instantly shoved to the side when more people come through.

Delyth and I are still linked at the elbows and Inara grasps her hand, tugging us along to catch up to Gregor and Keenan who've already started walking. "Alright, first I think we should find a tavern and get some drinks in us." Gregor scans the area, looking for a spot to do just that.

"Well, I want to do some shopping first," Delyth chimes, a bright smile lighting her face. Maybe one day her positivity will rub off on me. I can only hope.

"I second that," Inara adds, and another woman agrees.

My mouth quirks up as I take in the different shops we walk by, "I'm on the hunt for some candy."

"Then you ladies go do your shopping and we'll meet you back here in an hour and a half. We'll all go do something together after." Keenan is already backing away, Gregor and the other men starting to follow.

The four of us continue to wander, browsing the carts and stalls lining the street. A large clock tower is visible at the far end, perfectly in view to remind us when we need to meet.

"I bet you a coin they'll be late," Inara says while pulling us toward a cart full of jewelry.

I snort, "I'm not taking that bet. I already know they will."

Inara seems to find something that catches her eye and quickly pays for it, stuffing what looks to be a necklace into her pocket. We continue down the street, stopping every so often to look at different goods. Delyth no longer hangs on to me but walks by my side. Inara is behind me with the other woman, whose name I think is Melinda, but she's generally quiet and keeps to herself. Or, she sticks by Inara's side, which makes sense because I believe she's also a water fae.

The merchandise stalls start turning into food sellers and my eyes dart across each one, searching for any candy. I'm hoping that maybe they'll have the sour peach strings I love. "Looking for something in particular?"

I glance at Delyth, "Yes but I doubt they'll have them. There's this candy from the Earth Kingdom – sour peach strings, and I'm a bit obsessed with them."

Her ice-blue eyes widen and she gasps, "I love those!"

I smile, "Well then, keep your eyes open."

We stop by a few carts selling different kinds of fruits, I pick up a small carton of raspberries. Inara and I munch on them as we continue on. Thankfully, the sun is no longer beaming down on us, now hidden behind some clouds. People eat and drink under awnings that take up the sidewalk areas. It reminds me a bit of Qesa minus the smell of salty sea air.

A long line snakes from one side of the street to the other and we have to push our way past. Delyth gasps, "Ameria, look!" I whip my head in the direction she's pointing, where the long line starts. Squinting, I see what she's so excited about: My candy!

I grab her hand and yank her to the end of the line. "I hope this line moves fast or we're going to be late meeting the men."

"Eh," she waves her hand, "they'll be late themselves. Plus, this is more important." She clasps her hands in excitement.

"We're going to head back toward the meeting point, we'll see you there." Inara slips through the line in front of us, planting a quick kiss on Delyth's cheek.

My mouth curves into a crooked smile, and I raise a brow at Delyth. Redness was already starting to creep up on her pale cheeks. I knock my elbow into her side, "Looks like that's progressing, huh?"

She purses her lips trying to hide a smile and shrugs, "I guess. It's still new."

"I think it's nice that you two found each other here." The line begins to move forward.

Delyth makes a little satisfied hum. "What about you, anyone catching your eye?"

A bark of laughter slips from me, "Oh no, I try to avoid any romantic relationships."

She scoffs, "First, it can be just physical you know. Second, are you telling me you've never been in a relationship?"

Scrunching up my nose, I shake my head. "No, romance didn't really fit into the job description."

A man accidentally bumps into me and I stumble a little but the line moves again. "I know plenty of mercenaries that were happily married!" She throws her hands into the air.

"I guess I didn't feel like subjecting anyone to the possibility that I might not come home from a job," I lie, though not entirely off base.

We're finally next in line and as the man in front moves out of the way, my jaw drops. Not only are there the pink peach strings, but there are three different others as well. "What kind of flavors are these?" I wave my fingers over the ones I don't know.

The seller points to the red ones, "Strawberry," he motions to the yellow ones next, "Mango," and lastly points to the green, "Apple."

My mouth waters in anticipation, "I'll take a bag of each."

"Strawberry and mango for me." Delyth yelps. The seller excitedly scoops our candies into bags and we hand over our coin. "Oh, my Gods. You've got to try eating the mango and strawberry together." She moans over the candy stuffed in her mouth as we head to where we're supposed to meet the others.

"Only if you try the apple. It's so sour my tongue feels like it's shriveling up." I shift the bags around in my hands and pluck one out for her.

Her face scrunches up seconds after throwing it in her mouth, "Whew! That is…" Delyth shivers.

"I know," I say while chuckling at her reaction.

Turning the corner we find the whole group waiting. Keenan throws up his arms, "There you two are! We've been waiting for almost twenty minutes!"

Delyth ignores him and heads straight for Inara. I watch them converse and then she's shoving candy at her. I fight back a smile while I observe the interaction. Delyth seems like she doesn't belong in this competition. I can't see her being a mercenary and so I wonder what led her to enter.

"We found a whole square of games. I say we go play for a bit and then grab some grub before we head back," Gregor announces. Everyone nods in agreement and follows his lead.

Keenan walks beside me and questions what I'm eating. I hand him a sour green one. His face screws up and he begins to gag. "Fucking hell, Ameria. How do you eat that?"

I laugh and plop one into my mouth. "Haven't you ever had these? They're from the Earth Kingdom."

Keenan shakes his head and stumbles as a child goes barreling by him. "Not whatever that flavor is. We only had the peach ones." I smile and pull one of them out of the bag. His face lights up. "Gods I miss these. My wife used to own a shop and she sold these every spring and summer."

I begin condensing all the candy I haven't eaten yet into one bag, my stomach starting to hurt from how much I've had already. "So, that Starla woman you mentioned, she's your wife?"

He takes the empty paper bags from me and throws them in a nearby trash bin. "She sure is. Took me forever to gather the courage to ask her on a date." A smile stretches across his face, "We're hoping the mating bond kicks in at some point."

"What happens if it doesn't?"

"I can't imagine she isn't my mate. We haven't been together that long, but it just feels so right." I nod along, as if I personally know what he's describing.

We come to the square and there's archery, dagger throwing, ring tosses– pretty much every game one could think of. I share some coin with a few members before we break up into various groups. Keenan, Gregor, and I head straight for the dagger-throwing game. It's one I'm positive I'll beat their asses in.

Of course, all six of my daggers sink into the middle of the target. "Damn," Gregor whistles.

Grinning, I turn with a flourish. "Let's see if you can do

better than that boys."

Gregor steps up. He gets two in the bullseye. Keenan gets three.

"You may be small Ameria, but never let me get on your bad side." Gregor yanks me into his side and I awkwardly hug back with one arm.

The sun has officially started to set by the time we've finished the games. Our group strolls around the streets until we find a brown two-story tavern to settle in. The waitress grumbles at having to push together two tables, but does it anyway.

After a round of drinks, our food finally comes: A rabbit stew and a large platter of bread, meat, and cheese.

I fall back against the chair, my belly full, and let out a satisfied hum. "Well, well, well. Look who we found, Corro." The deep timbre of a familiar voice comes from behind me. Narses pulls up a chair and plops down next to me. Corro pulls one up on the other side next to Gregor. Narses reclines and props his feet on the table. "Looks like you guys found one of the best taverns in the city," he smiles smugly.

"If more of them find out, our favorite spot will be ruined." Corro checks out a waitress who walks by and snatches her wrist, tugging her into his lap. She giggles, her bouncy breasts almost popping out of her dress, and plants a kiss on his cheek.

"I'm working Corro." She playfully smacks his chest and tries to rise to her feet but he holds firm. I ignore the unwelcome feeling of jealousy and roll my eyes.

"Feet off the table Narses," says another who comes and swats him with her towel. He drops his boots to the ground and she also takes a seat in his lap. I see Gregor watch in awe as both men bounce annoyingly beautiful women on their knees.

"Bella my dear," Narses whispers into the woman's ear, "it seems my friend Gregor over there could use some company." She bites her lip seductively and hops up, sauntering over to him. My gaze darts to Corro who is flirtatiously smiling while the woman nuzzles into his neck, whispering. My stomach does a weird little flip at the sight of his beaming smile.

His eyes meet mine and shoots me a wink. I fight the urge to flip him off and turn my attention to Narses instead. "So, this is where you get your cheap thrills then?" The woman on Corro's lap shoots me a glare but I ignore her, somewhat satisfied with my small dig. I have nothing against women in this profession, I'm just annoyed that I'm annoyed by seeing Corro with someone else.

Narses leans in, "If you want a ride Ameria, all you have to do is ask," his mouth quirking up to the side.

I scowl, "Only in your dreams."

"You wound me," he places a hand on his chest.

The waitresses finally leave and Gregor raises his glass in Narses's direction and downs the rest of his ale. "You guys should probably hurry. Can't imagine the person assigned to this side of the gate will wait very long since it's about three minutes before they themselves head back and you're stuck here."

Everyone exchanges a worried glance while reaching for pouches of coin. "Aw, come now Corro. We shouldn't scare the poor souls. I think maybe just this once we can escort them back later. You're Ameria's trainer after all. It's the least you could do." Narses sends him a look I can't read and plucks a mug off the waitress's tray.

"Yeah, alright. Just this once." Corro stands, "In that case, I'm going to find Lynia." I watch him disappear into the crowd and through a door on the other side of the tavern. It might be hard to sway him with my body when he's got that kind of woman on standby. Who knows how many others there are? Plus, if he were interested in me he would be giving me more attention. This could put a kink in Callum's plans for collecting information.

I come back to reality after getting stuck in my spiraling thoughts to find Narses watching me. The side of his mouth lifts and his shoulders move with quiet laughter. With a wave of his hand, a mug appears and he slides it in front of me. I take it and down half of it in one go.

During the next hour, we manage to procure a deck of cards and play our usual game. I win a few hands but unsurprisingly, Narses wins most of them. "There he is," he mutters while standing. The tavern has gotten a lot busier, and the crowd is growing rowdy. I see Corro stalking his way back to our table, a hand running through disheveled hair.

"Alright, let's go contestants," Narses announces and we throw our cards on the table, following them out the door.

The night sky is cloudy, and lights strung from rooftops and awnings illuminate my surroundings. The smell of food is still in the air but now mixed with chimney smoke. People still roam the streets, drinking and hollering.

I haven't had a day like this since Haemir and I went to Qesa for a week. Even then, it didn't feel like this because I was constantly being watched. I may be stuck working for Callum but this is the most freedom I've ever had. Now that I've had a taste of what it's like to just let go and be with people who have started to feel like friends, the more I need to get out of this situation with the High Lord.

"You coming or what?" I blink and realize I've stopped in the middle of the street the gate is on. Corro is the only one left on this side, his eyes narrowing at me while waiting with his arms crossed. I swiftly close the distance and walk through.

Corro and I emerge on the other side, the others already a bit ahead. I feel him walk alongside me but I'm busy watching Inara pull the necklace out of her pocket and dangle it in front of Delyth. A small smile creeps across my face.

"I saw you drink tonight," Corro's voice is soft. Quiet.

Keeping my eyes on the ground, I watch for any roots as we continue to walk behind the group. "It was just two ales. I'm perfectly fine." He answers me with just a grunt. I wave my bag of candy, "You should probably be more worried about how I'll feel tomorrow after I eat the rest of these tonight."

His eyes narrow, "What is it?"

"Sour candy." I look up at him, "Want to try one?"

"Sure." He says with a shrug.

I fish out a peach one, "Here. This is my favorite. I used to get them from the Earth Kingdom in the spring and summer months."

Corro hums as he chews it, "It's good." He laughs, "My

sister would have loved these."

My brows shoot up. He's starting to open up more. "You have a sister?"

His face falls as he looks down at his feet, "She died when I was fifteen."

"Oh. I'm sorry."

He jerks his head in a nod, "Do you have any siblings?" And we're changing the subject from him. Got it.

Lights from the camp start to peek through the trees in the distance. "A half-sister." She's also my cousin, but I feel like that's too much information to drop on someone.

"You get along?"

"It's complicated." My brain replays the conversation Petra and I had before I left. More guilt settles in my stomach. It was wrong of me to treat her like I did, for not getting to know who she really is, for just leaving her there to fend for herself. I take a deep breath, pushing away the ache in my chest that has started to build.

We enter the edge of camp, "See you bright and early," Corro calls out, walking in the opposite direction of where I'm heading.

I sit on my bed, with my empty candy bag in front of me, and my chest continues to ache with the realization that Haemir and Mereena still have not written back.

Chapter Seventeen
Ameria

The weather is gloomy and gray, which perfectly describes my mood this morning. I tossed and turned all night, thinking about my two best friends and for some reason, my sister. I can feel my emotions rising and usually around this time I'd drown myself in alcohol but I'll have to settle for training. Inara convinced Delyth and me to train with the water element this week and we decided that we'll get together to practice every so often for the rest of our time here.

A disgruntled noise leaves me as I run a hand down my face. I need to get information from Corro, and I need to do it soon. I'll just amp up the flirtation and see what happens.

As I get closer to the clearing, I can make out two voices. When I enter, I see Narses standing with Corro, the former looking tense. "There she is." Corro turns his whole body to face me as I make my way over to them. "I've done the honors of choosing your next weapon, which happens to be Narses's favorite." He nods in his friend's direction.

Narses smiles smugly, "Every other morning this week,

you'll be training with me using the battle axe."

"So, you're an axe guy huh?" I cross my arms, looking him up and down. "I guess I can see that."

I catch Corro roll his eyes, "Don't fuel his already large ego." Narses snorts, "Did you decide which element you'd like to practice this week?"

"Yeah, water." I say with a quick nod.

"Perfect." Corro shoots a glance toward Narses – a look I can't decipher. "Get started on your stretches and warm-up exercises."

"Then, meet me over there," Narses points a finger to an area across the clearing.

I go through my typical morning exercises, adding a few more reps as I start to get stronger in certain muscle groups. My hamstrings are still tight and I fear they always will be.

I stride over to Narses as he waves to Corro who is heading out of the clearing, and then hands me a plain double-sided battle axe. "We'll start with the basics and then go through attacks and blocks," he announces while he readies himself in a stance that I copy. "Elbows out more." I adjust and he nods in approval.

"There are multiple kinds of axes: some you throw and some you wield with one hand while using a shield. Others are long handled ones like the one I have here. Yours is the most common double-sided axe for someone of your size.

I frown, "Is this going to be another weapon that puts me at a disadvantage because I'm smaller?"

Narses shrugs, "Maybe, maybe not. Depends on what weapon your opponent is wielding. If it's one like mine, then yes. If it's one like yours or the one-handed type, you're likely to be equally matched."

Straightening my back, I refresh my stance. "Okay, let's do this."

He runs through movements of swinging, jabbing, and so on. He also shows me how to block common hits and what to do if one of them is thrown at me. It may still be cloudy, but I'm soaked with sweat by the end of the session.

"This is a weapon for which we'll need to work on your forearm and grip strength as well." He turns toward the trees and sweeps his hand in a slicing motion. My mouth slowly pops open as I watch one of the thicker trees fall forward, leaving a decent-sized stump. Another sweep of his hand and the tree goes flying to the right side of the clearing.

"Holy shit," I murmur. He's one hell of an air wielder.

"Follow me." Narses makes haste toward the stump and I pull my gaze away from the tree he effortlessly flung, and hurry after him. "From now until lunch, you're going to swing down upon this stump repeatedly. This will not only allow you to build arm strength but also, prying the axe out of the stump will somewhat mimic the feel of yanking it out of a person. Every sixth time you pull the axe out of the stump, I want you to hold it at arm's length for as long as possible and then repeat it with your other arm. Then get back to swinging."

My shoulders start to slump. It's two hours until we break for lunch. "What happens when I need another stump?"

He snorts at me while swinging his axe up to rest the handle on his shoulder, "You won't need another."

For two agonizing hours, I swing my axe down, struggle to yank it from the stump, and repeat the motion. Over and over. The most frustrating part is that every time I pause for too long, Narses barks at me from across the clearing to keep going. One time I ignored him to take a tiny rest and he flung me ten feet.

My hands are bloody and my knuckles are permanently curled by the time I drag myself to where Corro has reappeared and is standing by Narses.

My axe falls onto the ground, "Please never leave me alone with him again." I sarcastically plead.

Corro chuckles, "Imagine being trained by him every day."

I cringe, "No thanks."

Narses leaves when Corro and I sit down for lunch. My eyes dart from the finger food to my bloody and blistered hands. He notices my hesitation and motions for me to hold them out. Water materializes, drenching my hands and I rub them together before wiping them on a few napkins.

"I've already called for a healer. She'll be here after we eat."

"Thanks." I pick up my turkey leg and my hand stings with the movement. I hold it as gingerly as possible with my fingertips. However, those are also sore so I double hand the bone with a napkin around it. "So, how did you and Narses meet?"

"He was another one of the contestants when I competed, except he was quite a bit older than me. We've been brothers ever since," He says over a mouthful of turkey.

"He has strong air magic," I comment, hoping he spills a bit more information about Narses. I'll take anything that's helpful for when Callum returns.

Corro just nods and continues to shove some food in his mouth. The wind starts to pick up as we fall into silence and I carry on having a hard time eating food with my beat-up hands.

The healer shows up and closes the blisters and small cuts, but she leaves the calluses. A drop of rain falls onto my cheek as she leaves. "Great," I mumble.

"Actually, the weather should be helpful," he says looking up at the sky. "More physical water for you to work with." I consider him and acknowledge that he's right. It's unlikely I'll be able to conjure water from thin air at first.

I stand next to him as he fills a hole he has dug with water. "Is this going to be as hard as it was for me to learn earth magic?" I ask, crossing my arms.

"Harder likely."

My eyes shoot to his, the rain now steadily picking up. "What? Why?"

"Water is a natural repellent of fire, so of course it's going to be tough for someone like you." I groan. "You're in such a complaining mood this afternoon."

I wipe away the stray hairs that have begun to stick to my wet face. "You can thank Narses for that."

Corro huffs a laugh but jumps right into the lesson, "Okay, all I want you to do is hold your hand over this puddle and try to draw the water up in a stream to your palm."

Rolling my shoulders, I hold my hand out and draw out the magic from the elixir. The surface of the water stirs but nothing else happens. My eyes narrow and I try again. This time I close my eyes to focus on feeling when the magic hits the surface of the water. When it does, I gently pull. "Alright, you've got it. Keep going."

My eyes fly open in excitement and I lose my concentration, the small trickle splashing back to the surface. I try again countless times but each time it's only a thin line reaching halfway up to my hand.

"Let's try something else," Corro steers me by the shoulders away from the puddle. "Get on your knees." I give him a pointed look, brows raised in amusement.

He lets out an exasperated breath while shaking his head, "Nice to see where your mind is, Ameria." He kneels on the ground himself and I suck in my bottom lip, biting back a smile at seeing him on his knees in front of me.

It'd be so easy for me to just hook my knee over his — no, nope. Heat rises to my cheeks and I bat those thoughts away for now and quickly drop down next to him.

"We're going to try and see if you can pull directly from the earth. Even if it's just a little bit."

I snap my narrowed eyes to him, "You think I can pull from the earth when I could barely manipulate water that was already there?"

"Yes, it might help with connecting more to the element," he says side-eying me. "Place your palm flat against the ground." I mimic him, splaying my hand against the soaked grass. "Close your eyes and search with your magic to find the water that exists within the ground. It should be easier since it's raining."

I let out a heavy breath and let my eyes flutter closed. My magic pierces the ground and I begin to search. After a minute or so, it finally recognizes the water that's there. "What do I do when I find it?"

"Draw it upward and try to create a small puddle around your hand."

I tug on the water, imagining sucking the earth dry but it barely budges. My nose scrunches up in annoyance. "It's not moving." I can feel my forehead begin to crease as I try harder, finally getting it to move toward the surface a smidge more.

I feel movement next to me. "Keep trying, I'm going to help you out a bit."

My mouth opens to ask how but the words don't come as Corro's hand gently wraps around my wrist. A jolt of magic flows into me. I ignore the way his warmth seeps into my skin and continue to work on drawing up the water. This time, it moves with more fluidity and I can feel it gather around my hand.

Opening my eyes, I see a small patch of water. "Ha, I did it!" I grin at Corro, who smiles back and slowly removes his hand from my wrist, the extra magic disappearing with his touch.

"Good," he hops up to standing, "now remember how that felt and try it on your own."

I practice most of the afternoon, the steady rain pelting me relentlessly. I manage to make a small puddle around my hand but still struggle with creating a constant stream. For the last hour, Corro goes through various defense techniques a water magic user would wield.

Corro lunges, landing a few blows to my arms. His fist strikes out, aiming for my chest. Anticipating the move, I knock it out of the way. His other hand reaches for me, pulling me by the front of my shirt to drag me closer to him. Hooking his foot behind my ankle, Corro sweeps my leg out from underneath me. With a curse, I begin to topple. I refuse to go down without dragging him with me, so I claw at his shirt and pull him down.

His weight crashes onto me, both of us grunting as we hit the ground. Corro's face is inches from mine. So close I can smell him, sweat mixed with, what is that, lavender? How does he smell this good when he's drenched in sweat and caked in mud from all the rain we had yesterday?

I go to shove him off me, but as swift as the water he wields, he slams my wrists against the ground next to my head. This is not helping the devious thoughts his scent was giving me. I try to buck him off but it's no use. "Well," his voice is low, "the good thing is you finally managed to get me on the ground." The corner of his mouth twitches, "Unfortunately, you're still at a disadvantage."

A smile spreads across my face, "Am I?" I call on my magic and heat my wrists underneath his hands. He begins to squirm but my victory is snuffed out as water drenches my wrists, leaving them to steam in its wake. My usual harmless defense is now useless, and I don't want to burn him, so I take advantage of the moment.

I'm supposed to seduce him, right? It's obvious my body is attracted to his. Maybe it wouldn't be such a terrible thing to attempt it, see what happens. I roll my hips against his and that's when I feel a bit of hardness. My eyes widen, heat flooding my core, and Corro lets out a deep groan from his chest. His grip tightens on my wrists, his mouth forming a tight line, and he pushes off of me.

"Go practice your axe for the remaining hour," he says over his shoulder as he stalks hurriedly toward the boulder he likes to perch on.

I remain on the ground, elbows propping me up. I thought that situation would have gone very differently but it seems he has more self-control than I'd assumed. At least now I know he has some sort of attraction to me, but it looks like I'll need to up my game, especially if I am supposed to get information out of him. With a defeated grunt, I hop up and grab my axe.

At the end of the hour, I'm winded and my hands are ruined yet again. I pushed myself a little extra this time, just to work out my pent-up sexual frustration. Corro is stuffing his supplies into his pack as I trudge over to him, dropping the axe into the chest that holds an assortment of other weapons. "How did my form look?"

Without looking up, he grunts, "Better."

Well shit, now it's awkward. We walk side-by-side back to camp and I worry my lip as I think. Maybe he's just embarrassed, or maybe he regrets the whole weirdly intimate moment we had. Either way, this silence won't do.

I clear my throat, "Two other contestants and I decided we're going to help each other train for the rest of the competition." I peer over at him as we continue walking, "Work on elements and what-not," I add with a wave of my hand. It currently stings from swinging the axe so much that I'll have to see a healer before dinner or else I won't be able to hold silverware.

"Sounds like a good idea," Corro replies, still not bothering to look at me.

"Yeah," I say quietly, the awkward silence continuing. I puff up my chest and whip my head toward him, "I hope you know that one day, I'm going to knock you right on your ass. I'm letting you know now so you can prepare yourself for all the gloating I'll do." He scoffs, the corner of his mouth raising. Now we're getting somewhere. "What, don't think I can do it? I'm not that far off."

Corro swivels his head, his eyes meeting mine. A crooked smile gracing his face, "Actually, I look forward to seeing you succeed," he winks and then quickens his pace. I don't bother trying to catch up, my goal of eliminating the awkwardness already achieved.

I find a healer to take care of the little cuts and open blisters. I leave the soreness so I can get used to it though, as well as the calluses. Holding a fork isn't too bad, but my stiff fingers make eating take longer. I briefly tune into the conversations happening around me, chiming in occasionally but mostly staying to myself. I'm busy being plagued by thoughts of seducing Corro, finding that this is feeling like less of a job and more of something I might truly enjoy.

Chapter Eighteen
Ameria

It has been two days and I've made zero progress in getting any information from Corro. Mereena and Haemir still have not answered and I've written to them every single night. At this point, I can feel myself starting to spiral. None of us have been able to get a drink lately and I've had to drown my thoughts and feelings in training.

This isn't a bad thing if I want to survive – I have to be at the top of my game. But without the alcohol, it has been harder to sleep throughout the night because I constantly wake up drenched in sweat, the lack of alcohol having its effect on me. Plus, the nightmares have returned. Every night I dream of something my father has made me do or has done to me. Last night I woke to find my tent completely covered in thick shadows. Thankfully it was dark out and I was able to reel them back in rather quickly. I don't know what I'd do if someone saw my magic.

Narses comes every morning now to help me with my axe skills, but today I had a nice break from his brutal training. I've tried to get Corro to tell me something about Narses but he was annoyingly tight-lipped about anything that had to do with his friend.

It became abundantly clear over these past two days that I'm not good at getting information out of people if I'm not torturing them. It's a sobering thought, to say the least. It's also clear that just being friendly with him is going to take too long and Callum needs something of note next time he visits.

Corro seems to be ignoring our intimate moment and has returned to treating me as normal. I, however, have not gotten over it. I may be shit at getting information out of someone, but I thank the Gods for my skill of being able to see through people's defenses well enough. It's something I acquired over the years of observing people and torturing information out of them.

I know he's somewhat interested, I just need to break through his walls. So, I've started to flirt. Every day, I get a bit bolder with him and I can see those walls crack a little as he's started to flirt back. I can't say I'm not conflicted by what I'm doing, but unfortunately, I have to push that part of me deep down — something I've done one too many times.

The water element has proven to be difficult and I'm grateful that our tenth day of sparring doesn't involve me having to actually wield it or else I'd be screwed. While I was finally able to draw a steady stream, I've struggled to do anything bigger. It irks me to no end.

My arms fly up in the air as a frustrated noise escapes me. "This is so fucking useless." I glare down at the puddle that I've been trying to transform into a ball of water. A trickle I can do, but apparently anything more is asking too much.

"You're not concentrating enough," Corro chimes in from behind me.

I wipe a bead of sweat from my brow. The sun has been blazing down on me all day without so much as a puff of wind. "I assure you, I'm concentrating enough," I shoot over my shoulder.

"Then maybe that's your problem. You're concentrating but not connecting."

With a huff, I spin around to face him. "I'm connecting as much as a fire user can connect to water."

He looks off to the distance for a moment, "Alright then. I think I know what you need. Follow me," he motions with a wave of his hand.

I follow him as he leads me out of the clearing and into the surrounding forest. "Where are we going?"

"To the lake."

My brows jump, "There's a lake?"

Corro looks down at me and smirks, "We trainers like to keep it to ourselves for as long as possible."

The lake is on the smaller side, surrounded by large rocks and more trees just beyond it. From where I'm currently standing at the edge, I can see the whole thing. "Get in," Corro motions to the water in front of us.

My head whips to him, "What?"

He cocks his head, "If you want to learn water magic, then you'll need to get in the water."

"Why can't I practice from right here?" I glare.

"You need to connect more with the element. Actually being in the element will help with that."

My gaze flicks back to the lake and my shoulders sag with resignation. Gently, I lower myself into the water expecting it to be ice cold but I find it's surprisingly warm. "See, it's not so bad." Corro chimes from behind me as I wade in deeper until it comes up to just below my breasts.

"Now what?" I ask, turning to face him.

He crouches on a rock on the shoreline, "Feel the water around you. Notice how it moves and flows. When you're ready, try creating a ball like we've been practicing."

I do as he instructs and close my eyes, letting my arms move lazily beneath the surface. Noticing what the water feels like as it passes through my spread fingers and around my arms. My eyes open as I raise one arm out and call to the magic within me.

The first attempt is met with only ripples, so I change my tactic. I'll start with just a steady stream and go from there. On my third try, I finally get a small ball of water. Thrill pulses throughout me and a smile stretches across my face. "Good, now raise it into the air as high as you can."

I bite my lower lip and begin to raise it. I can feel the magic give out the moment it loses its form, splashing back into the lake. I'd only made it two feet over the surface – which I should be proud of since that's the most I've been able to do so far. I'm still not used to failing, and especially without a traumatizing punishment.

Air whooshes out of me, my arm collapsing heavily back into the lake. "Try again," Corro encourages. So, I do. Multiple times in fact. While forming the ball gets easier, holding it for a long period and moving it at the same time is where I trip up.

After countless miserable attempts, my anger and frustration grow, "I thought you said this would help?" I snarl at Corro, who has been lounging on the rocks at the edge of the lake.

He sighs while throwing his head back, mumbling a string of words I can't hear, and slides down into the lake, striding my way, "You're letting your frustration get in the way. It's going to take time and practice." His hands grip my shoulders and spin me around so my back is facing him.

One of his arms comes into my periphery and a massive ball of water forms over the surface. It raises high into the air and with a flick of his wrist, it flies across the lake, hitting a tree on the other side.

"Show off." I mumble under my breath.

Corro chuckles while placing his hand back on my shoulder. "I'm going to help you," he says, leaning down to whisper in my ear. I don't fight the shiver that crawls down my spine. It's taking every ounce of self-restraint to not lean into his warmth.

One of his hands slowly slides down my arm to the elbow and lifts it. This time, I fight the chill that wants to rack my whole body. "Pull on your magic and feel it flow with the water like you've been doing." His voice is soft, calming.

I'm barely able to focus as I watch, feel, Corro's hand continue to slide from my elbow to my wrist. I can feel his chest move in silent laughter, "Breathe, Ameria." Apparently, I stopped breathing. How I'm supposed to focus at all right now is beyond me, with his body flush against mine, his calloused hand on my arm.

It takes me longer than I want to admit, but I manage to focus on the task at hand and feel my magic weave with the water. I sit with it for a moment, letting it flow with the natural movement. And then I feel warmth spread throughout my arm, another magic intertwining with mine.

With Corro's magic assisting mine, I pull a small ball of water from the lake. I pour magic and focus into it, making it grow larger. Corro's hand cups the back of mine and guides me to move the ball higher in the air. I smile as I watch it gain height, coming to hover above us.

I can feel his eyes on me and I twist my neck, our faces coming close enough to feel each other's breath, and he returns a smile. His hand leaves mine and with a feather-light touch, he trails it down my still raised arm. Past my shoulder and all the way down my side. Fingers hit the dip of my waist and my breath catches.

Corro quickly pulls away and the large ball falls directly on me. A bellowing laughter fills the air as I wipe water from my eyes, pushing the hair that's now plastered to my forehead to the side. "That wasn't funny!" I turn toward him, flustered and he's already hauling himself out of the lake, still laughing.

"Sure it was," he says, facing me with a radiant smile. "But for a moment, you held that in the air all by yourself. Until you got distracted by me of course." His smile widens. I avert my eyes, hoping that my reddening cheeks aren't noticeable.

I start to walk toward the edge to pull myself out when his voice stops me, "Where do you think you're going? You're not done yet. You need to learn how to do it on your own now."

Scowling, I turn on my heel as much as one can when submerged in water, and continue practicing. Hours pass before he lets me get out. He continued to sit on the rocks the whole time, occasionally instructing and annoying me. I never formed the ball as big as I did with his help, or move it as high, but I did better than when I first started.

Training ended a few minutes early so I could change out of my sopping wet clothes before dinner. Corro stayed to clean up at the clearing so I walked back by myself, grateful to have some alone time to go through the events of this afternoon.

Today was a big breakthrough. He not only flirted, he touched me – quite a bit more intimately than a trainer should. I try to convince myself this is a good thing but guilt and disgust floods me.

Corro

I can feel him before he even emerges from the forest. Hell, I don't even have to turn around to know he's here. His magic is overwhelming right now, which makes me wonder where he's been. "What has you all riled up?" I ask, throwing a look over my shoulder as I pick up the last weapon left on the ground of the clearing. Sure enough, Narses's face looks unhappy.

"How did training go with Ameria today?" A silent breath leaves me and I almost shake my head, I see we're skipping any questions about him.

"Fine. I tried to get a feel for her magic again, see how she uses it and whatnot." I chuck the last weapon into the crate and slam the lid shut, causing some birds to fly out of the trees and into the sky.

Narses crosses his arms, "And?"

My eyes meet his, "She has a hell of a lot more than she uses, I'm sure of that."

He seems to contemplate this while magic still radiates off him. He nods like he's come to a decision, "Have her practice one day with you. See if she's hiding how much she has or if she just doesn't know how to use it."

I sit on this for a moment before I answer, "I think she knows, but I believe she might be afraid to use all of it." A thought comes to me, "Maybe she just needs help learning it, do you think -"

Narses's hand comes flying up, "Definitely not. He has much bigger things to deal with. Plus, we don't want her to learn how to control more of it if she's working for someone against us. Which brings me to an idea I've been mulling over. I think we, meaning you, should feed her some false information. See what she does with it."

My shoulders tense, "Why?"

His eyes narrow at me like I've asked something ridiculous, "To see if she's working for anyone. If the information makes it out, we know she's in someone's pocket and we get a lead on who that is."

I avert my gaze, looking off into the trees as my jaw clenches. My hands seem to clench too. I still can't for the life of me figure out why I get so worked up when it comes to doing my job when Ameria is involved.

Maybe it's because I'm afraid to find out she is working with the wrong side, because that would mean - "What would we do then? Use her? Kill her?" My insides turn at that last one. Fuck.

"We'll figure it out when it gets to that point." I can feel him staring at me and my eyes flick to his. "She's really gotten you all messed up in there," he snorts, waving a finger at my head.

A deep annoyed growl rumbles from my chest and I shake my head, my hand running through my hair. I go to open my mouth to ask what false information he wants me to feed her but the unreadable look on Narses's face stops me and I ask a different question. "Why are you looking at me like that?"

He snaps out of whatever stupor he was in and shakes his head, his radiating magic easing away. "Nothing. I need to go speak to Rafael and the others. I'll let you know what information we'll give her later."

"Narses - " I start but he's already portaled, leaving mist in his wake.

Chapter Nineteen
Ameria

Training had been brutal today. Narses came back and made me work extra hard with the axe. As welcoming as the tub full of warm water currently in front of me looks, a better idea pops into my head. One that will hopefully gain me some traction in the assignment Callum has given me if I want anything of note to report the next time he comes to retrieve information.

I had come to somewhat of a conclusion last night. While I don't know how to get out of the mess I am currently being forced into, the longer I can keep Callum happy without fully screwing over the rebellion in the process, the better. I'll feed him the bare minimum that this bitch of a brand allows me to and just go from there.

That's as much of a plan as I have anyway.

Turning on my heel, I push back through my tent flaps and walk straight to Delyth's.

"Delyth?"

"Come in," I hear her pipe up cheerily from the other side.

Poking my head in, I find her sitting on her bed midway

through untying her boot. "Don't take those off just yet!" She looks at me with intrigue. "I have an idea of where we could go to have some fun that's not the tavern."

Delyth sucks in a breath and hastily re-ties her boot before shooting off the bed and following me outside. "Go grab Inara and I'll gather Gregor and the rest. Meet me by the northern edge of the camp," I point in the direction and see her nod.

"Gregor!" I call from outside his tent and his head pops out. "Want to go swimming?"

His eyes light up, "Hell yeah I do."

I snort, "Delyth is getting Inara. Help me gather the rest."

We round up everyone and meet Delyth and Inara at the edge of the forest. "So, where are we going Ameria?" the former asks, her hands clasped in front of her chest, brimming with enthusiasm.

I wave for everyone to follow me as I explain, "I found the perfect little lake to go swimming."

When we arrive at the spot Corro showed me yesterday, I find that I'm not the only one who has the idea to swim. It is the perfect clear summer night for it, after all, I should have known. It's crawling with most of the trainers – including Corro, who immediately turns in our direction. His brown hair is soaked and pushed back. His perfectly sculpted chest glistens with water in the moonlight. I'm ashamed to admit my breath caught for a split second. "I brought you here in confidence, Ameria!" he shouts.

I shrug with a half-assed innocent look on my face. Another trainer next to Corro shoots him a look while splashing water at him, "You brought a trainee here?" He tackles him and they begin to wrestle. Corro lifts him up and, *oh*, he's naked. My eyes dart around the lake and finally, I notice they all appear to be naked, except for a small group of women hanging out on the rocks to the side.

My cheeks heat at the possibility of seeing Corro naked. I've never been around so many attractive naked men, except for the one time an assignment brought me to a brothel to kidnap someone.

By the time I've stopped ogling them all, everyone has already gotten into the water, which leaves me standing here like a prude. I follow the lead of the women who have kept all their undergarments on. Though, as I'm removing my boots I notice Corro's gaze and decide that this is the perfect time to nonchalantly seduce him.

While I've always been confident with my body, something about this makes me oddly nervous. However, I swallow those nerves and take my time removing each piece of clothing. Letting all the handsome men, including Corro, take me in.

A quick dart of my eyes tells me he definitely is watching me. A thrill bolts through me and I drop the last piece of clothing. Striding to one of the rocks that points out into the water, I dive in. When I reach the surface, I see his gaze has strayed elsewhere but I don't worry as I had him the entire time I stripped.

Delyth, Inara, and I flounce about in the water, occasionally floating on our backs to look up at the stars. I watch the men in the group do all sorts of jumps and dives into the water. Gregor and Keenan aren't unattractive, but I could do without seeing their cocks flop about. Now and again I let my gaze wander toward Corro who is always wrapped up in talking or tussling with others. Though, I've caught him glancing my way a few times.

"Ameria! Get your little butt over here," Gregor bellows with a wave from halfway across the lake. Most people here started playing a wrestling game where teams would sit on one another's shoulders and knock the other team into the water.

I make my way over and he lowers himself, "Get on sweetheart and let's kick some ass."

He doesn't have to ask me twice. Grinning, I drape my legs over his shoulders with my thighs on either side of his head. As Gregor rises to his full height, his arms wrap securely around my legs and he begins to trudge to meet the other team.

We pass by Corro on our way and he's smirking with his arms crossed. I flip some wet strands of hair over my shoulder and lift my chin pompously. I've always been a competitive person and don't like losing, which probably has something to do with my upbringing, so losing to this team in front of everyone is not an option.

Gregor and I now face the other team, another woman sitting on top of a man's shoulders. "Ready...go!" a person shouts. Gregor holds his stance firm as the other team strikes forward. The woman and I wrestle with our arms, pushing and pulling at each other's hands and arms. I realize quickly that neither of us are going to go down like this, so I get an idea.

"Bring me closer." I yell to Gregor through the cheering crowd around us. His arms tighten on my legs and I hook my feet behind his back, giving me a sturdier hold. I'm practically nose to nose with the woman now and I yank one hand free. Wrapping it around her neck, I pull her head as close to my chest as I can.

Gregor catches on and I don't even have to tell him what to do next. He pulls us away while twisting his body. The man holding my opponent up loses his balance and together they topple into the water. Cheers erupt as Gregor and I raise our arms in triumph.

A smile stretches across my face and I pat him on the head while laughing. I haven't had this much carefree fun in a very long time and it feels good. Thoughts of why I'm really here and my assignment crack through my happiness, but I push them away before they can grab hold. I just need one night of feeling this good. Just one, and then I can think about all of it later.

The night carries on while Gregor and I beat team after team. As it gets late into the evening, all the trainers begin to leave and we decide to go as well. While everyone climbs out of the water, I find Corro, who is pulling his pants over his toned ass. Slipping quickly into my clothes, I shove my boots on and don't bother to tie them. When I straighten, he is already a speck in the distance.

I stop in my tracks as I step into my designated training area the next day. There's yet again another course waiting for me, seemingly bigger than the last one.

"Good morning, Ameria," Corro smiles, with a hint of deviousness. I had been thinking about last night on my way here and I need to play today cautiously. I have him interested, but I don't want to spook him and ruin all my progress, which would likely cause painful trouble with Callum. This situation keeps getting more and more frustrating. All I wanted to do was live a free life but apparently that's not going to happen for me.

I flash Corro a snarky grin, "Good morning, brute." The light breeze in the air wafts his scent my way. He smells like rain on a hot summer afternoon, and it floods my senses, making heat pool in my belly. I clear my throat, "So, new course?" My head jerks toward the expansive setup.

"One of three," he says looking over his shoulder at it.

My brows shoot up, "I have less than a month before the competition, and you think I can make it through three this size?"

Corro steps closer, coming to tower over me, "Maybe. I guess we'll see. They are meant to be quite difficult though."

"Challenge accepted," my mouth forms a tight line, showing I'm ready for it. I actually welcome it since I've settled on watering down my drinks — for now — and this is all I have to keep my stress and raging emotions at bay.

The course was, in fact, way more difficult than I had anticipated. I could almost feel Corro laughing to himself as I was knocked to the ground repeatedly. This one had all the elements I've practiced, minus air, woven throughout. It included flying daggers, swinging blades, and all sorts of pointy things that would certainly kill me if they were real.

To my dismay, it seems Corro has snuck in some real blades, one of which just jammed into my thigh, causing a strained scream to rip from my throat. I collapse onto my knees, sending more burning pain through my thigh.

"What the fuck, Corro!" I shout in his direction. "I thought these were all supposed to be an illusion," my head whips toward him, a glare painted on my face.

"You need to learn how to get hit and keep moving," he shrugs, "so, I threw a few in there."

My teeth clench as I flick my eyes to the small dagger sticking out of my thigh. Little does he know, I have experience taking a blade to my skin. Though, now that I think about it, I haven't ever managed to get stabbed. My father mostly used me for spying and kidnapping. The latter was always quick and easy and they never had time to fight back because rarely did anyone ever see me coming. I relied on my magic to do most of the work.

"What if it hit me somewhere vital? Or gouged my eye out!"

Corro holds up a finger, "One, don't be a baby. The blades are too short to do any real damage. And two," another finger raises, "they've been enchanted not to hit any vital areas. So," his hand drops, "get up and keep going. I have a healer on standby so I promise, I won't let you die."

Scowling at him, I take a deep breath and yank the dagger out. Sure, it was shorter, but not by much. I chuck it in Corro's direction and it lands in the grass at his feet. One day, I'm going to stab him and see how he likes it.

With the wound trickling blood down my leg, I hobble to a stand. I limp about five feet before a metal tube shoots out and hits me right where I'd been stabbed. The air leaves me in the form of incoherent garbled noises and I'm knocked to one knee. Unfortunately for me, the metal spheres don't stop and I'm thwacked to the ground.

I keep at it for the rest of the morning. By lunch, I hadn't even made it halfway through the damn thing. I'm a bit embarrassed by my lack of progress.

Sure, I've trained with Haemir and the few guards my father let me occasionally fight against, but it seems that compared to everyone here, I don't have as much preparation as they do. No one ever dared to stab me, and during my assigned missions, I just kept to my shadows.

In the afternoon, we took a break from the course and sparred with each other. I was happy to see that I've at least gotten better at fighting. I wasn't bad before, but I surely wasn't warrior status. My fighting improved as the day went on, particularly after Corro showed me how to incorporate the breathwork technique he taught me on the very first day.

He had also asked me to wield my shadows some more. I'd been hesitant at first, but the magic has been crawling under my skin lately so I figured releasing some of it shouldn't hurt. Corro had asked me question after question about my magic, but I told him all I could: I don't know how to wield more and I don't know where it came from. His last question though, I couldn't answer. At least not out loud, because part of me is afraid of what will happen if I use more of it.

"Good job today," he says as we walk back to camp together. The sun has already disappeared behind gathering clouds and the wind blows some stray pieces of hair in my face as I stare hard at the ground.

My lips form a tight line, "Thanks, but I didn't even make it halfway through the course."

Corro places a hand on my shoulder and my eyes dart to the contact. "You made it a lot farther than I thought you would have."

"Still, I should have been better. I can be better." My fists clench at my sides. If I can't make it through one course, how am I supposed to make it through the trials at the end of all this.

I catch Corro quickly glance down at me. "You'll get better, don't worry. It has barely been two weeks and you have plenty of time to improve before the end." His calloused hand runs through his sweat-soaked hair, "I'm actually quite impressed."

I watch him for a moment, a soft smile touches my lips. His eyes meet mine and I avert my gaze to the ground. "Thanks," I mutter.

The tenth day came once again. My friends still have not reached out to me, so I stopped sending letters. There must be a good reason why I haven't heard anything. That's what I choose to believe anyway. Even if they were in trouble, I have no way to get to them.

This time in magical sparring, I got lucky again and was paired against Inara. It went exactly like last time except she was very, very good. We volleyed back and forth, slowly increasing how much power we used.

I don't know anything about Inara's background other than she obviously comes from the Water Kingdom, but she was able to meet my full-force fire attacks head on. It was impressive but also made me wonder: Who is she? At the very least, she must be from a noble family with this kind of power. Perhaps a distant cousin of the royal family? I've only met the prince once, and we didn't exactly spend the time talking. Although, what would a cousin of the royal family be doing here?

That night, everyone became interested in sparring against one another. Gregor, Keenan, and I decided that we would go check it out. I might even participate since I could take all the practice I can get. We all stand at the edge of a ring, watching Lorik, the fire fae, go through opponent after opponent with a battle axe.

Luckily for his opponents, they're fighting with enchanted axes. That, however, doesn't stop him from attempting to burn them to a crisp. A water wielder trainer has snuffed out many of his flames already. It doesn't seem like he's going to leave the ring any time soon, and I need to practice against someone who would actually want to kill me.

I let out a heavy breath and wipe my sweaty hands on my pants. Before I can talk myself out of it, I step into the ring and snatch up an axe from one of the trainers waiting on the sidelines. Lorik grins menacingly as I step forward to face him and ready my stance.

His brows lower, his face going hard as he stalks towards me. "Why did the King send his dirty little pawn to this competition?"

He knows who I am? Impossible. I try not to react but my face falls slightly and he catches it, a grin returning to his face. Instead of answering him, I lunge. Lorik blocks it easily and pushes me back. My dark magic roils inside of me but I tamp it down along with my anger and anxiety.

I lean out of the way as his axe swings in a sideways chopping motion. As it comes down past me, I step forward and jam the top of my axe into his chest. The top of the blades don't pierce him but he stumbles back with a grunt. I silently thank Narses for endlessly making me chop into wood.

My feet move to get out of his swinging range. With a guttural growl, he runs at me and slashes. He misses as I duck. This time, I attack his left side but he swivels out of reach. I move against him before he can recover but he still manages to block it. Taking a chance, I slide my axe to the side with momentum. The bottom of my blades meet his, causing them to lock in a tangle. With as much force I can muster, I swing the axes in a downward circle and both of our weapons fly out of our hands.

Lorik and I watch them hit the ground and I assume the match is over, but I don't dare turn my back on him. I start to slowly retreat from Lorik, whose body is tense – a wolf ready to pounce. His head whips toward me, fury etched across his face. My feet stop in their tracks as fire lights in his clenched fists. I instantly summon mine.

"You can't burn me like your other opponents." I spit. It's true, he can't. Only my father's fire is strong enough to kill me. Perhaps Petra's may be one day as well.

A muscle in his jaw twitches, "Fine," he stalks toward me, his fire disappearing, "I'd rather kill you with my fists anyway."

A deep calming breath fills my lungs and I also smother my fire before getting into a fighting stance.

Lorik sends his arm out in a wide hook. My mouth twitches slightly at the mistake he's already made and I'm somewhat proud to know that I might not be as bad as I thought. I crouch a bit and his body falls forward slightly as his arm flies through the air. My fist connects with his stomach and I can hear him huff out air. My body swiftly twirls around his and I prepare for his next move.

He whips around to face me, veins popping out of his neck in anger. It's a mistake to let your emotions guide a fight. He pounces, and I knock him away with a sweep of the back of my forearm. My punch hits his face hard enough to hear the satisfying crunch of bone.

I back away as blood starts to stream from his nose. "I know what you do for the King. Tell me what his plan is for having you here, bitch." Lorik snarls as we circle each other.

We've gathered even more of an audience than before, which means he's outing me to the whole fucking camp. "There's nothing to tell Lorik. I'm no longer a part of his plans," I state plainly.

I take a few steps toward him and he meets me, striking at my side. I dip out of the way but not in time to evade his other fist, which connects with my jaw. I stumble to the side and in my brief haze, I fall to my ass. The coppery tang of blood fills my mouth. I hop to my feet and work on blinking away the dark spots clouding my vision.

My dark magic begins to rise again but I push it down. "I find it hard to believe that the Fire King's personal torturer isn't involved," Lorik spits.

How the hell does he know that? I worked very hard to conceal myself, and my father only allowed a select few to know what I did for him. "I don't know what you're talking about." I spring forward, finally out of my haze, and land a few blows to his arms while evading a few of his.

Lorik smiles, showing his blood stained teeth. "I know all about the deeds you do for your father, *Princess*." My eyes almost pop out of my head and my body freezes up. My heart sinks like a rock. His laughter is deafening. This is not good. "You think the rebellion doesn't have our own spies?"

He lunges and lands a strike to my arm. I snap myself out of it and jam an elbow into his ribs. "Good for you, but I don't particularly care. Because, like I said, I'm no longer aware of any of his plans," I snort, trying to play off how shaken I am.

I'm aware that the rebellion has nobles within it, which means I wouldn't doubt they were working in the palace somewhere. But again, only a select few knew what I did and even fewer knew that I was the King's daughter. This makes me wonder who the spy is.

Lorik's entire chest shakes with laughter, "You should care," he grins, "considering your best friend is one."

My head rears back. "What the fuck are you talking about?" I sputter. Lorik attacks, taking my shock as an opportunity to land some blows to my sides and stomach. I'm able to kick the side of his knee, making him wobble to the ground, giving me enough time to stagger away.

"Oh, he and Mereena hid it from you so well," he chuckles

as he stands. "They really played you like the fool you are."

My spine stiffens as my life with Haemir and Mereena flashes before my eyes. It couldn't be true, could it? My two best friends were part of the rebellion and they didn't even tell me? My emotions come rushing to the surface: anger, disappointment, violation. Every feeling one could possibly have spears through me like a sword.

I've lost myself enough to give Lorik an opening. His fist slams into my jaw again and I drop to the ground. Another blow to my face crushes bone. Blood drips into the back of my throat and down the sides of my face. Dark spots cloud my vision.

The last thing I hear before I lose consciousness is shouting and the I feel the weight of Lorik's body disappearing.

Chapter Twenty
Ameria

The beige color of the canvas tent ceiling comes into view as I blink awake. With a moan, I turn on my side and come face to face with legs. Tilting my head slightly, I find Callum, of all people, staring down at me, his expression unreadable. My pounding head collapses to the bed. "What do you want?" I mumble against the sheets.

He scoffs, "I'd be more considerate in your tone if I were you. I just cleaned up your little mess, however, much of the damage has already been done."

I flip over again and everything comes rushing back. My fingers find my nose and I can feel that my injuries have been healed but a headache and some soreness remain. Callum is right. This has turned into a mess. I should have never stepped into that ring.

I've been outed; my identity spread wide open to the masses. Not just what my position was in the Fire Kingdom, but also the deepest secret of all: That I'm the Fire King's daughter and technically the rightful heir to the throne, regardless of whether

I want it or not. Secrets have been revealed and that cannot be undone.

My friends, Haemir and Mereena. They lied to me. They were spies for the rebellion and they - a lump forms in my throat – they spied on *me*. They told their rebellion group everything about me. I force back tears that so desperately want to spring free. No wonder they haven't responded to my letters.

I clear my throat, "Well, my cover has been blown."

"Not entirely." I flick my gaze toward Callum, who's still casually standing at the side of my bed with his hands in his sleek pants pockets.

My eyes harden, "No one is going to open up about the rebellion to the daughter of the Fire King. I likely lost all the progress I've made. They might very well decide to murder me while I sleep."

He rolls his eyes, "Use your brain, Ameria. Spin the story. Offer up information about the King and convince them you're on their side."

I prop up on my elbows, wincing at some leftover pain in my ribs. "You're suggesting giving away information about the King? Aren't you two working together?"

A look I cannot decipher flashes across Callum's face but it's gone in an instant. "On the contrary, I'm not working with your father. We just happen to currently have similar goals in mind." He waves his hand in the air, "By all means, spill the secrets of King Toross. It won't interfere with me."

I blink in surprise, more questions flooding my mind. Sitting up fully, I eye him carefully. "And what exactly is your goal?"

"Now why would I tell you that?" Callum smirks. "I expect you to spin this unfortunate situation in our favor. If you don't, you're useless to me and I'll throw you back to your father." I flinch and immediately curse myself for showing such a reaction. A knowing look forms on his face.

Callum rests his hands on the bed and leans forward. "Isn't it sad, how the people we love seem to be the ones who betray us the most?" His voice is soft and gentle. I would have thought he was being sincere if it weren't for the malice dancing in his eyes. "How depressing it must be to find out the friends you've known your whole life lied to you. Distrusted you. Spilled your most confidential secrets." He slowly shakes his head and rights himself. Wisps of light gather at his feet and begin rising up his legs. "Makes you wonder if they truly were your friends. Or if they just consider you a job. A mission."

Light consumes him and he vanishes, leaving his taunting words to echo through my mind. He's wrong. There must have been a reason they didn't tell me – a good reason. Still, Callum's words continue to play over and over, making me doubt everything.

My head falls into my hands. My fingers tangle with my hair as I squeeze my eyes shut. Warring thoughts crowd my mind and mixed emotions squeeze my heart. My throat tightens and burns with the tears I refuse to release.

"You!" A voice startles me out of my breakdown and my head flies up. My eyes connect with a stone-faced Corro. Through my despair, I hadn't even heard him come in.

"Corro, I –"

"Stop." I clamp my mouth shut as he takes a step toward the bed. "Is it true?" My shoulders slump and my gaze falls to the bed. I lightly nod my head. "I figured you had to be from a noble family, with fire magic like that. But royalty? The Princess?" He spits the last word. I shake my head as he's talking, unable to accept the words he's slinging my way. His anger. I was the farthest thing from being a princess, but how would he know that. How would anyone know that. "You..." his voice turns harsher, "You *tortured* my people."

My fists curl, crumpling the sheets and I jerk my head up. Our gazes clash, "I didn't have a choice."

"Bullshit! We all have a choice."

I go to move but finally notice I'm fully naked under this sheet so I stay planted where I am. My voice turns cold, "Do we? You know nothing about my life growing up. Do not talk to me about choices. My life was decided for me at the age of fifteen."

Corro shakes his head, "Everyone is able to make a choice. It's a coward's way to be complacent." I rear back like I'd been slapped, my anger snuffed out by shame. "Are you still working for him?"

"No," the word comes out of me as a choked whisper.

He takes a few steps back. "I wish I could trust that answer." He turns to leave but I call out after him, making him pause with his hand on the tent flap.

"I didn't tell anyone because of this reason." I swallow, "I wanted to create a new life, untethered from who I was made to be. I wanted to be free." Not a lie. I do ultimately want freedom, however, that's all complicated now. I'm not surprised by his distrust, considering who currently owns me. I hate that word but it's the truth. Always an object. A weapon to use. Collared like a pet.

Corro doesn't say anything for a moment. His head dips slightly, "I hope you can prove your words," his voice soft. He doesn't look back as he stalks out.

I slump fully into the bed and curl in on myself, floating in and out of sleep. No one else comes in, thankfully, and eventually, the noises outside my tent wane as night settles in, leaving me to stew in the dark.

The morning commotion outside wakes me. My body is still curled in on itself and I slowly stretch out my stiff and cramping limbs, allowing my eyes to adjust to the light of day. Relief settles in my stomach as I realize that no one attempted to come in and kill me as I slept. I wouldn't entirely blame them for trying. Perhaps at the end of this, it is what I deserve.

Eventually, I bring myself to sit up, letting my eyes stare off into space. My thoughts flood with all the poor choices I've made in life. The things I'd done for my father and to where it's now led me — forced to be working for Callum. Dragging myself to the bathing area, I find my tub full of warm water and sink into it, bringing my knees to my chest. Any lingering soreness melts away. My head falls to rest on my knees and I sit there numbly, unsure of what to do now.

Everything Corro said was correct. I was a coward. Did I agree with anything my father did? No. Yet, I didn't help anyone. I followed his rules and allowed him to push me around, beating me into submission. I could have chosen to do something, even if it was just refusing and taking the punishment, but I didn't. Maybe that's why Haemir and Mereena decided not to tell me about their part in the rebellion. My stomach sours at the thought that it could have been one of them on the cold metal slab. My own hands carving away pieces of their flesh and making them bleed to death.

A shiver crawls down my spine and I hug my knees tighter. Would I have joined them if they told me? My heart says that I would have at least supported them, but my head tells me that I might have been too afraid, too fearful to do anything. A few tears manage to slip my guard and trickle down my cheeks. One of them hits the water, making soft ripples.

I'm aware of someone entering my tent. I should be jumping up to guard myself, preparing for a fight. Yet, here I sit defenseless, as still as a graveyard in the night, awaiting whoever has decided to come and bury me six feet under.

Soft footsteps make their way to where I am and a body enters my view. It crouches and a warm brown face with piercing green eyes comes into view. Inara's black and emerald braided hair is piled high on her head.

Where I expect to see anger and judgment on her face, I see a hint of warmth. Her hands rest on the edge of the bathtub as I feel her stare straight into my soul. "Are you here to kill me?" I whisper.

Her mouth forms a line, "No one will be killing you."

My eyes shutter as I let out a heavy sigh, "I wouldn't blame any of you if you did."

Inara's grip tightens on the edge of the tub, "Look at me." Her voice commands my attention and I force my gaze to meet hers, "Are you still working for your father?"

My nails dig into my legs with the words I cannot say, "No."

"Do you agree with everything he has done?" I shake my head. "Then I will not judge you. A person cannot help their family of origin. We all have a past and have done things we aren't proud of."

I look straight ahead, embarrassed and uncomfortable with the vulnerability I'm about to spill. "I may not believe in what he does but I didn't do anything about it. I was in a position to do something, anything, and I selfishly ignored it all. You do not think of me as a coward?"

"It does not matter what I think," I side peek at her from the corner of my eye and feel her unwavering gaze pierce me, "it matters what you think. Do you believe yourself to be a coward?"

"Yes," my voice cracks, my shoulders slumping with the weight of the answer.

Her brows lower, "And is that who you want to be?"

"No." I say through clenched teeth.

Inara jerks her head in a nod and stands, "Then prove to yourself that you aren't one." She stares off to the side in thought, "I have to return to training," her eyes connect with mine, "You've been relieved of your training duties today. I was informed that the King determined it's best if you didn't make an appearance in the camp right now. The others and I will be meeting before dinner. We have some things to discuss amongst ourselves, regarding you."

I flinch a little at her bluntness, though I've always appreciated that she cuts out the bullshit. "We'll come find you afterward." I nod my head, acknowledging that I hear her and she gives me the briefest of tight smiles before padding away.

The water has become cold and I quickly scrub my skin, harder than necessary. Once I've dressed, I plop down into the chair at my small desk. My weapons still clutter the top of it, my mother's sword sitting there, taunting me. With a scowl, I push it off the desk along with my two daggers and they clank to the ground between the wall and the desk.

My emotions are all over the place and I feel like I could vomit. I no longer belong to my father but my throat still burns with all the things I can't tell Inara. Or any of them. Anyone. They shouldn't trust me — I barely trust myself. I've given their names to Callum. I'm taking their secrets and spilling them just like Lorik did with mine yesterday.

At this point, my actions have proven I'm undoubtedly working against the rebellion. Disgust fills my bones and I slam a fist on the desk. I'm stuck on the wrong side. My eyes dart to the brand on my wrist and my hand clenches even harder, my nails digging into my palm.

My forehead thumps to the desk and I let out a long groan of despair. My thoughts are making it so hard to concentrate. I take a couple deep calming breaths, like Corro taught me.

Inhale, two, three, four.

Exhale, two, three, four.

"One thing at a time Ameria." I mutter to myself. Lifting my head, I scramble around for a piece of parchment and the fancy writing utensil. I scribble one sentence.

Why didn't you tell me?

With a flick of my wrist, I send off the letter. My knee bounces and my fidgeting fingers rest on my lap. I'm going to crawl out of my skin. I abruptly stand, unable to just sit here anymore. I need to do something. Scooping up my boots, I shove my feet into them.

I need to get this pent-up energy out along with my magic, which has been simmering underneath my skin, ready to burst. I don't have alcohol and I have no one to spar with. I'll have to settle for a long run.

Carefully poking my head out of my tent, it seems everyone has left for training so the area is clear of foot traffic. As I weave through the lines of tents, I can hear the magical and metal-on-metal sparring. The sky is full of looming dark clouds, ready to let loose anytime.

The sparring noises and chatter mix with all the emotions whirling about in my head. Finally, I see the tree line and portal with my shadows into the forest to avoid walking through all the pairs who are training. My magic seems to sigh at finally being released. It's been getting restless lately.

I run. I tear through the trees, whipping through short brush and jumping over roots.

I run from having to face my emotions.

I run from the consequences of being complacent.

I run from the truth that my friends never trusted me.

I run from having to make a choice.

I can't handle this. Not now. It's all too much.

The screech of an owl, chittering birds, and the rustle of leaves fade into the distance until all I can feel is the wind on my face and my feet thudding on solid ground.

My pounding steps carry me even when my chest feels like it's caving in and my breath becomes so heavy my lungs feel like they're being squeezed. I'm soaked head to toe from the clouds that opened up a while ago, yet I still run through the forest.

My pace finally slows to a trudging walk and my gaze lands on the view beyond the trees ahead. I come to stand on great cliffs overlooking the restless ocean. I don't know how long I ran for, but I made it to one of the furthest edges of the island.

The wind is brutal, sending droplets of water stinging across my skin. Goosebumps rise on my bare arms and I tuck my loose wet hair behind my ears. Sinking to my knees, my eyes flutter closed and I let the sound of the ocean settle me.

I kneel for who knows how long, letting the wind continue to pelt me with rain. The cold has sunk far into my bones and I'm shivering enough that it convinces me it's time to head back. Rising on shaky legs, I turn on my heel and ram right into a hard chest.

Rough hands grip my arms, "Quite far from camp are we?"

My teeth grind and I try to shake Callum's hands off me but they only tighten, "Twice in twenty-four hours, lucky me." My voice drips with sarcasm and at the moment I have little care if he wants to reprimand me for the disrespect.

"I'm in need of your expertise." I open my mouth to spit some snarky retort but we're quickly consumed by light and the next second I'm standing in a dark stone hallway. It smells like wet rot and the sewer. It smells like every dungeon I've ever been in.

Callum turns my body and I stumble a little but catch myself. He gives a little shove to indicate that I need to walk forward. I don't move but a harder shove makes my feet budge. "What would you have done if I was at training? Just snatch me up in front of Corro?" I spit over my shoulder. The hallway is adorned with gemstones embedded into the stone walls, lit with yellow-tinted light.

"I knew you weren't training today." His nice shoes scuff the stone flooring as he trails behind me, making this walk down the hallway even more eerie.

Of course he did, "How? And where are you taking me?" We continue to walk down the cold bare hallway.

"You'll see."

I roll my eyes at his response. My dark magic floods my senses and simmers restlessly beneath my skin, on high alert. My spine straightens at its increased attention. Finally, in the distance, I see a plain wooden door.

I glance over my shoulder at Callum, whose eyes are already on me. Mine narrow at him and his mouth curves into a cruel smile. We reach the door and with a wave of his hand, locks click and it flies open. Callum's palms come to rest on my shoulders and he slowly guides me into the pitch black room.

The minute we cross the threshold, the same gemstone lights adorning the hallway flicker to life, one by one, around a plain circular dark gray stone room. My stomach bottoms out.

At the center of the room is a recessed circle, where a man lays strapped to a table made of sleek polished stone. I shake my head and whip around in Callum's grip, "No. No, don't make me do this. My hands have caused enough death this way." My palms begin to sweat as my heart rate increases and I attempt to push Callum away from me.

His hold on me is firm and he pushes me further into the room, causing me to trip over my feet and I hit the floor. Hard. I'm still shaking my head, in denial enough to think that if I beg, he won't make me torture another soul.

"You do not have a choice. I own you, remember? It is what you are, the Shadow of Death." My fists curl, my jaw clenching at his reminder of what I am and the use of that fucking nickname. His weapon. His pet. The door behind him slams and the locks click in place.

"I refuse." I spit up at him. Blinding, searing pain spreads from my wrist to the rest of my body. I collapse back to the cool floor. The breath is knocked from me by the immense torment radiating throughout my body and my eyes well up automatically.

"This is pathetic." Callum says with a snort. Through my tear-stained vision, I see him crouch before me. "End this, now."

"I'd. Rather. Die." I choke out, my fingernails bleeding from clawing into the floor so hard.

"So help me, Ameria. If you do not submit, I will collect every single person you care about and force you to slowly rip them open and then I will heal them and make you do it over and over until there's so much blood you're drowning in it."

No. He couldn't force me to do that. I'd refuse, like I am now. But the look in his eyes tells me otherwise. I think of all the people he'd make me hurt, of all the people I love and have grown to care about dying at my hands. Just when my vision starts to dim around the edges, I submit.

I haul myself up from the floor and reluctantly follow Callum like the dog I am toward the man strapped to the slab. My body is trembling from the ghost remembrance of pain and now from having to torture someone.

I stare down at the unconscious man where bands of light restrain him. The tools I'm all too familiar with lay on a standing metal tray next to me. Callum takes his place on the other side of the body, his hands casually resting in his pockets. He looks down at the man, his golden brown eyes flash molten and the bands of light around the prisoner glow brighter.

The man's eyes fly open, a scream tearing through his throat. I back up a step, gaze darting between him and Callum.

"Oh good, you're awake," he teases, "This will be far less painful if you just simply answer some questions for me, Garrick."

"Go to hell!" the man, Garrick, spits.

Callum grins, "Been there, not my cup of tea." He flicks his cruel eyes up to mine, "Begin, my little Shadow of Death." Garrick pales and slowly turns his head toward me. "Oh, it seems our friend here is familiar with you. Good, so you know how this will go if you don't answer."

"Y-you," Garrick's voice trembles. His wide eyes lock onto mine and his dilated pupils are filled with fear. Hopelessness.

I've seen this look too many times to count.

I look away, eyes fixating on one of the light gemstones on the wall. I can't do this. My dark magic rises to caress me, soothing my growing panic, and offering to help take some of the burden. My magic and I have done this before, and this time I readily agree to what it wants. It floods me.

And I become the name that is whispered across the lands. The Shadow of Death.

Chapter Twenty-One
Ameria

My focus is honed on the fae that lies before me. The essence of death lingers in the air yet, no, this one won't die today… but soon. The High Lord is staring at me, wonder sparkling in his eyes. I've seen that look from the Fire King the first time I came to the surface. My weak side does not want to watch, but I make her. In time, she will realize I am her and she is me. Until then, I will do what she cannot.

The fae on the table starts to shake and plead. I ignore him and pluck up a small scalpel from the tray. The High Lord is still staring at me but I keep my eyes on the body.

I begin by taking one of the fae's fingers and digging out his fingernail. Screams echo throughout the chamber and after he's gone quiet, I can still hear the phantom remnants of pain. Dropping his hand, I wait for the High Lord to begin his questioning.

"Tell me, Garrick. Where were you going with that stash of magic crystals we found on your ship?" The fae does not answer and the High Lord flicks his eyes to me. This time I remove one of his toenails.

"I told you, this will be much less painful if you just answer."

The fae shakes his head, refusing. I internally sigh, knowing that this one will be stubborn. I do not care for the theatrics of torture unless it is well deserved. It's the death that I revel in. When the soul leaves its body — that is what sings to me.

Stalking to the tools, my shadows skitter over them deciding which to use next. Perhaps some broken bones will work. Taking up the mallet, I turn and survey the fae's body.

My inky black fingers run over his lower ribs until I find the one I'm looking for. "One," A finger traces over the first rib, "two," another trail of my finger, "three," the fae tenses as I run it over the third rib. They always expect me to do it on three. I glide to the fourth rib, "four." The mallet slams against the rib with a satisfying crack. Piss leaks from him and dribbles off the side of the stone platform.

The High Lord wrinkles his nose and resumes his questioning. Still, the fae refuses to answer. I ram the mallet against the same broken rib. Surely another hit will cause his diaphragm some trouble. We need him to be able to speak, so the next time he does not answer, I shatter his shin. And then his hand.

This lasts for a while and I'm starting to get bored. The High Lord is getting restless, and so am I. With the scalpel back in hand, I cut a strip of skin from right above the rib that's been demolished for maximum pain. "Okay, okay!" the fae wails. Finally. Holding the bloody scalpel aloft, I wait. "We were heading to the Water Kingdom. A small port there."

"And where did you get this large supply of my crystals?"

The fae does not talk, so my scalpel meets skin again. Surprisingly, he lasts through my expert removal of two more rectangles of flesh before he breaks. "I don't know where they came f-from, okay," the fae lets out a shuddering sound. "I was just the person in charge of moving them. They we-were already on the ship when I got there."

He's lying. I move to his feet and sever his pinky toe. "It seems my friend here believes you're lying. I'm inclined to agree with her," the High Lord states. The urge to ram my shadows down his throat because he referred to me as a friend is strong. However, I resist. Perhaps one day, but not now. I am not strong enough to face him yet.

I'm beginning to tire of this. It's taking far too long. I cut off his other pinky toe and before the High Lord can ask another question, I swiftly come around the table and gently dig the scalpel into his pubic bone near his cock.

"Fine!" He's blubbering now. "I didn't see what they looked like. They were concealed by their hoods, but they were definitely built like men. I t-tried to sneak a look at their faces but they were covered with m-magic. They delivered the crates and left." Sounds familiar. Perhaps it is the same pair of men we came across on that rooftop.

"I want names," the High Lord demands.

"We use code names. Everyone's always masked when we meet. Please," anguish fills the fae as he pleads for his life, "Please, I don't know who anyone is. I'm just told to move things and I do."

"Well," the High Lord says, "this was useless." He turns

with a wave of his hand, "Knock him unconscious and let's go."

I knew he would not die today. I do not know if that is a mercy though, as whatever the High Lord has planned for him may turn out to be worse than death. A squeeze on one of the pressure points makes the body go limp. I return the scalpel to the tray and examine my bloody hands. The weak part of me doesn't want to come back to the surface, refusing to face her reality. But I cannot live life for her. She must fully accept me, which she will need to do soon as I grow more restless by the day. However, if she refuses too long, the madness that comes will be difficult to undo.

The cool air fills my lungs as I take a deep inhale, the stench of bodily fluid stings my nose. My resolve almost breaks as I take in the state of Garrick. I've had enough of this torture business; I can't do it anymore. My magic took over but it made me watch the whole time. I can feel it simmering in my well, disappointed with the lack of death. I, however, am tired of it. Yet, everywhere I go, death follows me.

"Let's go, Ameria." Callum's voice skitters across my skin and my fists clench. I start to pull my eyes from the body but they snag on symbols carved into some of the stone beneath Garrick. They're a similar style to the ones engraved in the gate archways. Except these are brimming with freshly spilt blood.

My magic perks its head up as my gaze traces them and my feet move forward a step to get a closer look, but Callum clears his throat and the brand slightly burns. Annoyingly, I follow his command and make my way to where he stands, holding the door open for me. He motions to exit and I do but not before I throw him a glare on my way out.

"You're welcome," he mutters under his breath.

I ignore him and begin walking back down the long single hallway but a hand on my arm stops me. I'm yanked into Callum's chest and light consumes us. It blinds me for a split second and I blink away the spots to find that we're back on the cliffs overlooking the ocean.

It's no longer raining but a light fog creeps from the forest to spill over the edge, the sun almost practically gone beneath the horizon. Tugging my arm from his grip, I spin on him. "I refuse to torture another person. For you or for anyone."

Callum rolls his eyes, as if I'm some petulant child. "You will if I tell you to."

"Next time, I'll just let myself die." I spit.

His face gets in mine as he lets out a dark laugh, "That brand won't kill you. You'll just pass out from pain, over and over, until it's so agonizing you eventually submit," he grins.

"Fuck you." My anger gets the best of me and with all my might I shove him. Callum stumbles back a step, his brows raised.

It's only when I see his smile fade that I instantly regret my rash decision. He could crush me like an ant. With this brand, he could make me do anything he desired. Callum grips the front of my shirt and yanks me off my feet. My hands scramble, clawing at his arm. "I may have been lenient with your attitude, but push me too hard, Ameria, and I'll make whatever your father's punishments were, look like child's play." With that, he drops me back to my feet and is swallowed up by light.

I'm frozen, staring at the spot where he disappeared. The weight of my situation is setting in – a situation from which I so desperately want to be freed. My hands are still covered in the prisoner's blood, and I collapse to my knees. Furiously, I run them through the wet grass and wipe them on my damp, crusty clothes. My breathing turns fast, heavy, as I rip off my shirt and wipe my face, chest, and arms: All the spots where I can see blood or suspect it's splattered.

Tossing my shirt down, I brace my hands against the ground and try to calm my breathing before I go into a full panic. My magic thrums against my chest. If I can't hold myself together, it's going to escape and I can't deal with that right now.

I just tortured another rebel. What would I have done if it were one of my friends? I've been lucky enough to not have someone I care deeply for end up on that table in front of me. I fear for when that luck runs out.

How can I face my new friends and Corro after doing what I just did and act like it never happened? My fingers curl in the grass, trapping dirt underneath my nails.

Something white under my discarded shirt catches my eye and I reach for it. I slide out a small folded piece of wet parchment. My hands shake as I unfold it.

We were going to tell you before we parted ways.

H and I considered telling you many times over the years, but we couldn't risk the King finding out.

We decided it was best to keep you in the dark.

We're sorry for not telling you.

A restrained sob escapes me and I squeeze my eyes shut, the soggy paper crumpling in my curling hand. *It was best to keep me in the dark.* That's it then, they don't trust me. That's what Mereena means. Why would they, after everything I've done for my father without any resistance? I just about folded to his every command. Bolting up in a rage, I ball up the letter and chuck it over the cliff, watching the wind carry it out of sight.

My dark magic boils to the surface. Shadows leak from my hands, blanketing the ground around me to mix with the white fog. Some of them cascade over the edge in front of me. A defeated scream rips from my throat. A few tears fall down my cheeks.

I can't stand by and do nothing any longer. Corro said everyone has a choice, so I'm going to make mine. A choice I should have made over a hundred years ago. My shadows stir restlessly and a twig snaps somewhere from behind me. My magic sucks back into my body and I whip my head around, surveying the woods. They seem unnaturally darker.

"Who's there?" I shout. No answer, yet it feels like someone or something is watching. I swiftly tug my shirt back on and call fire to my hands. "Are you going to just watch or are you going to face me, asshole?" I yell into the darkening forest. Still, no answer, but something comes out to meet me. Magic.

The air gets heavier — thicker — and magic surrounds me. I can't see it, but I know it's there. I feel it caress my skin, poke at my chest. My dark magic rises to meet it. Whatever it is, it's calling to my own.

This aura of magic, it's like nothing I've ever felt. I should be afraid but it feels calming, somehow. The panic I had been feeling just moments ago eases away a bit. The fire in my hands dies, my eyes flutter, and I let out a heavy shuddering breath. The strong magic retreats slowly and I watch the forest in front of me lighten back to its normal dim light.

Cautiously, I take my first steps into the trees. "Hello?" Again, no answer. Whatever was here is gone and I no longer feel like I'm being watched.

I decide to jog back to camp and as I trudge through the fog-filled forest, my boots squelching in random patches of mud, I go over the decision I've made. It's time I do something – anything – besides sit around and pretend I have no choice. I may be stuck in an almost impossible situation, but that doesn't mean I can't try everything in my power to make things right.

I already know that I can skirt around certain information when telling Callum about the rebellion, so I'll continue to do that. But in this position, I can also be helpful to the other side. To the rebels. While I have to play spy for Callum, I can also play spy for them, offering whatever information I can provide, warning them if there's to be an attack or if someone is in trouble.

My stomach bottoms out at the fact that I'll be getting this information by possibly torturing the poor people. This brand is really throwing me for a loop, but I'm going to do my best.

Regardless, I can do something other than just bitch and moan. That's what's important. I can't be complacent any longer.

Corro

The agitation in this cramped, dusty backroom of the inn we've acquired for an emergency meeting is getting out of hand. I don't blame them; it's daunting to find out we have the Shadow of Death in our midst, in the competition no less. My heart, mind, and cock are all fighting against each other with warring emotions. I should have known by her other magic and the fact that she has the firepower of a royal. I feel like an idiot for not even suspecting anything.

"Can you imagine having that kind of power on our side though?" Bear's voice cuts through my thoughts, bringing my attention back to the heated arguments around me.

"Please, you really think she'd help the rebellion?" someone else spits.

Bear gets into one of the newer recruit's faces, "I bet you she would with the right incentives."

"Everyone calm the fuck down," Vel bellows across the room and instantly it's quiet. When did he get here? The meeting has been going on for almost an hour now. Where the hell has he been? "We know who she is now but the questions of what she's doing here and to which side her loyalty leans still remain."

"Actually, I believe I can help with that," Serpent, of all people, stands. "I went to visit her before training today. I believe her when she says she's not under her father's control anymore, but I sense there is something deeper. With that being said, perhaps it would be beneficial for us to sway her. Get her to join our cause."

"Since when have you become her best friend?" someone spits at Serpent, and if looks could kill, he'd be dead on sight. A knock sounds on the door, meaning we only have a few more minutes to wrap up this meeting.

Rune finally speaks up, "I don't trust her, and I don't think we all should fully. But, I think Serpent might be onto something. I think her loyalty hangs in the balance and can be swayed to our side if we play it right." I can feel him looking at me but I keep my head down, eyes on my boots.

"What do you suggest we do?" Gild asks, "If we get Ameria on our side, how are we to test her loyalty?"

"We can get her to divulge important information. Anything regarding the Fire King, his Kingdom, major players. Anything," Bear offers as he leans against the wall. Two knocks sound on the door. Time is almost up.

"Ask her if she knows anything about Callum. It's assumed that he and King Toross are working together. Any information regarding that would be valuable, " Vel adds.

Three knocks, which means this hell of listening to people argue over what to do with Ameria is over. Unfortunately, the hell continues when I'm pulled to the side after leaving through the back door. Two hooded figures, shadows obscuring their faces, come into my view. "What do you two want?"

Vel crosses his arms as Rune speaks, "We wanted to thank you for feeding Ameria that false information. It worked."

My eyes roll and I look off to the side toward the narrow alleyway wall, "Congratulations. Anything else?"

"We wanted to let you know that we confirmed that she is feeding information to someone, but not all of it."

That gets my attention, "What do you mean?"

Vel speaks this time, "She gave them the wrong area. We thought that maybe she just got mixed up but it was the complete opposite side of the island."

"Which is good for us if we want her to join the rebellion. And, Corro, we need her on our side, more than ever now," Rune adds.

My eyes narrow at them and I cross my arms, "Your point?"

Vel shifts his weight but Rune is the one who answers me, "We need you to be the one to sway her. You can achieve that more easily than the others."

"What makes you think I can do that?" I scoff.

"Because it's clear both of you are interested in each other. Use it. Flirt with her, romance her. You don't have to sleep with her." Vel makes a low growling sound from behind Rune, who continues, "Actually it might be better if you don't sleep with her but regardless, romantic interest goes a long way. Make her feel special and whatnot."

My jaw almost cracks with how hard I'm clenching my teeth. I shake my head, "I don't," I sigh heavily, "I'll think about it, I need to go."

I've already turned around and started walking down the alleyway when Rune calls out. "Please do think about it, Corro."

My thoughts are warring even more now. Ameria is making the effort to misdirect whoever she is informing. But why is she doing that in the first place? I run my hand through my hair as I exit the alleyway and join a throng of people. I need to think. I need to go home.

Chapter Twenty-Two
Ameria

My pace quickens as I exit the forest and go into the fields surrounding camp. I don't care if anyone stops me, but I do walk hastily toward my group of tents. I don't miss the blatant stares and whispers that follow me as I do.

The area around my tent is clear and quiet, and I'm grateful that I'll get a moment of peace and the opportunity to clean myself off before I look for the group. I slip inside and that feeling is snuffed out. They all stand in front of me, minus Delyth, and their attention snaps in my direction.

My feet halt and take in all the faces looking at me. Analyzing me. Judging me.

"You look like shit," Gregor says, breaking the silence, his arms crossed over his chest.

My mouth forms a tight line, "I feel like it too."

He glances around the room before his eyes land on me again, "Inara told us about your conversation this morning." I take a deep breath in, uncomfortable with the fact I was so vulnerable and now everyone knows. I nod and stay quiet, waiting for him to continue, but it's Inara who steps forward and speaks.

"We don't judge you for what you've had to do in your past. It would have been nice to not be blindsided by this information but we understand why you didn't want to tell anyone. Gods know I understand." There's a quick glimpse of softness on her face and then it's gone.

"But," Keenan cuts in, "we don't trust you. That trust will have to be built back up and you can start right now by telling us about your father, proving that you're not on his side, and answering any questions we ask."

"I understand," I answer with a jerk of my head. "I'm not a very open and vulnerable person. It has been something ingrained into my brain as weakness." I sigh and my shoulders slump, "It's something I've been told I need to work on, and I'm willing to do that right here, right now. With you all." They wait for me to go on.

So, I do. I offer up everything about my father, the Fire Kingdom, secret entrances to the palace... everything. I avoid talking about my personal life and relationships. That kind of information I choose to keep locked up tight.

When I'm finished, everyone but me huddles into a tight circle, whispering amongst themselves. I wait, uncomfortably shifting my weight while clenching and unclenching my fists. Finally, they turn and face me.

"We have more questions." Inara is the one to speak first.

"Okay."

"Do you have any information about the High Lord of the Sun Court? Is he in league with your father and aiding him?"

Gregor asks.

"Well, they seem to be working together in a way. I'm not sure how or why, but from what I gather, they have the same goal in mind. What that goal is, I have no idea."

My body physically relaxes as no burning pain accompanies my spilling of information. I wasn't sure if it was going to happen but I'm glad it didn't, which makes things a smidge easier for me.

"The two people Lorik mentioned, they're rebels?" Inara squints at me.

I swallow a lump in my throat, "Yes, apparently they are."

"Have you talked to them about it yet?"

"Briefly. "They confirmed it."

Inara nods and motions for Gregor to speak, "Would you kill him, if you had the chance? Your father? No hesitation?"

"In a fucking heartbeat." I practically snarl, years of abuse boiling to the surface. Sparks of flame dance on my arms and I have to tamp them down, my anger getting the best of me.

Everyone exchanges a look, "Would you take the throne from him?" He asks cautiously.

My head rears back, not expecting that question. "No, no." I shake my head, "I don't want his crown. It's not mine to take anyway."

"What do you mean it's not yours to take?" Gregor's eyes narrow as he sits in the desk chair.

I snort, "I was raised as a secret weapon, not a Princess who would eventually become Queen. That's my half-sister, Petra. It was supposed to be a secret that I was the original daughter, the rightful heir, but apparently that information was spread by my friends. Everyone thought I was just a relative to the crown. At least, they likely still think I am."

"Your sister, is she like your father?" Gregor crosses his arms.

The conversation I had with Petra flashes in my mind. "I don't know, to be honest. I thought she was but," I shrug and look down at my feet, ashamed by the way I treated her while growing up. I might be more like him than she is. "Based on a conversation with her before I left, I'm not sure anymore. We didn't exactly get along." I lift my head, "Mostly my fault."

"So, you don't really know much about her then?" Keenan asks.

"No." My answer is soft, my insides dripping with disappointment and guilt. They all seem to nod, satisfied with my answers.

Inara steps forward and takes up a spot next to me, surveying the group. "Where do we go from here?"

My spine straightens, "I was going to come talk to you guys about that." Inara's head turns toward me. "I want to help in any way I can. I've sat on my ass and have done nothing in the past. That's not something I want to do now." I look each of them in the eyes, "I want in on the rebellion."

Dinner last night was tense – not with my group – but with everyone else at the camp. The entire pavilion went silent when I entered. Gregor made a heated speech defending me, which ended up getting the rest of the contestants to resume their meals. I couldn't help but internally cringe at him speaking up for me. I may now be joining the rebellion, but I'm still stuck also working for the Sun Court. The other side.

Beforehand, we all continued to talk about the rebellion and what each person's role is. They didn't share who else here is involved, but they filled me in on the basics, including their codenames. Apparently, you don't get one until after your first meeting. They informed me that the next would likely be within a week.

The ground is still wet and my boots are already covered in mud as I hike through the forest to the clearing for training. My heart thumps heavily against my chest. Anxiety builds as I ready myself to see Corro, what the dynamic is going to be and whether I've lost all my progress with him. If he sees me as a part of the rebellion, that might help.

He doesn't trust me right now, which is fair, but it also means it's going to be harder to get close to him. It's an order from Callum that I can't break. If I can't produce more information for him, I'm afraid of what he'll do to the people I care about.

My mood sours at the thought of using Corro to get information. I can't say I'm against using my body, because I'm accepting the fact that I do desire him in that intimate way. But the underlying situation makes the whole thing feel…dirty.

The clearing comes into view and I take a calming breath before stepping through. Except, Corro is not who I find there. Instead, it's Narses who stands there with his arms crossed, waiting. I had forgotten how intimidating he can be. My feet slow but I manage to keep them moving.

"I'll be taking over your training for the next three days," he announces as I get closer.

Disappointment settles in my bones and I respond with a small, quick nod and tight smile. I begin my warm-ups while uncomfortable silence fills the space between us. Eventually, he speaks, "As you know, I am proficient in air magic. So, I expect you to take advantage of learning the most you can from me. You'll also be learning how to use a bow and arrow this week. Not my weapon of choice but," he smirks, "I'm still highly skilled at it."

I click my tongue with a roll of my eyes at his inflated ego. "Where is he?" I ask the question that's been gnawing at me.

Narses side eyes me from where he's setting up different targets, "Back in his home court taking care of some business." I hum in response. "He won't be upset with you for long, you know."

I stop my exercise and look over at him from my spot on the ground, "I think he made it pretty clear yesterday."

"He's just big on trust." Narses states as he continues what he's doing, "Finish your warm up." With a grunt, I do as he says.

"I said aim for the target, not the tree behind it," he hisses.

"It's my first time using this weapon. You'll have to excuse my lack of aim," I snark back, lowering the bow to my side. My eyes harden on the tree in the distance as I knock a new arrow. Another miss. I grumble in frustration and knock another.

"Your elbow keeps falling." Raising the bow, I aim. "Hold." Narses orders. He puts a hand under my elbow, moves it up a little and holds it there. "Now shoot." The arrow sails through the air and finally embeds into the target. It doesn't go anywhere near the ring of circles he's carved, but at least I hit the right spot.

"You're good at throwing daggers accurately, so this should be easy for you."

I glare at him while readying my bow again. "This is entirely different than flinging daggers." I let my arrow loose and it hits the ground right before the target.

"That time you dropped your bow hand."

After a while, I get the hang of it and begin hitting the different circles within the target. I have yet to hit the bullseye despite my progress. In the afternoon, he teaches me the basics of air magic along with different attacks and defenses.

"It's just pulling from the air around you. It's the easiest element to learn but also the strongest, deadliest."

My brows shoot up, "Really?"

Narses smirks, "The possibilities with air magic are endless, depending on how strong your magic is of course. It's also the hardest to defend against, especially if your opponent is a strong wielder. They can rip the air from your lungs in seconds."

I think of Torvin and how he used his air magic on me. To suffocate me and lock the shackles around my wrists, putting me in this position. Anger simmers in my gut and my dark magic stirs but I force it away. "How are you supposed to defend against that?" I ask, wanting to make sure the next time someone tries that on me, I'm prepared.

"Most can't. However, if you're equally matched in power, it's possible to fight back. If they rip the air from your lungs, that means the magic has to weave itself into your body, just like a water wielder who would try to drown you from the inside, or a fire wielder wanting to heat your insides. You can use your own magic to force theirs out. Takes a lot of practice, though."

Three days pass and finally Corro shows back up to training. Things between us are tense and awkward. Air magic was simple enough and I learned the bare basics, but all my attacks and defenses were flimsy.

Once I got the bow down, shooting was a lot easier. Narses had me practice on moving targets, which I got the hang of rather quickly. I learned how to defend against someone shooting arrows at me, with magic and without. Narses continued to teach me the air element and said that these wielders are fond of the bow and arrow as they can adjust an arrow if it's off course.

I never wrote back to Mereena but she has sent a few letters since the first reply. I have responded to none for multiple reasons. It still stings that they, my best friends, didn't tell me and give me the option to join them.

Inara, Delyth, and I have practiced together every night since I joined the rebellion. I asked Inara why Delyth wasn't a part of it and she said she is, just in a different way but it's not her story to tell. I haven't gone looking for any answers. It's not my business and if Delyth one day wants to share, then that's good enough for me. I've been helping them up their game against my fire attacks since I can use my full-force magic now, no longer needing to hide my strength.

Stepping into the clearing this morning, I find Corro standing, looking as menacing as possible, in front of what looks like a new course. Gods, I fucking hate the courses. My nose scrunches up as I point to it, "Is that a new one?"

"Same one, just a few things moved around here and there to keep you on your feet." His tone is bland, "Begin your warm-ups and start on the course."

I go through my usual routine in the tense silence between us. Corro has barely spoken any words to me outside of ordering me around since he got back yesterday. But today, Narses isn't here to fill in the gaps. I've tried to lighten the mood, turning toward our old familiar, friendly banter but it looks like he's no longer interested in that.

I make it halfway through the course before the damn vines get me again, except this time they have thorns that embed into my skin. With a hiss of pain, I shoot him a death glare but use my continued practice of earth magic to unravel and wilt the vines.

Finally, I make it past the cursed vine area but a wooden club comes out of nowhere and whacks me in the face.

I wake up grumbling as the healer is just finishing up. "Thanks," I mumble while righting myself and glancing toward Corro, who is sitting on his usual boulder sharpening a dagger. "How long was I out?"

"Only thirty minutes." He doesn't look up.

The healer finally finishes mending my broken nose and jaw and takes a seat against a tree, pulling out a book from her satchel. I start to lay back down for a small rest but Corro grumbles at me, "Get up and try again."

I prop up on my elbows and stare at him incredulously,

"Fuck, Corro, am I not allowed to rest for a damn moment?"

"Technically," he looks up at me, "you just rested for thirty minutes. Now go."

My lips press into a tight line and I will myself not to cuss him out while marching back to the beginning of the course. I worked at it the entire morning, and by afternoon, I finally made it all the way through.

The healer left when we broke for lunch. Then, it was just us and a lot of tension. I worked on conjuring up a wall of air that was thick enough to block most simple magic or light weapon attacks. The hour before training ended, I worked on creating stronger gusts of wind, all while Corro either barked orders or ignored me.

The next day of training was just as miserable as it was the day before. Corro continued to only yell his commands at me and I tried to push away the building desire to punch him in the face, instead focusing my attention on completing the second course he set up.

I've made it almost all the way through, and I can see the finish line. Just a few more feet I tell myself as the coppery taste of blood fills my mouth from the stupid wooden club that swung into my face earlier. Just when I thought there would be no more surprises this close to the end, a dagger slams right into my side. I should have known.

Even though it's a short blade, it still hurts like hell. Inhaling a gasp of air, the blade twitches inside me and I collapse to my knees. I grit my teeth and yank it out. Blood begins leaking out of the wound. My head becomes woozy and dark spots fill my vision, but I'm determined to finish this damn thing. I push my hand against my bleeding side and crawl across the finish line before everything around me fades to black.

I find my back leaning against a tree when my consciousness returns. I'm already healed and Corro stands a few feet away from me holding a longsword. "You made it through the second course - barely — but it still counts. You start the third tomorrow. Now get up, pick up a longsword, and meet me in the ring."

I mutter in frustration, not surprised that he'd give me only a few minutes to rest. Slowly, I stand up from the ground and wince. Although mostly healed, my body is still covered in bruises and my bones ache.

Upon stepping into the ring, he lunges and swings his sword at me. I'm able to duck and block the second swing with my sword. With a shove, I knock him back a few steps. My eyes narrow at him. Gods, this man is extra moody today.

He attacks again but I'm ready. Lowering into a crouch, just missing his sword, I swing my leg and knock his feet out from under him. Hitting the ground, Corro easily rolls and springs to his feet. A flash of surprise crosses his face but it's gone in the next moment.

With a sly smile, I whirl the sword in my hand. I charge. He swings his weapon down and I drop to a knee, blocking it. A slam of his foot has me falling onto my back. "And you're dead." Corro stands over me, pointing his sword right at my heart. "Nice spar though, you're getting better."

In that moment, my anger gets the best of me and before

he can move, I surprise him by kicking his knee. He topples to the ground and I pounce, pinning his arms against the grass. "Would you stop being an asshole for one fucking minute?" I snarl in his face. "I get it, you hate me, you don't trust me, but I'm trying. I am."

Corro wiggles beneath me, "Enough. Get off me."

"No!" I scream in his face, "I didn't tell you or anyone for this reason. I get that I could have made a choice to stand against my father but I didn't. You're right, I was a coward. But I'm trying not to be one anymore. I'm trying."

A muscle in his jaw twitches, "Gods dammit, Ameria. I want to trust you, I do."

"I'm not asking you to trust me. I know I don't deserve it. But I'm asking you to believe in me. Believe that I'm doing the best I can." I swallow thickly, "We were becoming friends, maybe even -" I cut myself off and avert my gaze. Leaping up, I take a few steps back and clench my teeth. Frustrated that I almost admitted my feelings for him.

Corro stands slowly, "If you want me to believe in you, I need you to give me something. Anything that shows you're on our side," he says softly. My gaze meets his and I release a breath at the hopeful look he's giving me. I tell him as much as I can, everything I told everyone else. Except this time, for him, I include personal details. A small step toward being more vulnerable.

He searches my face, likely looking for any way to not believe me, but then he nods and closes the distance between us. "Okay, I believe in you," he says, outstretching his hand. We grip each other's forearms and Corro smiles, "Took you long enough, but welcome to the good side."

I fight a smile but lose. "Does this mean we're back to normal? No more awkwardness, no more of you being an asshole?"

"Sure, we're back to normal," he grins and with a yank, I'm pulled into his chest. I gasp in surprise and he leans down to whisper in my ear, "Can't promise I won't be an asshole though." Corro backs away and drops my arm, the grin still plastered on his face. "Come on, let's get back to sparring."

Chapter Twenty-Three
Ameria

The feeling of being shaken wakes me from my slumber. "Ameria, wake the fuck up!" My eyes shoot open at the commanding voice.

"Gregor?" my voice cracks with grogginess. He's half kneeling over me, his hands gripping my shoulders. Above him, trees stretch high into the night sky. I jolt upright and take in my surroundings.

"What the hell?" We're in the middle of a forest. Just us two.

"Thank the Gods you're awake." Gregor stands, yanking me up with him. We're dressed in our training clothes, his sword gripped in his hand and my daggers strapped to my hips.

"What is going on?" I seethe, my eyes slowly adjusting to the darkness. Tonight had been the first night I'd fallen asleep within minutes of hitting my bed.

Gregor holds his hands up defensively, "I have no clue, but it can't be good. And it's just us out here. I woke up on the ground just moments before rousing you."

A howling noise echoes through the forest and we exchange wide-eyed looks. I waste no time unsheathing my daggers,

"Sounds like it came from that way," Gregor jerks his head in the direction behind me. I whirl around, scanning the surroundings but all is quiet again.

"This has to be some sort of test, right?" I whisper.

He groans and I hear the leaves crunch under his boots as he comes to stand at my back. "Our elixir has worn off too. We only have the strength of our main elements and our weapons," he snorts and I glance over my shoulder, "Boy, am I lucky I'm out here with you. You know, having royal magic and all."

My eyes roll as I bring my gaze up to the canopy of trees and scan all the patches opening to the night sky, "Let's just get out of here as quickly as possible."

"And where exactly is here?"

Still scouring the sky, I answer, "My mother taught me how to read the stars. I've been practicing ever since." I pause, there it is. "Part of that constellation," I point, "looks familiar and if I'm right, which I believe I am, the tip of it faces East. Which is that way." Gregor follows my finger.

"That means the star that points North should be about," I spin, "there." It wasn't much to go on, and a lot of it I had to guess based on the camp's layout and the parts of forest I've traversed. I know the cliffs I found were to the West, which means… "Well, I have some unfortunate news," I announce, my arm dropping while turning to face him.

"How fucked are we?"

"You know how they told us the furthest part of the Northern forest was off limits? Well," I gesture with my hands, "we have to go that way to get back." I nod my head in the direction the howling came from.

Gregor lifts his sword, "Off we go then."

We head south with stealth rather than speed since we aren't entirely sure why this part of the forest is off limits. We've been walking for a while now and have heard various noises that made us pause in our tracks, but none too concerning. Until now, because the howling resumes and it sounds close.

"That can't be good." The snapping of a branch has us whirling around. Another snap off to the left. "Okay, this definitely is not good," Gregor hisses.

"Whatever it is, it's surrounding us." We move into a fight stance, back to back. The bushes to my right rustle with movement. In front of me, a creature shows its face: A giant wolf, larger than any I've ever seen before, comes prowling out of the brush with two smaller ones trailing it. "Three," I say softly, not making any sudden movements.

"Two," Gregor replies tightly, informing me how many he faces. Five in total, unless there are more hiding. Could be worse. "Get ready," he mumbles.

My palms begin to sweat, my mouth going dry. I adjust the grip on my daggers and lift them. Taking a deep breath, I light them on fire. Except, my magic doesn't come. My stomach sinks, "Um, Gregor. Is your magic working?"

Mumbled cursing tells me his isn't working either. As the pack leader in front of me howls into the night sky, the two behind it lunge. Looks like I'll be putting my training to the test. I duck from the one on the right while swiping my blade upward on the other. A direct hit. A flicker of movement from the corner of my eye tells me Gregor has also begun fighting.

The one I dodged attacks again. I tuck and roll, slicing into its hind leg. It snarls and turns back to face me. The wolf I'd hit earlier is struggling to get up off the ground. With that one taken care of, I pour my focus on the one in front of me.

We circle each other, and then it leaps. My foot catches on a rock and I stumble. Searing pain lashes throughout my arm as its claws make contact. Clenching my teeth, I let out a muffled scream. Careful not to alert any more creatures lurking around. I fix my stance but my arm shakes from the pain, blood dripping from the gashes.

Just as the wolf crouches, a crippling screech ripples through the air. The wolves curl in on themselves from the sound. My daggers drop from my hands as I cover my ears and fall to my knees. My jaw clenches, eyes squeezing shut, as the screech pierces my ears.

It stops, my eyes opening in time to see the wolves scatter. I find Gregor scrambling for his sword. Swiping my weapons from the forest floor, I rush over to him. Before I can get a word out, a loud thud booms throughout the forest. The blood drains from Gregor's face as it goes slack, terror flooding his features.

My body stiffens and I slowly turn around.

A giant, pure white beast resembling a lion emerges from the trees. It has to be at least ten feet tall, eyes glowing like molten gold. Drool drips from its mouth, leaving a patch of the forest floor sizzling. The beast's claws are black, the size of a large kitchen knife — big enough to rip someone to shreds with one swipe.

"Holy Gods," Gregor breathes.

"Run," I choke out. "Run!" I kick my legs into gear and take off in the other direction, dragging him with me. With a glance over my shoulder, I find it's started charging at us. There's no way we'll both make it. Splitting up will give at least one of us enough time to get out and maybe find help before the other dies.

"Split up. Go right Gregor!" I shout. He sends me a look that displays how crazy he thinks I am, but I give him a solemn, tight-lipped smile and bank left. Thankfully, he listens and I hear him go off in the other direction.

My heart thunders and I push myself as hard as I can to get away, but I'm losing blood. I don't know how long the adrenaline will hold out. A line of bright white fire whizzes past my head, hitting a tree in front of me and blasting a hole through it. Fuck me. Of course I'm the one it follows. I can't catch a break.

I twist my head to see the beast gaining on me. The only thing I have to my advantage is size as I can fit through small gaps between trees. If this is a taste of what the trials are going to be like, I might be in trouble. What the hell is this thing?

My legs are getting tired and my lungs are on fire from pushing myself so hard. A small selfish part of me wishes the beast didn't choose to chase me. I attempt to pull on my threads of magic, even my dark magic, and I don't get a single spark or whisper of shadow.

A burning sensation sears into my back causing me to falter and hit a tree. A scream rips my throat raw. I collapse to my knees and scramble to the other side of the tree, hiding myself behind it. My breathing is heavy as the thundering steps slow. The smell of brush and trees burning fills my nose.

My body is trembling. I beg my breath to even out and will my body to stop shaking. The beast's steps get closer and I pray to whatever Gods or Goddesses there are, whether or not I truly believe in them. This cannot be the end, the way I go. I wish my dark magic wasn't dampened, I could use the calmness it gives me when I let it take the reins. Hell, I could portal the fuck out of here if I had it.

A drop of sizzling spit falls to the ground next to my boot. My stomach bottoms out as I slowly lift my head. The beast's glowing eyes hover above me and it snarls. Its jaw opens wide, a white glow builds in the back of its throat. I lift my hands in front of me and yank on whatever magic I can pull, hoping that I break whatever is holding it back. A blood-curdling scream tears from me and I erupt.

My shadows shoot out along with some of my fire magic. They tangle together, creating a burning black flame. The beast screeches as my magic hits its eyes. With all the adrenaline I have left, I leap from the ground into a sprint. As my feet carry me forward, I feel magic. Ward magic specifically. It has to be the barrier of the northernmost part of the forest.

I hear the booming sound of its paws behind me but I don't bother to look. I can't chance it. Expending every ounce of energy I have, I run as fast as possible. My magic is completely gone. Whatever I did back there was all that I could muster. The only choice I have is to keep going and hope I make it.

Voices reach my ears. I can make out Gregor yelling as

well as someone else. The magic of the barrier gets stronger, its humming thrums against my skin. Another hot searing pain hits my back. I cry out but don't stop running, pushing through it all with tears streaming down my face. Someone is yelling my name now. Gods, I'm so close.

A familiar magic falls over the forest, like a heavy blanket draping across the land. The air is thicker, my surroundings darker. It feels like life is being drained from everything around me. I don't have time to wonder, I need to keep going.

The beast's steps falter and a small outcropping of grass comes into view along with the vibrating feeling of the barrier. I push forward, across the final few feet and fling myself through it, tumbling onto the ground. In the darkness, I make out four forms. Three I recognize.

"Ameria!" I hear Corro shout. He's on me in a second, pulling my weak body into his arms. I hear more yelling as I'm being moved but my adrenaline has faded and my vision is blurry. There's roaring and screeching from the beast as well as a deeper voice saying something that I can't make out through the chaos.

"Go, take them back to camp." Narses. I know that's him speaking.

I try to say something, to warn them, but my mouth can't form the words. I've never been so exhausted. "I've got you. I've got you, just hold on, Ameria," Corro's whispers make it past my deliriousness. "You're safe, you're okay." I feel my body go entirely limp a split second before my vision fades.

"Here, drink this. It'll help you heal," says the healer, Tabitha. I'd finally learned her name after the hundredth time she'd tended to me. She hands me a cup of something nasty smelling but I down it anyway. My back still burns with pain from whatever that beast did to me. I'd woken up in Corro's tent with him and another trainer holding me down as two healers worked on my back. The pain had me drifting in and out of consciousness, but it's now late morning and I'm feeling quite a bit better.

Corro and Gregor had apparently come to check in on me repeatedly but I can't fully remember the conversations we had. "Ugh! That stuff tastes as bad as it smells." My tongue smacks against the roof of my mouth and I shiver at the aftertaste while handing back the cup.

She chuckles, "Yes, it's not pleasant but works wonders." Tabitha places the cup back on the tray of herbs and liquids that sits on the desk. "Your back should start feeling normal in a few hours. There's not much we can do about the scarring it left though."

I play with the edge of the blanket, remembering hearing one of the healers saying something about permanent splotches of white on my back. I can feel it. One on my lower spine and one on my left shoulder blade. According to Tabitha, the spots look like someone splattered white paint at me. I have no interest in seeing my back look more scarred than it already was. Not right now at least.

She helps me settle back into the pillows and re-covers me with the blanket. "I'll let Corro know you're fully awake. I believe they have some questions for you if you're feeling up

to answering them." I nod and Tabitha pats me on the head –
oddly soothing – and leaves.

A few minutes later, Corro rushes in and sits on the edge
of the bed next to me. "How are you feeling?" he whispers,
dark circles shadowing his eyes. Their mossy green looks duller
than usual. Something in my stomach flutters at the sight of his
concern.

"Not as bad as I looked before, I'm sure." I smile, trying to
lighten the mood. I really do feel fine, a bit sore still but I'm
ready to get out of this bed.

He snorts but his smile doesn't reach his eyes, "I'm so sorry
Ameria. The test was supposed to be you and another contestant
fighting wolves and finding your way back to camp," Corro
shakes his head, "There shouldn't have been anything other
than the wolves, Beor made sure."

My nose scrunches up, "Yeah, about that." I smack his arm,
"What the hell! What if one of us died?"

With a grimace, Corro rubs the back of his neck and shrugs,
"if someone can't handle a couple Western Isle wolves with a
partner, they definitely won't survive the trials." I glare at him
even though that's a good point.

My mouth turns dry remembering the creature that almost
killed me in the forest, "If it was only supposed to be wolves,
then what was that thing?"

He begins to answer but a different voice does it for him, "A
Dranoq." My gaze drifts to Narses standing at the entrance of
the tent along with King Beor right next to him. He continues, "A
creature of legend and myth from back when the Gods roamed

the realm of the living."

I shift uncomfortably, my heart dropping with the fact that a mythological creature decided to come after me. I can't even begin to think about unpacking all of that right now.

"Beor has some questions for you and he'll try to answer any you have." Corro gives my hand a light squeeze and then moves to stand next to Narses. Seems he's being extra attentive, which is good for my mission, but it gets harder each day to follow through with it.

Beor approaches the bed and I right myself to sit taller. He clears his throat, "I have already heard Gregor's account of the events that took place, but we need to hear what happened after you two parted ways." I nod and relay the events, leaving out what my power did. The black flames — I internally shiver. Whatever that was concerns me but I can't say I'm not grateful. It saved my life.

"Is it dead?" I ask, shaking away the memory of what my magic achieved.

"We got rid of it," Narses answers. "According to legend, it's hard to kill. You have to send it back to where it came from but," he pauses, "unfortunately, we are unable to do so. We locked it away."

Beor stares at me, an emotion flashing across his face that I can't decipher, "We noticed it had been blinded. Were you the one to do that? With your d-" he catches himself, "other, magic." A small twitch at the corner of his mouth tells me he already knows the answer. They all do because they're the only ones here who know I have this dark magic.

"Yes," I speak plainly, no need to hide it. But, I keep the specifics to myself.

His gaze doesn't leave mine, "You're very lucky. Get some rest, Ameria." With a dip of his chin, he turns and exits. Narses jerks his head quickly and starts to leave.

"Narses, wait!" He pauses and glances over his shoulder, "I have so many questions but I'm only going to ask this one for now. Was there a reason it went after me?"

His eyes dart to Corro then back to me, narrowing slightly, "That's something I'm still figuring out." He stares for a second longer and then leaves.

Corro informs me he's going to let me rest for a while and we'll train for only a couple hours if I'm feeling up to it. I argued of course, stating that I was already in perfect condition to train but he wouldn't hear of it.

Finally, in the early evening two hours before dinner, we trained sword to sword and I felt invigorated. If I can survive a mythical creature, then I can survive this competition and whatever comes after.

Chapter Twenty-Four
Ameria

Corro and I are walking back from training, soaking wet from the rain that drowned us all day, when he turns to me, "How would you like to attend your first meeting tonight?"

My eyes widen, "Really?" He gives a quick nod, "I'd like that."

"Get cleaned up quickly after dinner. I'll leave some clothes on your bed for you." He breezes past me and heads off toward the tents. My insides jump. I can't believe I'm being allowed to go to a meeting already. I must have managed to convince them enough that I'm no longer a threat.

My head is swirling with emotions: excitement, anxiety, and nagging guilt. I'm looking forward to finally being a part of something, especially if it's against my father, but I'm nervous that I'll blow it when Callum comes knocking. He cannot find out that I'm aiding them.

As I walk past the mirror still in my towel, I jerk to a halt. I still haven't looked at my back yet, afraid to see how much more scarred it is. My eyes flutter as I take a deep, readying breath.

My towel slips off my body and I turn my back to the mirror.

Among the three deep scars, there are now two stark white splotches of skin. One on my shoulder blade and in the middle of my lower back. Tabitha's statement was accurate – they look like someone flung blobs of paint at me. It seems like all the color was sucked out of me in those spots. My head sags between my shoulders, two more scars to add to the collection.

Corro comes flying into my tent and I gasp. He stops in his tracks, eyes bugging out of his head. Releasing a strained noise from the back of his throat, he whirls around, facing away from me. "Uh, sorry. I, um, I should have -"

I slip my towel on as he blabbers, "It's okay! I'm covered, it's fine." Heat rises up my neck and as he turns to face me, his cheeks have gone pink.

"Thought you might have changed already. There's a long-sleeve top, cloak, and mask." He points to the pile of black fabric on my bed.

I scramble over and snatch them up. "Thanks, I'll change quickly now."

"I can leave you to it." He begins to back away but I stop him.

"No, it's okay," I say as I slink behind the bathroom curtains, "I'll be quick."

Corro clears his throat, "We hide our identities at most meetings. That's what the mask is for." I slip the black shirt on and tie the laces on my pants as he fills the somewhat awkward silence.

"Makes sense." I come back out while drying my wet hair

with the towel.

He motions to it, "You'll have to tie that back. It's a pretty distinguishable color."

I style my hair into three braids on top and thread them together so they merge into one that falls down my back. This way the front pieces are more secure and unlikely to fall free. Slipping on my boots, I clasp the cloak and scoop the mask up from the bed. Following Corro out, I find familiar faces surrounding the fire in the middle of our tents, all dressed in the same black clothes.

Corro motions for us to head out and I fall into step beside Inara as we're led out of camp and into the surrounding forest. "So, what are these meetings like?" I whisper to her.

She shrugs and tosses the core from an apple she was eating. "We usually discuss any ongoing missions, exchange information and talk about anything that needs to be discussed in person."

"You'll probably just sit and observe for the first couple of meetings at least, since you don't have anything to add at the moment," Gregor cuts in from behind us.

I almost protest, thinking I might have something to offer about Callum, but I realize then I don't honestly have that much they don't already know. If I did, they would wonder how I acquired it. I jerk my head in a nod, "Got it."

We finally reach one of the gates and Corro lays a hand upon it. It sparks to life with a shimmering wave expanding the inside of the archway. Everyone covers the lower half of their faces and flips up their hoods, so I follow suit.

I walk through the gate, Corro right beside me, and emerge onto a bustling street. I recognize it immediately as the same city we came to on an off afternoon. It's evening now, the sun having dipped below the horizon a while ago, and the streets are flooded with people.

My eyes scan for the others as a hand wraps around mine. I jolt at the contact but settle as I realize it's Corro, who is now tugging me away from the gate.

We push through drunk couples, women outside brothels flaunting their goods, and shady figures lurking in the shadows speaking in inaudible whispers. Corro and I weave through different back streets and alleyways, his hand never leaving mine.

"Where are the others?" I ask as we turn another corner. The stench of bodily fluids gets stronger, making me push past a gag.

His soft green eyes flick to mine before he ushers me along faster. "We split up and all convene at the meeting place separately. Just in case." I nod to myself, the logic making perfect sense.

It becomes abundantly clear that I have no idea what I'm walking into and I wish I had been a bit more informed beforehand. For the first time since leaving the Fire Kingdom, I'm nervous, but I swallow the anxiousness and continue to be led down the now less crowded side streets.

We slip down a small alley and stop in front of a wooden door. Corro lets go of my hand and turns to me, "Just sit and observe. Don't talk to anyone. If someone directs a question at you, let me handle it." He shifts on his feet and pulls my hood down a bit more, adjusting my mask slightly even though I know it's securely in place. He's fidgeting.

My eyes narrow, "Why are you nervous?"

He scoffs and rolls his shoulders back, clearing his throat. With one hand on the door, his other grabs mine. "Ready?" I nod my head once and he pushes the door open, dragging me along behind him.

I'm led down a hallway to a wooden spiral staircase. We climb, Corro never letting go of my hand. I don't know if he's doing it intentionally because we're both anxious but I'm glad to have the small comfort.

So many things could go wrong and doubt swirls in my stomach. Maybe I shouldn't be here. Maybe I'll end up doing more harm than good. Callum could force me to tell him everything, including this meeting spot and more blood would be spilled. My feet falter at the top of the steps.

Corro stops with me and stares into my eyes, which flare with panic. He gives me a gentle reassuring squeeze. "I'll be next to you all night. I promise," he says softly, mistaking the source of my panic. I swallow my guilt and square my shoulders, ready to face whatever comes from this.

A tall figure blocks the door at the top of the stairs. As we approach him, Corro speaks a word that makes the figure move aside. The small room is full, with around fifteen people, all dressed exactly the same. I can feel their eyes on me and I try not to squirm under their watchful stares. I itch to let go of Corro's hand, afraid it might make it seem like I need coddling. Might make me look weak. I try to unlace our hands but his grip only tightens on me.

"We're just waiting on Vel and Rune. As usual," one of them says while we take up a spot against the far wall. Corro snorts at that.

A few minutes later the door opens and the room quiets. My dark magic stirs but I stomp it down and see the two others we've been waiting for. My spine snaps straight and my stomach sinks. Standing in front of the now-closed door are two large and looming figures, dressed in all-black leather with no markings. Hoods up. Instead of a mask hiding their identities like the rest of us, darkness covers their entire faces under the hoods.

My heart hammers as I face the two men who caught me on the roof spying for Callum. This is bad, very bad. They could recognize me any second and it'll blow everything. I might be murdered right here in this room, my guts splattered on the walls.

Their heads turn as they scan the room and stop when they reach my direction. I can't see their eyes, but I know they're looking at me. That's it, it's over. I'm dead. And you'll deserve it, my inner monologue chastises me and I clench my jaw. My grip tightens on Corro's hand and he squeezes back.

Both of them stand there staring in our direction, their arms crossed. The one on the right cocks his head slightly. Corro rubs his thumb over the back of my hand before letting go. "Always late you two," a familiar voice drifts across the space. Inara's calm tone brings lightness into the room.

The one on the left huffs a laugh and leans against the wall on one side of the door. The other mirrors him. "If I recall, Serpent, you were late to the last meeting yourself."

Inara, apparently codenamed Serpent, clicks her tongue from where she's sitting at a small table. "Apologies for my one late arrival in years, Vel." Okay, so the one on the left is Vel, meaning the other whose shoulders are moving in what appears to be silent laughter has to be Rune.

"If we could get started, my partner is already pissed at me for missing the in-laws tonight," A man says in annoyance, a few others snickering at him.

A deep voice rumbles from one of the back corners, "Well, as you know our shipment of crystals has been apprehended along with the captain. I assume this was Callum's doing."

Around the room, people nod in agreement. My stomach sours with the knowledge that it was his doing and that I had a hand in it. I wipe my sweaty free hand on my pants and I feel eyes on me. My gaze snaps up to see Vel and Rune with their heads facing me.

I inhale deeply and continue to listen, ignoring the fact that I have their attention. "It took months to get all those crystals, so this is a huge setback," someone chimes in.

"We should have separated them into different shipments. What happened to the guy who was supposed to watch them leave the dock?"

A sigh leaves a woman standing by Inara. "Dead. And we did separate them. A few crates made it to their destination but not as many as we would have liked."

"It was a mistake to have the shipment leave from the Sun Court. It's a lot longer of a journey to the Water Kingdom from the other courts, and only half our ships are successfully making it there." Vel says steadily.

"We need a new spy since our last one was killed."

"Agreed. Especially since the captain was likely taken, I wouldn't put it past Callum to convince him to work for the Sun Court. He can be quite convincing," Rune's voice drips with disgust.

"We need someone more equipped this time. Someone who won't get caught on a simple lookout mission," Inara pipes up, her gaze flicking to mine so quickly that no one else would have noticed but me.

She's suggesting I volunteer. I take a moment to consider as a few people throw out different codenames. Technically, I do have a leg up and it would make it a lot easier to share the information I get from my time with Callum and not have anyone question how I got it. There's a slight possibility it could make things entirely worse though, but I have to try. Maybe if the lines blur enough between the two sides I'm on, it'll become easier to skirt the truth when reporting to Callum.

"Who else could we—"

"I'll do it," I cut off the man who started to speak. Every head whips in my direction. I see Rune straighten and I can feel Corro's eyes glaring a hole through the side of my head.

"Corro," Vel commands his attention.

I hear him mutter a curse under his breath before he responds, "She does have the certain set of skills one would need."

"You vouch for her then?" someone asks.

"Yes," he grits out, throwing a searing look my way, telling me he's going to let me have it once we're done here.

"I do as well," Inara adds, ever so slightly nodding her head to me. My chest tightens a little.

"Same," a familiar voice croaks from across the room. Slowly, my gaze finds the person who spoke. Recognition floods my body. I'd know those brown eyes, that voice, anywhere.

Everyone begins to agree and I distantly hear Corro agree to something regarding me and the chatter continues. But I can't rip my gaze from the brown eyes that belong to my best friend. *Haemir.*

The rest of the meeting has various information being traded and solutions to problems being made. I try to pay attention but knowing that Haemir and I are standing in the same room makes me want to jump out of my skin. No matter how angry I am with him, I can't help but want to tackle him in a hug and never let go.

People file out of the room when the meeting ends and I turn toward Corro. "Can I meet you in a moment?" There's someone I need to talk to."

His eyes dart between me and Haemir, who hasn't moved from where he's stood all night. "I'll be downstairs."

I mutter a thanks and then it's just me and my best friend, alone. He tugs his mask down and I do the same, tears welling in both of our eyes. Haemir meets me halfway as I fling myself into his arms, his cinnamon and clove scent filling my nose. "Oh, Ameria," he mumbles into my hair.

We don't let go of each other for a while but eventually I

peel myself from him and blink away the blurriness. Some of my anger resurfaces then, and I give him a small shove. "You lied to me for years!" He takes it, lets me yell and push him. "We were supposed to be best friends." My teeth clench as I wipe away more tears.

"I'm so sorry," Haemir croaks out, his face full of regret. "I wanted to tell you, for so long but I couldn't risk your father finding out."

I shake my head, "I would have kept your secret. Unlike you, spilling all of mine," I throw at him.

He averts his gaze, lips drawing into a tight line. "I deserve that."

"You do. You spied on me, your best friend!" I spit and take a deep inhale, trying to calm myself as my magic is beginning to get riled up at my distress. "How long?" I choke on held back tears.

It takes Haemir a moment before he turns to look me in the eyes, sadness clouding his features. I know right then that it's going to be longer than I expect. And it's going to break me. "Since your mother died."

All the air leaves my lungs. "You- you…" My chin trembles and I look away. I can't bear to look at his face right now. "You've lied to me since I was fifteen." My voice is raspy. "I could have done something then, I wasn't who I am now. I could have…" In my peripheral vision, I see him take a single step toward me but my hand flies up as I take a step back, "Don't."

Haemir stops. "I was so young when I joined. I just listened to the adults and I—"

"Stop." I cut him off and his mouth clamps shut. "Even if you were young then, you've had over a hundred years to tell me and you didn't." More tears roll down my cheeks as I stare at the only real family I ever felt like I had. "I don't know how to get past this right now Haemir." I say softly, all of the fight in me leaving.

He gives me a smile that doesn't reach his eyes, "Take all the time you need. I'll do anything to make it right, Ameria. I love you." He murmurs, "I'll wait for however long you need."

I close my eyes as I inhale through my nose, attempting to clear my head from all the information and betrayal. I hook my mask back over my face and head for the door, avoiding eye contact with Haemir. I stop with the door partly cracked open. Slightly, I turn my head enough to see him out of the corner of my eye, "I love you too," I whisper. Yanking the door open the rest of the way, I head for the stairs.

Chapter Twenty-Five
Ameria

Corro and I walk back through the gate and into the forest surrounding camp. All the others must have had someone else escort them back. I don't know if Corro is aware of whom I was talking to, but he's kind enough to not poke at it. As we walk in silence, I can feel the slight tension in the air between us. I'm sure it's about me volunteering to be their new spy but, in this moment, it just makes sense.

He escorts me back to my tent and follows me inside. Yanking off the mask that's been sitting around my neck since we arrived through the gate, I chuck it on the bed and sit with a huff. "You're angry."

Corro lets out a long sigh while running a hand through his hair, "I'm not angry, just," he pauses and then his gaze reaches mine, "The High Lord is tricky, Ameria." He hisses in a whisper. I snort, well aware of how tricky he is. "I mean it, he's as cruel as they come."

"Clearly, you haven't met my father."

His mouth thins, "If Callum catches you…"

Oh. Oh. The corner of my mouth curls up and I stand, propping my hand on my hip. "You're worried about me," I taunt. "How flattering."

A muscle twitches in his jaw. "Of course, I'm worried."

I let out an exasperated breath and close the distance. "I'll be fine, I can handle myself. I don't need babying. I want to prove myself to everyone, so you'll have to deal with me doing this." I mean what I say, even though I'm technically being forced to play both sides. I choose the rebels, which is something I should have done a long time ago.

Corro's shoulders slump, "Your assignments will come through me. Because you're in the competition, you'll need an escort to and from the city each time. You will only be spying within the main city, Nyasa."

"Sounds good."

"I'll see you tomorrow."

I stop him as he turns to leave, "You were extra kind tonight. Thanks for that." My stomach churns with the softness I'm allowing him to see.

Looking over his shoulder, Corro shoots me a sad smile before he exits.

My night is plagued by thoughts jumping between "what if's" and I begin to question everything. Worry comes flooding back. Will my involvement make things worse? What will I do once I'm out of the competition and still have to work for Callum? What if he catches me spying and I'm forced to kill everyone? I stew in my thoughts all night, flitting in and out of sleep until I fully give up and peel myself from bed to go for a run, hours before the blare of morning horns.

Today was our final day sparring against one another, the next being the day before the trials. I didn't get to spar against Delyth this time, but she and the partner chosen for her were next to me and I was amazed at how lethal she could be if she wanted to.

I survey the course Corro has set up this afternoon for Inara, Delyth, and me to train together. I'd convinced him that it might be helpful and he readily agreed, saying it's important to learn how to work with others as a team. Now that I'm looking at the course, I regret my idea. A healer – not Tabitha – sits under a tree off to the side. Luckily, Corro got us some small doses of the elixir we've been taking every morning, so at least we'll have access to the other elements.

"Alright ladies," Corro grins and my stomach sours, definitely regretting my request for him to do this. He stands in front of the course, hands clasped behind his back, "You're going to have to work together. You won't only need to look after yourself but also one another. When it comes to battle, you won't be alone. You'll be surrounded by other warriors so it's important to learn to work as a unit. Now, stretch it out and then line up at the start."

As I stretch, my eyes constantly wander to Corro. The lines are becoming more blurred by the hour. I've come to find that I genuinely enjoy his company and having to report on him, use him, is gnawing at my insides.

What makes things worse is the small seed of emotion that's begun to sprout within me. I'm starting to care for him more than just feeling sexual attraction. In the past, alcohol has helped push away any intimate feelings I'd felt for someone until I eventually got over it, but I haven't had any in a while. All my feelings are starting to surface and it's a nightmare. I'm a ticking clock and I'm afraid of what will happen when it stops and I shatter, letting out everything I've safely kept hidden away. I rub my eyes and groan, shoving it all behind that locked door of mine.

"Maybe we should have a strategy," Inara suggests, knocking me out of my haze. She bends down into a squat, warming up her legs.

I nod, my hands on my hips as I begin lunging in place. "I agree."

"Well, we know each other's strengths and weaknesses when it comes to magic. If a part of the course involves, say, blocking metal spheres from flying at us, I'll throw up air shields since that's my specialty. We'll just have to work together when it comes to the earth element," Delyth states confidently while stretching her legs on the ground.

Inara begins to lunge around, "That's a good place to start."

"And, once we know what to expect from the course, we'll wing it from there." Delyth gazes across the clearing at the looming course, larger than the ones he's set up for me before. She grimaces, "No way we'll be getting through it in one go."

We line up at the start where a stone structure stands tall in front of us. "Go!" Corro shouts.

Springing into action, we climb the stone wall. Simple enough, we make it to the top. "Instead of wasting time and energy climbing down, we can jump and I'll slow down our impact with my magic. From this height, we won't even have to tuck and roll," Delyth says while looking down at the ground. "Jump on three. One, two, three!"

Flinging ourselves off the wall, we plummet to the bottom. My stomach rises into my chest and just as I think I'm going to surely break my legs, a strong gust of wind knocks into my feet and slows my descent. My knees barely take any impact as I hit the ground. "That was incredible!"

Delyth grins proudly, sending me a wink. "You haven't seen anything yet."

"I think we'll all have to shield ourselves for this next one and not rely fully on Delyth to cover us all. How are your air shields?" Inara asks over her shoulder.

"Good enough, but I don't know how long I'll be able to hold them."

They both nod, satisfied with my answer and we step forward single file to head through the portion of spinning metal tubes and flying spheres. Delyth leads us and I take the rear. There are a few close calls as we maneuver around each other, blocking and dodging the spheres.

A high-pitched cry comes from Delyth and I whip my head up in time to get nailed in the stomach by one. "There are flying daggers?" she cries.

I straighten with a wince while clutching my stomach, waiting for the air to return to my lungs. The course comes to a halt and my narrowed gaze shoots to Corro, "You put the fucking daggers in here?" I yell across the clearing. The bastard just shrugs, a smirk plastered all over his stupid handsome face.

Inara is already pulling out the short dagger that has embedded into Delyth's thigh as I rush over and cringe, "Sorry, if I had known those would be in here I would have warned you."

"You mean these are normal?" Delyth blanches, a hand covering her bleeding wound.

"Unfortunately. They're small enough not to do too much damage though, and spelled not to hit any major arteries or the face."

Inara chucks the dagger on the ground and shrugs, "It's smart. Teaching you to take a stab wound and keep going afterward." Delyth makes a disagreeing noise.

"We have two options. Either we keep going as far as Delyth can make it or go take care of the wound now. Either way, both options end in us having to start from the beginning." I look over to Corro who is still grinning, obviously happy with himself.

Delyth groans and starts to hobble off the course, "Let's just take care of it now."

We're able to make it through the flying daggers, spheres, and spinning tubes on our second go. My air shields hold and come quicker now that I've warmed up. I warn them that the part we're approaching likely has vines that shoot from the ground.

Which, indeed, the minute we step into the small muddy patch, vines wrap around various body parts, bringing each of us down. I immediately burn them all and then help Delyth while Inara makes quick work of hers.

We nod to each other, communicating we're all good, and continue. A blast of heat hits us in the face when a large wall of fire appears, blocking our path. With a confident smile, I manipulate the flames. Creating an opening we can walk through.

I'm about to take a step when more vines snake up my legs and shoot to my wrists. I burn them off with haste and find my friends have also become restrained. I help Delyth again, Inara takes care of hers with impressive speed. By the time we're all free, I try parting the flames again but more vines come at us. The three of us let out a collective groan.

It took two more tries to make it through the vines and wall of fire. To our annoyance, Corro made us restart the course over again both times. We're currently on all fours on the far side of a deep pool of water, dripping wet and panting after clawing our way out of it.

We'd tried to use Inara's water walking ability – which I had no idea was a thing – but Corro decided to make it harder for us and we were swallowed up by the gross, slimy water. In the pool, Delyth had used her ability to create air bubbles around our heads, Inara blocked and deflected balls of water that came at us from all angles, and I did my best to help her.

Thankfully, water magic has become easier to wield since I have practiced every night while in the tub, until the elixir wears off. "I hope I never have to fight in water," I heave. "That was miserable," Delyth grunts in reply as she gets to her feet.

We're finally at the last part of the course. A ladder rises high into the sky and I can barely make out a small walkway at the top that connects to another ladder in the distance. Inara whistles, tipping her head back to take it in, "Fuck, that's high."

My face scrunches, "I wonder what happens if one of us falls off."

She cringes, "I'd rather not find out."

"If anyone falls, we should all go together. That way I can help ease our landing a bit," Delyth offers.

My brows shoot up, "That's a pretty big drop, can you really do that?"

She nods, confidently meeting my gaze, "It's the timing that will be tricky as we'll likely be falling at different heights, but I can manage it."

It takes us hours to make it through the last part. Climbing the ladder was exhausting on its own and the walkway at the top was covered in ice. I'd been able to melt it but it would re-form almost instantly so we'd each have to use fire magic on the spots in front of us.

Strong gusts of wind would knock into us and we'd go flying. Turns out Corro had spelled the area around the bottom to stop us right before we hit the ground. We had figured that out when Delyth's timing was off slightly and I was sure that it was going to be my end.

Even though it was spelled, we decided to fall together anyway. It was my first time working as a team, other than my assignments back home with Torvin. But, I wouldn't call what we did teamwork. It was more like forced partnership.

The sun has fully set by the time we finally finish the course and my arms are so sore I can barely lift myself off the ground. We drag our beaten bodies to the pavilion to grab some late dinner. "Will you teach me that air bubble trick?"

Delyth smiles at me, "Of course! Burning the vines off would be nice to learn since air magic takes a lot longer to get them off."

I nod, "I can teach you that easily, you just have to be careful not to burn yourself."

"We should get together once more before the competition. We all have pretty strong magic and can teach each other as much as possible before the elixir wears off," Inara says. My mind wanders to what family she comes from. Delyth too, considering how strong her air magic is. They both must be from powerful families because I've never heard of a commoner having power equal to what nobles and royals can wield.

Delyth's voice brings me back to the conversation. "I agree. Maybe mid-week would be good."

We reach the pavilion as others have already started leaving. "What do you think these last ten days of training will look like?" I ask them as we sit at our usual table, our empty plates and bowls discarded in front of us.

Inara shrugs, "I assume we'll continue to practice all the elements and work on our fighting."

Delyth shakes her head, "There has to be more. We're competing to become a Western Isles warrior. Magic is different here. I bet we'll at least learn about the courts and their magic."

"You're right, that does feel like important knowledge. I don't think we'll get all those details though, not until we've actually joined one."

"We might not even get to pick one. My trainer told me that we could be hired by anyone in a court. However, I've been told that the High Lord of the Astral Court has heard about my skills and has an eye on me. So, I'll probably head there."

"And I'll go wherever Inara goes," Delyth adds, sending her a longing smile.

A smile of my own forms, small though it may be. Seeing them fall for each other has been a surprisingly sweet reprieve amid all of this chaos. My shadowed heart aches with happiness for them but a deep loneliness resides there too, wishing mine too could beat alongside another.

"Well," Inara breaks the tension building between the two of them, "we have a feeling where you'll go, Ameria."

My head rears back and my brows scrunch in confusion, "What do you mean? I haven't thought that far ahead."

"Oh, please," Delyth rolls her eyes. "You don't think we can't see what's forming between you and Corro?"

I scoff, "There is nothing building. We're just a trainer and trainee who happen to be friends." I'm in complete denial, and I know it, but I'm not ready to admit that yet.

"I saw the way you two came into the meeting the other night. I don't know many trainers who would hold hands with a trainee," Inara smirks in my direction.

"I was nervous," I mumble, shifting on the bench.

"Ha! I was nervous the first time too, but the person who brought me didn't hold my hand."

I click my tongue, "Whatever."

Neither of them push any more, for which I'm grateful because feelings are not something I'm used to talking about. On our way back to the tents, Gregor and Keenan manage to lure us away with their plan of relaxing in some hot springs with bottles of wine they managed to acquire.

The hot springs are far out on the Eastern side of camp and we have to hike through heavy brambles, bushes, and plants. When we finally make it, I nearly gasp at the steam wafting off the surface. My muscles long to sink into it.

Fae lights and the floating orbs of light from our tents illuminate the area. Not surprisingly, Corro and Narses are here. Looking around, I can also see a few smaller pools hidden around the main one. My friends choose the large pool where most people are and I can feel both Corro's and Narses's eyes on me as I strip down to my undergarments.

I let my orange locks fall free from my braid, hopefully hiding my scarred back, and slink into the water, submerging myself to the chin. I take up a spot next to Inara, Delyth, and Gregor, my body entirely relaxed against the edge of the pool. Keenan is behind us chatting the ear off of some trainer.

Gregor opens up the bottle of wine by pulling the cork out with his teeth, spitting it out into the brush surrounding the pool. I'm handed a metal cup and he fills it to the brim. My appetite for alcohol is strong, and the possibility of drowning my feelings and sorrows is appealing. But my gaze flicks to Corro across the way, deep in conversation with Narses, the fae light casting a shadow across his chiseled jaw.

I glance back down at my cup and frown. Maybe I shouldn't. If I'm going to be a part of the rebellion and play this situation with Callum carefully, having a clear head is smart. My desire for alcohol wars with the logical part of my brain, as always. It's pretty much screaming at me to say, "Fuck it," and down ten cups right now.

"What's wrong, Ameria?" I snap out of my torment as Inara scooches closer, glancing between me and my untouched cup.

Maybe having someone help me through this would be beneficial, and I'm always with Inara when alcohol is around. Surprisingly, I trust Inara completely with this embarrassing confession. I bite my lip as I scan the immediate area, making sure no one is too close to overhear my admission of weakness. "I was uh, I think -"

Inara raises her hand to cut me off. My mouth snaps shut and she reaches for my cup, snatching it out of my hand. She turns her back toward everyone while downing half the cup and then fills it with crystal clear water. She hands it back to me with a knowing soft smile.

My lips purse, "You're more observant than I thought." Inara smiles smugly and her brows jump up, clinking her cup with mine.

The watered down wine is still disgusting, but I will hold onto the hope that I'll get used to it. It could also be that this wine wasn't very good to begin with because it tastes worse than the stuff they have at the camp tavern.

Hiding my grimace every time I sip is a challenge and whenever Gregor sees that my cup gets low, he pours me more. Inara is right there to drink half of it and replace the other half with water. At one point, I had to swap spots with Delyth because Inara started to get too drunk drinking for the both of us.

I take a moment to clear my mind and focus on relaxing my

sore muscles and bruises. My head falls back and rests against the edge of the spring. Pushing the noise of everyone chatting and yelling into the background, I gaze up at the stars through a small opening between the tree canopies.

Someone squeezes my thigh lightly and I snap upright. Delyth motions with her eyes and I turn my head to see Corro slowly making his way over to me. I side-eye her and she just happily purses her lips and jumps back into a conversation with Inara and Gregor.

Corro sinks into the empty space next to me, propping both elbows back onto the ledge. His wet chest glistens in the small amount of light. I lick my lips as my stomach flutters at the sight. "Enjoying the view?" My attention snaps away from his body and I take a sip of my disappointing drink to busy myself. "You're drinking," he says.

"It's watered down," I grumble while looking at him out of the corner of my eye.

He laughs, "Gross, isn't it?"

Turning toward him now, I prop my elbow on the ledge and let my head rest against my fist. My nose scrunches up, "Yeah, I can't say it's too pleasant."

"You'll get used to it," he shrugs, "Though, it's better with good wine. I think the stuff your friend has is the cheapest shit you can get." I snort and take another sip, not hiding the grimace that crawls over my face from the aftertaste. "So, first the lake and now the springs. Are you trying to steal all my relaxing spots?"

"I take responsibility for spilling the secret about the lake, but this time is not my doing."

"Fair enough."

In my periphery, I see Narses stand and I do a double take. Water drips down his perfectly sculpted physique, completely stark naked. His butt is – damn. If the Gods do exist – which being chased by a mythical creature pretty much almost confirms they do – I would expect them to be built like him.

"Like what you're seeing?" Corro's husky voice pulls me out of my trance and my mouth, which is hanging open, slams shut.

I twist my head in his direction, a satisfied smile plastered on his face. I suck my teeth, grateful for the lack of lighting to cover the blush that I'm sure is forming. "I assume you're naked again too?"

"Would you like to find out?" His eyes turn heated and he leans forward, crowding my space. "If you want to see me naked, Ameria, just say so," Corro grins.

My heart beats faster and I swallow thickly, my core heating even more and I squeeze my thighs together. I take a big sip of my drink to distract the influx of arousal. "Someone thinks very highly of himself," I manage to playfully get out.

He leans even closer, and I can feel his warm breath on the side of my face. He's getting bolder, and my body is betraying me by liking it so much. Maybe my desire will go away if I just find someone random to sleep with.

"Why shouldn't I? You certainly enjoyed looking at me naked last time." My breath catches.

"Corro, come on. Let's go!" I hear Narses yell from across the way. He's fully clothed now, which is kind of a disappointment.

Corro holds up a finger to him.

"For the record, I enjoyed looking at your body as well." Corro lifts himself out of the water next to me and I get a nice side view of his half-hard cock swaying with the movement. My mouth goes dry as I watch him walk away.

Chapter Twenty-Six
Ameria

I'm braiding my hair for the day when I see swirling light appear behind me in the mirror. My shoulders stiffen as Callum steps out, dressed in matching beige pants and jacket, this time the jacket left open to show off his toned chest. A gaudy necklace sits on display. His silver hair is coiled in tight locs and wrapped neatly on his head, one piece dangling to the side of his face. If I didn't know what was hiding beneath the pretty exterior, I'd have blushed at seeing him dressed so finely.

Instead, anger and disgust roil in the pit of my stomach, my dark magic tensing at his presence. "To what do I owe the pleasure of your appearance?" I exhale through my nose and finish tying off my last braid.

"Checking in, of course." His eyes roam up and down my body. "I assume you were able to turn the situation around?" Callum casually waves a hand in the air.

Gritting my teeth, I turn to face him. Time to test the brand's limits, "Yes." I answer tightly.

He raises a brow, "And?"

"And what?" My eyes dart nervously to the entrance of my tent, hoping it's too loud outside to hear the conversation and praying no one comes in while he's here. Or else I'm screwed.

An exasperated breath leaves Callum as he stuffs his hands into his pants pockets. "We've been over this, Ameria. I come calling, you answer. Now, tell me what I need to know."

I nibble on the bottom of my lip, quickly scanning through what I know and what I can tell him that won't completely compromise the rebels or out me as now being on the inside. I clear my throat, "Well, I know they're upset about their shipments of crystals that went missing." Callum continues to stare at me expectantly. "They're positive it was you."

"Of course," he nods at me to continue.

"Some made it to their destination though," I reluctantly spill, figuring it's okay since they're already there.

"How many?"

"I don't know." The brand thankfully doesn't burn at my answer, I take that as a win. My heart is ready to beat out of my chest. I know it was a few crates but I don't know exactly how many and it seems the limits of the brand accept that.

Callum takes a single step forward, "Where did they send them?"

"The Water Kingdom, but other than that I don't know."

A muscle twitches in his jaw. "Did you find out anything useful?" he spits.

My eyes flick away from him and I stare nervously at the tent wall. Gods, I really should have paid more attention in the meeting, but Haemir being there distracted me. It saved me from having to spill important information, but I can't decide if that's a good thing. Not with Callum currently stepping into my space, his powerful form towering over me.

"What about Corro? Have you at least made progress there?"

"Yes," I pause, swallowing a lump in my throat, "but I don't think sleeping with him is the way to go about it."

Quick as lightning, he grabs my chin and studies me intently. His golden brown eyes flash molten for the merest of seconds before a grin breaks out across his face. Callum bursts into laughter and my stomach drops. I grab his wrist, attempting to remove myself from his grip but his hold on me tightens.

"Well," he cuts his laughter off but his grin remains, "isn't this interesting." His face gets into mine, "Are you starting to have *feelings* for the Moon Court boy?"

My heart sinks like a rock but I immediately snap my walls up, scoffing in defense, "No, I'm not."

I must have not convinced him because he laughs and nudges my chin a bit roughly before dropping his hand. "You cannot lie to me, but clearly you can lie to yourself." He shakes his head and takes a few steps back, "You should know better than to show such weakness, Ameria. I figured your father would have taught you that." My fists ball up at my sides.

"Be careful there. Who knows what others would do with that information." The corner of his mouth twitches as light begins to crawl up his body. "Be ready for me to retrieve you after dinner."

I watch with sweaty palms as Callum disappears, my insides souring. I plop onto my bed and rest my elbows on my knees. A long groan climbs up my throat as I rub at my temples. Really, what have I gotten myself into. This is all such a mess. I can't even begin to think about the Dranoq, a mythical creature that's not so mythical, or even the current riff between Haemir and me. It's all going to have to wait until after the competition.

"Morning, Ameria!" I jump at Delyth's voice and my hand flies to my chest with a curse. She grimaces, "Sorry, I didn't mean to startle you."

"It's okay, just distracted with my thoughts."

My lungs beg the air to return to them as I lay on my back in the mud. The rain that hasn't stopped all day pelts my face. I can feel the warmth of the blood that's trickling out of the small holes punctured in my chest by the thorn-wrapped wooden club that just walloped me.

Once I get my breath back, I stand, determined to finish this last course. It resumes its assault and I manage to duck the club that previously hit me. I have half the course left, and it involves wielding multiple elements at once. Corro thankfully informed me of that bit this time.

Vines instantly fly out of the thick mud and wrap around my legs. I'm able to get rid of them quickly before a ball of fire comes rushing toward me. I fling it out of my path with a strong gust of wind as more vines shoot from the ground. While I'm wilting those, multiple metal spheres fly at me and I throw up air shields to block them.

I miss one and it slams into my arm. Releasing a hiss through my clenched teeth, I ignore the pain as best I can and continue to block more of them as I finish getting rid of the vines. I manage to make it a couple of steps further before more blasted fucking vines appear and wrap around my arms. Taking a breath to calm my rising anger, my fire burns them to a crisp. Again I take a few steps when a wall of fire suddenly erupts in front of me, knocking me back a couple of paces.

My fire magic thrums inside me as I part the flaming wall down the middle and sprint through. My feet catch on something on the other side and I tumble to the ground, my hands just catching me before I get a mouthful of mud and flip onto my back. Vines snake around my entire body, securing me to the ground. These things are going to be the death of my sanity.

I begin to burn them, but not fast enough. Water comes pouring out of nowhere above me and flows right into my nose and mouth. My eyes start to tear up as I choke on the water trying to drown me. My body seizes a split second before I thrash around in the hold of vines.

"Don't panic, Ameria!" Corro shouts from the side.

His voice snaps me out of it. I can do this. Fighting the panic and lack of air, my borrowed water magic comes rushing to the surface, stopping the flow of water and reversing it. It rushes out of me and pools onto the wet mud around me.

I turn my head to the side as I vomit the rest of it and gasp for air. The vines retreat back into the ground, likely orchestrated by Corro because I'm still coughing up liquid. His boots come into view, "You made it quite far." I grunt in response, my entire body exhausted. Next thing I know I'm hauled up into his arms and he carries me over to where Tabitha is waiting.

He dismisses the healer when she's done and turns to me, "We have some time left to spar."

I look up at him from the ground, "Five minutes, please."

Corro lets out a laugh but nods, "Fine, but only because you did well today."

My body sags fully against the wet grass, my already soaked, mud-covered body not caring about getting more gross than I already am. The rain has slowed to a drizzle, but the canopy of the tree I'm lying under provides almost total shelter from it.

My thoughts drift to Haemir and whether I'll see him at the next meeting. What would I even say to him? Mereena has stopped reaching out. I'm sure they've communicated since our interaction. I pull myself to a sitting position and stick to the decision I made about dealing with it later.

"Ready?" Corro calls out.

I head to the box of weapons and pull out a longsword. Walking toward the sparring ring while twirling the sword around in a circle, I taunt him, "Ready to kick your ass? You bet."

My sword meets Corro's swing for swing, block for block. He may be faster, stronger, and bigger, but I can use my size and agility to my advantage.

"I've been thinking," I heave out between breaths as he shoves me backward with force from the blow I just blocked.

He gets into a stance and motions for me to attack, "Oh? What about?"

I lunge, swinging at his open side. He blocks it. "I don't know much about the Western Isles, besides what we're told in the Elemental Lands." Corro raises his foot to kick me in the knee and I jump back to avoid it.

"What would you like to know?" He comes at me with a series of swings, none of which find their mark..

"Well," I shove him back, "I know there are three courts. Sun, Moon, and Astral. None of them include this island. I'm curious why the King lives here and not on any of the other islands. Also, what are the other courts like? The magic systems included." I swing and grunt from the force of him stopping it. "What are the other High Lords like?"

Corro swipes with his sword and I duck. He pulls away and before I have time to register it, a giant ball of water propels its way toward me. I land on my back sputtering out water. "You didn't say magic was allowed."

He comes to stand over me and I take his outstretched hand, letting him help me up. "I also didn't say it wasn't allowed. You should expect that in a real fight."

"Yeah, yeah," I mumble.

"As for your questions," he stabs his sword into the ground and crosses his arms, "the King lives here because he doesn't belong to any court. He mostly lets the High Lords do what they want but makes sure that there aren't warring tensions between courts." Corro shrugs, "He's old. I don't blame him for not wanting to rule over all of them completely."

I nod my head, taking in everything he's saying. This basically tells me Beor has stopped caring, especially since it seems the Sun Court is going rogue.

Corro continues, "As for the magic of other courts, you'll

learn about them when you're a part of one. Aside from that, everyone here has an elemental magic as well. Basic magic, like sending letters for example, is close to the same. I mentioned before that sometimes the land gifts magic when one is either born here or officially becomes a citizen. Our healers have magic that yours don't. It's not a profession one can just decide to pursue. It's gifted."

"You said your magic was gifted by your High Lord. Can they all do that?" I recall the conversation we had the first day I met him.

"No. The High Lord of the Moon Court is different."

My eyes narrow, "What do you mean by that exactly?"

Corro smirks, "He's special, and his magic reflects that." His cocky grin dies and his eyes go hard, "Ameria, the High Lords are on a whole different level of power. The four of them are the strongest, most powerful fae to exist in a long time."

I blink, "Four?"

"Yes, the Astral Court has two High Lords." I open my mouth to ask why but he raises his hand, cutting me off, "Before you ask, I don't know why. They just do."

"Are they more powerful than the Kings and Queens of the Elemental Lands?"

His mouth forms a tight line, the trees shake from a gust of wind and I squint my eyes at the sudden change in weather. "Yes. If they were to fight each other, they probably would level not just the Isles, but the main continent as well. That is how powerful they are."

A shiver slithers down my spine, and it's not just from the

wind hitting my rain-drenched body. The fact that four fae capable of destroying an entire continent have been living here in the Isles makes my mouth go dry.

Corro yanks his sword out of the ground and wipes the tip on his pants. "Enough questions for now, let's get back to sparring. This time, you may use magic."

Chapter Twenty-Seven
Ameria

Wonderful, you're ready. Let's go, we have a busy evening." Callum snatches me up from my bed where I've been waiting for the past thirty minutes. He didn't say when he was arriving so I hastily bathed and changed after dinner, letting myself sit with racing thoughts until now.

Callum flicks his hand and cuffs appear. He slaps them down on my wrists and my magic floods out of me. "What the hell?" I mumble while toppling into him as my head gets dizzy.

We blink out in his blinding light before I can gather myself after getting shackled. When the light disappears, I find myself on a ship in the middle of the ocean. I instantly feel nauseous from the roaring waves, loss of magic, and the memories of what happened last time I was on one. "Wait to get sick, will you? We're not there yet." Callum states and I look up at him incredulously.

"Can't really help when I get sick," I hiss through my teeth.

He rolls his eyes and then we portal again, this time to a busy trading city I know quite well. "No," I mutter. Nausea roils in my stomach and it's not just from all the portaling. It's from where I suspect he's taking me. We portal one last time and Callum drops me hard on cold stone. I vomit all over the polished beige floor of my father's office.

"You have two hours. No more, no less. I'll be back then to retrieve her." I see a flash of light in my periphery signaling that he's left me here. This is the first time I'll lay eyes on my father since he sold me for a fucking sword.

I gather myself up on my hands and knees, the magic-nulling cuffs clanking on the floor, and I lift my head to face the monster who raised me. "Hello again, pet." His fire-red hair is loose, falling just past his shoulders, a smug smile stretched across his face. My sister Petra stands behind him, not an ounce of emotion on her face, as usual. Maybe I was wrong about her.

"I'm not your pet," I spit out while slowly getting to my feet.

He waves his fingers that rest on the arm of the chair he's sitting in. "I only have a couple of hours with you so," he stands and I'm reminded how small I've always felt in his presence. Toross whistles and two guards come rushing through the doors, "Let's go."

They grab hold of me and start hauling after the King and my sister. Down and down we go, through the dungeon halls. The door at the very end taunts me as we get closer. I struggle against the guards but one punches me in the ribs and I deflate as they continue to carry me. I don't even have to ask where we are going, I know these halls like the back of my hand. My father only ever wanted me for one purpose and that's likely why I'm here. To be his weapon.

We reach the door and Toross turns, a smug expression expanding across his face. "So good to have you back, even if it's temporarily." He turns the handle on the torture chamber and it opens with a heavy creak.

My eyes blink away the blurry surroundings. Bickering can be heard in the background but I'm more concerned about why my face is plastered against beige stone and what the hell happened. Releasing a groan, I turn my head and pain radiates through it, like I've been hit. Maybe that's why I'm on the ground. It still doesn't explain why I don't remember a damn thing after Toross opened the torture room door and how I came to be here on the floor of his study.

More pain hits me as I attempt to move, but this time it's coming from the scars on my back. I hiss through my teeth and the room quiets, those present apparently now realizing I've awoken. The first person my eyes land on is Petra, who looks a bit pale and pity pools in her eyes. My stomach dips at seeing emotion on my sister's face. Oh Gods, this is not good. My gaze finds the two others in the room, Callum and Toross. I swear the earth trembled a little with the looks they exchanged.

"What happened? Why can't I remember anything?" I croak through my sore throat. It feels stripped raw. I must have been screaming.

No one answers me and the two of them continue to throw each other looks that could level the palace. As I'm slowly peeling myself off the floor, Callum moves to grip my arm and hauls me up. "We're leaving."

With no questions answered and my body exhausted from whatever Toross inflicted upon me, we portal out of his office. I'm back on a ship and I try to gather my bearings against the rocking. I dry heave and Callum makes a noise of disgust, letting go of my arm so I collapse to the floorboards.

After a few deep breaths, I'm able to take in my surroundings. Callum is speaking hushed words to some crew member, a captain perhaps. My legs are wobbly as I stand and make my way toward a railing. The cuffs I still wear clank against the worn wood as I rest my forearms against the rail.

I can't see anything in the dark besides the waves hitting the side below and two vessels straight ahead, rapidly getting closer. My fingers rub at my head. Why can't I remember anything? My nausea only builds as I try to piece things together but no memories come. Not even a sliver of a moment.

Callum comes to stand beside me, gazing out at two ships that are slowly getting closer. "Why can't I remember anything?" I grind out, my hands clenching the rail in frustration.

He waves a jeweled hand in the air, "Don't ask me, you were like that when I arrived." My brows furrow, this is going to drive me insane. I know my magic didn't completely take over. I'd have known as I always do. Plus, I'm still wearing the cuffs. I can't feel a drop of power.

"You see those two ships there, Ameria?" My eyes dart between Callum and the vessels he's talking about.

"Yes?"

"Those are rebel ships leaving from the Moon Court." My eyes blow wide. Those are ships they talked about in the rebel meeting. They've been disappearing. I glance around at the people on board and everyone seems relaxed. Too relaxed.

My eyes find Callum who is smugly staring down at me, "You see, every vessel has to pass by my court to make it to the Elemental Lands. The waters are too treacherous around the King's Island to sail that way, so they must always go one of two ways."

I swallow thickly, "Your point?"

He grins, "It means that I can easily stop them in their tracks. The rebellion won't have whatever it is they're smuggling to the Water Kingdom, whether that be weapons or just people to aid their cause."

Callum grips the back of my head, pulling my face closer to his. "I want you to watch as I end every single one of their lives. Hear their screams as the flesh melts off their bones. Watch as they jump ship only to be swallowed by the sea." He shoves me into the railing of the ship and I whimper in pain as my rib collides with it.

He climbs up onto the rail with surprising balance. "No, no," I choke out as I watch him lift his arms, his crazed eyes meeting mine. "Watch as they all burn."

My face crumples as fire begins to crawl up both ships. Callum's waving hands match the flow of flames I see lighting every inch of the vessels. Screams rip through the air and cries of help ring out. People fling themselves from the crumbling ships to the raging ocean below. There's no way they'll survive. They're all dead.

And now I know Callum has fire magic, not just his light. He uses it as if it's nothing to him, a small bit of power used to raise hell upon the rebels.

Two more waves of his arms and the ships explode, giant plumes of smoke and fire blending with the night sky. He's laughing in a way that makes my stomach clench. I drop to my knees as he hops down from the rail and crouches next to me.

"Do you hear that, Ameria? Get used to that sound, as it's what you'll hear when people decide to go up against me, decide to go to war with me. They'll all burn. They'll all disintegrate to ash, and next time, I'll make you do it." His eyes are bloodshot, and they turn molten again, staying that way for longer than I've seen before. All but one speck though, that is as dark as the horizon in front of us, clouding part of his left golden iris.

Callum lifts me up by the arm and makes me continue to watch the burning of the ships, the aftermath of destruction. So this is how he's making the shipments disappear. By leaving nothing but ruin. All the evidence hidden in the depths of the sea.

I'm sobbing while trying to get the guards off me. My mother's body lies lifeless across the room, her unmoving eyes still staring up at me. The guards pull me out of the room and restrain me against the floor. "No! No!" I shout through my thick spit-filled mouth, tears streaming uncontrollably down my cheeks. My vision blurs more. I try to get up, to run to my mother, but they continue to hold my body against the cold stone. "You're lucky I made her death quick," says my father, standing over me.

We're in the dungeons now, the guards still gripping my arms. A bloody and beaten body is restrained to the table before me, my mother's lover apparently. Toross is yelling something from the other side of the room, but the words sound as if I'm under water. Something hard hits my cheek, snapping me back to reality, the sting of it spreading across my face.

My father stands in front of me, holding out a knife. I shake my head, "No…no, I won't do it. I don't want to do it."

The cold blade presses against my throat, flames burst from the crown on his head, his eyes glow red like hot embers. "Then let me show you what will happen every time you let your emotions get in the way, every time you refuse me," he spits.

I wake with a gasp and shoot upright. Beads of sweat roll down my neck as I grasp at my chest through my soaked nightgown. I grimace. It has been a long time since I've dreamt of that horrid day. The first day my father marred my skin. The first time I ever tortured someone. My dreams flitted between that day and what happened tonight.

My body trembles as I hug my knees to my chest and a strangled sob escapes me. The emotions I've been pushing away for the past couple of weeks are starting to come rushing back and the memories are beginning to taunt me again. Thanks to cutting out the alcohol, I no longer have anything to keep them at bay.

I worry about my new friends and about the rebels who are risking their lives against rulers like my father and Callum. My worries drift to Haemir and Mereena as well. Burying my face in my hands, I groan, trying to hold back everything that's bubbling to the surface. I don't want to feel these things. I want to feel nothing.

It's still dark and I'm unsure of the time, but I need to get out. I need to move. Throwing on my training clothes, I start walking with no destination in mind. It's a pleasant summer night, not a single cloud in the night sky, and I find myself wandering in the direction of the lake.

Absent-mindedly, I play with my fire magic, expelling some of it before I light the whole camp on fire. My dark magic is also restless but I'd rather not release it right now, especially since anyone could be wandering around. It's been on edge since Callum brought me back to camp, removed the cuffs, and left without a word.

The nearly full moon reflects in the still water and I settle down on a boulder at the edge of the lake, bringing my knees to my chest. My gaze falls to the calm surface and I work on my breathing techniques.

I jolt at the sound of crunching leaves behind me. My head whips around to find Corro catching himself from tripping over a root. Our gazes crash as he looks up.

"Oh, I didn't think…"

"I can leave."

We speak at the same time. I nibble my bottom lip, "I can go, leave you by yourself," I say while starting to stand.

"No," Corro steps forward, clearing his throat, "you can stay."

My butt sinks back down. "If you're sure."

He takes a few long strides and sits next to me. "Yeah. I just come here to think sometimes. When I can't sleep." He side-eyes me, "I'm glad to have your company this time."

I give him a tight-lipped smile and we sit side-by-side in silence for a moment, overlooking the calm lake.

"So, you couldn't sleep either," he says, still staring out in front of him. I hum in answer, not feeling like spilling all of my problems to him.

Corro abruptly stands and starts to take off his shirt. "What are you doing?" I send him a narrowed look.

"Going for a swim like I usually do when I come here." He kicks off his boots and starts untying his pants. My attention turns back to the lake, ignoring the fact he's getting naked right in front of me. Out of the corner of my eye, I see him dive into the water.

Corro breaks the surface, shaking his hair out before running a hand through it, and sends one of his dazzling smiles my way. "Care to join me?"

"Uh, I'm good."

"It'll make you feel better, I promise," he coaxes, arms lazily flowing beneath the water.

My head falls backward with a sigh, why not. Maybe this will help, I'll try anything to escape my thoughts at this point. I strip everything but my underthings and dive in.

Leaning back to float, the warm water seeps into my bones as I stare up into the night sky. "Told you it'd make you feel better," Corro chimes in as he swims up next to me.

I let my lashes flutter closed as I take a deep breath. "My body is relaxed but my mind isn't."

"It gets easier, you know," his voice comes softly from beside me.

One eye opens to peek at him before I close it again. "What does?"

"Cutting out alcohol." He pauses. "It sucks for a while, having to deal with everything you worked so hard at pushing away but, slowly it gets more manageable."

I right myself and face him, his gaze sliding to mine. "How do you make the feelings go away without using alcohol?" My voice comes out weaker than I want it to.

Corro snorts, "You don't. You feel them and then you move on. That's how having emotions works, Ameria."

I turn my back to him, breaking our eye contact. My jaw and fists clench. "I know, I…" A disgruntled noise forces itself from my throat, "I just grew up being taught that emotions other than anger were weak. How am I supposed to reverse more than a hundred years of people forcing that lesson on me." I don't know why I'm telling him this. I'm being vulnerable, and I'd be beaten senseless if I showed this kind of weakness in front of my father. Yet here I am, opening up to someone I've only known for a short period.

His voice is gentle as he nears closer, "Little by little. It's not something that will happen overnight," A finger traces down the scar along my spine. I stiffen, sucking in a breath. "Is that how you got this?" Corro whispers.

My mouth goes tight and my head falls forward, emotions hitting me like a raging sea. His body comes into view, fingers hook beneath my chin, bringing my gaze to meet his. My eyes line with silver as he stares at me intently. "Let yourself feel everything, just for right now." Corro's hand moves up to cup the side of my face, his thumb gently stroking my cheek. "And then we can move on like it never happened." A strangled sob blubbers out of me, a single tear betrays me and falls.

His other thumb wipes it away, cupping my face between both hands. Leaning his forehead against mine, he speaks tenderly, "Let it all out, and I'll be here to catch you as you fall." My chin trembles. I take a deep inhale and then I shudder as more tears begin to fall, years of emotions releasing all at once.

Corro wraps his arms around me, pulling me flush against his body. I shake as the tears turn into violent sobs. My legs get heavy but he holds tight, keeping me upright. I bury my face into his warm chest, "My heart feels like it's going to crack into a million pieces," I manage to blubber out.

He hugs tighter, "I know."

"It fucking hurts," I choke out between sobs, "I hate it." I'm practically clawing my nails into his chest at this point but Corro never lets go, never complains. He doesn't even move or flinch.

My breathing become shallow and rapid. "I," gasp, "can't," gasp, "breathe."

His hand starts to stroke my head, "You're hyperventilating. Focus on controlling your breath like I taught you."

I violently shake my head, "I," gasp, "can't."

"Yes, you can. Do it with me. One big inhale, two, three, four. Now exhale, two, three, four." My body shakes but eventually I manage to get some big breaths in as he continues to guide me through it. "Good girl," his hand still caressing the back of my head.

I sniffle and release a painful hiccup bubbling up from my chest. My heavy sobs turn into silent trickles of tears, and then fade to nothing. Corro still holds me tightly as for the first time in a very long while, I allow myself to feel things instead of using something to drown them all out.

Chapter Twenty-Eight
Ameria

As Corro promised, we didn't speak a single word about what happened at the lake. We stayed there until the moon disappeared and then we parted ways. Training was normal and while I felt embarrassed and awkward about the whole thing, he treated me the same as always.

The group decided to go out to the tavern this evening and I jumped at the chance to go with them. I don't want to sit and stew alone in my tent, and while I won't really be drinking, the tiniest bit of wine I allow myself is better than nothing.

"Ha!" Gregor laughs while shoving a finger in my direction, "No one matched your number, again. Drink up babe!"

I grumble but down the rest of my watery drink and slam it on the shabby circular table. Gregor, Keenan, a few of the other men, and I are playing some dumb drinking game one of them made up. You throw up a number, one through five, to your forehead and whoever doesn't have someone else matching their number, has to drink. It's a game purely based on luck and a quick way to get drunk.

"Looks like I need another drink fellas!" I bellow over the noise of music and laughter while wiping my mouth on my arm.

I push out of my chair and stalk off to the bar for a refill of my trash drink as the rest of them continue to play. As I wait, my eyes wander around the room. It's packed tonight, full of competitors and trainers. Some of the healers are here too and apparently they're all proficient in music, currently playing tunes off in the far corner.

People dance or play games, groups howl with laughter, and a few couples are kissing and fondling around the open room. It seems the remaining days are affecting everyone. Who knows how many of us will be dead in nine days, including me. My drink is filled and I take a sip, my gaze catching on Inara and Delyth, dancing with various people. A small smile spreads across my face and I nudge my way to them.

They yank me into their arms and we begin to dance. My drink empties quickly, thanks to Delyth making us cheer to friendship and some other drunk nonsense that came stuttering out of her mouth. Half of my drink ends up on the floor rather than on my stomach.

The music is lively, and I find myself laughing while getting lost in the beat. Switching between dance partners, I drink up the energy and let myself push away all the thoughts that have been swarming me.

The tavern is still packed when I head to the door for some fresh air. Beads of sweat drip down my back and face and I'm so out of breath from non-stop dancing that I stumble out the front door. The air outside doesn't make much of a difference. It's one of those midsummer nights when the air is muggy and sticky, so thick that it feels like every pore is suffocating.

An owl hooting somewhere in the distance, the muffled party noises from inside, and the swish of the long grass around my ankles are the only noises that reach my ringing ears as I trudge my way to the edge of the tavern.

I lean up against the side of the building that is out of view from the entrance and close my eyes, letting my head thump back as I try to fan myself with a hand. As much as I wish I could get drunk with all my friends, I'm glad I won't be as miserable as they will at training tomorrow.

The brush across from me starts to rustle and my eyes shoot open, my stance snapping straight. Corro stumbles out of the woods, getting his leg stuck along the way, and tumbles forward, almost falling on his face. I try to stifle a laugh but fail and his surprised eyes dart to mine.

"What are you doing in the woods?" I snicker.

He rights himself with a cocky grin, "Can't a man just enjoy the outdoors?" He swings his arms out wide.

My brows furrow and I cross my arms, "Are you drunk?" Shock floods through me, as he's told me he very rarely indulges.

Corro grunts, "Blame it on the shitty conversation I had recently." He stalks his way to me, stopping so close I can smell the alcohol on his breath.

I peer up at him, "You're going to have one awful day tomorrow."

"Oh, I'll be fine." He winks and places a hand on the wall next to my head.

"So, who pissed you off enough that you decided to get drunk?"

Instead of answering, he leans in and lets his mouth get dangerously close to mine. My heart rate picks up, my gaze darting between his hooded eyes and parted lips. "Corro…" It comes out as a breathy whisper, a warning or a plea. I'm not entirely sure.

He closes the distance between our bodies, trapping me between his solid form and the wall. Corro's lips gently brush mine and I shudder, my lashes fluttering from the contact. "Gods, Ameria, you are all I can fucking think about anymore."

I inhale a shaky breath and my gaze meets his. This shouldn't be happening. I mean, it's good for the whole Callum situation but every day it feels ickier. The lines get more crossed day after day, and it feels deceitful even though I'm pretty sure I have started to fall for him. Ah hell, I'm not pretty sure – I definitely have.

All thoughts leave my brain when his free hand grips my hip to hold me still and he grinds his body into mine. "Do you feel how hard you make me, Ameria? All the Gods damned time." I release a whimper when he does it again.

Corro's mouth crashes into mine, our tongues meeting desperately. We devour each other like starving animals, frantic and hurried. He grips my ass to lift me up and my legs wrap around his waist. My fingers tangle in his hair as he grinds his hardness against my core over and over again.

I moan into his mouth when one of his hands finds my breast. The heat of him thrusting against me and the pinch at my nipple have me becoming increasingly wet. His hand wanders from my breast down to dip below my waistband. Corro's fingers slide over my clit and I buck against him with a breathy gasp.

The tips of his fingers circle it and then move to my entrance. "Fuck, you're so wet already." He nestles his face into my neck and groans, the vibration of it causing me to shiver. I moan huskily as he slides two fingers into me and moves them deliciously slowly. I roll my hips with the movements.

His fingers pick up speed and he nips at my throat. My grip on him is tight and I pull his body as close to mine as it can get. Corro's fingers continue to assault me in a steady rhythm, curling occasionally to hit that sweet spot.

"Oh Gods, Corro," I heave out between heavy breaths.

His tongue travels up the side of my neck, stopping to nibble on my ear. "That's it, Ameria. Be a good girl and come for me."

"Corro!" Someone calls.

He growls low in his throat but doesn't stop the movement of his fingers, "What?" He snaps, glancing into my eyes before popping his head around the corner of the building.

"Let's gooooo, we're heading baaack now!" A heavily drunk man yells out.

Corro continues to finger me, almost pushing me over the edge. He presses his forehead against mine, "I'll be right there, start walking."

Footsteps get further away and Corro moves my hand to my clit, and I begin to work it. My release pours out of me. He muffles my sounds of pleasure with his mouth as I come, clenching around his fingers. They slow and then stop fully when my orgasm peeters out.

Our breathing fills the air between us as he removes his fingers from me. Corro's eyes tear into me as he brings the same fingers to his mouth, sucking them one by one. His eyes shudder and he groans. "Damn, you taste good."

Corro drops my feet to the ground and sighs. Grazing his thumb along my swollen bottom lip, he slips it past my lips and I suck on it, giving it a swirl with my tongue. He lets out a pained noise and pulls his thumb from my mouth with a pop. He pauses, looking me up and down, shakes his head, and walks off in the direction his friends must have gone in while adjusting himself.

With my back slumped against the wall, my heavy breaths calm. I listen to his steps get further away while sliding down until my butt hits the ground. My fingers brush over my lips, everything inside me roaring with how bad of an idea that was. But, I can't get the taste of him out of my head — or the feel of his hands on my body.

My hope is that this was a one-time thing, something to release the tension, and then we forget about it. When the competition is over, if I still live, he will see how much of a traitor I am.

A pang rings through my chest — I don't want him to forget. I want to get lost in him again and explore more of his body. The emotional side of me wants Corro deeply. There's no denying it. I stay on the ground until I can settle all the thoughts running rampant in my brain.

After trudging back into the tavern, I instantly head for the bar to grab another watered-down drink. I stand there waiting, my fingertips drumming along the surface as I shift my weight back and forth. Maybe one cup of real wine wouldn't hurt, right? My teeth nibble on my lip as I debate my choices. It's not like one glass is going to get me drunk. There's no way my tolerance dipped that low in such a short time.

The internal debate is for nothing as the bartender puts down a mug in front of me. I take a sip and grunt at the watered down taste. It's probably for the best. I return to the table where all my friends are now playing cards, including Inara and Delyth, and join in, spending the next hour or so listening to their rowdy stories – and beating most of them at the silly card game. It's enough to distract me, for now.

Breakfast is full of unhappy people. Even Gregor and Keenan are too hungover to jab at one another. The trainers will put them all through hell today, that's for sure. I tossed and turned all night, regretting not asking for a cup of real wine, but this morning I've come to be grateful that I didn't. I was able to be level-headed in my earlier decision that the best course of action is to pretend nothing happened between Corro and me. Maybe he'll say nothing and I won't have to force distance between us.

My knee bounces under the table as I push around the muck on my plate, my heart warring with my brain. Logic tells me to sweep it under the rug and move on, but my heart is telling me to throw caution to the wind. As I lay sleepless in bed last night, I thought about what Mereena always said to me: It's not a weakness to let love in, but a strength. I was raised to see it otherwise, however. Not that I love Corro, I just met him, but the possibility of it turning into something could maybe be a reality.

My brain reminds me that there is no future for us. Not when I'm chained to Callum. The minute Corro, or any of my new friends, find out about that, everything will be ruined. That is, unless I can find a loophole in how this brand works and run away, but it's doubtful. Is this what the rest of my life will truly be? A rehomed pet trying to run away from another man who just wants to use me as his weapon? I scowl, nearly throwing my fork down onto my plate and pushing it away. My head thumps onto the table. I've really gone and gotten myself into a bunch of deep shit, haven't I?

The second I step into the clearing for training and find Corro grinning at me, I know instantly he hasn't forgotten about last night. "Good morning, Ameria."

I send him a clipped smile as I breeze past him and start on my morning exercises. "So, what's on the agenda for today?" I see his grin falter and I have to ignore the twist in my stomach.

He recovers quickly, "Well, I thought we'd work on sparring with just elements for the first half of the day."

"Okay, sounds good," I say as I begin my walking lunges.

"Ameria, I think -"

"I feel like we should work on sparring with weapons and elements again. But this time, I will use just my fire and you can use the others," I cut him off.

I catch him shaking his head out of my periphery, but I continue my exercises. "Yeah, sure, fine. But, Ameria -"

"Maybe I should throw in my other magic too, you know. I

think it has its benefits in fighting, like portaling behind someone for a surprise attack. I feel restless lately, not using it enough." I cut him off again to ramble some more. Anything to get him to not bring up last night.

"Ameria." His tone is impatient, but I continue anyway.

"Those kinds of things could be important in a fight, I think -"

"Ameria!" Corro shouts while taking a step in my direction and I wobble mid-lunge in surprise. "We need to talk about last night."

I shake my head and look anywhere but him, "No, it's fine. There's no need. It was a mistake, I understand, it's best to move past it."

He grabs my chin, forcing my attention to his. "I don't want to move past it." So much for sweeping it under the rug.

Swallowing thickly, I bat his hand away and take a large step back. "Well, I don't feel that way about you, so..."

Corro snorts, "That's not what it looked like last night."

"It's not a good idea. It won't work out. We should just pretend it never happened and things won't get complicated. No one will get hurt."

He prowls toward me, "And what makes you think it won't work out?"

My eyes narrow at him, "Because I could die at the end of all this. Or because I wouldn't put it past my father to try punishing me for leaving. Because you're my trainer and..." my voice trails off as Corro's hand snakes to the back of my neck and grips it.

"Got any more reasons?" His eyes dart down to my lips.

"Because..." I lose some of my resolve as his lips brush ever so lightly over mine.

"Because?" He breathes upon them.

"I'm not a good person."

"I disagree."

My lashes shudder with a shake of my head, "You don't know me."

Corro's grip tightens, "I want to know you."

His mouth crushes mine in a deep kiss and I fully let go. I choose to throw caution to the wind. I've never had this before and I want it. I want it desperately. I know it will only be for a short time, and it's selfish of me to string him along when I know there isn't a future for us. But, I can't let my one chance at experiencing romance pass me by.

I wrap my arms around his neck and pull him closer. His hands are everywhere. Gripping my ass, he moves me until my back hits a tree. Corro unties the laces of my pants and then spins me around, pushing my front against the rough bark.

Glancing over my shoulder, I watch as he slowly pushes my pants and underwear down. And then he kneels.

His hands drag up the sides of my thighs to grip my hips and I arch my back, giving him full access. Something wraps around my wrists, and I startle as small branches come to life and gently restrain my wrists securely to the tree. I open my mouth but the words never make it out as Corro's tongue slides from my clit to my pussy. My entire body sighs as I slacken, the restraints holding me up.

He spreads me wide, circles and sucks on my clit. My head

falls backward with a moan. "Oh, fuck yes." His mouth feels so good. Better than good. Corro begins to devour me, thrusting his tongue deep inside. I want more, need more. I push my ass further back against his face and he makes a deep rumble from his chest.

My breaths get heavier, shorter. I can feel my release right around the corner and Gods do I want to come. When he pulls away, I can't help but whine, missing the feel of his tongue. Corro chuckles while his hands trail up over my backside. As he stands, they continue over my ribs to cup my breasts through my shirt. He rips it down and plays with my peaked nipples.

Leaning against me, I feel his cock press against my core. He must have pulled it out when he was feasting on me. The thought of him stroking his cock while he did so makes me even more aroused. Teasing me with the tip of it, he presses a kiss into the crook of my neck. "I dreamt about tasting more of you all night."

My entire body is ignited in heat, from him and from my magic coming to the surface. Corro kicks my feet further apart and wraps my braid around his fist, lightly tugging it. So agonizingly slowly, he pushes himself halfway inside me, eliciting groans from us both. He draws out and then thrusts into me fully.

A choked gasp rips from my throat and he pauses, seated deeply inside, allowing me to adjust to his size. Corro tugs on my braid again and sinks his teeth into my shoulder, "Gods, Ameria, your pussy feels as good as it tastes." I let out a shaky breath and push my ass back, signaling my need.

Gripping my hips with both hands, he finally begins driving into me. It starts with a steady rhythm, but he gets needier and I get more heated. Corro thrusts faster, harder. The smell of smoke wafts into my nose and from my hooded eyes and I catch a glimpse of the branches securing me crumble to ash.

The bark digs into my forearms and my fingers grip the surface to hold me up. "Don't stop," I choke out. My legs shake as Corro continues to pound into me and my climax starts to build. His fingers reach around to play with my clit and I lean further back, opening my legs wider.

"You like that?" his voice comes out husky.

"Gods, yes," I cry out. My fingers dig so hard into the bark that I can feel it draw blood.

"Tell me how good my cock feels inside of you."

I whimper, "So fucking good. Make me come, Corro."

And he does. I utter a string of short moans as I clench around his cock, my eyes rolling into the back of my head with my orgasm tearing through me. Corro keeps me upright while continuing to fuck me through waves of pleasure, his balls slapping against me. A guttural groan rips from his chest as he spills his release.

He remains inside me as we catch our breath, his forehead resting against my spine. "Shit, I shouldn't have come inside you." He says between his slowing breaths.

"I'll start the contraceptive tonic again." Corro wraps his arms around my middle and slowly pulls out.

Lifting my pants back up over my hips and tying them for me, he leans me back against his chest and nuzzles into my neck.

"You should probably drink the abortive tea tonight just in case though." I almost argue against it, knowing that I don't need the tea. But I nod to avoid any questions about why. Of why I can never have children, how the choice was forever taken away from me. Not that I'd be a good mother anyway.

"You get five minutes, and then we start sparring." Corro murmurs, pressing a kiss to my temple. I groan at the reminder that we have a whole day's worth of training ahead. "You're lucky I'm letting you have a break at all," he chuckles.

I turn in his arms and roll my eyes. A soft smile forms on his face and he leans down, giving me the most gentle kiss that makes my insides flutter. And they've never fluttered, not like this. Releasing me, he smacks my ass causing me to yelp and then heads to the trunk where all the weapons reside.

Taking a deep breath, I lean back against the tree and close my eyes. I've definitely just made everything way more complicated, but I don't care. I'm done caring because this is the first time I've ever felt anything like this. And I don't want to lose it. Not yet anyway.

Chapter Twenty-Nine
Ameria

Tabitha came last night with the abortive tea. I drank it anyway – not like it'll do anything. This morning, Corro and I decided that it was best to draw some boundaries for the remaining six days, separating whatever relationship this is from our training. This was only after he bent me over his favorite sitting boulder and railed me from behind.

I was the one who enforced the rule. With everything I'd gotten myself into, I needed a time I could focus on the competition with no distractions. Just being around him made it difficult when all I wanted was to lose myself in him.

I've avoided thinking about the future consequences and inevitable fallout between the two of us. Unfortunately, that time is just around the corner.

Inara, Delyth, and I sit around a crackling fire we built in the middle of one of the fields near camp. I look forward to my time alone with them. Even though they are obviously together, I've never felt like a third wheel.

Inara was just talking about her trainer being one of the top

Western Isles warriors and how she's determined to surpass her one day. I have no doubts when it comes to her achieving such a thing.

"Ameria, why did you just now decide to leave the Fire Kingdom?" she asks bluntly. I can always count on her directness.

My stomach dips and the silence stretches between us while I think about whether I should tell the truth, lie, or even answer at all. I decide there's no point in lying and so I answer honestly. "I had thought about it for a while, but I worried about leaving my two best friends behind, knowing they'd take my punishment for leaving." I swallow thickly, "Mostly though, it was just fear and complacency. I never thought I'd succeed in escaping."

My jaw clenches with the fact that I actually didn't succeed. Yes, I got away from my father, but was shoved into the hands of someone equally as cruel. Although, it seems my father can still call upon me through Callum, so did I ever escape him at all?

I didn't notice the tear that had fallen until Delyth's finger wiping it away jolted me. She flings her arms around me and I instinctively stiffen but am able to relax when Inara, not surprisingly a non-hugger, pats me on the knee. I don't deserve friends like these two, but I'll take advantage of their companionship while I can. Until my world eventually implodes.

Inara and Delyth depart for a quick dip in the springs together and I debated on finding Corro's tent for a late night distraction but figured if he wanted to see me, he could find me on his own. Visiting him would only deepen our intimacy and I wasn't ready to face all that yet. All I can think about right now is crawling into a hot bath and passing out.

My plans are instantly ruined when I step into my tent and find Narses standing in the center, looking harsh and imposing. My thoughts whirr with hesitation and worst-case scenarios. I can't get my feet to move from the spot where they're planted, my stomach tightening at the possibility that he knows everything.

"You have five minutes to get changed and then we're heading out on your first mission." Narses's brows remain narrowed as he looks me up and down and then marches to leave the tent.

"I thought Corro was in charge of my assignments?" I question him with a look over my shoulder.

He tenses but doesn't bother to turn around, "He's busy," and then storms out.

My face scrunches up as I watch the tent flaps flutter closed. What the hell is his problem? My mind falls again to the possibility that he knows my secret, but if he did, I'm pretty sure I'd be dead by now.

I'm out of my tent in five, dressed in the black outfit and cloak Corro gave me before my first meeting. The mask hangs tied around my neck but my hood is up, covering the braid I hastily redid. Narses is by the fire, staring deeply into the flames. I approach and his head snaps up, expression still stone-faced.

"Let's go," He nods his head in the direction I'm to follow him. I almost have to run to keep up with his quick strides.

Thick tension fills the air between us, but I don't utter a word until we pass the tree line and enter the southern forest. "Are you going to tell me what the assignment is?"

His jaw twitches before he answers. "We caught sight of the captain who had been captured the other week. He's been acting shady and hasn't been in contact with any of the rebels so we have to stake out all the places he's been seen."

My face jolts up to his, a flurry of conflicting emotion running through me and my feet catch on a root making me stumble. I manage to catch myself before hitting the ground, "He - he's alive?"

Narses nods once sharply. What if I have to confront him, will the captain recognize me? How is he not dead in the first place? Surely Callum would have killed him or he would have die from his injuries not long after I left.

My brows jump, "Wait, we?"

"The leaders have agreed that I should accompany you on your first few assignments." His rough stare meets mine. "That's not going to be a problem for you, is it?"

I swallow thickly and shake my head, "No."

"Good."

We continue through the forest to the gate. It's clear he and the leaders don't trust me, which is fair. My guess is that Narses thinks I'm hiding something. Again, fair. He activates the gate and grabs my upper arm, dragging me through with him.

I don't recognize the area I'm in and I wonder how many gates there are in a city. We stand at the top of a hill, large townhouses lining both sides of the street. Each house is bathed in yellow-tinged light from tall lamp posts, showing off the small grass patches behind each house gate. It's exceptionally quiet, which unnerves me.

"Pull your mask up."

I do as instructed and Narses tugs me to the right, toward a small alley between townhomes. I flick a glance at what is behind the gate we came through. A manicured garden full of sunflowers, tansies, amaranth and much more that I can't make out beyond the floating orbs of light scattered throughout. Golden benches adorned with red rubies and spiral designs are spread along the paths and a fountain sits in the middle.

My steps slow as I squint at the statue in the center of the fountain. I snort when I realize whose likeness it is. Out of the corner of my eye, I see that Narses has stopped and is looking at me funnily. I dart my eyes between him and the statue of Callum, suddenly realizing I'm not supposed to know what he looks like and quickly change what I was going to say. "Who's full enough of themselves to have a statue made of them?"

Surprisingly, his chest moves like he let out a silent laugh. "The High Lord." He continues onward, toward the alley. I take one last look at the garden, silently cursing the statue, and resume following Narses.

We're in the dim space between houses when he stops and turns my way, pulling out a folded parchment from his pocket. I look back to where we came from and a shiver crawls down my spine. "Why is this street so deserted?"

"It's a new development the High Lord specifically created. For what exactly, I'm not sure but it's entirely gated." He raises his gaze to mine. "There are markings etched into the fence surrounding the street, so I assume at some point it'll be warded as well."

"Interesting," I mutter. He grunts in reply. Closing the distance, I look at the parchment he's studying. It's a map of the Sun City, Nyasa, with circles and crosses drawn in certain spots. Narses flips it over, mumbles something under his breath about someone named Damien and his barely readable handwriting scrawled there and then flips it back over.

"We have to get here first." He points to a circle on the map, "It's where Garrick, the captain, was last spotted."

I nod, "Okay. And where are we right now?"

He points to a spot all the way across the city, close to the palace. "Well," I sweep my hand out in dramatic flourish, "Lead the way." I catch him roll his eyes as he turns and walks down the alley, stuffing the parchment back into his pocket.

The whole area is surrounded by tall gold-spiked iron fences. At this point in my life, I'd be content with never having to see gold ever again. All it does is remind me of the two men who have owned me.

I portal us to the other side of the fence and I notice there are indeed carvings etched into every other gold spire, similar to the ones on the gates. We rush down the grass hill on the other side and maneuver our way through back alleys at first. Once the streets become more crowded, I shimmy up an escape ladder on the side of a building and up onto the roof, Narses on my heels.

We jump roof to roof, with the occasional portaling to one further away, finally making it to our destination. My legs shake and I heave myself into a crouch to catch my breath. It'd been a long day and all this extra physical activity has made me want to lie down and sleep right here.

"This is the first location we need to scope out," Narses states, kneeling next to me, his eyes staring daggers at the building across the street.

"And how many are we planning to hit tonight?"

"All of them," he says, not taking his eyes off the building.

I glare at the side of his face, "How many would that be?"

He flicks an annoyed look in my direction, "Six." I try to imagine the map in my head but can't recall how far apart the circles were.

This first location is a decent-sized warehouse with a rusted brown metal roof. Small rectangular glass windows line the upper portion beneath the eaves, light emanating from them. They look big enough for me to shimmy through but I doubt Narses would be able to even fit his legs.

"What's the plan?" I ask while cracking my neck and knuckles.

Narses pulls out the map again and I scurry over to take a peek at the circled points. All but one aren't too far from where we are now. My tiring body is grateful for that. He flips the map over and reads more of whatever is on the back. He wasn't wrong: This person's handwriting is atrocious.

"How can you read that scribble?" I squint my eyes at the notes.

He snorts and folds the paper back up, slipping it into his pocket. "I'm used to his handwriting," he mumbles. Narses jerks his head in the direction of the warehouse. "His notes say that the guards are on rotation every fifteen minutes and they increase in number when the lights go out, which is in about," his head whirls around looking for something and stops on a clock tower in the distance, "about thirty minutes."

"I assume we'll need to get inside the warehouse?" I survey the guards walking the perimeter on the ground, then move to the ones on the roof that have been occasionally turning in place. One at each of the four corners. They're not in any uniform I've seen before, black with hints of gold throughout. From where I am, I can't see any markings.

"Which is where you'll come in."

"We will need to get close enough to where I can see a point inside." I'm only able to portal to places I've seen or been to before and clearly, I've never been to this warehouse.

He nods, "How much sound can you conceal within your shadows?"

I grin, "Even the loudest of screams can't pierce through my magic." Narses doesn't answer so I dart my eyes over to where he's crouching and find him narrowing his eyes at me. My grin falls into a scowl, "What?" I hiss.

"Just wondering how you found that out."

My tongue clicks with annoyance and I bring my attention back to the targets. "Once the lights turn off, I can portal us to the small metal balcony around the windows. I'll get us inside after I get a good look." I nibble on my bottom lip, "What if there's a tripwire for intruders?"

"Well then I guess it's a good thing you can portal isn't it." I throw him the most exasperated look I can manage through my eyes.

We wait and watch the guards change at the fifteen-minute

mark. Fifteen more minutes go by and they change again, while the lights go off inside. A group leaves the front entrance and I suck in a sharp inhale. "What is he doing here?" I hiss.

"Who?"

My mouth tightens as I watch my father's closest confidante shake hands with the party of people. "The Grand Duke of the Fire Kingdom. Caid." My eyes trail him as he saunters down the street alongside another figure and out of view. The urge to sneak up on him and jam my dagger through his throat is strong.

"I guess that confirms that the Sun Court is working with the Fire Kingdom."

My hands curl into fists and I whip my shadows around us both, portaling onto the balcony on the right side, and peer into a window. I find a spot inside that's hidden in darkness and within seconds, we're there, my shadows still concealing us. Just in case.

With a tug on Narses's sleeve, I stalk forward and peek my head out of the aisle we're in. The main space is full of wooden crates, stacks of rolled parchments, weapons, and various artifacts.

"What exactly are we looking for?" I look up at him.

"Quite literally anything. If it looks like it could aid the rebellion, take it." He walks forward and starts looking around the space. I drop my shadows and do the same.

All the artifacts look ancient and if I had more time, I would examine them all. But statues and trinkets don't seem like they'd be helpful for our mission, so I skip past them and head to a stack of rolled parchments.

I unfurl one after the other, all of them maps of the elemental lands but each with different border changes. The dates on the bottom state they're from well over a millennia ago since they show the creation of each kingdom. I find another and it's a current map of the Elemental Lands. The next one is the same, but the borders have changed. My eyes dart to the date and widen with a sharp inhale.

"What did you find?" I hear Narses whisper, his feet rustling over to me.

"It's a future map of the Elemental Lands." I hold it out for him to see and his eyes flare and then flick to me. "I think this is what the Fire King is planning."

"Hold onto it and we'll bring it back with us." I roll up all the other maps I looked at and place them back onto the shelf. Slipping the band back onto the one we're bringing, I head toward where Narses is examining a few crates. "Give me your dagger."

He holds out his hand and I unsheathe it, plopping the handle into his waiting palm. "Can you surround us and this crate with your shadows? I need to make a bunch of noise to pry it open."

With a flick of my wrist, shadows conceal us and the cracking noises he makes prying the lid off the crate gets swallowed by the darkness. While he does that, my eyes rove over the plain wood. I do a double take at the bottom left corner and drop into a crouch, running a finger over the symbol carved there. Four overlapping circles. It looks incredibly familiar but, where have

I seen it before?

The lid pops up and I hear a curse, "I think these are the crystals that went missing."

My face falls slack, "The King's symbol." I say under my breath.

"What?"

My gaze clashes with his and I point to the symbol on the crate, "This. It's King Toross's symbol. He and his stupid loyal followers use it. I remember seeing it a few times pinned to some nobles' jackets."

"Looks like some of our missing shipments are being sent to the Fire Kingdom."

My lips thin as I look into the crate of crystals in varying colors – white, yellow, and blue. "Do these crystals happen to amplify magic?

"That and more."

I sigh, my stomach sinking. "We can't let my father get his hands on these. He may already have acquired some but he cannot get any more."

"We need to get all of these out of here. Tonight. Follow me and keep your shadows up." I trail Narses around the warehouse, pointing out the ones marked with a symbol and he pries them open. We leave the others alone after finding out they only contain simple weapons. In total there are twelve crates full of crystals.

We begin to discuss how we're going to get them out and how I've never portaled anything this large when the doors to the warehouse burst open. I immediately smother us with my magic.

"I told you I thought I heard voices in here." One of the guards that entered says.

"Look!" Another shouts, pointing in our direction, "Some of the crates have been tampered with."

"Quick, send word to the High Lord. You five, with me." The leader of the group orders. "The rest of you, search the perimeter."

"Shit." Narses curses. "We need to get these out now, it's our only chance." He shoves my dagger back into my hand, "You need to distract them."

"You want me to fight off six guards?"

"Think of it as a good training exercise." He gives me a push and hides behind a crate, "You can drop your shadows around me."

"What are you going to do?"

"Don't worry about me and go!"

I grit my teeth and chuck the rolled-up map I've been holding onto an unopened crate. I mark each location of the guards in my mind and portal to the one that's a bit further than the others. Stepping out of my shadows, I bring my dagger to his throat and slice it open, not bothering to cover the noise since I'm supposed to be a distraction.

Shouts ring out and a few men charge at me while others shoot beams of what I presume is light magic my way. "Fuck," I curse. I'm swallowed up by my shadows, appearing behind the ones flinging their magic. I'm able to slice at one's ankle, causing him to cry out as he falls to the floor, and portal again back to where I originally was.

"They have special magic!"

"Shadow magic!" Someone shouts and I internally kick myself for using it so openly, but I have barely used my fire magic to portal and it's not as discrete as my shadows. Now that they've seen it, they'll have to die.

"What the hell is that?" One of them yells, pointing in the direction where I left Narses. A figure covered in a cloudy mist stands tall, casting that same mist all over the opened crates. And then the figure dissipates, taking the shipments of crystals with it.

My jaw drops. Not only can Narses fucking portal, but the bastard abandoned me! I let out a frustrated groan which pulls the guards' attention back to me. More shouts echo from outside. Gods fucking dammit.

I portal to the back of the warehouse and blend in with the darkness, just in time for ten guards to come rushing through the open door. I whistle, attempting to lure them back to where I am. A split-second plan to get myself out of this predicament comes to me. It will cause enough chaos for me to slip away and also kill them all in the process.

Most of the guards stalk toward me, two staying behind but far enough away from the doors for my plan to work. Portaling to the entrance, I slam the doors shut, leaving everyone inside with me. I whirl around and transport myself to the middle of the room. Throwing my hand out, I cast a towering wall of flame that blocks the doors.

The guards start shouting but I don't pay attention to them.

Everything must burn. Including the priceless artifacts, which makes my insides sink, but it must be done to hide my identity and save my ass.

I start spreading the fire from the front door and ignite every interior wall of the warehouse. My hands whirl about, manipulating the flames and bending them to my will. I light the artifacts, weapons, and parchments. Everything is blazing and I'm sure the heat is beginning to become unbearable, but I'm used to it and my fire cannot burn me – but it can burn them.

One by one, I ignite each of the guards in flames. Their cries of agony sing a song only my soul can hear. My dark magic dances inside me, thrilled to be delivering such death. The creaking of the building burning to ash fills my ears.

I've never destroyed something like this before and it feels… incredible. I continue to burn the place down, reveling in the destructiveness of my power. My father, Callum – neither of them will be able to salvage a thing from this place. This is my first act of revenge. This is the start of the payback Callum deserves for killing all the rebels on those ships the other night.

My limbs shake and I stagger a step. I drop my arms to rest them on a nearby crate that is about to be smothered in flame. My vision darkens around the corners as I try to catch my breath. I briefly notice what must be happening - I'm burning out. I've never used this much magic before so my body isn't used to it. I'm too satisfied at the ruin I've created to worry though, and laughter bubbles up from my chest.

The air next to me cools and I hear someone curse. My head turns slowly, still crazed with laughter. Narses stares wide-eyed at me and the crumbling building around us. My laughter dies as I meet his wild expression and my body finally starts to sag against the crate that's now almost entirely covered in flame.

I hear him curse again and his arms wrap around my middle from behind. That's when I notice the map I left on top of this crate. With what little strength I have left, I snatch it up and then I'm swallowed by the mist.

Chapter Thirty
Ameria

My body hits solid ground. The gray mist clears and a familiar beige canvas comes into view. The arms holding me disappear and I roll onto my back, the map clutched to my chest. My breathing is heavy and beads of sweat drip from my forehead as I try to blink away the dark spots that pepper my vision.

Rushed voices bicker and then there's movement on the floor next to me. I try to focus on Corro's frantic face, "What happened?" My voice comes out more gravel-like than I expected.

"You almost burnt out," Narses speaks plainly as he comes into view on the other side of me and hands Corro a cup of water. Just as I suspected, I used more magic than my body could handle.

I'm helped to a sitting position with my back leaning against a bed, and even though my vision is still a bit hazy, I can see we're in Corro's tent. I chug the water as if I haven't had any in days, some of it dribbling down my chin. They refill the cup and

I down half of it instantly.

My vision starts to clear but a splitting headache is forming and my limbs barely want to move. With my returning vision, anger comes with it.

"Ameria…" Corro starts but I cut him off, my head whipping toward Narses who is standing a few feet away.

"You could portal this whole time?" I hiss.

His face hardens, "My power is mine to disclose when I want to."

"And yet you're entitled to know all about mine?" My fist closes tightly around the cup. Corro pries it from my grip before I break it.

"It's different," he states matter of factly.

"How?"

Narses takes a single step forward, fists clenched at his sides, "I outrank you, which means it is my business to know about anyone and everyone."

My jaw clenches but he makes an annoyingly good point. One that I refuse to admit. "You left me there. You could have taken me with and you didn't."

"You couldn't go where I had to take the crates. Plus, I figured you could handle yourself." I gesture at my current state and he rolls his eyes, "Well, I didn't think you'd burn down the whole warehouse in the few minutes I was gone."

"Wait, what?" Corro yelps but we both ignore him. One of us can fill him in later.

"They saw my magic, so they had to die. And getting rid of everything inside was a good decision and you know it."

Narses averts his gaze, a muscle twitching in his jaw, but he remains silent. He knows I'm right but it's clear his ego doesn't like admitting it. We seem to be alike in that regard. "I'm surprised you almost burnt out from just setting fire to a warehouse. And so quickly," Corro says, the air of a question attached.

"I've never used my magic at that power before." I've also never lost mental control like that either, but I bite my tongue on that.

Narses snorts and if I still had the cup in my hand I'd chuck it at him. "That's something you'll have to work on. We can't have you burning out so easily." I nod and slump back against the bed. "We have much to discuss, Corro," he says while calling the rolled-up map I took to his waiting hand. "She needs to rest anyway."

He jerks his head toward the exit, motioning for Corro to follow and then leaves. Corro's arms slide underneath me to scoop me up like a limp noodle, and he sets me on his bed. I'd object and insist I sleep in my own tent but I'm so exhausted I can't be bothered.

Corro

"So, I take it the mission went well? Besides what happened with Ameria, of course. You're back earlier than I thought you guys would be." I walk alongside Narses as he leads us to his tent

"The first warehouse had all the recent shipments that went missing." He parts the flaps of the tent, allowing me to go in first. "All the crates were marked with a symbol the Fire King uses among his loyal followers. Ameria also recognized the

Grand Duke of the Fire Kingdom there as well. It seems Callum and Toross are working even closer than any of us realized."

"Shit." I mutter, running a hand through my hair. "Do the others know?"

Narses nods and unfurls the map, "I brought the crates straight to Rafael."

"Good." I stride over to his desk where he lays out a map of what looks to be the Elemental Lands. "What's this?" He points to the date at the bottom and my stomach drops. "Oh shit."

"My thoughts exactly," Narses says. "It's not surprising to me that Toross is going to claim the Earth Kingdom as his own. But, I'm surprised by the Air Kingdom."

My brows furrow, "I thought last we heard Queen Samira wasn't on a side?"

Narses straightens and crosses his arms, still studying the map. "Either Toross has recently convinced her to join him, or he's very confident he can. Either way, we should prepare for the worst."

"Rafael needs to see this."

"I agree. I'm about to head to the Moon Court in a few minutes." His gaze lifts from the map to bore into mine, "I wanted to talk to you before I left."

My stance widens and I cross my arms, "What about?"

"You know what about, Corro."

I scoff and look away, I can't believe this shit. "I was told to get close to her, you should be happy that I've done that."

He takes a few steps in my direction, "You were also told to separate your feelings from it."

My fists clench, "It's not exactly easy doing that Narses."

"I just don't want you to get hurt." His tone is a bit calmer now, gentler.

My eyes flick back to him, "Who says I'm going to get hurt?" His face has pity written all over it, and I don't want any of it. "I know what I'm doing."

"I'm not saying that you don't, it's just, she could die. Or what if she's not who you thought she was after all of this? What if she has a mate out there? Did you think about any of that before getting involved with her? I still don't entirely trust her."

I shake my head and back up a couple steps, "Stop it Narses, just let me have this. And what makes you so sure she's not my mate?"

"I'm just trying to make sure you look at this logically."

"I don't care if it's logical or not. It feels right to me and I'm going for it. If I only get five days with her then so be it. I'll regret it if I don't. This is the first time I've felt anything like this and I'm not going to give her up. So, either get on board or just leave it alone."

I turn and storm out of the tent. I'm pissed as hell at Narses for trying to ruin the limited time I have with Ameria. Logic be damned. He mutters a curse behind me but I can't be bothered with his extra protective attitude right. Rafael will support me – he already said he would. I just don't understand why Narses won't.

Ameria

My eyes adjust to the daylight streaming in. A crash startles me and my heart leaps into my throat as I jolt upright, reaching under the pillow to grab my dagger only to find it missing. Corro stands at his desk, the chair laying on the ground. I sag with a sigh and calm my beating heart. I forgot I'd fallen asleep in his tent.

I rub at my sternum, realizing I was changed out of my dirty clothes at some point. Corro grimaces, "Sorry, I didn't mean to startle you awake."

"It's fine. I was already awake."

He joins me, sitting on the edge of the bed, "You were out for a full day."

My eyes blow wide, "A whole day?" I yelp and practically leap out of bed, stumbling over my feet in the process. Corro lets me run to my tent to freshen up and I meet him in the clearing to train.

"I can't believe I wasted a whole day sleeping. There are only four days left!" I nervously bite my lip as I block one of his water attacks.

"Uh, yeah. About that, you only have three days to train." He hurls a force of wind at me and I throw up an air shield to stop it.

"Three? What do you mean three?" My fire whip breaks one of the large rocks he's just thrown my way and it shatters to pieces.

"Everyone gets the last day off. You know, to enjoy what could very well be their last day alive." This time I send a line of fire right toward him. He stops it in its tracks, dousing it with water. "That's enough element sparring for now. You still have the last part of the course to get through, why don't you do that. We also need to talk about what you can do to keep from burning out so quickly."

I half run, half stumble across the finish line and collapse into the dirt. My entire body is screaming in pain and I can feel myself getting woozy from the loss of blood. I really pushed myself to finish this damn course today and now all the adrenaline I relied on to ignore the bleeding wounds is starting to wear off.

Corro carries me over to Tabitha who heals my wounds and leaves. "Congratulations, I didn't think you would finish that today."

"Well, I was determined. Especially since I missed yesterday." I stand up and prop myself up against the tree.

He saunters up to me, resting his hand against the tree above my head. "Now that training is over, I can think of a good way to reward you for completing it."

My lower stomach warms with heat. "I thought we had to talk about my burnout."

Corro groans deep in his chest and leans in to nip at my throat, "That can wait until later."

"No, no," I playfully shove him away, "We talk now, play later." My smile is smug.

He rolls his head dramatically but agrees. "The thing I don't get is you have royal fire magic. You shouldn't have burned out with the amount of power you have, whether you used it too quickly or not."

I shrug, "I don't know what to tell you. I mean, I used my dark magic a bit more than I usually do. It's possible that complicated it."

"Either way, we're going to need to train you to use that much power over longer periods of time. It'll have to wait until after the trials though. I'm not the right person to help with that."

My heart cracks a little, knowing that after the trials, no one will be training me in anything. I'll lose everyone because of my forced hand in working with Callum. "Speaking of after the trials," Corro begins, "since I'm higher up in the ranks at the Moon Court," he shifts on his feet, "I could hire you and you could come live there."

My arms slacken at my sides, "You…You want me to come with you?"

He rubs the back of his head, "Honestly, Ameria, more than anything. I want to explore us, I want to…" Corro closes the distance and caresses my cheek, "I want you to come live life with me."

I can't stop the tear that falls from my eye. I'm being offered a home, a life. Freedom. And I can't have it. I don't get any of it, because I'm eternally cursed to live as a weapon for cruel men. Once Corro finds out I've been working for Callum, the damage will be irreparable.

"I want that too. "It's not a lie, I want nothing more than to go with him. His smile is radiant, hopeful, and it cuts my heart up even more. In a few days, he'll learn the truth. And he'll never smile at me like that ever again.

Chapter Thirty-One
Ameria

The day before the trials came quickly, a blur of intimate moments with Corro, training, and sitting around the fire with my friends. Corro continued to talk about his home court every day, which crushed me to no end. I could see the light in his eyes as he talked about a future with me, naming off the places he'd show me. How I'd stay in his home with him. Listening to it was unbearable – a special kind of torture. The guilt has been suffocating, the heavy burden of it presses down on me like I've been buried alive.

My tent mates and I sit around a table at the tavern sharing stories of our time here and stories from back home. "Ah, hell. I'm grateful I met all you assholes!" Gregor cheers holding up his mug, his occasional softness coming out tonight.

"Here, here!" Keenan chimes.

One by one, we raise our mugs and down them. Tonight, I allow myself to have real wine, not the watered-down shit. I at least deserve to get drunk one more time with everyone else if there is a chance I'm going to die tomorrow. Plus, we were all informed we'd get a hangover elixir in the morning. Everyone was ecstatic about that.

"Whatever happens tomorrow, I'm glad I got to know each of you," Delyth smiles at everyone around the table.

Gregor burps, "Alright you saps, let's play a game and get drunk!"

We played the stupid number game they made up until we were all good and plastered. Then the dancing came, and by the time I left the tavern, I was drunk and sweaty and really craving a snack. The snack being Corro.

I head for his tent while thinking about how this is likely the last night I'll spend with him. My heart sinks but I try to push away those thoughts for the moment. I want to enjoy this. One last time.

Corro

I sigh heavily as I trudge through camp to Narses's tent. We reconciled the other night, which makes things a lot less stressful for me. We've been friends for years and he's taught me almost everything about fighting and life in general.

Ameria is off with everyone else at the tavern and it takes everything in me not to turn around and head there instead. She deserves a night of revelry with her friends. I scratch the back of my neck, Gods I really am a downright fool for falling for her. I haven't felt this way in a very long time though. I know mates are a rare occurrence, but what if she's it?

I take a deep breath before striding into Narses's tent. He's sitting at his desk, reading various parchments scattered across the surface of it. His space is the same size as every other trainer's, but the contents are a lot nicer because he brought everything from his home. Animal skin rugs lay throughout, and the curtain behind his bed is made from the darkest black material I've ever seen aside from the warrior uniforms we all wear. His bedding is ten times nicer than mine, made up of furs and silk. Silver candlesticks with black tapered candles litter almost every surface. Narses wouldn't admit it, but he does enjoy his life of luxury.

We've been friends since before I even entered the competition at fifteen. He was the one to save me when I was dying in the Water Kingdom. He'd been the one to help me overcome my drinking problem, and he was the one who got me noticed by Rafael. I owe him everything. Narses is like the brother I never had.

He looks up from his papers and smiles, leaning back in his chair. "Well, to what do I owe the pleasure of your company my brother? I thought you'd be balls deep in Ameria."

I snort and look down at my feet, "I've come to ask you for a favor." When I look up, Narses is squinting at me. Moving further into the room, I pour myself and Narses a glass of his whiskey from his drink cart. He rises to meet me and takes the glass I offer him.

"Alright, out with it. What do you want?" He leans against the small table that sits by the drink cart, taking a sip of his alcohol.

"I want you to guide Ameria through the trials tomorrow. Beor said he'd pick out a trainer for her but I want it to be you."

Narses sets his glass down and crosses his arms, "I don't

understand, why aren't you doing it?"

"Rafael called me for an important meeting back home. Apparently, it's urgent."

"If it was so urgent he'd want me there. How come I haven't heard anything?" Narses pushes.

Letting out a groan, I run my hand through my hair. "He hasn't told me the particulars. If you want to take it up with him, by all means."

He stands straight and grabs his glass, drinking the rest before putting his hand on my shoulder. "Fine, I'll do it for you. Also, Ameria deserves not to be assigned some random trainer."

"Thank you." He waves me off but I continue, "No, I mean it. I sure as hell don't say it enough."

"Alright, alright. No need to get chummy you fucking sap," Narses laughs while taking a seat back at his desk.

"I'll be back at some point before or during the second trial. I don't know when but I'll come find you as soon as I return."

He nods and goes back to reading his parchment, "Will do friend." I pat him on the shoulder before leaving the tent.

The walk back to my own is short. I kick off my boots and strip my clothes before sinking into the bath. Damn, I love these enchanted tubs so much. My mind begins to spiral about how nervous I am for Ameria, for her to go through these trials. All the trainers are told what the trials are at the beginning of the competition so we can train the contestants properly. I just hope I trained her well enough.

I climb into bed naked and stare at the ceiling, hoping she comes by tonight. Just as I close my eyes, I hear my tent flaps rustle.

Ameria

I pop my head into his tent and there he is, naked and lounging on his bed, the sheet covering his lower body. My eyes drink him in as I make my presence known. "Hey there," he smiles softly and I smile back while kicking off my boots.

Getting onto the bed, I crawl up and straddle him. He holds my hips and lets loose a heavy breath, circling my hip bones with his thumbs. "I didn't think I'd see you tonight. Figured you'd be out partying, and by the smell of it, you have been."

I bend down, planting a kiss on his lips. "I wanted to see you. I could die tomorrow and I don't want to waste one minute."

"Don't say that, you're going to live," he frowns at me.

"Well, it's hard not to think about."

A devilish grin graces his face, "I can help with that," he purrs, gripping my hips and grinding his hardening cock against me.

My head falls back, "Mmm, I believe you can."

Corro leans up and helps me remove my shirt, his hands dragging up my sides and cupping my breasts. He reaches behind me and unclasps my brassiere. Tracing my pebbled nipple with his tongue, he nips on it, my lashes fluttering at the sweet spike of pain.

I climb off him to remove my pants and underwear and then return to straddling him. He pulls my mouth to his, pushing his tongue against mine. Corro's kiss turns hungry and I grind into him over and over. He moves the sheet down, exposing his cock and I lick my lips while gazing at his perfect length.

The corners of my mouth lift and I bite my lip, flashing him a wink as I inch my way down. Grabbing him in my hand, I swipe my thumb over the already wet tip and pop it in my mouth. When I twirl his tip with my tongue, he throws his head back, hissing through his teeth. "Oh, fuuuck."

My tongue moves to the base near his balls and I lick my way up before sliding it fully into my mouth. My hands and mouth move together, up and down, my cheeks hollowing out as I suck his hard cock. Corro gathers my hair in his hand to slowly push himself into the back of my throat. My eyes close and I hum against him in approval. "Gods you look so good with your mouth around my cock."

He withdraws to his tip and then thrusts into my mouth. I gag as he continues to fuck my throat. We move together and with a grunt he releases himself. After sucking every last drop up, I remove my mouth with a pop and slide him a sly smile. Corro, still fisting my hair, gently pulls me back up and brings his lips to mine.

Moving both hands down to my hips, he flips us. Corro peppers my neck, breasts, and stomach with kisses. Making his way lower, he flicks my clit with this tongue and I quiver. He circles it and then spreads my legs wider, slipping his tongue into me. My back arches off the bed and I death grip the sheets at how good his mouth feels on me.

Corro's fingers slide inside me and his tongue goes back to sucking on my clit. Thrusting them in and out, curling around that sweet spot, he moves faster. Waves of pleasure flow through me, pushing me to my climax. Sucking me off his fingers, he hovers over me, nestling himself at my entrance.

My arms wrap around his neck and I bring his mouth to mine, "Fuck me hard, Corro." I murmur against his parted lips.

He releases a breathy laugh and slowly slides into me. Leaning back, he surveys my naked body. Pulling my legs up to rest on his forearms, he grips my hips and pulls out to his tip. Corro rails deep into me, in and out, pace increasing. My breasts bounce with every thrust and I want more of him.

"Deeper, Corro," I breathe.

He pulls out and flips me onto my stomach. My ass is yanked into the air and his cock is rammed right back inside me. I whimper at the pain of the impact. He smacks my ass as he fucks me deeper and I cry out in the ecstasy of pain mixed with pleasure. I can feel my orgasm building, its rise to the surface every time his balls hit me.

I can't hold out any longer and I move my fingers up to my clit, "Come with me."

Corro growls and fucks me so hard my back feels like it could snap from being at this angle. My walls tighten around his dick as my orgasm explodes. He groans and comes undone himself.

Leaning down, he presses a kiss to the middle of my back and gently pulls out. Collapsing next to me, he pulls my body flush against his and we lay there in comfortable silence for a while.

"What are you thinking?" Corro whispers after our breathing has long calmed down.

I stare at my hand that rests on his chest a moment longer and then peer up at him through my lashes. "Everything is going to change tomorrow." What I really mean is that everything is going to blow up in my face.

Corro hooks his finger under my chin, lifting my head fully. "It is."

"This is not how I pictured the competition would go. I feel like my whole world collapsed around me."

He pulls me up so we're face to face, bringing his lips to mine for a soft kiss. "Sometimes our world must fall apart before we can fully begin again."

Corro plants another kiss on my lips and then draws away to get out of bed. I watch him move to the cart across the tent that holds various drinks. My eyes roam over his muscled body, everything firm including that plump ass of his. They linger on a large brand on his back. Shoulder to shoulder, an owl with its wings spread wide. I've stared at his bare back multiple times and he's never had this before.

"That brand on your back. You didn't have it when I saw you at the hot springs." His body stiffens for the briefest of seconds but relaxes as he turns and hands me a glass of water. Corro sits down on the edge of the bed, his glass of water in hand.

He looks down at it, "I received it that day I got drunk at the tavern." He takes a large gulp.

I cock my head, yes narrowing, "The shitty conversation you had?" He nods with a grunt. "What does it mean?"

Corro lets out a breathy chuckle and places a hand on my knee, "Unfortunately, I cannot tell you the specifics."

That's something I can relate to. Internally I roll my eyes and try not to look down at my own brand. He grabs my glass after I drain it and sets them down on the cart. I rise and follow behind him, dragging my hand from his shoulder down to his hand and grab hold of it.

He faces me, tucking a piece of hair behind my ear. "However, I can tell you that it has to do with my High Lord. Which brings me to tomorrow," Corro's thumb reaches up to trace my cheekbone, "I can't be by your side tomorrow during the trials. There's an important meeting I need to be at."

My face falls, "Oh." I'm not sure what to say. I had hoped he could be there but I know that when your boss calls, you answer.

Corro drops his hand, "Narses said he'd guide you through them, and I might be able to get back either before or during the second trial."

I nod, "I wish you could be there with me but, I understand."

He sends me a soft smile, "It's late, and you need all the rest you can get."

"You don't want me to stay?"

Dropping his forehead against mine, he moves my hand up to rest against his chest and whispers, "Trust me, I would love nothing more than to spend the whole night with you. But we wouldn't sleep much."

I push up onto my toes and press a kiss to his lips. "I'm glad I met you, Corro."

"I'm happy that you wandered into my life when you did. I can't wait to bring you home."

My heart cracks when he says that but all I can do is smile and pretend that there will be an after for us. I take in his mossy green eyes, soaking up these last few seconds of what could be.

The walk back to my tent is long, thoughts consuming me with every step I take. The camp is more still than ever, the only sounds my heavy footsteps and an owl screeching in the distance.

Chapter Thirty-Two
Ameria

Iwake to the sounds of someone in my tent and I shoot out of bed, fists raised, dagger gripped in one. A woman standing by the desk yelps and I breathe a sigh of relief when I see it's Tabitha. My arms fall limply to my sides and I drop my stance. "Sorry, I didn't mean to startle you, Tabitha."

I chuck my dagger onto the bed as she makes a dismissive sound and waves her hands, "It's I who should apologize dear. I meant to wake you gently, but I dropped the cup while putting down the tray." She motions to the desk where food is.

"We're eating in the tents this morning?"

Tabitha nods and points to a pile of clothes sitting on the floor by the mirror. "When you're finished eating, you are to change into your new fighting leathers and boots. When you hear the horns, follow everyone else to the base of the stone palace and await the King's instructions."

My feet almost cry at the sight of new boots, I've beaten the shit out of the ones I've been wearing since training started. Right before she leaves my tent, she looks over her shoulder with a sly smile, "There's a box from your trainer on the other side of the bed." She purses her lips as if trying not to grin but fails and walks out.

I rush over to the other side of the bed and kneel at the wooden box, reaching for the letter that sits atop it.

These will come in handy, so use them well. And before you ask, I had them spelled with the same enchantments as your other ones.

Fight like hell, Ameria.

All my love,

Corro.

P.S. Try not to lose them, they were a fortune.

A small chuckle leaves me as I read it, able to hear Corro's specific exasperated tone. The latches open with a click and I lift the lid. My eyes widen as I take in the two beautifully crafted black steel daggers inside. The blades have a slight curve to them, my preferred style, and there are swirls of dark grey throughout.

The handles are wrapped in the same incredibly dark leather used for the warrior uniforms. The cross guard is simple, with etchings of the sun, moon, and an eight-pointed star. I stand while flipping them in my hands and make some simple attacks in the air.

They're light and impeccably balanced. These really must have cost a fortune. I'll have to thank him for these later, before my secret gets out and he never wants to talk to me again.

My stomach sours and it's hard to eat the breakfast Tabitha brought me. I force the food down my throat as I mull over what the day might bring me. My focus needs to be only on surviving and not what the end of these trials will entail.

With the shake of my head, I knock back the elixir that grants me the other elements as well as the hangover one, which makes me feel instantly better. This is not the time to think about how shit my situation is. It won't matter if I'm dead so I need to focus on winning this thing.

Standing in front of the mirror, I gaze at the reflection staring back at me. The black fighting leathers cling to every curve, looking every bit of a true warrior. I'm able to study the uniforms a bit better now. Vines are etched down the sides of the arms and legs, three designs displayed on the chest. With light hitting it at just the right angle, there's a moon, sun, and eight-pointed star.

My orange hair sticks out like a beacon against the stark black material. I styled it in three braids that run across the top of my head, gathering at the crown, and then falling loosely in a tail down my back.

Horns blare outside, startling me out of my haze. Gods, I'm jumpy this morning. With one last look, I take a deep inhale and release it, "This is it," I mutter to myself. Sliding my new daggers into the sheathes at my sides, I lift my chin and march out of the tent.

Everyone is quiet, the heavy footfalls of all the competitors following one another to the gathering crowd at the bottom of Beor's castle fill the tense silence. The sounds of weapons being sharpened echo through the air and I search for any glimpse of my friends but see none. My gaze falls to the bottom of the hill the palace sits on.

Beor stands in front of his black and silver velvet throne. His hands are clasped behind his back as he surveys all of us gathering before him. He doesn't wear a shirt but rather a crisp black jacket and pants, showing off all the brands that cover every square inch of his chest.

A hand gently grasps my elbow and I whirl around, finding Gregor looming over me with a smile on his face. My anxiety calms a little, thankful to see at least one of them before the trial begins. He gives me a wink and a light squeeze on my elbow. I return his smile, though less wide, and lightly pat his hand.

"Today are your long-awaited trials," Beor bellows over the crowd, pulling our attention. "Some of you may live and some may die. That is the risk you took when entering this competition. Now, let's officially begin the first trial."

This is it, it's starting. I thought I was ready but my quickening heart rate proves otherwise. What a horrid time for my panic to start. Closing my eyes, I go through the breathing technique Corro taught me.

Inhale, two, three, four.

Exhale, two, three, four.

I repeat that process a few times and my panic eases as much as possible considering the circumstances. When my eyes open, Beor speaks again. "For this first trial, you will be brought through the gates to a small, heavily warded island called Balrath." Murmurs scatter throughout the crowd.

He speaks over them, "You will be tasked with finding two objects. The objects have been spelled and will call to you. If you listen well, it will guide you to them. You'll all be sent out in groups, but you will be invisible to each other. You are on your own. Those who make it out with their objects will continue to the final trial." He pauses and scans the crowd until his eyes land on me.

My body tenses under his piercing stare as he holds my gaze. "Make no mistake. This will be difficult. Balrath has creatures and magic that have not been recorded or are known only in myth and story." He looks away and I release a breath, my shoulders sagging with it. My mind automatically goes to the Dranoq and I pray to the Gods I don't run into that thing again.

"You may use the weapon your trainers have chosen for you but the rest is up to your physical stamina and magical abilities. Let us begin."

A group of ten, including Keenan, are ushered by trainers into the forest in the direction of the closest gate. I wonder if the walk there is as daunting as it sounds, a long silent walk toward the horrors of Balrath. Toward life or death.

While waiting for the first group to return, everyone has the thrilling task of stewing in anxious anticipation. Some sit and continue to sharpen their weapons while speaking in hushed voices with their companions, but most remain relatively quiet.

I go through my usual warm-up exercises and stretches alongside Gregor, both of us surveying those around us. I contemplate looking for Delyth and Inara but decide against it. I need to focus on myself, keeping as calm as possible.

Time seems to pass painfully slowly but isn't that always the way it goes in the limbo of anticipation? Just when I think

I can't wait anymore, rustling comes from the forest. The entire camp seems to still as a man and trainer stagger out of the trees, the former clutching two objects. He's as pale as a ghost and covered in blood.

Beor motions for him to place the objects into a large wooden chest by his side and then he's led away toward a tent that likely holds the healers. Not long after, three more emerge, some looking worse than others. The next sight chills me. The rest of the trainers come striding from the forest without any of the competitors they brought in. Without Keenan.

I glance at Gregor, whose face has fallen. He meets my gaze, a silent mourning passing between us. I can't imagine how torn up he must feel right now. Losing a friend you've known for years. My heart breaks for him. "Gregor Windrak!"

My eyes widen but Gregor just smiles sadly at me with a nod and takes his place with the rest of the group and disappears through the trees.

I wait and wait, but after a while I can no longer sit still. So, I pace and go through some fighting movements. Finally, a competitor returns but it's a woman I don't know. Two more come through after that but still no sign of Gregor.

When my bottom lip becomes raw from my worrying it and my hope starts to drain, he comes barreling through the trees, the rest of the trainers on his heels. His skin is covered in inky black liquid, his clothes are drenched, and blood is smeared on his face around three large gash wounds that run from eye to chin.

I let out a big exhale and collapse onto the log stool, allowing the tension to ease from my upper body while dropping my head into my hands.

The relief is short-lived as both Inara's and Delyth's names are called for the next group. My body stiffens again and at this point, I may never fully relax. I look up to see my two friends walking hand in hand. My heart crumples at the sight of them striding into possible death together.

What if one of them doesn't make it? What if they both don't survive? "Oh Gods." I groan and drag my hands down my face. I was not as prepared for this as I thought. These waves of emotion are going to make me sick. The one thing I'm grateful for at the moment is the clouds blocking the beaming sun.

I continue to practice my breathing technique while forcibly willing extra tension to leave my body. I'm not used to seeing people I care about in immediate danger, and if I don't get a handle on my shit, it's going to leave me exhausted before I even begin the trial.

At long last, someone emerges from the trees. Inara. Gods I could vomit with relief. She looks worse for the wear but the confidence in her doesn't waver for a second as she strides right over to the trunk. Delyth arrives not long after and my entire body finally relaxes the most it has since this whole thing started. Her white hair is streaked with a mixture of blood and mud. Even with a limp, she makes her way toward Beor and, in typical Delyth style, gingerly places the objects in and grins up at him.

More groups come and go and I've finally relaxed enough to focus on running through movements and stretching. As more contestants go in, fewer come out. I wonder if more people going into Balrath has made it become more alive, causing fewer to survive.

It's my turn and I'm joined by nine others as the last group to go. We all pause to look at one another before being led into the forest. Narses strides up next to me and gives me a reassuring smile. Even though he's an ass, I'm grateful for his presence.

The walk through the forest to the gate is more daunting than I could ever have imagined. I have no doubt Beor did it this way on purpose, to test the mental ability of contestants. It's like we're now officially stuck between life and death. Stuck in the in-between. I wonder if this is what the walk into the afterlife is like.

The sound of our boots crunching the sticks and pushing through brush fills the thick air around us. My gaze follows a lone crow flying overhead in the same direction we're headed. I can feel the aura of unease floating around the others. One of them even trips over a root but catches himself before fully falling.

We reach the gate and Narses surprises me by encompassing my hand with his. My gaze snags on a large black wolf sitting off in the distance to my right. The wolf and I lock eyes and a sense of calm blankets me before I'm pulled through.

The minute we get to the destination, I'm hit with the intense magic of the wards. These have to be the strongest ever created because it takes me a minute to attune to them and even then, it's like a nagging presence telling me, *"Danger. Stay out."*

We're at the edge of the island where trees meet the coastline.

Narses gently grips my shoulders and turns me toward the wall of invisible wards. The sight makes my stomach bottom out and a shiver crawls up my spine as I face the forest in front of me. The nagging feeling of running away intensifies.

"Don't worry, that feeling will go away once you're past them," he says knowingly. I swallow spit that has thickly gathered in my mouth. "You are to retrieve a black chalice and a golden emerald necklace. Once you've acquired them, make your way back here."

Looking over my shoulder I give him a grim smile. I take my first step toward the forest and I flinch. Taking another, the feeling of the wards crawls over my skin.

"Ameria," Narses's voice is soft yet commanding. I twist back to find an expression almost resembling worry on his face "Trust your senses. If you think something is off, it likely is. Be ready for an attack at any moment. If you can survive the Dranoq, you can survive this. Don't be afraid to use your dark magic."

"Thank you, Narses," I whisper.

He gives me a nod, "Make sure you get back here. I don't want to deal with Corro's whiny ass if something happens to you."

I snort and turn back toward the wall of wards, thankful for his attempt at lightening the mood. Unsheathing my daggers, I roll my shoulders back and let my magic rise to the surface. Then, I take my first step past the barrier.

Chapter Thirty-Three
Ameria

It's not any better on the other side of the wards. Stepping through felt like ants crawling over every inch of my skin, making me want to spill the contents of my stomach. The air is thick and a light fog rolls across the ground. It's quiet – the kind so devoid of sound that it almost hurts your ears.

I take a deep breath and immediately regret it. Sulfur and decay burn the inside of my nose and the back of my throat. I'm barely successful at holding back the gag that forces its way up my chest.

Lifting my daggers, I begin to stalk through the forest. Everything here feels dead and alive at the same time. Corrupt. Almost as if this place has one foot in the underworld. Balrath has a dark blue and purple tint to it. The forest floor looks as if it's been burned to a crisp.

Half of the trees here stretch impossibly high into the sky with dripping wet moss and mushrooms clinging to them. Otherwise, they're nothing but bare limbs. The rest are smaller, adorned with patches of purple and black leaves. This place feels like it has been plagued by a disease. The brush and plants look like they've been doused in a slick oily film. I've never seen anything like this before. It puts me more on edge, making me wonder what creatures haunt this place.

I startle with a jolt as I feel another magic course throughout me and begin to tug at my chest. It must be one of the objects calling to me. I home in on the tug to decipher which direction I should go and begin moving quietly yet swiftly.

Along the way, I pause a few times, holding my breath as something seems to be moving through the brush around me. Stalking. Waiting.

The pull gets stronger as I reach a swampy area. The ground becomes increasingly muddy with small pools and puddles between large lumps of moss. I use the moss mounds to move around the water, boots squelching every time I take a step.

A murky pond glazed with green scum comes into view. Silently, I groan and my body deflates in the realization of where the object is: In the pond.

I've only been able to practice the air bubble magic Delyth taught me a few times, so I'll have to be quick. Sliding a dagger back into its sheath, I keep one securely gripped in my hand and grimace as I slowly sink into the water. The irony that I can peel skin from a living being unphased but be grossed out by pond scum is not lost on me.

Taking a deep breath, I close my eyes and dunk myself under. Instantly, I call the air magic up to my eyes and mouth. Under the water, everything is just as murky as it looks from above, but I continue forward and swim deeper, following the pull of magic.

Dodging tall pond weeds, I finally reach the bottom. It's clearer down here and I'm able to see bones littering the floor. Full skeletons are lodged into the muddy rock sides.

There, on one side of the pond, is a rotted water-logged corpse sitting on a rusty throne, a black chalice gripped in his hand. Dread fills my body as I assume the worst. Once I take the chalice, this corpse and all these skeletons are going to come to life. Any rational person would leave it alone. Of course, they wouldn't even be in this situation in the first place. However, I have no choice.

I'm no doubt running out of time holding these air bubbles, so I jump into action and swim to the sitting corpse. I ready my dagger and as quickly as one can move through water, I snatch up the chalice.

For a moment, nothing happens. But then magic ripples out from the corpse in front of me. It grabs the wrist of my hand that's holding the chalice, causing it to slip from my fingers. I swing my dagger, swiping at the waterlogged hand holding onto me. It doesn't do much in terms of damage but it releases me and that's good enough.

Calling to the water magic, I create a spiraling torpedo in front of me and shoot it at the corpse. It flies straight back into the wall, the torpedo ripping a hole right through its chest. I feel the air magic around my mouth falter a bit. Shit. It's still holding but I don't have much time. Using so much focus on the torpedo caused me to lose some hold on the air bubble.

The corpse has sagged to the ground and I waste no time in scooping up the chalice from the bone-covered ground. I launch myself toward the surface, success thrumming through me as I get closer.

A bony hand grips my ankle and yanks me back down. I use a force of water to push it off just in time for four more to shoot up from the depths. I knew this would happen.

This time, I form balls from the water around me and cast them one after the other, as if I'm a living cannon. More and more skeletons keep coming and firing balls of water is causing my air magic to falter. I force my hands out in front of me, one clutching my dagger, the other the chalice. Connecting with the flow of water like Corro taught me, I become one with it.

One of the air bubbles around my eyes pops and I silently curse, closing it quickly. I continue to manipulate the water of the pond, creating a long slender whirlpool stretching from the surface down to the depths below. The elixir they gave us this morning must have been a double dose because I've never been able to pull off something like this. It feels spectacular.

With a sweep of my arm, I direct the underwater tornado around me, knocking it into the skeleton army. Their bodies crumble, bones flying in every direction as the spout spirals into their path. I dispel the whirlpool, thinking I've gotten enough of them out of my way for me to escape. In good time too, because the air bubble around my mouth is failing.

I take a deep breath and hold, right as the bubble pops. My feet carry me toward the surface when bone arms wrap around my neck from behind. With a skeleton strangling me and only one eye to see, I start to panic a little and flail about. My lungs are beginning to burn already, and I know the breath I'm holding won't last for much longer.

Taking the chalice, I ram it backward into its skull. It loosens its grip and I use the opportunity to turn toward it. The jaw hangs open wide, releasing a soundless scream. Forming one last burst of water, I send it right into the thing's chest, and it breaks into pieces that slowly sink to the bottom.

I swim as fast as my arms and legs can carry me diagonally to the edge of the pond, where the water meets solid ground. Breaking the surface with a gasping inhale, I haul myself over the edge, staking the dagger into the ground to help drag and roll my body out.

I lay on my back taking heavy breaths, clutching the chalice tightly to my chest. Glancing over at the pond, the surface is still, as if I hadn't just been fighting for my life in there. There's movement out of the corner of my eye and I find half of a skeleton's arm still latched onto my shoulder.

With shame, and glad no one is around to hear me, I squeal in disgust. Sitting upright, I rip it off and chuck it back into the water. I take a few more deep breaths in an attempt to calm my nervous system after completing my first test. Standing on wobbly knees, I remove my dagger from where I'd shoved it into the ground.

I now realize that I'll need both hands free for my weapons and we've been given nothing to put the objects in. I maneuver the chalice stem under my belt and tighten it so it won't fall out. This will have to do. Now palming both daggers, I scan my surroundings, listening.

There's no way all that commotion didn't stir up something

around here. I stalk back the way I came through the swamp and lead myself deeper into the forest, waiting for the magic of the second object to hit me.

As I continue to move, more fog rolls in. It becomes so thick I can barely see five feet in front of me. I attempt to retrace my steps but the fog seems endless and I fear I'm just walking in circles now. All of a sudden, I'm knocked off balance by something whizzing by me. I fix my stance, my senses on high alert. Ready for an imminent attack.

The gusts of wind I conjure to try and clear the air around me are no use.

"Ameriaaa."

"Ameriaaa."

"Ameriaaa."

My heart leaps into my throat as my name echoes through the air in a haunting tone. A creature knowing my name unsettles me. I'm knocked to my knees when it zips by me again. The back of my neck prickles and my dark magic perks up for the first time since entering this place. Something is behind me, and there's a weird sense of familiarity to it.

I shoot to my feet with a pivot, daggers raised. The fog eases enough to see a figure creeping into view. It's a woman, with dark shadows cascading from her body, trailing behind her with every step she takes toward me. My feet move a few steps back as I try to distance myself. Her skin is so white it borders on translucent, and her wet inky hair flows all the way down to her hips, clinging to her shirtless torso.

A shiver crawls down my spine as the temperature drops,

and despite being surrounded by thick fog, I can make out my breath. An overwhelming sense of dread washes over me, making my knees wobble and hands shake. Clenching my jaw, I pull myself together as best I can when facing a creature that radiates death.

The woman lets out a blood-curdling scream that's almost deafening and before I get the chance to cover my ears, it's over and she's now mere inches away. I gasp as she towers over me, expecting an attack, yet all she does is stand there, staring down at me. I don't question what she's doing and swipe at her, aiming for the gut. I feel the blade slice right across the translucent skin.

I know I hit flesh but the woman doesn't even move, not even a flinch. Her expression seems almost, surprised. My eyes dart down to where the blade made contact and my face falls in confusion. There's no sign of damage, not even a scratch.

My gaze flicks back to the depthless black eyes of the creature before me. She sniffs and cocks her head, the corner of her mouth twitching upward. "You smell different than the rest." Her bony fingers flutter in the air as she waves her hand.

I jerk back, putting more distance between me and this thing. It's playing with me. If knives don't have an effect on her, maybe magic will. My resolve comes flooding back and fire ignites in my hand. Her gaze snaps to the fire and then back to my face, her smirk only widening as I hurl a fireball.

With minimal effort from the creature, shadows swirl around the fire, extinguishing it. Unease fills me as my dark magic slithers under my skin, intrigued at the familiar shadows leaking from this woman.

"Oh," a wide menacing smile spreads across her face, "that is why." She sniffs again, "So familiar." Her melodic voice croons while she peers off in another direction. A chuckle escapes her black and blue lips, "The Queen would be most interested in you."

My muscles lock up, "What queen?" I demand, oddly somewhat interested in where this conversation is going.

The creature doesn't respond and continues to speak, "Yes, most pleased she'd be." Finally, her gaze slips back to mine and with a flick of her hand, the fog retreats, the forest coming back into view. "You will meet with the Queen."

The hell with that. I fling another fireball at her but again, it's engulfed in shadow. She clicks her tongue, "Enough of that. Come." She lazily motions with her hand.

"I'm not following you," I spit.

The woman peers over her shoulder, "You and I both know you will. Your curiosity is piqued. Don't you want to know why our magic is so similar?"

My instincts and training tell me to fight, but she's right. I am curious, and it seems that my dark magic is as well. This could be a trap, but something in me rebels against fighting her. I could have conjured all of the elements and flung them at her, but all I've done is fling measly little fireballs at her.

My interest in knowing why I have this magic, what it is, and who this Queen is, wins out. And it seems she knows it did, "See? Follow me."

I'm still on edge. My hands grip the handles of my daggers and I'm ready for this to be a trap, but I follow. I keep a few feet behind her while my eyes dart around the area suspiciously. We walk long enough for the doubts to begin outweighing my curiosity. The thought of being led so far away from where Narses is at the barrier gets my rational brain moving. What am I doing? I'm in the middle of a competition for fuck's sake. I don't have time for this, I don't even know how long I've already been gone.

My mouth pops open, ready to curse at the woman and run back when we come upon a path littered with glowing stones. The trees lining the path bend at unnatural angles, creating a domed effect high above us. I inspect every single thing as my dumb ass continues to follow her. Vines have started to decorate the trees, some hanging down from the branches above. White asphodel flowers sprout from various spots, the first hint of anything natural looking I've seen since stepping into this Godsforsaken place.

I'm taken aback by the skulls that are embedded into some of the tree trunks, even though I shouldn't be surprised considering where I am. A faint whispering reaches my ears and I listen to the cacophony of ghostly chanting voices. My feet come to a halt, looking for the source of the sound but it seems to be everywhere all at once. "What is that?" I whisper, accusation filling my tone.

"Don't worry, they will not harm you. Only those who have not been invited in are corrupted by the decay of our plague."

My stomach roils with nausea at her statement. The decay of their plague? I shiver, not wanting to know what that means, but I assume that's where all these skulls came from. My pace picks back up, letting the whispering voices float over me.

They eventually stop and a disturbing part of me misses the sound because the air becomes deafeningly still. "Here we are," the creature in front of me announces. Thick fog blocks the path in front of us but she continues through it. I look back to where we came from, the long path now unsettlingly swathed in shadow.

"Well, Ameria, there's no going back now," I mutter to myself as I hesitatingly take a step into the fog.

I can't say what I was exactly expecting to find on the other side, but it definitely wasn't this. Tall, massive trees are scattered across a field of pure white grass. A large floating orb that mimics the sun spreads light throughout what looks to be a small treehouse town. Homes are built into the bases of the trees while more are suspended further up the trunks, bridges connecting them all.

Lanterns and smaller orbs of light hang from various branches. While the trees don't have the same slick oily appearance, the leaves are still purple and black. More of the white asphodel flowers grow throughout. How they got something to grow in a place like this is impressive, though based on the grass that seems to be leached of color, they can likely do many things.

There's no one else to be found. It's just me and the woman who continues to lead me through this small treehouse town to a path through more trees.

It doesn't take long to get to our destination, and I now know why I didn't see anyone else. About thirty women, all with the same translucent skin, are gathered in a small clearing. Some sit at short tables and straight ahead is a raised throne carved directly from a gnarled white tree. Bones adorn the bottom of the throne and stark black vines entwine with the branches.

Atop the throne sits a woman with chin-length black hair and eyes as red as blood. White silk covers her lower half, a slit cut all the way up to her hip to show off her slender legs. The barely-there top is made of finger bones strung together.

The second her blood eyes land on me, they widen a fraction. Hushed whispers echo around me, reminding me of the ones that I heard on the journey here. I hold myself tall, refusing to whither under her stare. "We've been waiting a long time for you," her voice projects.

My eyes narrow and I look around at the others staring intensely at me. My mind wanders to how long it took to get here…maybe time moves differently?

The woman on the throne stands and descends the few steps, the silk of her skirt trailing like water behind her. "We have a lot to discuss with barely any time to do so. My name is Serafelle, and you've met Visha." She motions with her long sharp red claw nails toward the woman who brought me here. "You're curious and have a lot of questions, so let me begin."

"You're wondering about your magic and why you're here. That's a loaded question so, I'll simplify as best I can with the information I'm allowed to give. You'll likely have many more questions as I speak but please refrain from asking until I'm done." I nod, unsure of what to say but it's clear they aren't planning to kill me so that's a relief. Against my better judgment, I slip my daggers into their sheathes as she continues to speak.

"Simply put, you're here because you are meant to be. Our small race here," Serafelle motions to the women around the clearing, "was created by the God of Chaos to serve. We do not bleed therefore we do not die. We are endless." A dangerous smile spreads across her face, showing off sharp pointed teeth. All my thoughts are now consumed by one: The Gods are real. They were real. My mother, the texts, it was all true. And now, I'm standing in a group of monsters created by a God that cannot be killed.

I open my mouth but she lifts a clawed finger stopping me and I slam my mouth shut. Serafelle slowly starts to pace, "I know our presence confirms that the Gods exist. It's best if you fully come to terms with that as it'll make things a whole lot easier for you." My head starts spinning with the knowledge.

"Your magic is similar to ours because it comes from the same place." She pauses to look at me, "I'd tell you more but you are not ready yet." Serafelle continues pacing, talking animatedly with her hands, "We have been stuck in this ridiculous place for too long and now, finally, we will soon have the chance to go home. Which you will help us do."

My face scrunches up as she comes to stand in front of me and grabs one of my hands. Hers feel like ice and I jerk a little but don't pull away. Serafelle gazes upon me with a flurry of emotions that almost crumble my hardened heart. These creatures may brutally murder people, but so have I. They're trapped just like me. I soften, feeling an odd kinship. But, I don't know what I can possibly do for them.

I take her silence as the go-ahead to speak, "I don't know

if I'm the person who can help you." I shake my head, "I don't even know where your home is, and breaking down the wards around this island is likely impossible."

She pats my hand and then drops it, "The wards will fall, and you will be the one to help us. You have some learning and growing to do, but it is you." My stomach drops at her statement, if these wards fall…

Serafelle's eyes land on another, "Malvolia, bring the stone." The woman disappears in a flurry of shadow at her command.

My mouth slowly falls open, "How similar is our magic?"

"Quite. Why?"

I take a small step toward her, "Can you help me understand it?" Hope blooms within me, if I can learn more about it then I can control it easier.

She gives me a small smile, "You will have to learn on your own. That is the only way you will grow. But I'll give you this: you need to embrace your magic. You're still afraid of it. Subconsciously, you're connecting it to the way you were forced to learn and use it. Sever that connection and you will have more power than you'll know what to do with."

I sink a little. I don't know if I'll ever be able to fully embrace this magic. It spreads a darkness throughout me that I'm afraid one day will swallow me whole. I feel the dreaded call to fully submit to it every time I use it.

Malvolia reappears and hands Serafelle a small silver and glass box. She turns to me and pops the lid open. Inside is a black marquise-shaped gem the size of my pinky. "Take it. You'll need it," She nods toward the gem.

I eye her skeptically but reach in and pluck it up with my fingers. Hushed gasps come from everyone and Serafelle's eyes widen. Was I not supposed to touch it? I palm the stone and bring it closer to my face, examining it. "What is it fo -" my sentence is cut off when the stone turns to liquid and absorbs into my skin.

Panic floods me and I claw at my palm where black lines begin to spread out. I watch in horror as they start twitching and then move up to my wrist, disappearing under my sleeve. Magic that I cannot begin to describe spreads through my body and up to my chest.

Collapsing onto my knees, I grasp at my chest where it feels like something is burning straight through my flesh. Ripping the belts and straps of my leather armor with hurried fingers, I manage to get them undone and fling it open to reveal my bare torso and brassiere.

I look down at my sternum and stare in pained dread at the sizzling, bubbling, and smoking flesh. A strangled sob comes from my throat as I watch something pushing itself out of the burning spot. My head bows and my hands dart out to grip the grass beneath me. My fingers rip up pieces of the earth as I let out a strangled scream when my skin breaks. Blood dribbles down and collects on the ground, a stark contrast against the perfectly white blades.

The pain ends abruptly and I'm left with a small, heated spot in my chest. I collect myself, breathing heavily, and sit back on my heels while quickly wiping the tears that gathered at the corner of my eyes. My gaze drifts to my sternum and my face crumples in fear. The black gem is now embedded into my skin just above the center of my breasts, the skin around it red and inflamed. I run a trembling finger over it and hiss at the pain.

My head snaps up and I stare furiously at Serafelle, "What the fuck is this?" I cry, "What did you do to me?"

"You are truly the one who will help save us all," she states in wonder.

Disgust spreads across my face, "What is this thing?"

Serafelle's face hardens and the voices of the others mix with hers as they speak as one:

"When the three come together, the gates will open.

But beware the corrupt son, who will release the cursed one.

Great sacrifices will be made to restore the realms.

For the fate of the universe rests upon destiny, luck, and death."

My angered eyes pierce her, "What does that even mean?"

"The prophecy is all I am bound to give. It is up to you and those around you to reveal its meaning." She gives me a sad smile and helps me to my feet. Her hand hovers over the stone in my chest, hope flashing through her blood-red eyes. When they flick up to mine, they harden once more, "The stone cannot be removed, not yet. But beware, others will try to use you to hold dominion over its power. Be wise with whom you trust."

Serafelle backs away. "We are almost out of time. I wish I could give you more, but I am limited with what I can share. However, I can tell you that," her head tilts toward the stone, "will only amplify your shadows and the magic they're connected to. Remember what I said. Do not be afraid."

I begin buckling my uniform back up, attempting to process

this overwhelming situation, but my brain can barely focus on one stream of thought. My eyes scan the faces of every woman here and land on Serafelle. "I don't know what to do with all this information. And now I have this thing in my chest that is going to make my dark magic more potent when I could barely even control it in the first place," I shake my head. "I don't know how I'm supposed to help you when I can't even save myself." The last part comes out as a whisper of admission.

"You will. Right now, just focus on surviving and worry about the rest later. In time, everything will make sense."

Visha comes to stand next to her, "It's time."

Serafelle nods, "Your time with us has come to an end. You need to get back to your trial. Visha will bring you back to where she found you."

I nod numbly and let my feet carry me after Visha. "Ameria," I glance over my shoulder at Serafelle, now surrounded by all the other women, "When you need aid in the future, call upon us and we will happily serve you." I swallow thickly and resume following Visha.

Chapter Thirty-four
Ameria

Turns out Visha could have portaled us the whole time. We pop back into existence right in the spot from which she'd plucked me, the aura of the forest seeping back into my pores. I throw an annoyed look her way, "Why couldn't you have done that before?"

She smirks, "You needed the walk." I scoff in response. "Before I leave I'll give you a hint. You'll need to go that way," Visha takes a few steps back, pointing her bony finger in the direction straight ahead of me and then disappears.

I stand paralyzed in a flurry of thoughts that I don't even know where to begin sorting out. I'm hit with an overwhelming storm of emotions: confusion, awe, fear, inadequacy, and dread. That last one is more prominent than the others at the moment. How I'm supposed to go back to this trial given all the information I just received and with an unknown magical stone embedded in my body is beyond me.

My fingers rub at my temples where a headache is starting to bloom. I attempt to do what I'm best at, which is shove everything deep, deep, deep down. My dark magic rises to crawl underneath my skin and shadows start to leak from my fingertips, cascading to the forest floor. Cringing, I shake my hand and yank back on my magic. *Fucking great.* It's more restless than it was before.

My chest still feels like it's going to cave in but if I continue like this, I'll end up dying and everything will have been for nothing. I really need to calm down.

Inhale, two, three, four.

I palm my daggers.

Exhale, two, three, four.

I stalk forward in the direction Visha pointed while doing my breathing exercises.

Soon enough, I'm as calm as one could be, and I feel the call of the last object. It's close. The tug leads me to the outskirts of a decent-sized outcropping of the burnt-looking ground, surrounded by trees and bushes. A figure stands at the other end and I swiftly tuck behind some brush.

I examine the figure: It has shapely curves like a woman but its skin is tree bark. Its hair is made of thick green, purple, and black vines. The creature turns and I can see, there on its neck is the golden emerald necklace.

After I'm done complaining about this situation in my head, I form a plan of attack. Common sense says that a creature made of the trees will have some sort of earthly magic, so that's out. Fire is my most powerful so I decide to start with that, hoping the necklace doesn't burn along with it.

I creep along the edge of the outcropping, aiming to surprise it from behind. But then my boot snaps a twig and I still, knowing I'm screwed. My gaze whips to the creature, who's looking straight at me with gaping holes where the eyes should be. Maybe I'll get lucky and it'll be blind.

It bellows a screech and starts sprinting right at me. Nope, not blind. I spring into action and rush into the clearing, slamming my fist into the ground. A line of fire heads straight for the creature and I'm able to singe part of its leg as it jumps out of the way.

As I go to form a ball of fire, vines shoot out from the brush behind me and ensnare my wrists, knocking both daggers to the ground. More rip through the earth and wrap around my body, sending me toppling. They begin crushing me, some of them piercing my skin with their thorns. My magic slithers across my skin, burning so hot that it wilts them all.

Feeling grateful for Corro and his relentless torment of vines during training, I leap up from the ground as the creature hisses and charges with an outstretched hand. I put one foot in front of me, ready to run if I need to or if this thing makes impact with me. Crossing my arms in front of me, fire snakes down them to gather in my hands. Bringing my arms down and out to the sides in one fell swoop, a crackling light of fire emanates from both my hands, creating great whips of fire.

The action is enough to stop the creature in its tracks. The smile that spreads across my face probably looks half crazed and I seize the moment to charge. The creature lifts its arms out to the sides and rocks of all different sizes raise up into the air behind it. My feet skid to a stop, my eyes widening. A rock the size of my head hurtles through the air and I twirl just in time for it to whiz past.

Another the same size comes at me. I fling one of my whips at it and a large crack booms through the air as it makes contact, shattering it to pieces. Dodging one of the chunks, I head straight for the creature. It doesn't hold back now and begins flinging rocks and boulders one after the other.

I don't falter and shatter each one with the cracking of my whips. The largest boulder rises into the air and I realize that there will be no way to break it, even with both whips. The creature stretches both arms forward and it comes flying. In a split-second decision, I create a plan that's crazy, a total shot in the dark.

Making both whips longer, I hurl them outward and wrap them around the boulder coming at me. I instantly shorten them and let my body soar toward it, dispelling the whips at the precise moment. The second my feet make contact with it, I leap off and call a gust of wind to help push me further through the air. I hit the ground with a roll right behind the creature.

Easily, I call upon the whips again to ensnare its wrists, yanking it to the ground, and it screeches while writhing to get free. I remove a whip from its wrist and slash across its stomach, burning the bark skin in the process.

It lets out another blood-curdling screech and I hastily transform my whips into pure flame, letting them smother the creature. I dispel the magic, finding that the necklace is half melted to its body. Through my labored breathing, I reach down and dig the pendant out of its burnt tree bark skin. The chain is unsalvageable so this will have to do.

I slip it into my pocket and stand. I need to get the hell out of here, now. Jogging over to where my daggers fell, I scoop them up and rush out of the clearing.

Retracing my steps, I head back toward where I came through the wards, trying to be as stealthy as possible but honestly, at this point, the faster the better. I'm almost there. I can feel the icky aura of the barrier. I push myself faster, ready to get out of here, when a howling comes from my left and a hound-like beast charges at me.

With my daggers still in both hands, I use my magic to light them on fire. Just as the hound leaps to attack, I stop in my tracks and take a large step back, allowing it to pass in front of me. I jab the flaming blades into its back and bend my knees, using the daggers embedded in its back to vault myself over it. As I do, I drag them through the torso with the weight of my moving body.

It howls and I yank the blades out when my feet hit the ground. The hound drops and I extinguish the burning blades as I turn and continue running.

In the distance, I can see Narses standing on the other side of the barrier, right where I'd left him. I let my guard down too soon and miss the snarl that comes from my right. Another hound tackles me to the ground, its sharp teeth sinking into my arm. Pain explodes throughout my body and I scream. My name rings out in the distance but the pain and growling beast muffle everything .

Its paw swipes at my head and I try my best to avoid it but a claw manages to slash the side of my face. I let out a sob-like scream. I can't die like this. Not when I'm so close. I replace my pain and fear with all the anger and adrenaline pulsing through my veins.

With the hound's jaws still wrapped around my arm, I look it dead in the eyes and yell right in its face while slamming the dagger in my free hand right through the top of its head and twisting.

It releases a whining yowl before it falls to the ground on its side and the jaws around my arm loosen. Yanking the dagger from its head, I drop it next to me and grab the beast's upper jaw to pry open its mouth. I pull my arm free from its teeth and with a grunt, I grab both daggers in my bloody hands and stumble to a stand.

I bolt the rest of the way, slamming right into Narses as I cross the barrier. His arms envelop me before I have the chance to collapse. I can feel the blood dripping down my arm and face. "Good job, Ameria. Let's get out of here." He hauls me up into his arms and rushes through the gate.

The minute we're on the other side, my body slackens in his arms and my daggers slip out of my hands. Gently, but quickly, Narses places me on the ground and I feel him slide my weapons back into their sheathes.

A pained howl echoes through the forest and my body tenses. I attempt to jump but the pain in my arm paralyzes me. "It's okay, it's just a wolf. It won't hurt us."

I nod at Narses's reassuring tone and relax as his arms snake underneath me. My body is exhausted, the pain and blood loss are causing black spots to cloud my vision. We must be close to camp because I can hear distant chatter and Narses sets me on my unsteady feet.

His hands grip my shoulders and his hard stormy eyes meet mine, "I know it hurts, but you need to pull it together for just one more minute." I answer with a shaky blink of my eyes.

I feel him dig into my pocket, pulling out the half-melted pendant and place it into my blood-soaked hand. My fingers curl hard around it as he also removes the chalice from my belt and shoves it into my other hand. "Stand as tall as you can. Push through the pain. You can let go once you make it to the healers' tent. Just fight through it until then."

He turns me by the shoulders and I do my best to roll them back, feigning courage, dragging my heavy feet through the trees into camp. I can practically feel everyone still at my appearance and I swallow thickly but manage to make it over to Beor, likely leaving a trail of blood behind me. The steady presence of Narses following me has my spine straightening as I glare at the High King and toss my objects into the chest.

Chapter Thirty-Five
Ameria

When my eyes blink open, I can make out a looming, person-shaped blob over me. My vision clears and Delyth's face brightens, a splitting grin growing. "She's awake!" She sings and moves her face closer to mine. "How are you feeling?"

Someone clicks their tongue and Delyth is yanked from my view, giving me room to breathe. "Don't crowd her Delyth," Inara says.

I gently sit up, the motion sending a shooting pain to my head. My hand flies to my forehead and my arm burns with movement. "Fuck," I hiss.

"The healer says the pain will subside before the second trial begins," Inara chimes in from the corner of the cot she sits on. I groan, the events of the trial flooding through my mind making my headache worsen.

Things I'll have to deal with later, not now. I can't get into that headspace at the moment. I need to stay as clear-headed as possible. "Glad you two made it," I say between pained breaths, the stone in my chest feeling sore.

"We're glad you made it too. You don't have a lot of time before the next trial begins. Let's get you some food." Inara pats my leg, motioning to follow her out of the healer's tent.

Climbing off the cot, I follow the two of them. My breath catches as I take in the remaining number of competitors. "So few are left," I mumble while plopping down onto a stump.

Inara hands me a plate of food, "Most didn't come back and the others had injuries so severe the healers couldn't save them."

I'm sure my face looks paler than usual and I consider myself extremely lucky. I finish the food on my plate and toss it onto the stump next to me. "I knew you'd make it outta there!" A voice rumbles from behind me. Startled, I straighten and turn to see Gregor standing there, smiling down at me. I shoot up and wrap my arm around him in a side hug.

He catches me staring at the now-healed scars across his face and waves a hand, "I'm good, the scars make me look tougher anyway." Gregor gives me a wink. "Glad to see your scar was able to be healed though, that looked gnarly."

I laugh and reach up to where the claw got me, "Yeah, I can't say it was pleasant."

The small crowd gathers around Beor again as he announces the final trial. "It is now time for the final trial of the competition. Whoever makes it will attend the closing ceremonies and officially become a warrior of the Western Isles. In this trial, you will face an opponent and only one of you will emerge victorious. You may use your chosen weapon and magical abilities. There are only two rules: No one is allowed to interfere with another person's duel, and it must be to the death."

Whispers scatter through the crowd with everyone exchanging glances. I'm sure we're all wondering the same thing, are we going to be facing each other? Beor continues, "You will be escorted to the ring by your assigned trainer. Once there, you'll be brought to a private seating box to watch until it's your turn."

With a nod of his head, all the trainers start escorting everyone to where the final trial will take place. Narses finds me and we walk together with everyone who's left, hushed conversations happening between other participants and their trainers blending into the background. I find him continuously surveying me, but I don't care to find out why. There's so much on my mind that I'd rather take this time to focus on getting ready for the duels.

We trudge through the forest for a good while until we reach a giant pit in the ground, made from clay and stone. I'm led down a spiral stone staircase and as we wind downward, I gaze into the pit. The drop into the actual ring is decent and the walls lining it are tall enough that there's no way someone could escape. If one were to fall into it, they'd have broken legs at the very least.

Above the walls are rows of little dark alcoves, which I assume are the private boxes. Narses guides me through a narrow hallway and into one of the alcoves. I plop down onto the bench and just a minute later, the duels begin.

I watch as contestant after contestant enters the ring. To my relief, we're not fighting each other. Instead, they seem to fight random warriors, none of whom I recognize. "Is there something special about these opponents?" I ask over my shoulder.

Narses steps up next to me and grunts. I glance up to see his arms crossed and brows narrowed, "Well, this one looks familiar. He's a commander in one of the court's armies." He clears his throat, "Looks like you'll be fighting some of the realm's best warriors."

I let out a long breath and continue watching the matches. As time goes on, more contestants than warriors lose their lives. The number left is slowly dwindling. Fourteen matches in and then Inara steps into the ring. I sharply inhale while gripping the edge of the bench I'm sitting on. I shouldn't be worried because she trained with one of the best.

She faces an unnaturally large man, but she gracefully duels him with sword and magic moving as one. In the end, she burns him to a crisp and then decapitates him for good measure. After watching her effortlessly beat the warrior, I have no doubt she'll be one of the greatest in history.

I get antsy as the matches continue. Corro still hasn't made it back and I'm afraid I won't get to see him before I either die or am exposed as Callum's pet. Delyth also still hasn't gone yet and it seems I might be one of the last to go, again. On top of everything, I can feel the stone in my chest pulsing occasionally, making my dark magic flutter every time.

Thankfully, Gregor emerges victorious. But Delyth is next, and that's when I notice a limp in her step still. Were the healers not able to fix it? My palms become slicked with sweat and I'm up on my feet, standing at the edge of the alcove gripping the rail.

She faces a tall but slender male and he wastes no time in charging at her. The clash of metal fills the pit as they duel it out. Both land an equal number of blows to each other and then Delyth is able to swipe the warrior's wrist, making him drop his sword. She lunges, but he side-steps just before her sword is able to impale him and lands a blow to her temple.

My grip tightens, my knuckles turning white. "Get up Delyth, come on. Get up." Delyth swings her legs around, knocking his feet out from under him which gives her time to scurry to her blade.

Vines sprout from the ground and grip her outstretched hand just before it reaches the sword. My breath catches. Fast as lightning, the warrior grabs his sword and slams it to the ground, cutting off her hand.

Delyth's scream fills the ring along with what I assume is also Inara's. Stumbling backward in shock, I clench my fist to my chest. Uselessly begging the tears not to fall, I drop to my knees. Gods, I'm going to puke. I feel the weight of a hand on my shoulder and I don't need to look back to know it's Narses. I hold back choked sobs, "No, no, no," I whisper. I was foolish to think I wouldn't lose someone I'd cared for. A friend I'd just gotten to know. The sweet, cheerful and positive Delyth.

A screech comes from the alcove we're in, startling me and Narses. Sitting on the railing is the whitest owl I've ever seen. Its head turns my way and blinks, then it screeches again before flying off. I glance up at Narses who looks pale as a ghost and then a scream of pain rattles the pit. Stumbling to my feet, I look over the railing.

There she is, lying lifeless on the ground with the warrior's sword sticking out of her chest.

Delyth is dead.

I start to collapse when strong hands grasp under my arms, Inara's cries still echoing through the arena. Someone shakes me, bringing my attention back to the present. My dark magic boils at my distress. "Ameria."

Through my blurry eyes, I see Narses looming over me. "Ameria, you need to pull it together. It's about to be your turn." His mouth is formed into a tight line, his eyes holding worry. "We have to go."

Right, I still need to fight. I can pull it together, I just need to shove it down with everything else. Focus now, worry later. It's the only option if I want to make it out alive.

He leads me out into the hallway we came in through and down deeper into the pit. The whole way, I try to get a handle on my spiraling emotions. We stop just before the arching entrance to the ring where another match is occurring.

My mother's sword weighs heavily on my back. I'd chosen it as my weapon for this trial, in hopes that it might give me strength. I draw the sword and it vibrates in my hand, reacting with the stone in my chest.

"I knew there was something off about you. Why are you radiating so much magic? I'd first noticed it when you came through the wards of Balrath," Narses pushes, his face as hard as stone.

"I don't know what you're talking about," I shrug him off.

His eyes scan my whole body landing on my breasts. I give

him an accusing look but he pushes forward. "What do you have around your neck?"

"I don't have anything around my neck, see." I motion while twisting so he can see there's nothing hanging around it. Hopefully he'll just leave it alone.

His mouth opens to protest but light flashes from the corner of my eye and there stands Callum. No, no no no no. Not now, don't out me now. "What are you doing here?" Narses spits in his direction.

Callum waves his hand, "This doesn't concern you brother. I'll only be a minute and then be out of your hair." My eyes widen as they dart between the both of them, just now putting together their similar features. Holy shit, they're related.

He grabs my wrist and yanks me so his face is in mine, "I want you to kill the other opponent as quickly and swiftly as possible so that this ridiculous competition can be over." The brand on my wrist burns and I hiss.

"We'll be watching, Ameria," Callum grins, sending a wink toward Narses before disappearing in his light.

Narses rushes over to me and grabs my wrist, pushing up the sleeve to see the brand. "When? When did you get this?" The brand burns as I attempt to tell him and he notices. "You can't say anything about it, can you."

My thoughts filter through anything I might be able to say. "I was told to do anything he'd ordered during the competition."

His eyes flash and he drops my wrist, "Ameria, I need you to show me why there's so much magic coming from right here." He points to my sternum, where the stone sits. I don't move, maybe if I wait long enough, this match will be over and it'll be my turn. "Now!" He barks in my face, and I jerk back, swearing I thought his eyes burned pure silver.

I drop my sword and unbuckle my leather armor enough to show him. His eyes widen to saucers and with a shaky hand, traces a finger along the raised skin around the stone. Cheers shout throughout the arena as Narses's eyes meet mine. He takes one large step back and looks out toward the pit, "It's your turn."

Callum

"Toross, I have told you multiple times. Ameria is mine. She is what you bargained the sword for. If you'd like to renegotiate after the competition, be my guest, but I'm not promising her return to you." I rest my ankle on my knee, sipping the wine his other daughter, Petra, served us. Timid little thing, yet something dangerous swims behind those eyes. And I intend to fish that out.

"Fine. We're here to discuss expansion plans anyway. We'll revisit after the competition. If she's still alive that is," the Fire King responds before knocking back the rest of the contents in his goblet.

I swirl my drink, "I think you underestimate her."

He scoffs and changes the subject. He's really regretting only bargaining for the sword. Toross has always been a greedy bastard. "The Earth Kingdom is already to be mine soon, but we need the Air Kingdom. You said you would be able to take care of that problem for me… have you?" He eyes me from across his ugly wooden desk.

A smug smile spreads across my face, "I already have the Air Kingdom in my pocket. In just about a month, it'll be mine."

"Yours? You were supposed to help me claim it!" Toross slams a fist on this desk, knocking the empty goblet over. I thought Petra surely would jump at that, but she stands still as stone. Very intriguing. I think I'll have her.

"I am helping you claim it, Toross. Once it is mine, you may take it by marriage." My gaze drifts to Petra. The little thing doesn't even look my way. That will need to be remedied.

The King follows my eyes. "You already have one daughter, here you want to take my other one as well?"

I shrug and down the rest of the wine. "What will you need her for? She's not truly going to ever rule. Why not use her as a chess piece in getting what you want." He seems to consider this and I stand, already running late. "You may think about it, but I know you'll come to your senses. But for now I must go, I'm late to watch my little pet finish the competition. It's going to be a glorious ending. You should come watch, be my guests."

My smile is downright devious and Toross seems to be intrigued. "I think both of us will join you."

"Wonderful."

I emerge from my light in the narrow hallways of the arena and I stalk down them, going over my perfectly laid plans in my head. I need to go give my pet orders. But first, I have some important pieces to move into place. He should be arriving any minute now, I know because that brand on his back will lead him right to me.

Sure enough, the little Moon Court boy comes sauntering

out of the dark. "What the hell are you doing here?" He stops in his tracks, afraid. As he should be.

I stuff my hands into my suit pants pockets, "How was your important meeting back home?" I ask, knowing that there wasn't ever one. He eyes me but doesn't answer, "Oh, right," I take slow steps, closing the distance, "There wasn't one, was there?"

"How would you know that?"

I chuckle, "Because silly boy, I was the one who put that information into your mind. That brand came from me, not Rafael. Of course, you don't remember." I reach out and snatch him up by the shirt, bringing his face to mine, "But you will remember, *now.*"

Ameria

This is it. I take a deep breath and step out into the ring, waiting for the person I'll duel to emerge. An owl's screech fills the air just as a silhouette appears in the entrance at the other end. Narses fled the moment I buckled up my leathers – where he went, who knows. He's learned my secret, and I'm sure he's off to tell everyone not to trust me. That I belong to the enemy.

The past forty days of training flash before my eyes as the person steps out into the ring. Panic rises within me and I have trouble catching my breath. Nausea pools in my stomach, bile stinging the back of my throat. I feel like I'm going to collapse. This has to be a joke, this can't be right.

His name floats past my lips in a whisper on the wind, "Corro."

Chapter Thirty-Six
Ameria

There he stands, now only a few feet away from me. His elegant sword in hand. I shake my head, unable to come to terms with what's happening, "What the fuck is this, Corro," I spit.

His face softens as he raises his sword, "I'm sorry, I didn't know. I couldn't remember until just now. It was a part of an unbreakable deal."

The brand on his back…I grip my mother's sword, my dark magic thrumming in my palm. I retreat a couple of steps, tears beginning to pool in my lash line. "No, no. I refuse to do this, this isn't right!" And then the brand on my wrist burns and I drop down to one knee as the pain from refusing an order spears through me.

"You have to, Ameria. You have to fight me and kill me or I'll have to kill you." He closes his eyes and lets out a heavy sigh. When he opens them, a mix of emotions flashes across his face and then he charges.

I submit to my order. "This can't be happening," I grunt,

throwing my sword up to catch Corro's blow and push him backward. He answers with a swipe at my left side. Twirling out of the way, his blade just misses.

"It's happening, Ameria. I know you've been forced to work with Callum this whole time, so I know you have no choice but to kill me as well. We can't stop now until one of us is dead." Corro springs toward me again, but I duck and leap around him. I slash his arm along the way and he lets out a hiss as he faces me.

"Why would you agree to this? Why didn't you tell me you knew what I was doing?" I scream as he makes another attack and just manage to block it from hitting me. A tear falls from the corner of my eye but I stop any more from forming. It'll only impede my vision.

Corro takes the opportunity to land a kick to my chest and I fall backward. I tumble but right myself quickly. His steps falter mid-attack like he's fighting the orders. "I can't tell you, the brand won't let me, I really wish I could say. Fuck...Callum, he" his face flushes with anguish as he tries to break through the magic of the brand.

Mine stings and forces me to jump into action, faking right and going left, slicing him across his other arm. A force of air is hurled at me, flipping me onto my back. The wind is knocked from my lungs and I gasp for breath as he comes to stand over me.

"You have to stop me, Ameria. I don't want to kill you." His blade comes crashing down upon me but I'm able to reach for the handle of my sword and stop it in its tracks.

"We're supposed to live, both of us. You would have never talked to me ever again once you found out, but you'd be alive." My voice comes out strangled while straining against the weight of him pressing down on my sword. Corro continues to press his blade against mine, getting closer to my neck. Summoning a force of air, I use it to help push and throw him off. Rolling onto my feet, I face him.

"We have no choice, Ameria. The magic of the brands will compel us until someone succeeds. It has to be you." He says solemnly while getting to his feet. "I just need to know, please, was any of it real? Or was it a command, to make me fall for you?"

"It was both." My voice cracks, "But every moment was real, even if it originally came from an order."

Corro opens his mouth to speak but closes it, and my heart sinks. I knew this would end in heartbreak. Embarrassment, anger, everything comes rushing to the surface. My insides feel like they're on fire and my darkness rises within me, trying to force its way out.

A part of me wants to just end this already, but it's Corro. The first person I opened my heart to. And, even though I made a mockery of it, my feelings are real. How could I kill the man I've grown to care deeply for?.

Water shoots out from his hands but I throw up a wall of my own just in time and it absorbs his attack, so forcefully it nearly knocks me backward. Spinning in a circle for momentum, I form a ball and launch it right back at him. Hitting its mark, Corro soars in the air and lands on his back, his sword clattering to the ground behind him.

Sauntering over to him, I stand at his feet looking down at the man I thought I would one day maybe, possibly, have a chance to love. "All my feelings were real, Corro."

He moves, swiping his legs under my feet and knocking me to the ground. Vines wrap around my wrists as Corro climbs on top of me. "I believe you, Ameria." He pulls back his fist and lands a blow right to my face.

I spit blood onto the ground and the darkness in me pushes even more. "Stop me, Ameria." Winding his fist back again, I turn the vines to ash in time to catch his fist with my hands. His other hand finds my throat and grasps it tightly. "I'm so sorry, Ameria." His head falls, "I was told to use everything I had to get you to kill me. The bond is too strong, I can't stop. I've already tried so many times."

His eyes pierce into mine, a look of pleading. Recognition floods me. He is going to use his power to siphon my magic. The hand around my throat tightens and mine loosen around his fist. "No, p - please." I choke out. My eyesight starts to cloud over as I writhe under his grip.

"Please, you have to stop me." Silver lines his now glowing green eyes as I feel his magic flood into me. I watch the elixir magic, my fire magic, even my dark magic, be dragged to the surface. My shadows hold on but everything else begins to flood out of my body into his hands, feeling like a piece of my essence is being stolen.

"No!" I choke out a sob, tears leaving the corners of my eyes. Placing my hands on his wrist, I use whatever last magic I have left before he takes it all and heat my hands until they burn and sizzle his flesh.

Screaming, he tumbles off me clutching his arm to his chest. Gasping for air, I roll to my side and crawl to my sword. Standing on shaky legs, I turn toward Corro, who is now racing for his own weapon.

"You - you took it," I rasp, my throat sore from his grip. All but my dark magic is gone, I feel empty. I watch as Corro's shoulders sag and tears stream down his face. This is it. All of this needs to end, no matter how much it will break me.

My eyes flutter closed and I let every memory of pain that I've experienced in my life flow through me. All the emotions I've kept bottled up since arriving here push to the surface. Instead of letting these emotions impede me, I'll use them as fuel – let them carry out this task I very much don't want to do. The darkness in me roils in anger, the stone in my chest heats. My eyes snap open and I let out a scream that holds a hundred years worth of anguish.

I slam my mother's sword into the ground before me. A crack splits the earth, running straight for Corro and stopping just before his feet. His eyes go wide as black inky snake-like vines come slithering out. They tangle around his body, slamming him to the ground.

Yanking the sword from the packed dirt, I stalk over to where Corro lies restrained. The pit around us is deathly silent save for the distant owl screeching. Every muscle and bone in my body aches, but I don't let it show. Stepping over Corro, I crouch down to straddle him.

I will some of the vines around his upper body to creep back into the earth. "I'm so tired," I whisper.

Tears fall from his eyes, "So finish it."

"It was all real, please know that." A tear rolls down my cheek as I lean down and press a kiss upon his lips.

"I know," He whispers in my ear.

My chin quivers as I flip around my sword, "I would have loved to make a home with you." I say sadly. And then I jam the black steel tip straight into his beating heart. All of the vines retreat while I sit here, my heart crumpling with fading dreams, and watch Corro draw his final breath.

The arena is filled with cheering as I stand and pull the sword from his chest. As much as I want to grieve the loss of Corro, I can't just yet. This isn't over. My anger boils. Callum made this happen. He inflicted a special kind of torture, just because he could. The ground slowly absorbs Corro's body, returning him to the earth. Just like it did with all the other deaths that have happened here.

Fifteen remaining contestants enter the pit, with High King Beor announcing the winners from somewhere within an alcove. Everyone is clapping and celebrating, but all I can do is stare at the spot where Corro's body disappeared.

My eyes scan the pit, looking for Callum. I refuse to bend to his will anymore. There, across the way, he strolls into the arena with my father and Petra on his heels. "Wonderful job, Ameria. I knew you could be as ruthless as the rumors say."

"Fuck you, Callum," I spit, my hand goes numb from

gripping my sword so tightly. My dark magic feels depleted, like I used every ounce of it to summon those vines. The missing fire magic makes my bones feel hollow.

"Now, now. No need to have a tantrum, pet. I did it for your own good. Now let's go." He heads for me, likely to portal me out of here but my father stops him.

"Actually, Callum, the competition is over and I'd like to renegotiate. Now. I want her back."

Callum's hand forms a tight fist, and he turns slowly on his heel toward my father. I take a few steps back. "We can discuss possible negotiations later on, for now she is mine."

"She's not going anywhere with either of you," Narses pops out of nowhere, inserting himself in the conversation between a High Lord and a King. They're all mad if they think I'm going to let any man decide what to do with me again.

My eyes catch movement, and I see Petra slowly backing away from our father. Her gaze catches on mine, and she points to her wrist. My brows furrow in her direction.

"Oh please, brother. As if I'm going to let you take her from me," Callum spits in Narses's direction. A heavy aura pulses from Narses, and both Callum and my father jump into action. Bedlam breaks out as the three of them begin attacking each other, flinging magic and blasting holes in the arena's walls. Stone and clay fly in every direction causing the alcoves to begin collapsing.

Everyone begins to flee to the nearest exit as warriors from all courts begin attacking one another. My eyes find Petra again who has found cover, she aggressively points to her wrist but I still don't understand. She mouths two words. The brand.

I drop my sword and my hand claws at my armor to roll up the sleeve. My brand, it's gone. I recall the words Callum spoke when he forced this upon me. He only branded me to make sure I did what I was told while I was in the competition. Not after. The competition is over, which means…I'm free.

I find Petra again, who's staring hard at me, "Go!" She yells at the top of her lungs. My feet spring into action and I scoop up my sword while running in the other direction, away from the three men fighting over who gets to own me.

"No!" My father yells and I look back to see all three of their eyes trained on me.

I ram right into a hard body and strong hands grasp my arms. "Take her!" I hear Narses yell. Gods please, I just want to flee. The hands on my arms move to envelop me in a strong hold and I'm swallowed by shadows.

I'm dropped hard onto black marble flooring with silver veins running through it. I groan as black shiny shoes appear in my view. My gaze climbs up the imposingly tall, slender, but built, man before me.

Pale as moonlight, dressed head to toe in black. A crescent moon lip stud underneath his bottom lip glints in the dim fae light, his jet-black hair showing the slightest red tint. Hoops and studs are punched in both pointed ears.

His voice skitters across my skin, "It's nice to finally meet you, Ameria. My name is Rafael. Welcome to the Moon Court."

The End.

Epilogue
Narses

My mist swallows me up and I portal straight to the Moon Court. I book it down the halls of Rafael's estate to his office, my boots thudding against the polished marble, and burst through the set of black doors with silver vines painted on them.

"Raf!" I heave through heavy breaths. The High Lord shoots up out of his chair and Damien whirls around from his place by the window behind the desk, "I found a stone."

"Where?" Damien commands.

"It's in Ameria's chest."

"What do you mean it's in her chest?" Rafael leans forward, hands braced against his obsidian desk.

"The damn thing is literally embedded in her."

His brows furrow and Damien takes up a spot next to him, "That's not possible. Is it?" He throws a questioning look at Rafael.

Raf makes a disgruntled noise, "Where is she?"

My stomach drops, "She's dueling in the final trial...against Corro."

He stills and looks off in thought. "Bring her here immediately after the trial."

"Yeah, that might be a problem." I rub the back of my neck as both Damien and Rafael snap their gazes to me. "She's been branded by Callum. She's been working for him since day one of the competition. There is a possibility the brand might be fulfilled but the only thing she could tell me was that she had to do anything he ordered during the competition."

"Then there's a possibility that once it officially ends, the brand will vanish," Damien concludes.

Rafael finally speaks, "We'll have to take that chance." He nods at Damien, "Go with Narses. There's one person who might have insight on her brand."

"Who?" I ask.

"I've had eyes on her sister. She seems like someone who knows more than they let on."

I portal us back to the arena and into the alcove where Ameria and I had started out. She and Corro are still in the midst of their duel, but we don't have much time. "What are you doing here?" A voice comes from behind us.

Damien and I whirl around to find Inara standing in the entrance of the alcove, her eyes puffy and red from crying over losing Delyth. "We need to get Ameria back to the Moon Court after her duel. Unfortunately, she's been branded by Callum," Damien answers.

"Shit," she mutters.

"Rafael says that her sister might know the details of her brand."

"She's here, with the King."

"Perfect," I say. "Damien, go with Inara and get whatever information you can. I'll head back down to the pit and be ready for when this all ends."

Inara

I lead Damien through the alcoves to the one where the royals sit. My heart aches with every step I take, cracking more and more every time my foot hits the ground. Soon, it'll be nothing but broken pieces, too tiny to ever fully repair.

We reach the alcove where the High Lord, King, and Petra are watching the competition. I turn, holding my hand up to Damien's chest, stopping him. His narrowed eyes glance down at me. "Let me do this on my own. I feel like she'll respond better if a woman approaches her."

He seems to consider this before nodding and taking a step backward to hide in the shadows. I poke my head around the corner to look through the entrance of the alcove. Callum and Toross are standing against the rail, deeply enthralled by the match happening below. Petra, however, stands a bit further away, still likely able to see into the pit but out of view from the two males in front of her.

Pulling my magic to the surface, I conjure a small puddle of water beneath her slippered foot. Her yellow dress is short enough to see that it soaks her slipper and just like I wanted, it catches her attention.

I manipulate the water to form into a single thread that begins to crawl from her foot back to where I stand right outside the alcove. She quickly glances at the two men in front of her before her eyes follow the thread of water.

Our gazes meet. She looks again to the rulers in front of her before slowly backing away. They don't even turn around, too entertained by Ameria and Corro fighting to the death. I feel bad for her, I couldn't imagine having to do that. Now that I know Callum branded her, I'm sure this is his sick and twisted doing.

I back away from the alcove, far enough where our voices won't reach her father or the High Lord but close enough for Damien to hear every word. Petra rounds the corner, stopping a bit further away than arm's length. "What do you want?" Her tone is harsh, short.

"What do you know about the brand Callum gave Ameria?"

She crosses her arms, "What makes you think I know anything about that?"

I can already tell this stuck-up bitch is going to drive me fucking crazy. "I know you do."

Petra's hazel eyes survey me, her expression hard as stone. "Are you going to help her?"

My head jerks back, I was not expecting that question to come out of her mouth. "Do you want me to help her?"

Her eyes squint. "My father found out that when the competition ends, so does the brand. That's when he's planning on catching Callum off guard and renegotiating to get her back."

A scream rattles the stadium. Petra's eyes widen slightly, "That's all I know." She says before hurriedly running back into her alcove.

"Damien?" I call out into the empty shadowed corridor. There's no answer and I assume once Petra gave up the right information, he portaled to Narses. I begin walking back the way we came, looking for an empty alcove to see what's happening down below.

I walk past one, where a lone figure stands and backtrack. Striding in, I take up a spot next to Damien. His jaw is clenched, hands balled into fists, as he stares at the duel.

My eyes drag from him to Ameria, who's now straddling Corro, her back facing us. I watch as she jams the tip of her sword into his chest and the black inky vines that surround her begin to crawl back into the earth.

My already shattered heart breaks a tiny bit more for her, for the fact that she had to kill Corro. She wouldn't admit it, but she was starting to fall for him.

Cheers erupt and contestants begin rushing into the pit. High King Beor is announcing the winners. This is it, the end of the competition. Callum, Toross, and Petra waltz into view down below. They're exchanging words when Narses emerges from his mist.

I track Petra, who begins backing away, signaling to something on her wrist. My brows pull together, and then I realize what she's conveying.

"Damien, Ameria is going to realize the brand is gone. She's going to leave, you need to grab her. Now!"

Chaos erupts in the pit, "Get out of here, grab Gregor and head to the Astral Court!" Damien orders before he slips away in his shadows.

Acknowlegments

I am unsure of where to begin with these acknowledgments because childhood Hannah can't believe it. To my mother, Vera, for being the most supportive mom a woman could ask for. Thank you for always believing in me and being there every step of the way. I could not have done this without your support.

Thank you to my childhood friend, Jordan, for cheering me on every single step of the way. I'm sorry it took so long to get the book in your hands. I hope you finally enjoy holding it after two years.

To my editor, Melissa. Without your guidance, Death Follows would not be the book it is now.

To my amazing cover designer, I can't believe how well you brought to life the scene from Death Follows for the cover. I am in awe.

To Allison for answering every single question about publishing a book as well as formatting this for me. You're incredible and thank you for letting me annoy you with my questions.

Finally, thank you, reader. Without you, this book would be nothing. Thank you for taking a chance on a new indie author. I cannot thank you enough.

Hannah Rachel writes adult dark fantasy romance in the mile high city of Denver, Colorado. She loves slow-burn romances, darker themes, and female rage. When she's not writing, you can find her running an alcohol-free tech-startup and managing social media for influencers.

Her debut novel, *Death Follows*, is a nod to her Baltic and Slavic heritage, and the main character represents some of the struggles she's dealt with in life including addiction.

CONNECT WITH HANNAH ON:
Website: www.authorhannahrachel.com
Instagram: @authorhannahrachel
Tik Tok: AuthorHannahRachel